Chosen Different

By Nat Kozinn

natkozinn@gmail.com

natkozinn.com

Thanks to: Mom, Dad, Adam, Colin, and EvalineEdits

To my wife.

1

Upon the establishment that any individual is a Different, that individual must immediately surrender themselves to the custody of the Defense Department, Section 26. The individual shall remain in the custody of Section 26 until such time as the extent of the individual's abilities are established and the individual is determined to be safe for the community.

Article 2 Section 1 of the Different Acts of 1986

It's hot in here. Why is it so hot in here? I need to calm down; this is important. I can't seem like a freak. At least not more of a freak than I am. It's probably part of the test. They want me to be uncomfortable. They want to see if they can make me crack. They want to make sure I won't go nuts and make the room explode or wipe the mind of everyone in the building. But I've already been waiting seven minutes and twenty-three seconds. They can't keep me waiting much longer in this heat. I'll pass out, anyone would. Maybe that's the point. Maybe I'm supposed to fail the test so they can justify keeping me under their control forever.

Sweat! I forgot to sweat. You'd think I'd have the hang of this by now. I do have the hang of this. It was just a momentary lapse. I can control my abilities. I am an asset to the community. I've got to get my sweat flowing, but I have to be careful. Huge pit stains aren't going to make me look good. I signal the various sweat glands around my body and have them up my perspiration. I can feel my body cool almost instantly.

The door opens and a short, bald, middle-aged man walks through the door. His suit is cheap, and his glasses are clearly the basic model his government employee insurance covers. He has a folder in his hands that contains the sum totality of my existence, condensed into a few short pages. He has just used the information in that file to make a decision about the rest of my life. Now we are about to have a perfunctory conversation informing me of that decision. I don't know why all this is necessary. They could just give me a letter telling me where they've decided I'm going to work. The man sits down behind the desk, faces me, and begins looking through his papers.

"Hello Gavin, my name is Scott Wooling, and I'm your Adjustment Counselor. How are you today? Not too nervous, I hope?" Scott says without looking up from my file.

"No sir, just excited to see what opportunities await me," I say back evenly.

That was too calm. I'm about to find out what I'm going to be now that I'm all grown up, so I can be nervous. I should be a little nervous. I'll fidget, that's how people show they're nervous. I wiggle my left arm.

"I have to tell you, Gavin, I have been waiting to meet you. As you can imagine, I see many Differents and I thought I had seen every possible ability. Your Differentiation is unlike any I've heard of before. I find it remarkable to read about what you have gone through, what you have had to overcome to get to where you are. I applaud you for your accomplishments."

That's a good way to start this conversation. Scott seems genuinely intrigued by me. I think he's impressed by me like someone is impressed by a dog standing on its hind legs, but impressed nonetheless. I'm probably being too harsh. I can't read him well enough to know what he thinks. Maybe he's being genuine. How long has it been since he talked? I should have responded by now.

"Thank you, sir. I have a lot of people to thank for getting me to where I am today," I finally say.

I can tell by the look on Scott's face that I took too long to answer.

"And congratulations are in order for completing your high school curriculum. I see here you managed to recover from your... condition and post straight A's in your junior and senior level courses. You ended up just a few months behind the rest of your classmates," Scott says.

"My Differentiation helped me catch up. My memory is just about perfect," I shoot back.

My Differentiation also makes it difficult for me to grasp the passage of time. I have to get it together. I gave that response too quickly. He had barely finished speaking. I breathe deeply and concentrate on keeping track of time.

"Let's talk about your Differentiation. The powers that be are calling it Anthropomorphic Control. That's an entirely new classification. What does it mean?" Scott asks.

"Don't they tell you in there?" I point to the file. I'm quite certain it contains an attempt to explain me.

"They do. But it says what they think you can do. I want to know what *you* think you can do."

"I can control my body, sir. Completely, and in ways no one else can imagine. I can consciously direct processes in my brain that the unconscious mind controls in other people. This allows me to run those processes at an accelerated rate. I heal from cuts in hours and broken bones in a day or two. I can control my muscle growth, putting me in peak physical condition. My abilities allow me to run and perform at maximum effort for hours. I do not sleep..."

I can tell from the look on Scott's face that was too arrogant. He's heard too many Differents try to talk up their abilities to get a better job, and he's not buying it. Also, it's time to move lunch down from my stomach into my small intestine.

"Sounds like you think you've got some real gifts. So explain to me why, when you first Differentiated, you were classified as a Zeta?" Scott asks.

Zeta. Scott may as well have said that I was born with Devil horns. Zeta means useless, worse than useless, a drain. It means that your Differentiation is a disadvantage. It means you'll need extra food and medical care for your entire life. It means every other Different has to pay a tax to keep you fed and well.

I have to slow things down here. I should take my time and be sure I say exactly what I want to say. Good thing I can make time.

Well, stretch my perception of time anyway.

"It's the nature of my Differentiation. As my conscious mind took control of my unconscious systems, there was some difficulty adjusting to the changes. I had to teach myself a completely new set of skills. I had to figure out how to properly regulate my body's endocrine system, my digestive system, my nervous system... I could go on and on. It took me countless hours of studying human biology just to understand what was happening to me, let alone learn to control it."

"Tell me about when you first learned that you were a Different," Scott asks.

That question came out of left field. What does that have to do with what job I'm qualified for? I have no choice but to answer him. I think back, and I remember it well.

#

I was twelve years old. I was with my mother and father, waiting for the 32-Line Slug. I was beaming because all of my childhood dreams were about to come true.

"What about flying? Wouldn't that be great?" my father asked me.

"I don't want wings. It's supposed to hurt when they grow in. Besides, all they ever do is work as delivery guys. I want to help people," I answered.

"Maybe you're a Healer. No one helps people more than they do," he followed up.

"That's not exciting enough."

"Maybe you can blast cold? You used to want to be a fire-fighter."

"Yeah, just like every six-year-old, dad. And they don't generate cold. They absorb heat."

"Good to know... Maybe you can make crystal structures like Maceo. We need to build more train lines. The Slug gets slower and slower every day," he said and stared down the tracks.

"No, I don't want that either. I want something no one's ever had before, something that'll make me a hero, like BlueHawk."

"Maybe you'll be able to eat anything, and they'll have you clean up after dogs," my no longer silent mother chimed in.

Her face showed a blend of terror and sadness, with a strong hint of anger. Emotions exactly opposite mine.

"Helen! Can't you just let him be happy?" my father barked back.

Some of the other people waiting for the train stared at us, and then pretended to look away when I spotted them.

"Or maybe you'll be a Cooler. You can spend your days making sure rich housewives don't have to be uncomfortable. That's helping others," she added.

"It was only the screening. He's probably just a carrier like you. Stop being so dramatic, and let your son enjoy himself," my father said.

Nothing could keep me from enjoying that day. I was going to be tested and told that I possessed a special ability. I never even considered the fact that eighty percent of screening hits are simply carriers. I was a Different. I never doubted it. The test I was about to take would only confirm what I already knew.

"That's right, who cares if it's just a pack of lies. It makes him happy. Maybe we should give him some Tranq too. That'll make him happy," my mother said. "Your son is excited at the prospect of being a slave. A slave, Roy! This doesn't upset you?"

"Lady, why don't you keep your wacko thoughts to yourself before somebody shuts you up," a man yelled from behind us on the platform.

My mother whirled around and sized the man up. He was big and mean and looked like enough of a scumbag to hit a woman. Even worked up, my mother knew enough to zip it and look forward. I could hear her teeth grind.

We stood in awkward silence for a long time. I embraced it and dreamt of what abilities I might have. The Slug came and we stepped onto the train car. It was full so we had to stand.

"Maybe you can time travel? No one's been able to do that yet," my father finally managed.

"Let's stop talking about it," I said.

"Come on, who cares what the chances are? It's fun," my father said, even though it was pretty clear that no one was having fun.

"Most people don't Differentiate until they are fourteen or fifteen. There'll be plenty of time to imagine what I can do between now and then."

We hardly talked again for the rest of the Slug ride. The near silence continued all the way to the testing lab. After the test proved me right, my father tried to pretend to be happy for me, but I could tell he was crushed. It was fun to talk about what I might become when there was a two in ten chance of it being true. Faced with the reality, my father struggled to keep his smile on for my sake. My mother said nothing.

The next day when I returned home from school, my mother was gone. She left a note: "Gavin, you may put the collar around your own neck, but I do not have to stay and watch. My only satisfaction comes from knowing that God will one day punish those who enslave you, just as he once punished the Egyptians for enslaving the Israelites. I know you'll be too hurt to believe me, but I'm doing this because I love you so much. I can't watch what they are going to do to you. Love, Mom."

#

"I didn't believe her."

"You've had no contact with your mother since that day?" Scott asks.

Now I understand this man's purpose. They hide it behind the Adjustment Counselor title, but his real job is something else entirely. This is a psychiatric evaluation.

"None. She couldn't even wait the three weeks until I was officially enrolled in Section 26."

I make sure it seems difficult for me to say by fidgeting my hands and stammering a bit in my delivery. I don't like talking about my mother, but if I have to, I need to be conscious of my body language so Scott knows it is difficult for me. I don't want him to think I'm a monster.

"And your father? It says here that he died three years ago in a fishing accident. How would you say you handled that?" Scott asks.

He doesn't even blink as he asks me another incredibly probing question.

"I didn't handle it, not at first anyway. It happened when I was comatose," I reply.

"Why were you comatose?"

"I'm sure my file tells you. It was a side effect of my Differentiation first developing. I almost died."

"Why don't you tell me about that? When your Differentiation first developed?"

#

I was right about my abilities not showing until I was fourteen. Two days after my fourteenth birthday, at three in the morning, I woke up for the last time in my life. I was gasping for air. I could not breathe. I cried out.

Suddenly, what had been my dorm room transformed into a prison cell/reverse bomb shelter. Walls made of Maceo Steel came down all around me. This is why I was there, in Section 26. When Danny Libdo Differentiated, he destroyed most of the Minneapolis Metro Area. The Maceo Steel walls were indestructible. They could have contained anything. Even if my Differentiation had been splitting atoms like Danny's Differentiation was.

The authorities saw my distress over the feed they used to watch me sleep.

"What are you experiencing?" a voice asked over a loud speaker.

The voice knocked me out of my panic. I focused on my breathing. In and out, I started to feel better.

"It's nothing. I must have had a bad dream or something. I felt like I couldn't breathe for a second. I think I'm fine now," I answered.

"Okay, we will keep the protective unit down and continue to monitor you just to be safe," said the voice.

I spent the rest of the night focusing on my breathing. Every time I started to drift off, I woke up gasping for air. In the morning, I went to the medic. I had almost choked while brushing my teeth.

The medic was like most of the employees in Section 26,

overworked and under-resourced. He was unshaven and needed some sleep. That's what happens to you after years of helping Differents with complaints ranging from the common cold to the growth of new limbs.

"It's hard to explain. I wouldn't call it difficulty breathing, more like I can't breathe if I don't focus on doing it," I told the Medic.

He shined a flashlight in my eyes. It was incredibly bright. I pulled away.

"That hurt. That thing is too bright," I said.

"That's because your pupils are dilated. Have you taken any medication or other substances?" the doctor asked. It was not a friendly question.

"No."

"As your doctor, I can only treat you if I know what's in your body. You're sure you didn't take anything? Maybe some Tranq? You kids and that poison, I don't know how you manage to get it in here."

"No, I haven't taken anything. I just woke up in the middle of the night and couldn't breathe."

"If you really aren't on anything, there is another explanation. Panic attacks. I'll set you up an appointment with the therapist. She'll be able to help you. Has anything else been bothering you?"

"Yeah my stomach has been hurting for the last couple days."

The medic pressed his hand on my stomach. It hurt.

"You're as hard as a rock. When was your last bowel movement?" he asked.

#

"It had been a week since I'd taken a dump," I explain to Scott.

Maybe that was inappropriate. I wanted to emphasize my point, but that language might have been too much. Then again, maybe most people lose control a little when they are talking about difficult periods in their lives. Maybe it was perfect.

"And you continued to deteriorate from there. It says here that you lost the ability to eat and drink, so you had to be put on an IV and feeding tube for several months, is that accurate?" Scott asks.

"I'm sure it is."

"You're sure it is?"

"I don't remember."

"I thought you had an almost perfect memory?" Scott asks.

This guy is a jerk. That's why he's good at this. It's more than just a job to him. He genuinely enjoys needling young Differents to see if he can make them crack.

"I didn't have my improved memory yet. My unconscious mind had ceased forming memories automatically. I don't remember anything from a few days after I went to see the medic until a few months after my sixteenth birthday."

"Okay then, what's the first thing you do remember?"

"I remember Larry Rosen trying to do a back flip and breaking his glasses."

#

Larry stared up at me from the floor. One of his glasses lenses had popped out and the other was smashed right up against his eye socket. He looked ridiculous, especially with his big red afro. He had chosen to be five feet, two inches tall and two hundred fifty pounds. He made an excellent choice considering he was trying to be memorable, but he could have looked like anyone he wanted. He was a Morpher.

We were in a hospital room in Section 26. I had an IV feeding into my arm. All of my hair had fallen out and my skin was peeling off in sheets.

"I don't know how else to put it, but I think you have to focus on remembering, just like you focus on your breathing. While things are happening, actively try to remember them. Like if you wanted to memorize a phone number, but for everything that happens to you," Larry said.

"I've never used a phone," I replied.

"Okay wise guy, then like a date you need to remember for a history test."

That's just what I did. I thought about Larry doing his flip and how ridiculous his face looked right after it hit the floor. I ran the image over and over again in my mind. Then I focused on remembering to remember.

"We have to talk about something else for a while. What did you want to be when you were growing up, before you found out you were a Different?" Larry asked.

"You said you work with me all the time. Maybe you've asked me this a hundred times before."

"No, I mostly had you tell me every embarrassing thing that happened to you when you were a kid. So answer my question, or I'll tell everyone."

"I wanted to be a Different."

"You wanted to be a Different? No one wants to be a Different," Larry said.

"I did. I never cared about Cabot or the Plagues or The Different Acts. As soon as I learned about BlueHawk, that's who I wanted to be. I wanted to be a Different, and I wanted fight the Russians and save the world," I replied.

"The Ruskies aren't able to put up much of a fight these days."

"I think they have enough to stop me," I held up my IV-ridden arm.

"Maybe, maybe. Hey, do you know how I broke my glasses?" Larry asked.

"You were trying to do a back flip," I answered.

#

"Once I discovered I could control my creation of memories, just like I could control any system in my body, the world reopened to me. After nearly a year of being an invalid, I was able to begin functioning again. I could build off what I had learned the day before and figure out how to make my body work again. I'm just lucky I figured it out before my heart stopped beating on its own," I tell Scott.

Why do they have a normal human doing this interview? Why don't they just have a Telepath turn my mind inside out? Find out everything I ever thought or felt? Maybe they know I can hide from Telepaths.

"That seems like quite an achievement. May I ask why, after such a great accomplishment, it took you another two years catch up on your studies? I imagine a perfect memory would be quite the advantage in school," Scott Wooling asks.

I'm just being paranoid. It doesn't have anything to do with me, not specifically. The government wouldn't trust a Different with such an important task. Scott is the last line of defense, the last person who can figure out if I'm a danger to society. We Differents can heat their homes and grow food for their children, but the humans don't trust a Telepath to turn on their own kind.

I have to handle this question carefully. He's probing me again, trying to make me reveal one little nugget that can justify marking me as too dangerous to release or prove that I'm too useless for any job.

"The truth is, I have Larry to thank again," I say.

#

"I had the worst day yesterday," Larry complained. "I got woken up at five this morning because the couple next door was fighting. Something about how he's always spending their money down in Santa Monica while she pays all the rent and COL obligations. Anyway, I've been working with this kid. He's thirteen years old, early bloomer. His Differentiation makes his body produce this sticky green substance. They were hoping he could be used to produce an adhesive. The problem is his body needs carbon-rich materials in order to live, which is not exactly the most common thing in the world, thanks to Cabot. I was hoping we could teach him to focus and stop making the goo, but we couldn't figure it out. They had to put him under a Tranq-coma so he wouldn't die. The point is, by the time I made it home, I swear to God that day lasted as long as most weeks."

"I don't get it," I replied.

"And when I think back to when I first met my wife, back before the Plagues. It seemed like those early days just flew by."

"I still don't get it. Now hold on, I have to breathe," Larry waited while I took several deep breaths so I could listen to him for another thirty to forty seconds.

"My point is that time might not be under your control, but I think you might be able to control how you perceive it. If you recreate whatever happened in my brain that made yesterday seem so long, you'll have all the time you need to focus on blinking, or remembering, or growing your hair, or all that other stuff you always have to do. We can talk without you having to take breathing breaks every thirty seconds."

#

"Larry was right. The way we experience time is controlled by our brains. By slowing down life, by recreating the way time feels when you're stuck in a boring class or the moments during an accident when time seems to stand still, I gave myself time to manage the systems of my body while still interacting with the outside world. While you and I are talking, I am actively managing my endocrine system, my digestive system, my muscular system, my nervous system, my respiratory system... I could go on and on. By stretching my perception of time, I can effectively give myself time to manage those systems while also answering, listening, talking, and wondering what I'll eat for dinner. I needed more time, and I figured out how to make it," I explain to Scott.

"That's quite a story. You really have overcome many hardships caused by your Differentiation. You're an example to other Zetas out there. Maybe they too can make something of themselves, if they work at it. I have one more question for you, and it is important. Is there any element of your Differentiation, no matter how minor you consider it, that has not been brought to the attention of Section 26 personnel?" Scott asks.

And there it is, the question he had really been asking me the whole time, spit out it no uncertain terms. Are there any elements of my Differentiation Section 26 do not know about? Of course there are. I'm not sure if I gave them all the information they needed on how exactly I move fecal matter into my bowel or how hard it is to get blinking timed right. I still blink too often.

There is something I know they would want to hear about. I can fool Telepaths. I can feel them in my mind searching and probing, but I can control their view. I can let them see only what I want them to see within my mind. I lied to the Section 26 Telepath and got away with it. When I told this to Larry, he made it quite clear I should keep that fact to myself. He said they'll never let me out of Section 26 if they know I can hide from mind-readers. He knew because he can fool Telepaths himself. Apparently some Morphers can manipulate their minds as well as their bodies. Section 26 doesn't know about that.

"I can't think of anything, sir. Except that I have you guys to thank for saving my life. If I hadn't had the help and support of Section 26, I would be dead. I'm going to have a life thanks to the people here," I finally answer.

"I'm glad to hear that you feel that way, because now comes the painful part. We need to discuss your Cost of Living Obligations," Scott says.

Save me then bill me. It's quite a racket they have here. It's not like I asked them to keep me on an IV for months... not that I didn't want them to.

"When we add up the eighteen months you had to be kept in isolation before you Differentiated, the medical cost of keeping you alive, food and clothing costs, including the tax on higher than average food consumption, your contributions to the Different Assistance fund, and various administrative and personnel fees, you owe $386,236.74. Hey, that's not too bad!"

Sounds fantastic. My father didn't earn that in his entire life.

"There's more good news. I've decided to approve you for non-government housing, so you will be free to live outside Section 26. A mark of Differentiation will, of course, be required. Now, let's discuss your employment prospects. Based on your Cost of Living Obligations and interest rates, you will be required to make minimum monthly payments of $850. Your profile received one bid for service. It is from the Unified Logistics Technology and Research Applications Corporation. The pay is fair, more than enough to make your payments. You'll be working in the Oasis

Burger Research and Development division..."

"Ultracorps? Was there any interest from the Office of Exceptional Cases?" I interrupt.

"What in God's name could you do for the OEC?"

"I told you. I'm in peak physical condition, I have an incredible memory, I can heal at an accelerated rate, and I could master several forms of martial arts if I studied them."

"Sorry, Gavin. The OEC has no need of your services. If we can get back to the Ultracorps position..." Scott continues.

"Maybe you can have them review my profile again?" I plead.

"That isn't possible. Your responsibilities at Ultracorps would center on the testing and implementation of new foods and recipe changes for Oasis Burger. They believe you will be able to provide invaluable feedback on the effects of chemical additives."

"Maybe you could talk to the OEC, tell them you think I have potential. Tell them that I would make a good agent."

"That is not going to happen. Your safety will always be the program's top concern."

"I don't want to be a lab rat for fast food. I want to do something useful. I want to work for the OEC."

"Enough, Gavin. It's the Office of Exceptional Cases, not cases of freaks with no talent. You think you're strong? You think you're fast? There are dozens of Differents who can toss a Slug-car like a baseball or run faster than you can throw one. You think you're smart? I've seen twenty Differents this year who could recite the Bible cover to cover. You think you heal quickly? A hundred Differents out there can grow an arm back in five minutes! You may be a Different, Gavin, but you are not exceptional."

Boom. Just like that, my childhood dreams are crushed. I knew the OEC probably wasn't going to want me, but I still hoped, somewhere deep down. I didn't even know I still had a deep down. I just wanted some way to help people.

2

I speak to you plainly. This time there will be no confusion, no questioning of my will, and no quibbling over translation. I shall make my proclamations known explicitly and directly. These are the words of your Lord, spoken in your own tongue so that all may understand my third missive.

Chosen Sons: 2

David Gabbert has to hurry. The last Slug of the night pulls out of the station in six minutes. His feet cannot take another two mile haul to the central line. He gathers a mass of papers from his desk and stuffs them into his brown leather briefcase. He grabs his overcoat and heads out of his office.

The street is empty. Everyone else has the good sense to be home by now. Ten o'clock is too late for anyone to be out, let alone a sixty-seven-year-old bureaucrat with a potbelly. The one "person" on the street is a Walter, mindlessly sweeping the sidewalk. Even though the clones of Walter Reynolds have been a fixture in the Los Angeles Metro Area for almost ten years, they still give David the creeps with those empty, soulless eyes.

David still cannot believe his office was moved all the way out to this pit. It is hard to believe there is even a government building this far from the Metro Center. David knows she did it. Not that it was a tough case to crack. One day he took a stand against Nita's plan to have Ultracorps take over management of the Los Angeles Metro Area's water system. The next day there was emergency construction required in David's suite of offices, and he was "temporarily" relocated to the boonies. All because he had the audacity to oppose giving more power to the Ultracorps Librarians, which really meant giving more power to the twelve-year-old girl who is their leader. She already controls the Metro Area's transportation and heating systems. He does not care how smart Nita Martinez is. A child and her human computer friends should not control the entire infrastructure of a Metro Area.

Taking a stand against Nita hadn't worked, either. The Metro Council subcommittee overruled David, and Nita and Ultracorps got the contract. Overruled and exiled, it has been a terrible month for David Gabbert. It will get even worse if he misses that last train. He speeds up his pace.

Half a block away he hears the Slug pull out of the station. Breathing heavily, he sighs at his useless rushing. If David were paranoid, he would think Nita did this too. Ultracorps does run the trains after all.

He does not want to be paranoid. More importantly, he does not want anyone else to think he is paranoid. If they think he is paranoid then they won't listen to his opposition to Ultracorps. They will just dismiss him as another crazy old coot that is afraid of change, like one of those old men who used to complain about television back before the Plagues.

Maybe that's Nita's plan, to keep pushing David until he loses control and says something crazy in committee. Then they will ignore him forever, or until he is replaced. Then there would be no one left to stand in her way. He is the last one, especially since Lauren disappeared. Without her organizing protests, public opposition to Ultracorps is melting away. The LA Metro is just the beginning. Ultracorps—Nita—wants control of the utilities in every Metro Area. Then she will have control of the whole country.

Stop! David yells inside his head. No more crazy thoughts. A much more sensible plot would be for Nita to have sent David out to the boonies and hope some punks would murder him. He now has to walk two miles to the central line. They are not scenic miles, they are two of the most crime-addled miles in the Metro Area. David gets stared down by thugs every time he has to walk. It's only a matter of time until one of them does something more than glare.

David is distracted from his paranoid thoughts by a crippling pain in his foot. He's due for another Healer-Blood transfusion to manage the pain, but he has not been able to find the time. He has to sit down and finds a stoop to plop on. Taking off his right sock and shoe, he massages his foot. He has to stop the spasms if he wants to make it home.

David looks down for a mere second, but when he looks up there is a man standing a few feet away from him. David cannot see the man clearly in the shadows, but the man is the size of a mountain. A mountain staring coldly at David.

"I don't have any money or anything else on me worth stealing, friend. If you want my clothes you can have them, but I don't think they'll fit you," David says.

"I ain't here to rob you. I've got some good news. The Lord has chosen you to be saved," the mountain says.

"Oh, you're one of those. Sorry sir, not interested. I'm happy with my God. Maybe if my feet keep hurting…"

"But if you don't listen, you won't know eternity in heaven is waitin' for you after I eat ya."

"What did you say?" David asks, even though he heard the man clearly.

The mountain pulls out a book from his jacket and reads.

"There is but one way for my Forgotten Sons to return to my grace. They must serve my new race, my Chosen Sons, in any way possible. They must tithe to the Chosen, and submit to their every whim. They must be willing to sacrifice anything and everything for them. If my Forgotten Sons do this, they will be welcome in my kingdom for eternity."

"So what do you say? Are you ready to be held in the arms of the Lord?" the mountain says and steps forward into the light.

Now David can see that the mountain is not a man. Men do not have six-inch claws and massive canines that stick out from their jaw. Men do not have hair all over their body. Men do not weigh as much as bears. He is not a man. He's some sort of Beast.

"My God, it's you, The Beast. I always knew they were lying. They didn't really stop you in Chicago," David whispers to himself.

"I can't be stopped. The Lord has given me divine purpose. He's got a purpose for you too. Right now, He's calling you up to heaven."

Most of David's brain is frozen, unable to comprehend what is happening, but some primitive part of his mind takes over as he turns and breaks into a full sprint. His foot does not hurt anymore, and he forgets he's missing a shoe. *Run* is the closest thing to a thought in David's mind.

The Beast watches for a few moments as David scrambles away. Eventually, the creature bends his knees and pounces. The Beast jumps fifty feet through the air with ease and slams into David, knocking the poor man into a pile of old concrete. David can feel some ribs crack.

David picks himself up off the ground and begins to sprint again. Each breath feels like fire, but it reminds him that at least he is still breathing. He makes it around a corner and thinks, just for a second, that maybe he will get away. The Beast's claw shatters that fantasy. His nails tear through David's back like tissue paper and the man crumples into a bleeding pile on the ground.

The Beast stands over David, waiting to see if there is any fight left in the man, but there is not. David curls into a ball, whimpering.

"I knew I was right. I knew I was right," the terrified bureaucrat keeps repeating.

No wonder God has given up on his race: the Forgotten Sons are pathetic. The Beast licks blood off his claw. The blood tastes sweet, and the rest of David will taste even sweeter. He closes his eyes to pray over his bounty.

“Lord, thank you for giving me this chance to atone for my sins. I’m going to make sure nobody finds any of him, just like you said. Did I do good Lord? Can you tell me if I’m gonna be redeemed?”

The Beast keeps his eyes closed, waiting for a response. There isn’t any. He sighs and throws the old man over his shoulders. He grabs the man's briefcase. The Lord commanded The Beast to leave no trace.

3

All costs and expenditures associated with the care and evaluation of the Different shall be the sole responsibility of that individual. Upon release from Section 26, the Different individual will be required to pay the debt, such as they are able. The interest rate and terms of the debt shall be determined by the Federal Reserve.

Article 2 Section 2 of the Different Acts of 1986

I walk out of the Maceo Steel gates that contain the only world I've known for the last five years. All I take with me is a small bag full of clothes and a couple of childhood possessions. In a way, it's like I'm walking into the world for the first time. I can remember being outside when I was a kid, but it's almost as if they are someone else's memories. Compared to the memories I form now, my old ones are faint shadows. There are things I wish I could remember from before, but I can't, and there are thousands of things I can remember but don't care about. I don't know why I can recall the theme song from some radio show I didn't even like when I was a kid, but not what my dad said to me the day my mom left. The human brain has some flaws.

Now the memories I form are perfect. Every sight, every sound, every thought, every feeling. When I see a sign for Oasis Burger down the street, I instantly recall all the information I have stored about the chain. I remember all the different catch phrases: "Refresh Yourself," "Take a Break from Your Journey," "Discover the Oasis." I can also recall everything I learned about Oasis Burger from the article on think.Net.

Before the Plagues, Oasis Burger was called McDonalds. When Cabot's Plagues spread and the world food supplies dwindled, most of the McDonalds had to close. In 1987, McDonalds merged with Ultracorps, which re-launched the restaurant chain as Oasis Burger. The company spread quickly and is now the largest restaurant chain in America. It employs over a million people. Starting Monday, I will be one of them.

I consider stopping in the store and having a bite. I’ve used up most of the calories from lunch six hours ago, but they said there was a train waiting for me. I head towards the long stairwell that leads to Section 26's Slug station. I take deep breaths as I walk. The air smells different out here than it smells inside the building. There are more pollutants: carbon dioxide, methane, and hundreds of other things I can't identify. It's a little overwhelming, so I focus on my breathing and ignore my sense of smell.

When I get to the station, the small train car is indeed waiting. No one else is in the train, not even at the controls. I sit down inside on an uncomfortable seat and wait. It has been a long time since I’ve ridden the Slug. I always liked it as a kid, even with the smell. They call it the Slug because the fuel the train burns looks like a bunch of worms, or slugs. It's actually a by-product of a bacterium grown by a Different. The bacteria eat sewage, garbage, anything organic really, and leave behind the carbon-rich "Slugs." It is a better fuel source than oil or coal ever was. It burns longer and cleaner, but then there is the smell. The big problem is that the Different who produces the bacteria only grows so much.

I wait eleven minutes, but I make it seem like it's just a few seconds. Time flies when you're having fun. Or when you force your brain to recreate the experience of it.

I stop making time go by when a man in his early thirties walks onto the train. He’s wearing an ugly blue uniform. He must be the conductor, but his appearance doesn't inspire much confidence as a driver. He needs a shave and his uniform is a mess. He has a light behind his eyes though. He’s taking in everything he sees.

"You Gavin Stillman?" he knows the answer is yes, but he needs something to say.

"I am."

"Your chariot awaits, my friend. You've got the whole place to yourself. This train's heading straight to the Barracks."

He goes into the control booth and shortly thereafter, we head off towards Ultracorps employee housing, or the Barracks, as everyone calls it. It's on the south side of the Los Angeles Metro Area. The woman in charge of housing arrangements laughed at me when I asked if I had to live in employee housing.

"Of course not," she said. "You are authorized to live wherever you choose. Of course, every landlord in the country requires Differents to buy insurance. As long as your father is some sort of prince or the CEO of Ultracorps, I'm sure you'll be able to afford the premiums and rent in addition to your monthly COL Obligations payments and your mandatory think.Net account. If your daddy isn't rich as the Pope, you'll be living in the Barracks."

My dad was a fisherman and now he's dead, so I headed for Ultracorps housing. Maybe I can afford to live outside the Barracks if I save up for forty years, considering my salary and Cost of Living Obligations.

As for the mandatory think.Net account, it doesn't have to be mandatory. I couldn't imagine not having an account. It let me talk to my father for the last time on my fourteenth birthday. He saved for weeks to buy some think.Net time, just so we could talk. I can't remember much of what he said, but I remember how happy it made me.

Think.Net is made up of a series of over a thousand Telepaths who form a network that blankets the entire country. Using the network is easy, you just think about going on it. Then you think about contacting anyone you'd like to speak to, anyone who has authorized you to call or "knows" you. You can even call the other Metro Areas, except Houston of course. Long-range calls cost a small fortune though. There's just a handful of Telepaths powerful enough to reach that far.

But think.Net does so much more than let people talk. There are the Librarians, super intelligent Differents who are essentially living encyclopedias. The think.Net Telepaths can tap into the Librarians' memories and share what they know with us. The Librarians form even more perfect memories than I do. Between them all, they can recall almost every book or scientific paper that's ever been written.

They also provide think.Net shows for entertainment and even some Pre-Plague television shows and movies, anything that any Librarian has ever seen.

More than that, almost every store in Los Angeles does business on think.Net. They usually charge an extra fee if you pay with cash. I remember because my dad had to pay it all the time. I think the money is the main reason the government requires Differents to maintain a think.Net account. You can learn pretty much everything there is to know about a person by looking at how they spend their money.

It seems like overkill to me. It's not like it's easy for me to hide. I look down at the tattoo they put on my right hand after my meeting with the Adjustment Counselor. It's illegal to conceal it.

The tattoo is a big black D that takes up most of my hand. Inside the D, in tiny letters, it says, Gavin Stillman: Anthropomorphic Control: GAMMA.

Gamma is written in larger letters than the rest. It means they consider me no more dangerous than your average human, not a ringing endorsement of my abilities. Better than Zeta, though. They put it there so if the cops ever stop me, they have some idea of what they're dealing with.

I could remove the tattoo if I wanted to. The ink is stuck in my second layer of skin, and the cells there don't need to reproduce very often so the ink is stable. But I could have my body respond to the ink like it's a toxic invader, pushing it out of my skin like a pimple. The problem would be that I have no way to get the tattoo back on. It'll be useful if I ever have to flee the country, otherwise it's just a one-way ticket to Great Basin Prison. I should think about something else.

It will be a long ride to employee housing. The Section 26 compound is ten miles west of the Metro Center, which itself is another seven miles from employee housing. In those seventeen miles we'll pass by almost twenty million people. I remember hearing that people used to complain about Los Angeles being too crowded back before the Plagues. That was when there were only three million people.

When the Plagues devastated the nation, the government struggled to provide relief. Transportation was the most difficult obstacle. Cabot's bacteria ate up the world's fuel supply, making it almost impossible to transport what little food the government could manage to get its hands on. Since it was too hard to bring the food to the people, the government decided to bring the people to the food. The entire U.S. population was ordered to relocate to the Metro Areas. Those who refused to move were left in what are called the Non-Assisted Areas. While technically still the United States, the Non-Assisted Areas are outside of the government's control.

The Plagues killed around half of the United States population from 1980 to 1985. Still, that left about one hundred fifteen million people, divided into nine Metro Areas. Add in population growth and there are one hundred seventy million people divided into seven Metro Areas. There are about twenty million people in Los Angeles. Twenty-five million if you count people who live outside the official Metro Area border.

There must not have been anyone else getting out of Section 26 anytime soon if they're wasting the Slug on just me. The single train car is designed to hold sixty. I settle into the uncomfortable seat and make time breeze by. After what feels like two seconds later to me, but was fifteen minutes in the real world, the Conductor interrupts my space out. He's opened the door to the control booth and stands half in, half out so he can talk and keep an eye on the track. Guess he's bored enough to chat with the cargo.

"So what kind of work did they give you?" he says.

I hone in on his name badge and focus my eyes. His name is Ben.

"I got an offer to work for Ultracorps. I'll be working in the research department assisting in the collection of data to further nutritional development," it sounds better than telling him I'll be a lab rat for a fast food joint.

"An offer, hah!" Ben snorts. "Offer implies you had a choice. The good news is that Section 26 is letting their mitts off you, that counts for something. Even if they have you working as a lab rat—I mean nutritional developer—at least you get to sleep in a bed you own."

"Thanks. I guess."

"I'm just messing with you. It's not so bad. Wait till you see the Barracks. It's a palace. There's Hoovers in every apartment. They got a pool on the grounds and each building has their own Cooler. You will love them come August. I've got four people living in my one bedroom condo and our Hoover tube is on the first floor. I hurt my back carrying the garbage down last week."

"But, like you said, I'm a lab rat."

I hadn't realized employee housing was so posh, but maybe he's still just messing with me. I focus in on his carotid artery and watch it pulse. His heart rate is elevated. Maybe he's lying, or maybe he eats too many fried foods.

"Lab rat, that doesn't sound so bad. You think my job is so glamorous? After I drop you off, I'm supposed to head out to the depot and pick up a Slug tanker. I will have worked a sixteen hour shift by the time I get home. I'll work five more of those this week, and I'm lucky. There are a dozen other guys who would kill to get my shifts. Believe me, lots of those guys would kill to be a lab rat too."

"What about COL Obligations? You don't have some huge debt placed on your head just for existing. I didn't ask to be put in Section 26. I was just born a Different."

"That's true kid, that's a crummy situation there and there ain't no two ways about it. I hate to break it to you though, but all of us are in a crummy situation. I got rent, credit card payments, preschool, think.Net accounts, and three hungry mouths counting on my paycheck. Some might call those Cost of Living Obligations too."

"I know I don't have it so bad. I know it could be much worse. I just always hoped I'd get to be somebody special, someone who made a big difference, someone who mattered in the world."

"You and me both, kid, you and me both," Ben says dismissively.

Then he acts as though he sees something that requires his attention and heads back into the control booth. I think he's heard enough of my whining.

I make time fly through the outskirts of the Metro Area until we get close to the LA Metro Center. Once the Metro Center comes into view, I make time move as slowly as I can.

I've always loved the Metro Center, and seeing it for the first time with my new eyes only makes it more beautiful. The Shimmering Tower still stands shining brilliantly over the whole Center and right next to it are the Hanging Gardens, the most amazing thing I've ever seen. So much green in one place doesn't seem possible. It's like a miniature heaven floating in the clouds. I can't believe how the whole thing just hangs there. Even if I focus my vision as far as I can, I still can't make out the ForteSilk strands that hold the Gardens up.

ForteSilk, another moneymaker for Ultracorps, which of course, employs the Different who makes strands a thousand times stronger than steel. A strand as thin as a thread can hold up an entire building. A couple dozen of those and a bunch of Maceo Steel spires, and you can hold up a whole floating island.

As we continue through the LA Metro Area, away from the Metro Center, the neighborhoods get progressively uglier and uglier. Maceo Steel and ForteSilk give way to buildings made of B-Crete and others patched up after they were left barely standing from the Plagues.

Thankfully, the housing complex looks nothing like the surrounding neighborhood. It's made up of several different buildings, all built by Maceo himself. I try to focus on the beauty of the crystalline structures Maceo produced and not the fact that the material is unbreakable, and therefore makes the perfect prison walls.

Ben heads out from the control booth.

"This is you. Good luck."

"Thanks, you too," I say and step off the train.

I take in the Slug station I will be seeing twice a day for my foreseeable future. I turn back to look at the train, and through the window in the control booth, I see that Ben is speaking. Out of curiosity I amplify my hearing, and I can just barely make out what he's saying.

"I was thinking, kid, there is a difference between you and me. Yeah, we both got a pile of crap to deal with. But, if I decide to say the hell with it and run off, it'd just be my wife looking for me. You run off, you're breaking the law. We both have our responsibilities, but I'm the only one who is free," Ben says as if I was standing right next to him.

As he finishes his speech, he puts the train in motion. How did he know I could hear him? A normal person wouldn't have been able to make out a word. I run as fast as I can towards the doors, but he's already closed them. The Slug pulls away down the tracks.

#

The inside of the administration building is just as incredible as the rest of the grounds. It's all lit by skylight, and the sun sparkles off still pools of water dotting the lobby, which is shaped like a hexagon with a single reception desk in the center. I feel like I've stepped into the future.

I approach the desk and glance at the receptionist's right hand. No D. I guess some regular humans work here. She doesn't notice me approaching. Her eyes are open, but they aren't focused. She's in the think.Net stare, lost in a world inside her head. Her lips are moving, she must be talking to someone. I clear my throat.

"Hello, my name is Gavin Stillman. I'm supposed to check in here."

Her eyes focus in on me for just a second, and she puts on a smile. Then she goes back to the think.Net stare.

"Hello Gavin, my name is Theresa. Let me be the first to welcome you to Ultracorps employee housing. We are happy to have you stay with us, and we trust your stay will be a happy one," she says without looking at me.

"Thanks."

"I've been instructed to confirm that you are capable of turning off your hearing. Can you, in fact, withstand incredibly loud noises that would damage a normal person's ears?"

"I can. Although, I can't turn off my hearing exactly. I am capable of controlling the fluid level in my Tympanic Cavity, allowing my eardrums to adapt..."

"That's a yes?" she interrupts.

"Yes."

"Then it's your lucky day. You get the Penthouse, Tower 3. Your roommate's name is Nicholas Werden. Here's your key."

"Why all the questions about my hearing?"

"I'll let that be a surprise. Have a wonderful day."

#

Tower 3 is yet another miracle. It's over forty stories high. Each floor is elliptical and they alternate, quadrupling the number of balconies. It's amazing what can be built with unbreakable materials. Thank you very much, Maceo. There are gardens on every balcony. Things are definitely looking up.

I head inside and find the elevator, but I don't hear any movement when I hit the button. I spot a sign: "ELEVATOR HOURS: 6-9AM, 6-11PM." It's two in the afternoon. The Strong-Man Different who runs the elevator must have a day job. Strong-Men eat a lot, which means they need to earn a lot too.

The whole area sounds just about empty. I guess everyone around here is at work all day, something I have to look forward to soon. I see the sign for the stairs and walk down the hallway. There's a man mopping the floor.

"Hello," I say with a friendly smile.

The man looks up at me, and I see soulless eyes and a familiar face. He's a Walter. They used to terrify me when I was a kid. Clone of a clone of a clone of Walter Reynolds, who is another fellow Ultracorps employee. The clones can't speak and they'll do whatever they are told. They make a perfect source of free labor. They're the janitors for the entire LA Metro Area. I heard that Ultracorps wants to expand them to the other Metro Areas. I wonder if there is a limit to how many copies Walter can make.

I open the doors to the staircase and make my way up forty flights of stairs. I have my lungs absorb as much oxygen as they are capable of and speed up my heart rate so I don't get winded. I turn up my sweat production to get rid of some excess body heat.

I find my apartment on the forty-first floor. It was easy to find because it's the top of the building and the only apartment on the level. I hear sounds of life inside the apartment. Someone is listening to the radio.

"The search continues for noted Ultracorps opponent Alderman David Gabbert. Alderman Gabbert has been missing since last Thursday. Anyone with information regarding the disappearance is encouraged to contact Metro Police. This follows the disappearance of other noted Ultracorps opponent Lauren Conrad six months ago. Ms. Conrad was the leader of Idle Hands, a pro-human labor lobby which supports Alderman Gabbert…"

Is my roommate home? I would think he'd be at work during the day like everyone else. I insert the key and open the door while knocking. I figure that's the polite thing to do, even if it is my house too now.

"Hello, Nicholas?"

I enter and take a scan of the apartment. The living room is large with nice furniture. There's a dining room set and a comfortable-looking red couch. The couch is covered in dirty clothes. Seven socks, four shirts, and six pairs of underwear.

I hear a shower turn off, then the radio. My God, we have our own bathroom in the apartment. This place is getting nicer and nicer. The door to one of the bedrooms opens and Nicholas, I assume, walks out in a robe. He's tall with dirty blond hair. He looks like he is twenty-three or twenty-four. He has a small gut forming, and his body is going to keep storing fat there as he gets older. It is not going to be attractive.

"Uh, hello?" Nicholas stammers. I don't think anyone told him to expect me. "Can I help you?"

"Hi, I'm Gavin Stillman, your new roommate," I drop my bag and walk over to shake his hand.

He seems stunned by the news for a moment, and then he puts his hand out and shakes. He drops his towel. I ignore my optic nerve signals.

"My roommate? I don't believe it. They've been threatening to give me a roommate for four years. I just never thought they'd do it. Well, it's nice to meet you Gavin, I'm Nick Werden. Wait, can you hear me?" he asks while pulling up and securing his towel. He doesn't seem happy to have a roommate, but who would be?

"Yeah, of course I can hear you. Why?" I ask. What's with all the questions about my hearing?

"You're not reading my thoughts or something? You can really hear?"

"I can hear."

"Sorry, I just figured if I ever got a roommate, he'd have to be deaf. They did their best to insulate the sound, but it still gets pretty loud down here."

"Sound?"

"Didn't they tell you who I am? Of course not, that lady at the desk is evil. I'm the Metro Area's alarm clock," Nick proclaims.

He raises his hand up to his face, giving me my first good look at his tattoo. Nicholas Werden: Sound Producer: BETA. Beta means he's powerful. His Differentiation makes him a threat. It also means he probably makes a lot more than me.

"I'm a Screamer. Three times a day I go up on the roof and scream loud enough for the entire Metro Area to hear. Seven a.m. wake up, noon lunch, and seven p.m. quitting time. The city runs by my voice," He seems pretty proud of that.

"That's cool. What do you do the rest of the time?" I ask.

"Relax... or do ads. I make emergency alerts, too. What's your Differentiation?"

"Anthropomorphic Control."

"In non-government speak please."

"I can control all aspects of my body consciously. I can make myself heal, or make my hair grow, or protect my ears from loud sounds. I think that's why we're roomies," I explain.

"Lucky me. I'll have to clean out your room. I never thought they'd find someone. There's stuff all over the place."

"Thanks. You mind if I take a shower myself? I've never had a private shower."

In our apartment growing up, we had a communal shower that everyone in the building shared. In Section 26, all the guys on my floor had to share the same shower.

"Your room's on the left. And you have your own bathroom."

I walk into my new room and turn the WormLight on, but nothing happens. I look into the light, and the Manna cube is all eaten up.

"Hey Nick, do you have any Manna for the light I could borrow?"

"Uh, that thing burned out like two years ago. The worms are dead for sure. You'll have to buy a new one."

They aren't worms. They're actually strands of bacteria produced by a Different. Those strands generate light, as long as you keep them fed, but I keep that fact to myself. No one likes a know-it-all.

Good thing I can adjust my eyes to the dark. I dilate my pupils, which intensifies the low ambient light and lets me see the room. There are a few dirty clothes and empty boxes on the floor. It's a bunch of stuff Nick didn't feel like dealing with. Looks like he's lazy. Everyone loves a lazy roommate.

I drop my pack on the floor and make my way to the bathroom, which is also a mess. I see specs of vomit on the rim of the toilet. Nick might be partier, another highly desirable trait. I open the door to the shower, which is relatively clean, and realize that there are two knobs. Hot water! There is hot water! I haven't had hot water since I was eight and we stayed in a hotel on our trip to the Miami Metro Area to see my uncle.

"Hot water. I can't believe it," I yell to Nick.

"You know it. The Heater lives a couple floors down, he's a cool guy. You're not living in the Section 26 dorms anymore. We've got our own Hoover too. Don't have to walk out to the hallway to take out the trash."

I disrobe, turn on the water, and step into the shower. The hot water should not matter to me. I can make myself feel whatever temperature I want to feel. Still, there's something nice about just letting my nerve signals go and feeling the heat.

I remember my dad saying there used to be hot water everywhere before the Plagues. There were heaters that ran on oil in every home. I wonder how much one of those heaters would cost to run now, after Cabot's bacteria ate up most of the oil and coal.

"Hey dude, I've got to go up and do an ad, be back in a minute. Plug your ears or make 'em fall off or whatever it is you do," Nick yells.

I hear him head up a staircase that must lead to the roof. I prepare myself for the noise by flooding my Tympanic Cavity with fluid. This should insulate my ear from damage while still allowing me to hear whatever lovely corporate message Nick has to share.

"Are you lost in a desert of bland food and high prices? Come to a lush and delicious land. Come to the Oasis. Oasis Burger. We all need a rest."

Right at the end, Nick lets out a sound which almost ruptures my eardrums, even with the insulation. The sound is at such an incredibly high frequency it makes a small crack in my shower door. What happened?

I hear Nick come back down and yell the answer to the question he didn't know I asked.

"Sorry, dude. Ultracorps tells me what pitch and volume to read it at, I just do whatever they tell me. Somebody should get fired for that."

I hope he's the one who gets fired, considering the crack in my shower door. I heard that the New York Metro Area's Screamer can somehow make it sound like she's just standing right next to you when she does her thing. I bet she makes a better roommate.

4

From this death and destruction, my new race, my Chosen Sons, will rise. From the rubble, they will build a new world. It will be a world filled with wonders that can scarcely be imagined. It will be a world built to my glory.

Chosen Sons: 22

"I want to share with you all something that has been weighing on me lately. Most of you are old enough to remember the days before Cabot changed the earth, the days when the entire world's concern was the Cold War and the Soviet Union. We practiced hiding under our desks and questioned the loyalties of those closest to us. We were so afraid of the Soviets and their creed Communism, we would have done anything to fight it," the heavyset, bald pastor says to his mostly elderly congregation. The old grade school auditorium looks almost empty with only the four dozen or so parishioners. The pastor speaks loudly and forcefully, as if the auditorium were full of hundreds.

"Communism does not believe in liberty, does not believe in a man's right to bear the fruits of his labor. The state, the cold, hard, unloving state, is Communism's sole purpose. They believe that the individual should sacrifice himself, his well-being, for the good of imaginary lines in the ground. Communism is the enemy of individuality, the enemy of liberty.

"It is liberty that made America great, liberty that was the greatest gift from our Founding Fathers. We became the most powerful nation on earth because of liberty. Our love for the individual and his right to keep what he earns turned a country of wilderness into the world leader of industry, a country of poor immigrants into the wealthiest nation on earth.

"This nation's love of liberty compelled us to meet the threat of Communism head on. We built bombs and amassed armies. We started rebellions and supported any foe of Communism. We questioned our leaders and entertainers, making sure none of them bore the stench of Communism.

“We were not just scared for our own lives or the lives of our children, we were afraid for our way of life. We were afraid that the Russian's disease of Communism would spread onto our shores and extinguish the flame of liberty that made this country great. The fight was long, but victory was ours if we stayed the course.

"Then Cabot came with his Revelation, the so-called Plagues. The Plagues rotted the guns so they could not fight, the crops so the soldiers could not eat, and the fuel so the tanks could not move. Mankind was meant to move on from the petty political bickering and focus on the advancement of God's Chosen Sons, but as we know, most chose not to follow God's plan.

"It is but thirty years since the Revelation, and Communism is now the norm in America. Most of this country lives and eats Communism. The entire Metro Area runs on the back of Communism. We do not call it Communism. We call it industry. We call it Ultracorps. The Chosen grow our food, build our houses, and dispose of our trash. But the Chosen do not get to live off the fruits of that labor. Instead it goes to us, the Forgotten Sons.

"The Chosen are told it is their duty to provide for the Forgotten Sons, their duty because they were born strong, and we were born weak. Does that creed sound familiar? The Soviet Union is in shambles. Its cities lie in ruin, and its people struggle to keep themselves fed. Even still, it appears Communism won the war.

"Cabot is the way out of the darkness, the only hope for eternal salvation. Cabot told us that the Chosen are the next step in God's plan. We were meant to serve the Chosen. They were not meant to serve us. If we serve them well, the Chosen can lead us all to paradise. Cabot knew this, we know this, and if we are faithful, the whole world will know it too."

Pastor Newman finishes. Sweat pours from his graying brow, his bald head drenched. His round cheeks are red from the effort.

The crowd says "Amen" in unison and starts filing out the door.

The pastor begins saying hellos to congregation members but stops when he hears a banging coming from the roof.

"I'm sorry, you'll have to excuse me," the pastor says to the old woman he was speaking with.

He heads through the back door on the church stage. It leads to a hallway with a staircase to the church tower. The pastor knows his guest prefers meeting away from prying eyes.

It takes Pastor Newman a full two minutes to climb the stairs to the tower. His guest was probably able to reach it in the blink of the eye. He pauses a moment to catch his breath. His old body is winded from the short trip.

He opens the door at the top of the stairs.

"Hello Pastor," The Beast says to him as soon as the door opens a crack.

The pastor hurries inside the small room and closes the door behind him.

"How nice to see you, Your Grace," the pastor fumbles.

He tries not to tremble at the sight of blood on The Beast's claws. He should be used to it since he's seen it dozens of times, but it still fills him with fear. The fear is God testing his faith.

"Evening, Pastor. Nice sermon. A little depressing though," The Beast replies.

"You're right, of course. I must admit that it can be difficult to stay positive in light of the troubles my parishioners face. Most go to bed hungry. Unlike you, I see," Pastor Newman says back.

"It was more than a meal. It was a calling. The Lord had another soul He wanted up in heaven. I gave the man salvation," The Beast says.

"What a fortunate soul," the pastor says, forcing a smile. "How did the Lord appear to you? A vision?"

"A voice in my head, just like always," The Beast snarls back.

"Of course. It's just hard to believe that I could be so blessed as to know someone who speaks with God directly," the pastor stammers in response. "I never imagined I could be so lucky."

"Well, you are. The Lord spoke to me when I stopped to prey on a different meal. Some nice old lady who I saw giving out candies in her neighborhood. The Lord told me there was some government man who had been fighting for the Chosen Sons. He had done good, but his part was over, and now it was time for his reward. I made sure to take a few bites of the old lady too. She seemed like she deserved to go up to heaven," The Beast says.

"How kind of you, and how fortunate you are. You took another step towards your salvation. Did the Lord say anything about your redemption? How many more souls will you need to claim?" the pastor asks.

"He didn't say," The Beast says and hangs his head. "I don't know why. He never says anything after I claim whatever soul He wants. All I do is go around hunting and praying and hoping this is the night the Lord speaks to me. When He finally does, I ain't even that happy. All I can think about is how it's going to be months until He talks to me again. I feel like such a sinner for complaining."

"You aren't a sinner, Your Grace. I think you might be struggling to enjoy the Lord because you don't have anyone to share His love with," the pastor says.

"You mean a woman. You're gonna need to find me a pretty devout girl."

"No, not that," Pastor Newman says back. His mouth gapes in horror. He quickly composes himself. "I meant a friend."

"Are you saying we ain't friends?"

"Of course we are. I mean one of your own kind. I'm blessed to be able to help you in whatever small way I can, but I cannot understand you. I don't know how it feels to have a spark of the Divine inside you. You need to connect with one of your own kind."

"I want to, Pastor, but I'm scared. You know what happened the last time I saw some of my own kind. I'm still trying to redeem myself," The Beast says. Tears start to form in his eyes.

The pastor sees the water in The Beast's eyes and his knees start to quake. He doesn't like it when The Beast gets so emotional. It might just be a matter of time until that emotion turns to anger.

"I know it can be difficult, Your Grace, but you must trust in the

Lord. If you live how He has commanded you, He will reward you. Your task is to be patient and careful," the pastor says.

5

No business that employees more than one individual will be allowed to hire or maintain the employment of any Different individual if that individual is employed for the use of their abilities. Businesses exempted from this provision listed under Addendum i.

Article 1 Section 1 of the Different Acts of 1996

"Unified Logistics Technology and Research Applications Corporation (Ultracorps)."

Addendum i of the Different Acts of 1996 (in its entirety)

I snap out of the Zone at 6:55 a.m. The Zone is what I call my version of sleep. I don't lose consciousness, but I spend a few hours alternatively resting the various systems of my body, even parts of my brain. Dolphins do something similar while they sleep so they can keep returning to the surface for oxygen. I don’t have to do it every night, but it does help. Even if I can generate the chemicals my body needs to emulate sleep, muscles weren’t meant to run twenty-four seven, and neither was my visual cortex. It also helps pass the time. Life is pretty boring at four a.m.

I like to start getting ready for work before Nick does his whole alarm clock bit. A petty victory for sure, but I like knowing I have control. I go take a shower even though I don't have to. I can make my body odor non-existent, but I'm a sucker for the real hot water, even if it does slow me down.

The Doctors aren't usually ready to feed me whatever we are testing until after lunch, but they still get mad if I'm late. They spend hours and days preparing a sample and it only takes me minutes to tell them the results, yet they still go ballistic if I am not waiting the second the sample is ready.

My head erupts to tell me someone is trying to call me on think.Net. The caller has no ID, but that's the same thing as telling me who it is. There is just one person I know who can block their

ID: Nita.

I don't know much about her. She's been contacting me occasionally since I was sixteen. Sometimes she talked to me for hours, other times she asked me a single question, like what enzymes the body uses to process lipids.

I think she's a child, maybe ten or eleven, although sometimes it seems like she must be eighty. She's a Librarian, the head Librarian. The Librarians are the human encyclopedias that work with the Telepaths to run think.Net. Nita can think ten thousand thoughts in the time it takes a normal human to think one.

It's hard to guess how old she is because I've never heard her voice. On think.Net, calls come in using the voice inside your own head. It's like your internal monologue is having a discussion. My dad never got used to it, and he complained the handful of times he made a think.Net call. He liked the telephone better, where you spoke out loud. Hearing other people's phone conversations sounds incredibly annoying for everyone involved if you ask me.

I think about accepting the call, and my eyes glaze over as I go into the think.Net stare.

<<<Hello, Nita.

>>>Gavin, I hope all is well with you. How do you like working at lab 207? The work you are doing on iron enrichment is invaluable. Around 65% of America's children are anemic.

<<<Invaluable. I guess I never thought of taste testing Palm Fries as invaluable. Job placement isn't something you could help with, is it?

>>>You are in the position best suited for you now. Excuse me for ending the pleasantries, but I have an important question for you. What is the accepted standard for the concentration of sodium in drinking water? The medical Librarian is down momentarily.

<<<Forty milligrams per liter. I'm glad all the hours I spent studying human anatomy are making me useful for something besides Palm Fries.

>>>Thank you. Feel free to take your time getting ready. Your trains will be waiting in their stations. Smell you later.

And she's gone. She really is hard to get a read on. I can take my time though. She'll deliver on her promise of the trains. If it didn't seem so crazy, I would swear she runs the entire Metro Area.

I get dressed and head into the kitchen. I put a kettle on the stove to boil some water. I'm hungry, and I've got myself a treat: some genuine oatmeal. Cost me a fortune, but it's worth it. I eat Manna all day. I can't stand the thought of having to eat it for breakfast too.

I try not to think about it, but Manna is just human Maple Syrup. It's produced by a Different who's basically a Maple tree as big as a house. They pump her full of sunlight and water and her body produces the calorie-rich substance through photosynthesis. Manna may feed the country, but it still creeps me out.

I go on think.Net and read the news until my kettle whistles. The Metro Area Council granted a contract to Ultracorps to take over the Metro Area's water system. Was that why Nita was asking me about salt levels? I take the kettle off the heat and head into the pantry to get my oatmeal. The oatmeal has moved since I ate it yesterday. Sure enough, the box is light, nothing but dust left inside.

Nick! I've already talked to him twice about eating my food. He's going to buy me a new box. I don't know why he won't buy his own. He makes enough being town crier. Lucky clown. Ultracorps pays him a ton and he has barely any debt to boot. He's solar powered, not metabolic, which basically makes him a lottery winner. A few hours a day in the sun is all it takes to keep him energized. He only needs to eat multivitamins and salt, but I guess he likes oatmeal too.

I suppress my anger and pour myself a bowl of Manna Bites. I can make it taste just like oatmeal, but that's not the point. Oh, the joys of having a roommate.

I finish eating and purposefully leave my dish out. I know it pisses Nick off even though he lives like a pig himself. All part of some healthy roommate passive-aggressiveness. I turn my stomach on to get the Manna Bites all mashed up and the acid flowing. Even though it was a big bowl, it was only three hundred calories. I'll have to eat again when I get to the lab.

I head out of my front door and hit the button for the elevator. It comes right away, and I get to go straight down. I'm sure the other Differents waiting to go to work are wondering why the elevator just skipped them. While I head down, I go on think.Net and call the elevator Strong-Man to say thanks.

<<<Hey, Gary. Thanks for the express. Making any deliveries today?

>>>Yeah, you're my first stop of the day.

<<<Sounds good, see you then.

Making friends with Gary the elevator operator was a great decision, not that I did much to make it happen. Gary saw me walking around the employee housing courtyard one day and just started talking to me as if he'd always known me. He said he recognized me from his deliveries at the lab. Now, I have my own personal express elevator.

I head out of the lobby, past the Walter doing his cleaning, and make my way to the Slug station. Nita kept her word. I'm not sure how she knew when I'd get here, but there's a 3C train waiting for me at the station. The doors close moments after I get on. The car is almost empty, and I get a seat. I never get a seat. I bet she ran extra Slugs just so this one would be empty.

The ride usually takes around thirty minutes, but it's been taking longer and longer every day. Everyone knows it's the P-Trains, private mini trains for the wealthy who do not wish to mingle with the masses. They're clogging up the system, but they raise a fortune for the government in fees so they aren't going anywhere anytime soon.

According to my dad, before the Plagues, most people had cars, not just police and firefighters. People drove themselves wherever they wanted to go, whenever they wanted to go. It sounds great.

We make good time to Wilshire. I suspect Nita is giving me a hand with the signals, too. Sure enough, there's a 16A train waiting for me at the Wilshire Station. I hope she needs favors more often. I end up getting to work twenty minutes early and have plenty of time to get some food.

Ultracorps keeps the lab kitchens stocked with food. Not great food, most of it is Manna products, but lots of food nonetheless. People would freak out if they saw how much food we have. The truth is we need it. Most of the Differents who work here are metabolic. It takes massive quantities of food to keep us going. The average human needs two thousand calories a day. There is a Strong-Man in the lab who needs to eat upwards of five hundred thousand calories a day. No wonder there are anti-Different riots every time there's a food shortage.

I could use a few hundred calories myself. I can get by on almost nothing if I have to, but I'll be eating a lot today, and it will go more smoothly if I can get my metabolism ramped up ahead of time. I head towards the kitchen, but stop when I get a whiff of perfume. It's Sarah, and she's in the kitchen. I'd remember her smell even if I didn't remember everything. Now I would have gone into the kitchen even if I didn't need food.

"Hey, Dummy," I'm not being a jerk; Sarah's nickname is Crash Test Dummy.

"Oh, hi Gavin," Sarah answers.

She puts two different kinds of Manna Cold Cuts on the table and grabs some bread, continuing to make her sandwich as she talks.

"What they got you working on today?" she asks.

"They're still trying to perfect that iron fortification for the Palm Fries. Sixty-five percent of children in the country are anemic."

That has to make her like me more. Who wouldn't like a guy who is helping kids?

"That's good... except they have to eat fries," she says even though she can eat whatever she wants and count on her metabolism to keep her body perfect. Well, maybe not quite perfect. I'd add another one, maybe one and a half, percent more body fat if I controlled her anatomy like I do mine. But I should try not to think that way. I don't think it makes me pleasant.

"Yeah, I guess. They're having problems getting non-lethal amounts of iron to stick to the fries. Luckily, I can stop my body from processing it," I say.

"Good luck with that," she says. "I have to get back to the range.

They're still working on the changes to the collision systems on the new P-Trains. I hope it doesn't break my spine again, that takes forever to heal. See you later."

She shoves one of her two sandwiches in her mouth and heads out the door.

"See ya!" I yell at an awkwardly high volume.

By taking forever to heal, she probably means forty-five minutes. Maybe an hour. That's her Differentiation, she's a Regenerator. They use her as a crash test dummy to test out new train designs. She gets hurt and the lab techs take notes, she's also on call as an organ donor. She makes a lot more money than I do.

That pathetic little interaction is why I've been eating in the “Big Kitchen” for the last month and a half. I call it the Big Kitchen to justify why I’m here, even though there’s another kitchen much closer to the lab that's the exact same size. I’ve even been trying different combinations of pheromones to try to get her interested. Nothing is working. I make a sandwich and eat it as I walk to the lab.

I see Dr. Cole and Dr. Wilson talking in Dr. Wilson’s office. I give them a half-hearted wave and head to the file room. I know better than to ask them if they have anything ready yet. They don’t. They spend their mornings bickering about inane biological theories and then get to work at about ten-thirty. It's as routine as everything else in this place.

While I wait for them to make samples, I file reports and make the time fly by as fast as I can. Even at a blur, it takes too long. I pause when the ground starts to shake. A thousand-pound man tends to do that. Gary is here.

Aside from running my apartment elevator, Gary works as a delivery man for Ultracorps. He carries around multiple tons of food, medical supplies, metal, whatever Ultracorps needs moved. He's also the one real friend I have at work, and he only makes deliveries twice a week.

"Hey, Gavin, just dropped off two more tons of Manna. Hope you enjoy."

"Thanks. I'm going to use it to generate some gnarly farts I'll leave for you in the elevator."

"Maybe you'll be taking the stairs for a while. You see Sarah this morning? She was looking particularly fantastic."

"I saw her. I made a pathetic showing of myself in the kitchen."

"What happened to 'I don't get nervous unless I want to get nervous'?" he asks mockingly.

"I didn't get nervous. I just took a poor approach."

"If you were a normal person, you know, with normal emotions, I would tell you that you have to give up. It's crushing you. You need to expand your horizons, there are a lot of fish in the sea," he pauses. "Me and P-Dub and Jason are going out on Thursday, you should come."

I swallow the urge to correct his grammar. People don't like that.

"Where are you guys going?" I ask.

"The K-Spot. It's a human bar, but they're Different-friendly. The ladies are very friendly, I hear. A bunch of Cabotists, you know what they believe," he says and gives me a wink.

Cabotists believe Cabot was right, that Differents are in fact destined to inherit the earth. They think Cabot made the Plagues in order to prepare the world for the glorious rise of Differents, or the Chosen Sons, as Cabot called them. Women who follow this religion believe it is their duty to help propagate the Different race by being… friendly to Different men and having their children. Cabot taught that serving the Chosen Sons is the one way for humans to get into heaven.

I always say no to these offers. The one time I went out with Gary it was awful. He's fine enough, but Peter Warsall, or P-Dub as he demands to be called, is terrible. All he does is make rude comments to women and talk about how awesome he is.

He's an Energy Producer, a Heater to be exact. They use him to provide the activation energy for some chemical reactions. Being an Energy Producer means he has more money than he knows what to do with. Jason is not much better. He's a Cooler, a personal one for some Ultracorps bigwig who doesn't want to get too hot in the summer. I hate being with Jason because you can just tell he's being watched by Ultracorps. I stay off think.Net when he's around.

"Hey Gavin, you're doing it again. Us people with a normal sense of time are getting bored. Are you coming or not?"

"I'll come. What time you guys meeting?" I hear myself say. I had resolved to be more social. I guess I'm holding myself to it.

"You will? All right, this is going to rock!" Gary yells. I already regret agreeing to go. "Nine o'clock at my place. Don't wuss out," he adds as he heads out the door

How pleasant. Although, to be fair, I have wussed out on him before. I don't do well in groups. There are too many people to keep track of, too much to analyze. I tend to lose track of time. I'm going to keep being a freak if I don't learn to handle groups better, though. As Larry taught me in Section 26, everything takes practice. Everything.

I spend a few more zoned out hours filing before Dr. Cole comes to get me. Am I making myself younger by forcing myself to experience time more quickly to get through this boring work? Normal people have to live through the tedium. They sit and contemplate or twiddle their thumbs. I fly through the tedium as if it doesn't really happen. They live a more boring life, but it is still a life.

"I said, Mr. Stillman, we are ready for you in the testing room. Please come along if you're feeling up to it," Dr. Cole says slowly and sincerely.

He knows I was once classified as a Zeta, so he treats me like an invalid. Never mind that I've corrected him on the synthesis of organic compounds.

"Sorry, Dr. Cole. I'm coming," I say subserviently.

I follow him into the testing room and sit down at the table. I see Dr. Wilson working on a sample so I get my salivary glands and stomach pumping. I have to get ready for what's coming. It's the same thing as every day for the last month: Palm Fries and tons of them.

Palm Fries are the most popular product at Oasis Burger. The fries are a mix of 80% Manna, 15% potatoes from the Fertile Belt, and 5% a blend of a dozen different spices. Then they're deep fried in vegetable oil and covered in a mix of salt and sugar. They are sweet, savory, delicious, and I hate them. I've already eaten 32,795 fries and will eat another thousand today.

When I was a child, I remember eating at Oasis Burger with my parents. My mom would always say that we shouldn't go, that it was unhealthy, but we usually went twice a week and mom always got a double Oasis Burger, large Palm fries, and a vanilla Manna Shake. She was never happier than when she was dipping her fries in her shake.

"Mr. Stillman, I think we're getting close. I don't like the alkaline levels, but everything else is just about there," Dr. Wilson says. He is humoring me. They are still weeks away, and we both know it.

"I'm sure you are getting close. You're both doing such great work," I say. Scientists like having their egos stroked, and these two are my bosses.

"It's all thanks to the data we're getting from you. I hardly remember how we worked without you. I haven't had to turn on a Bunsen burner in months," Dr. Cole says.

"I better get to giving you that data then."

Dr. Wilson puts a plate of fries down on the table in front of me. I turn off my olfactory sense. I can't stand the smell anymore. I grab a handful of fries and shove them in my mouth. I close my eyes and imagine that I'm eating baked clams. I had those once when my parents took me out to dinner on my birthday. I'm not sure if I'm remembering the taste correctly, but it's better than fries. Once I finish the plate, it's time to start spitting out the data.

"Blood sugar level 2.2%, sodium level .015%, iron levels .094% and rising." I say as Dr. Cole and Dr. Wilson carefully write down everything I say.

I spend the next fifteen minutes providing blood levels at thirty-second intervals while the doctors listen with fascination. How they can be interested in the iron levels of fried Manna is beyond me. I can literally force myself to be excited, and I still find it difficult.

Ultracorps knows how to place their personnel.

After a thrilling fifteen minutes, they bring out another plate of fries and we repeat the process, then another and another. I end up eating twenty large orders of fries. We have to be sure some moron doesn't kill himself by switching to an all-fries diet.

I give my final data analysis and Dr. Cole and Dr. Wilson head back into their offices. They keep telling me we are almost there. We are almost there if every Oasis Burger customer weighs six hundred pounds. I don't know why they're having such trouble getting the iron levels down, but they can't seem to do it.

They won't let me in the back to work with them on the recipe. I've tried to show them what an asset I can be. I can recall and process the data almost as well as the Librarian they use, and they won't have to wait in a queue with all the other Ultracorps researchers to use me. The Doctors are just worried that if they let me help them do their job, they'd soon be obsolete themselves. They aren't wrong. I bet if I wanted, I could do this job better than they can. I'd be more upset if I cared about the job at all.

As it is, I'm just ecstatic that another work day is over, even if my stomach does feel as hard as Maceo Steel. I head into the kitchen anyway, the Big Kitchen, just to see if Sarah is there.

She’s not. I smell the air and can make out just a few molecules of her perfume. I missed her by five, maybe six, minutes.

It's probably for the best. If she was in here, I'd have to force myself to eat something just so I didn't look like a weirdo. I already have enough calories I need to burn off. I have my metabolism working overtime to digest those fries. I can make myself burn calories quickly, but the energy doesn't just disappear. If I don't do some sort of physical activity, my body temperature goes through the roof and I start fidgeting like a madman. Time to spend my evening the same way I always do: in the lab's gym, running on a treadmill while I watch the nightly news on think.Net. Thrilling.

6

I have given my Chosen Sons more than I ever gave the Forgotten. I have given them more of myself. I have given them a taste of my power. From that power, the Chosen will know my love.

Chosen Sons: 25

The Beast is tired, but he cannot sleep. What the pastor said is stuck in his mind. The Beast feels empty because he is alone. The pastor tries to be a friend, but The Beast can smell the fear pouring off the man. The poor old fool can't help it. Like the pastor said, he does not know what it is like to be a Chosen Son.

The Beast has been chosen by God. Not only was he blessed to be born a Chosen Son, God has picked him to do His holy work. The Beast gets to hear the voice of God. He is just like Moses or Cabot. If only people could know. If only The Beast had someone who knew that he isn't really a monster, that he is doing the Lord's work. But there is no one to tell. There is no one to be proud. The Beast is alone, but that wasn't always so.

He was not always The Beast.

#

He was born Thomas Calhoun in the Houston Metro Area. He grew up in a well-to-do neighborhood called the Fish Market, named for the wealthy fishing tycoons who inhabited the homes there.

Tom's father, Oren Calhoun, owned and operated a single fishing boat before the Plagues. He struggled to eke out a living. That all changed after Cabot wreaked his destruction. With crops failing around the globe, fishing became the main source of sustenance for what became the Houston Metro Area.

Cabot designed one of his Plagues to devastate life in the oceans and lakes. Many fish died of disease, so the Plague worked in the short term, but the other Plagues devastated the human population and destroyed ship fuel, causing human fishing operations to all but cease for a time. The drop in the fishing industry worldwide more than made up for those fish killed by Cabot's Plague.

Oren Calhoun was able to turn his fishing boat into a sailboat, making him one of the first operating fishermen in Houston. Then, he used the money he made from his first boat to buy a second boat and a third. Soon, Calhoun Fishing had the one of the largest fleets in the newly formed Houston Metro Area.

After Calhoun Fishing rose to prominence, Oren married Lilly Banks. Lilly's father owned the company that constructed Oren's boats. The match was perfect, and the two had a rapid courtship. Not long after they were married, Tom was born.

Tom's parents paid little attention to him growing up. His father spent his time at the office, trying to grow the Calhoun Empire. Tom's mother spent her evenings socializing and acting as the public face of Calhoun Fishing. A series of nannies and tutors raised Tom.

As a young child, Tom displayed no particular skills or abilities. He was not smart or athletic, and his art looked just like all of the other children's art. Tom's parents considered him a bit of a disappointment and didn't attempt to hide their thoughts.

That all changed a few months after Tom turned fourteen. Puberty hit him like a ton of bricks, or so it seemed. He grew a whole foot taller in just a year. With the growth spurt came a newfound athletic ability. A once clumsy kid became graceful and powerful, seemingly overnight.

Texas had always been known for its high school football, and as soon as they could, the leagues restarted after the Plagues. By the time Tom was fourteen, there were over thirty schools competing in the Houston Metro Area. The high school in the Fish Market was a perennial powerhouse. Oren Calhoun led the team to a championship as a running back in the 1960s. After the Plagues, the school resumed its winning ways. They had won the championship two of the last three years before Tom tried out for the team his freshman year.

Tom shocked himself, his parents, and his entire school by making the team as a freshman. He was the first freshman to make the team since the leagues had restarted. He shocked everyone further during the fourth game of the season. The starting running back and his backup were both injured, leaving Tom, the third-stringer, as the only healthy player. Tom was able lead his team from behind in the fourth quarter, rushing for three touchdowns including the game winner as time expired.

Tom was carried off the field by his teammates. After celebrating with his compatriots, Tom went home. His father had heard about the game, he was waiting with two cigars.

"Winners get their reward," Oren said as he handed Tom the lit cigar.

"Thank you, sir," Tom replied.

He put the cigar in his mouth and breathed in deeply. He then immediately turned green and nearly coughed his lungs out.

"You keep winning and you'll get used to it," Oren told him.

"If you say so."

"That was some performance out there today. You looked like your old man back in '68. You're a little bigger than I was, but you don't quite have my speed."

"Thanks. I was just happy they finally let me play," Tom replied. He was nervous. He couldn't remember a time his father talked to him aside from telling him dinner was ready or the like.

"I'm not too surprised. You've got my blood in you. It was just a matter of time until you cashed in on your potential. Your mom had Martha take some steaks out of the ice house. We're going to celebrate another Calhoun football star tonight," Oren said and put his arm around Tom's shoulder.

The two spent an hour looking up at the stars and talking before heading in for dinner. Tom grinned the entire time.

He continued to grow in size and athletic ability as time went on. By his sophomore year, he seemed unstoppable on the football field. He scored a touchdown half the time he touched the ball. He was the fastest, biggest, and strongest player on the team. Would-be tacklers just bounced off him. He played as the starting running back and the starting middle linebacker, playing every down of every game.

Opposing teams started to question whether Tom was going through a normal growth spurt. Rumors circulated that Tom might be a Different. The Genetic Incongruity scan was not yet available for public use, so there was no way to verify the suspicions. Oren Calhoun had been a star player in high school, and Tom was simply taking after his father. They both managed to convince themselves of that explanation. They chose to ignore the fact that Tom was eating five times more than even the most voracious teenager.

Oren Calhoun could not have people believe his son was a Different. The Houston Metro Area was dominated by believers of Sapienism, a sect of Christianity, similar in many ways to Baptists, but with one essential change. Their central tenet was that Differents were sent by the Devil to torture and test mankind. If people believed Thomas Calhoun was a Different, Calhoun Fishing could be finished. Oren Calhoun started fights in the stands with anyone who suggested his son was a Different. He even sued a rival school after its newspaper printed an article suggesting Tom was a Different.

As much as Tom won on the football field, he failed in the classroom. Tom was constantly getting into fights with other classmates and even teachers. To Tom, it seemed like they were all challenging him, challenging his position, challenging his dominance. A beast was growing in Tom, and the animal inside him could not stand to be challenged. If Tom had not been the star of the football team, the school would have expelled him many times over.

As it was, Tom led the team to an undefeated season his sophomore year, and his team made the Houston MA High School Championship game. Tom's father and mother watched the game proudly from the stands as they had watched all of his games that season.

In the championship game, the opposing team focused on Tom as no other team had. The entire defense would run towards Tom as soon as the play started, ready to tackle him even before he got the ball. They dared the other players on the team to beat them. Tom's teammates were out of practice. They had relied on Tom all year and could not make even the simplest of plays.

The strategy was working. Tom's team was losing by six points with only thirty seconds to go. His team had the ball. He demanded they give it to him no matter what. Tom had been getting more and more frustrated as the game wore on. By this point, he was shaking with rage. The beast in Tom could not accept this challenge to his dominance.

The quarterback hiked the ball and handed it off to Tom, who let out an animalistic scream and charged forward into the pile of players rushing to meet him. All eleven players converged on Tom, but they could not bring him down. He pushed the pile, letting out screams that turned into roars as he moved forward. He swung his arms, tossing players on both teams around like rag dolls. Tom broke into the open field and trampled a player trying to tackle him like a bug. When the last defender tried to stop him, Tom grabbed him by the facemask and threw him aside.

Tom ran into the end zone and spiked the ball, screaming and howling. He pounded his chest. Tom suddenly realized he was alone in celebrating and looked back at his path of destruction. Two boys lay on the field motionless. A few others were struggling to get up, and one had a broken bone that stuck out of his arm far enough to be seen by the crowd. When he saw what he had done, Tom knew what everyone in the stands knew. Tom was not human. He was a Different.

7

By the authority vested in me as President by the Constitution and statutes of the United States and in order to combat the rampant famine and disease that is crippling the nation, all citizens and permanent residents are hereby ordered to evacuate their homes and report directly to the closest designated Metro Area. Failure to do so shall constitute a violation of law. Citizens are advised to contact their local authorities regarding transportation to the designated areas.

President Ronald Reagan Executive Order 13578
March 17th 1985;
Mandatory evacuation to the Metro Areas.

"These ladies are going to be easier than kindergarten," P-Dub exclaims.

"That's what you said about the place last week and it was bull. It was just a bunch of prude private school girls with Ultracorps fat cat daddies," Jason counters.

P-Dub, Jason, and Gary have been having this same basic conversation for the entire Slug ride. I'm suddenly wondering why I made myself go out with them. I don't think I was really missing anything. Hearing P-Dub list his sexual exploits is not my idea of a good time. Besides, I can tell he's making up half his stories because his pupils dilate and his heart rate goes up. That's what your body does when it knows you are lying.

"They were hot. Anyway, this will be different. No prudes for us Chosen Sons. God commands them to get with us," P-Dub says.

"Yeah, Chosen Sons, I do like that name better than Differents. How'd you find out about this Cabotist bar anyway?" Gary asks.

"Keep your voice down bro, don't say that so loud. A bunch of Differents headed to a Cabotist bar isn't going to be too popular. There's probably a mob waiting to burn the place down as soon as they find out where it is," Jason says.

"So what? Who's going to mess with four Differents, even if one of them is Gavin? Anyway, as soon as we're gone, they can burn the place to the ground for all I care. I'll have gotten what I need," P-Dub says smugly.

I listen in silence as we ride the train to the outskirts of town. I need to be more social, I tell myself, that's why I'm doing this. I need to get better at social interactions, and practice is the only way to improve at anything. That's why I'm hanging out with P-Dub. Plus, I'm learning the important skill of being able to stomach people I can't stand.

"So, answer. How'd you hear about this place?" Gary asks.

"I heard about it from some dude in Santa Monica," P-Dub answers.

"What were you doing in Santa Monica? You can't get enough of those Morpher girls, can you?" Jason says.

"I found something better. Telepath girls. They can do things you can't even imagine, without even touching you. It's all in your mind, but it feels just like real life. They cost a ton, but it's worth it, and I can afford it," P-Dub replies.

I like P-Dub less every time he speaks. I'm discovering new depths of loathing hidden deep within my brain. I tune him out as he describes in detail the imaginary fantasies he'd had fulfilled by Telepath girls. I think about whether I can take him in a fight. P-Dub's an energy producer and a Beta at that. He generates heat, probably enough to kill me, but still, I bet I could take him out before he could get hot enough to do any serious damage. This is a weird thing to think about. I should stop.

"And let me tell you, she is as hot as can be. Blonde hair, nice rack, unbelievable," P-Dub says, and I somehow manage to dislike him even more.

"For all you know, it's a fat old dude and he's just making you think he's a woman the same way he makes you think your fantasies are coming true," I chime in.

Gary and Jason look at each other and break out laughing. P-Dub laughs too, but I can tell it's pretend. Being the butt of a joke is not the kind of attention he likes.

"Gavin, coming in out of nowhere with the slam! Awesome," Gary says and slaps me on the back.

"All right, come on, the next stop is ours," P-Dub says.

The Slug pulls into the Robertson station and we get off. I've never been to this part of town. It's far from the Metro Center, and there isn't any reason to come out here. The buildings are all rundown Pre-Plague structures. Most of them look like they are barely standing. The majority of the buildings are abandoned. There are only a few windows with lights on inside. Not many people live this far out.

"It's just a few blocks from here," P-Dub assures us, and we start walking.

"Man, its spooky out here, all these empty buildings," I say.

"What's the matter, need a tampon?" P-Dub says back, seemingly just to make sure I continue disliking him.

"Someone's still upset because he's been getting mind-screwed by a man," Jason says.

"Gavin is right. We should be careful. The Beast might be on the prowl," Gary says.

"You been reading the think.Net tabloids again?" I ask. Gary loves to read that smut. It's all made up news. The people writing it and the people reading it all know it's fake, so I don't get why anyone likes it.

"No this isn't from the Enquirer. The people out here are actually still afraid of The Beast. I was out here a few weeks ago, dropping off some old Manna to a soup kitchen. The guy who ran the place was harassing me to hurry up because he wanted to get home before dark. He said that Lauren Conrad woman who ran all those protests had been killed out here by The Beast, and he didn't want to be next," Gary answers.

"He couldn't have been serious?" P-Dub asks.

"Some people are just looking for an excuse to be afraid of Differents. If that means they have to imagine that some psychopath who was killed ten years ago is still on the loose, then so be it. That way they can justify voting to increase COL fees," Jason says.

"The Beast's Feast was only five years ago..." I say but then I trail off. We've finally gotten to the bar.

The block's activity stands out like a sore thumb. There's a giant WormLight on the outside of the bar that lights up the whole street. We can hear the voices inside. I focus and can make out what each individual is saying. There is a lot of disturbing talk about Cabot. These people are nuts.

We head inside and into a thick cloud of smoke. So far it's just like the only other bar I've been to. I take a quick scan and spot a few other D tattoos in the crowd. The other Differents look away when we make eye contact. They know we should be ashamed of what we are doing here.

I think if I could feel guilt and shame, I would be feeling them now. I came in with a bunch of guys who are here to try to take advantage of confused religious fanatics. I have to practice being social, I tell myself. I fight the urge to leave and follow the other guys to the counter.

"Four Manna Beers please, ma'am." Jason says to the attractive, late twenties, brunette bartender. She looks a little like Sean Young. I've had a crush on her ever since my ninth birthday when I got to watch the movie *Blade Runner* on think.Net.

She goes to the cooler and grabs four bottles.

"Here you go. Enjoy," she says with a smile.

"Thanks. What's the damage? You guys don't charge to think.Net do you?" Jason says as he reaches for his wallet.

"On the house, fellas. We don't take money from the Chosen here. Eat and drink all you like, we would be honored," she answers.

"Seriously?" P-Dub asks.

"Well that settles it. This is my new favorite bar," Gary adds.

We open our beers and lift them to cheers.

"Let's get stupid," P-Dub says with class.

We clink bottles and take a sip. I remember my dad claiming he hated Manna Beer, said it tasted like crap, that it couldn't compete with the real thing. Then he'd down another bottle, so I guess he didn't think it was so bad. It tastes gross to me, overly bitter. I don't think the taste is why people drink it, though.

"If everything is free, let's get some shots too," P-Dub says. "And some for the ladies at that table."

There's a group of four women sitting at a table close by who were already staring at us before P-Dub ordered them drinks. They happily accept the offer and come over to talk. They seemed to have us picked out already and separate to talk to us one on one. A cute blonde-haired woman approaches me.

"Hi there, my name's Jenny. What's yours?" Jenny asks me.

#

"Then I told them if they didn't get me a table, I'd make the bar so hot it would turn into sauna. We got the table," P-Dub says proudly.

He's full of it. There's no way they let him into Studio 54. That place is all Pre-Plague money. They would not let a Different into the club, and if a Different ever threatened them, that Different would go to jail for a long time. Lucky for him, the girl on his arm doesn't care what he's full of. Her religion has blinded her, and she'd go for any Different, even P-Dub.

Not that I should talk, Jenny has been pretending to like me for the last two hours. She's doing a good job of hiding it, but body language is hard to mask from me. It's nothing too awful, I think she just finds me boring. I can't blame her, I think she's boring too. We don't have much in common. The only thing she wants to talk about is a bunch of radio programs I don't listen to. Why would I? I can afford think.Net.

"I'm going to go grab another beer, do you want one?" I say and suddenly realize Jenny and I have been standing in silence for four minutes.

"I'm still nursing this one, thanks."

I make my way to the bar counter. The place has cleared out as the night has progressed. We are the only ones left in the bar besides the brunette bartender. She's cute and she’s older than me. I like that. She moves with more confidence than women my age do. There’s fire behind her blue eyes, not fear. She's working hard to clean a big pile of dirty glasses. I like the way the sweat looks on her brow.

"Excuse me ma'am, another beer please."

"You sure? You've already had a quite a few. Nervous about your date?" she says without really looking up from her cleaning.

"No, it's my Differentiation, it helps me process alcohol. I'm not very drunk at all, and I can be sober in two seconds if I want to be."

"Sounds useful. Does it save you from hangovers, too?"

"Sure does."

"Now that is what I call a Chosen Son."

"I feel like an ass. We've been getting free drinks from you all night and I don't even know your name," I make my cheeks turn red so she knows I'm embarrassed.

"Yeah, that was pretty rude, but I'll blame it on your jackass friends. I'm Becky," Becky says with a smile.

"A pleasure to meet you, Becky. My name's Gavin. You're right, my friends are jackasses."

"Lots of friends are."

"We aren't keeping you here too late, are we Becky?"

"No, it's okay. The owner makes me keep the place open till two every night, even though no one is ever here that late. Besides, it's my sacred duty to serve you however I can. Keeping the bar open seems like getting off easy."

"Then I'm sorry for all of the other nights that you have to stay till two for no good reason."

"I can't complain, really. The owner is my dad. The part I hate is walking home so late. My dad usually comes and meets me, but his leg has been acting up lately."

"Are you afraid of The Beast?" I ask.

"No," she says flatly. "There are too many real threats to waste time thinking about the Boogey Man. The usual assortment of murders, rapists, and thieves is more than enough. The cops never come out here so they can pretty much do whatever they want. My dad has been trying to get a neighborhood watch started, but nobody cares, or they're too scared."

"Doesn't seem like the cops help anywhere. I could wait and walk you home, if you'd like. I don't think the scumbags would mess with a Different."

She eyes me for a long moment. I think she's already decided to say yes, but she wants me to sweat. Which I should do, I'm getting a little warm.

"I guess so. But, so you know, it's just going to be a walk. I don't care what my religion says. I am a lady and expect to be treated like one. Plus, you're just a kid and I'm not the type to take advantage."

"Understood."

"Gavin, come on! We're all heading back to Lora's place. We're going to keep this party going," Jason yells.

I turn around and see P-Dub, Jason, and Gary standing with their arms around their girl's waists. I can see Jenny eyeing me sheepishly behind them.

"No thanks. I'm going to stay here a little longer. Have a good night," I answer.

"Screw that. You're coming. Jenny is Lora's sister. She'll be upset if her sister is lonely. I don't want anything upsetting my girl," P-Dub says. He is very drunk.

"Yeah, Gavin. You gotta come with us. You can't be alone out here at night," Gary pleads.

"I'll be fine. You guys go on. Jenny, it was a pleasure to meet you," I say.

I can see the relief in the girl's eyes. She's happy to be spared from doing the Lord's work with me tonight.

"You're wussing out, I can't believe it. Don't you know you're denying this girl a divine experience?" P-Dub says.

"Come on, let's just go." Gary says and pushes P-Dub lightly on the shoulder, which sends him stumbling forward ten feet. That's about as gentle as Gary can be.

"See you later, wimp!" P-Dub yells as he walks out of the bar.

"See you next week, Gavin," Gary says and stumbles out.

I'll be surprised if the bar is in business next week, considering how much Gary had to drink to get that drunk.

Becky and I are alone. She starts clearing the table where we were sitting, and I help. We work quickly and silently, cleaning up the bottles, wiping down the bar, bagging the trash.

"We've got to take this out back. The closest Hoover is over a mile away. A Strong-Man comes and gets it every other week," is all Becky says.

We cut off the Manna to the WormLights, making the bar dark, and head outside. She locks the door behind us.

"You sure you want to do this? I've walked home alone every night this week. I'm sure I'll be fine," I don't think she means it, but she doesn't like being a bother.

"Of course. I don't have anything better to do." I should have come up with something else to say. I always tell everyone I can't get nervous, but I'm starting to think wanting desperately to succeed is pretty much the same thing.

"It's this way," Becky says and points down a dark street.

We walk the first block in silence. The only sound we hear is someone coughing inside a half-collapsed building. He has a large buildup of phlegm in his lungs, maybe COPD. I shouldn't be thinking about this. I should be trying to make conversation. That's the normal thing to do.

"So, have you lived in the LA Metro your whole life?" I ask, even though I know it’s a cheesy question.

"No, I was born Arizona. Flagstaff, Arizona."

"You were born in a Non-Assisted Area? What was that like?"

"Well, it wasn't a Non-Assisted Area when I was born. It was a year before the Plagues started, or got bad anyway. It was just a regular city back then."

That means she must be thirty-two, maybe thirty-three years old. I thought she was twenty-eight tops. I guess I'm not quite the anatomy expert I imagine myself to be.

"Wow, I wouldn't have thought... it's just you don't seem that old... I mean you look great," I say.

I stretched time to come up with something good to say and even then, that's the best I could do.

"Oh, come on... thank you. Not a bad recovery for a pup," Becky says and blushes. I guess I didn't do so badly.

"I can't believe you lived through the Plagues. The way my dad talked about them, it sounds awful. I can only imagine what it would have been like to be a child then."

"It wasn't so bad. I was a baby through the worst years. I don't remember much. It was hard for my dad..." she trails off. This is upsetting her, but I get the impression she still doesn't mind talking about it.

"I'm sure. It was hard enough for anyone. I can hardly imagine what it would have been like with a baby. It's amazing that your parents got you through it. I remember reading that less than a quarter of the children born during the Plagues lived to adulthood. They call you the Missing Generation."

"My dad is amazing. My mom was amazing. She died when I was six. We were living in a government camp outside Las Vegas, and there was a cholera outbreak. It was bad. My mom had just gotten over pneumonia, and it was just too much. It only took a few days. We thought she was lucky. The whole camp was sick, and there was no medicine and not nearly enough food or water. We were all waiting around to die. Then he showed up, the Wandering Angel. I remember him like it was yesterday. He took my hand in his. He was so tall, and his hands were so warm. I woke up a few hours later completely better. He healed the whole camp," she says.

"He was real? I always figured he was made up to give people hope during the Plagues."

"He was real and he completely changed my dad. He was just so grateful I was still alive. One of the other guys in the camp had a copy of The Book of Cabot, before it was banned. He started reading from it, calling people who were Differents 'Chosen Sons.' As far as my dad was concerned, he had just seen an angel come down from heaven and save his daughter. He was ready to believe anything. He and a bunch of others from the camp formed a group around Cabot. I think they were just desperate for something to believe in."

"Sounds like you're not that much of a believer yourself."

"I don't have time to worry about what I believe in. I do know that the Church probably saved our lives, and it gives us a community, which is not something many people have in this world. There must be something true and good about the religion if it does such good things," she says, almost pleading.

She doesn't believe what she's saying, but she desperately wants to. If she was like me, she could make herself believe it.

"I can see the logic in that," I say. I've found people don't like it when I point out what they are really thinking, even if it's true.

"And besides, I've got a job because of them. They helped my dad buy the bar, and we're doing pretty well now. If I have to go to church a few times a week and praise God for the Chosen, it seems like a good trade," she adds.

That part she believes. I nod in agreement.

She stops walking in front of an old house. It's run down, the paint is long gone and there are B-Crete patches everywhere all over the house. Still, it's in a lot better shape than most of the homes around here. I guess they're doing okay.

"This is me," Becky says.

"It's nice."

"Look, like I told you before, it was just a walk. I don't care if it's God's command or anyone's command. I am a lady, and I am not doing anything with a kid I just met."

"I know, I know. I remember. I remember everything. I just like you and I wanted to walk you home. And, I might be a kid, but I'm mature for my years. You can use my friends as a point of comparison."

"You're right, plenty of guys just like your friends come to the bar every weekend. You are a different Different; you're an old soul. Will you be able to find your way back to the Slug from here?"

"I'll be just fine. Could I call you sometime? Maybe I could come out and walk you home again?" I don't know where that confidence came from.

She waits five seconds to respond, and I cannot possibly make time move fast enough.

“I suppose you earned a second date,” she finally says.

I go on think.Net and send her a knowledge request.

“Okay this is going to take a minute. I never use the thing. Nobody out here can afford any call time,” she warns.

She goes into the think.Net stare. It takes her at least three times as long as it should to accept the request. I remind myself that she didn’t want to be made fun of. Now we know each other on think.Net, that means we can call each other.

“Okay, well I’ll wait to hear from you then, and I’m not just being coy. My think.Net balance is zero, you have to call me,” she says as she comes out of the stare.

"Will do. I bid you good evening then," I bow and kiss her hand. I immediately feel cheesy.

"Thank you for walking with me," she says.

We stand silently for a moment as she looks into my eyes. I can tell she's going to do something, but I don't know what. She closes her eyes and pouts her lips. My God, she's going to kiss me. I don't know what to do. I just purse my own lips and receive. I feel just a tiny tip of her tongue in my mouth.

She looks embarrassed when she pulls back. She turns and walks off into her house before I can think of anything to say, not that I have any idea of what to say. I've never been kissed before. I watch the door close then turn and walk away.

I can barely think straight as I make my way back to the Slug. I just kissed a girl. Lying in bed at fifteen, trying to figure out how to make my kidneys function, I never imagined I'd be able to recover and get to this place. Maybe Cabot was the tiniest bit right. Right now, I do feel like a Chosen Son.

A shriek that pierces the night interrupts my bliss. Even without my enhanced senses, I'd have heard it clear as day. As it is, I can tell it is a woman around my age, and she is utterly and completely terrified.

I take off running toward the sound. I don't even think of what could be causing the scream until I turn onto the next block. The woman is still two hundred yards away, and three young men are after her, howling with laughter.

The woman keeps screaming as they chase her. They seem to be toying with her, letting her get up and run away before they chase her down and knock her over again.

"Come on girlie, you were all over me back when you thought I was holding," one of the guys yells. "You only wanted me for my Tranq? Do you have any idea how much that hurts my feelings?"

She screams again and tries to run, but he grabs her by the hair and drags her down.

"You may not be getting any Tranq tonight, but you'll be getting something else. In fact, I think we've all got something for you," he says and laughs. His friends laugh too.

"Help!" the woman screams out again. I think it is the last one, she doesn't have any more screams left in her.

"Yell all you want. Nobody out here's going to help you. This is our turf. Nobody would step to a Ripper," he says with confidence.

"Leave the girl alone," I find myself yelling in my most booming voice. It sounds impressive.

"Who said that?" one of the guys yells, and they all turn up the street to face me.

I'm not sure what my plan is. I don't usually find myself saying things I didn't mean to. It shouldn't be possible. Nevertheless, I said it, now I have to do something about it.

I've already broken the law. Article 3 Section 1 of the Different Acts of 1996: "It shall be unlawful for any Different individual, regardless of intention, abilities, or classification, to take action against any criminal or crime he or she witnesses or is the victim of unless that Different is protecting himself or herself from an imminent deadly threat."

They pounded that law into our heads during Rules and Regulations in Section 26. They made sure we all knew about what that moron "Captain Freedom" did in the Chicago MA. Although I'm pretty sure I'm not secretly strong enough to cause an earthquake that kills thousands of people.

I'm not about to destroy half a city or start some kind of race war. If I act, I could help this woman. On the other hand, I could run away and let these dirt bags kill her, rape her, or both. When I think of it that way, running away should be the illegal thing to do.

I should try to hide my identity though. I relax the muscles in my face, making everything sag. It will not completely change the way I look, but it should make me look a lot older. These guys probably won't go to the cops, but if they do, at least they'll be looking for a Different who's a lot older than I am. There's only one question. How in God's name am I going to stop these guys?

"Come on out here and get your ass beat," the first guy yells.

It's time to go take them up on their offer. I turn off the part of my brain that tells me I have no idea what I'm doing and that they could be armed. Instead, I listen to the part of my brain that says I'm six feet, three inches tall, two hundred pounds, and a built like a brick wall. I can run faster and lift more than any normal man. But it just so happens that I've never really put my athleticism to the test.

"I told you to leave the girl alone," I say in my most booming voice. It is quite effective. I can see one of the guys shudder.

I step out of the shadows and whatever intimidation factor I had immediately disappears. The dirt bags' faces all turn to grins.

"Take a walk, old man, before something bad happens to you," the lead man says. He twists the woman's hair, making her whimper.

"Can you believe this geezer?" the other talker says.

Now I know I successfully changed my appearance. Perhaps I went too far, a six-three, two hundred pound geriatric isn't going to scare anyone.

"Leave her alone, or there will be trouble," I say firmly and hold up my right hand, making sure they all see the D.

That's my last card. These dirt bags can't be drunk or stupid enough to mess with a Different. For all they know, I can melt them or make them think they're chickens. They would be crazy not to leave now. The leader starts to laugh. I don't think that's a good sign.

"We ain't the ones in trouble here, freak. You think anyone cares about another girl getting what she deserves? We tell the cops that some freak was out acting like a hero, and they'll hunt you down like a dog. They won't care what we were doing. I tell you what, how about you get the hell out of here. If you're lucky, we won't tell nobody about this and you won't get your ass thrown in Great Basin," the leader yells at me.

I'd like to think he's wrong, but maybe he's not. Maybe they would hunt me; maybe they would stop at nothing to track me down. Maybe I wouldn't get a slap on the wrist for a first offense, maybe they'd lock me up for life in Great Basin. I don't want to rot away in an impenetrable fortress built into the side of a mountain, designed to hold Differents.

My resolve starts to waver until I look the woman in the eyes. There's no question about what will happen to her if I leave. No one else will help her. There is only me with my maybes and her definite pain. I have to choose.

"I'm not going anywhere. Now, why don't you get out of here so I don't have to deal with three corpses and some real problems?" I say with intensity.

"Bull, if you could do something, you would have already done it. I bet you're a weak little freak who's just got a tiny arm growing out of his ass. Or maybe you're just a scared old man who drew a D on his hand and now thinks he's a tough guy."

The leader steps right in my face, trying to stare me down, and I see his lackeys moving in, surrounding me. I haven't been in many fights before, but I don't have to be Sun Tzu to know you don't want to be surrounded. This is about to go south, fast. I turn on my adrenal gland and have it pump full bore. I can feel the surge almost immediately.

"I warned you," I say.

I cock my hand back and make a fist, aiming at the leader. I make sure my tendons and muscles are as compressed as they can be. Then I let go, surging my hand forward. I can feel my bones aligning, generating just about as much force as my arm is capable of. This is a beautiful punch.

The problem is, my aim is not beautiful. I was focusing so much on aligning my fist that I didn't realize my target moved. My punch connects directly with his shoulder. I feel my wrist snap as three bones break and a couple of tendons shred. Nerves fire, making sure I'm well aware of what happened.

The blow to the shoulder pushes the leader back, but it's hardly more than a shove. Meanwhile, my wrist is hanging limply. I'm not exactly Mohamed Ali.

"It looks like what this freak can do is shatter like glass," the leader says.

I see one of the other guys lunging at me from the corner of my eye, trying to tackle me. I step to the side and give him a shove in the back as he goes by me. He crashes into the ground, hard.

I turn just in time to see a fist from the third guy flying at my face. All I can do is close my eyes. The punch connects in the middle of my cheek. I feel some blood vessels burst, but there's no structural damage.

The guy has his hands up, ready to deliver another punch and covering up his jaw pretty well. I decide to kick him in the shin. It hurts like hell and few people are prepared for the pain. There are a ton of nerves in the shin for some reason.

As soon as I kick his leg, he drops his hands. I use that opening to deliver another beautiful punch with my good hand. This one connects directly with his chin, snapping his neck back. The neck snap is what causes the knockout. I remember my dad telling me that when he taught me about boxing. The dirt bag goes down for the count.

"Run!" I scream at the girl, which snaps her out of her shock. She gets up and takes off running down the street.

"You done it now," the leader says and comes at me, swinging his fists wildly.

I cover up, trying to make sure he doesn't get a good hit on anything important, and his fists bounce off my forearms. I try to step back to buy some time to think, but he keeps after me. One of his punches catches me in the nose, busting a whole bunch of capillaries. Blood starts spurting out of my nose like a fountain.

The sight of my blood gives the thug confidence, and he winds up for a big punch. He throws a haymaker right at my kidney, which connects squarely, and I can feel his knuckles causing hemorrhages all over the organ. If I were a normal person, I'd double over in pain. Luckily, I'm not normal.

The thug's punch was wild. Even though it connected, it made him lose his balance and stumble. I see his clavicle exposed and punch it as hard as I can. I feel the bone snap under my fist and the man screams in agony. The blow also broke my ring finger. Now, both my hands are hurt, but I don't think I'll get any sympathy from this guy. He collapses to the ground, writhing in agony.

I taught three punks a lesson, and I'm still standing. Not too shabby. I have to say I impressed myself, maybe I'm not crazy, maybe I can make a —

8

My new race is blessed, but this does not mean life will be easy for my Chosen Sons. It will not. Much hardship awaits the Chosen in this new world. If they are righteous, if they persevere, the wonders they create will be worth paying any price.

Chosen Sons: 53

Tom looked back at the football field and saw his path of destruction. He was not a teenage boy going through a growth spurt. He was not a gifted athlete. He was a Different. He was a freak. He was a tool of the Devil. He looked at the crowd and saw their faces and their fear. He felt his own fear. The beast in Tom started running, and his body moved of its own accord.

Tom jumped over the stadium fence, then ran as fast and as far as he could. He ran away from the stadium, out of his neighborhood, out of the entire Metro Area, and into the swamps that surrounded Houston. Tom ran for six hours straight until he could not run any longer. He looked around and finally realized he was safe. No one was going to find him so deep in the swamp. He was exhausted and scared. He ended up falling asleep propped up against a half-dead tree.

Tom spent the next few days in the swamps, wondering when the Houston Metro Police were going to track him down. After five days, Tom realized that there was too much ground for the police to cover. They were not going to find him.

Tom pondered his options. He did not want to spend his life hiding in the swamps. He had not meant to hurt those other players. It was not his fault he was born a Different. He just wished it would all go away. He was a confused and scared fifteen-year-old boy who needed his parents.

Tom decided to make his was back to Houston, back home. He knew his father would be able to fix this. Maybe they could hire a lawyer or get Tom out of the country. There had to be something. The Calhouns were one of the richest families in Houston, there had to be some solution.

Tom waited on the outskirts of the Metro Area until nightfall. He quickly made his way through the edge of the city and into his neighborhood. He approached his house cautiously. He realized his fear was warranted when he spotted three Houston Metro police officers waiting out in front of his massive house. He also saw a light on in his father's study.

Tom made his way around the inattentive officers and climbed up to a second story window into his house. Tom went down the hall to his father's study and did something his mother had told him not to do ever since he was a boy. He knocked on the door.

"Damn it, Lilly, not now!" Oren yelled in response.

Tom sheepishly opened the door anyway.

"Dad," Tom said with tears in his eyes.

"Oh, it's you. I was wondering when you would show up. You have made a real mess here, Tommy. Do you have any idea what you have done to me? To this family? Because of you, I could lose everything I have ever worked for. Are you happy, Tom? Are you glad you won your little football game?"

"Dad, I'm sorry, I didn't know. I didn't mean to hurt anybody."

"Don't you call me 'Dad.' You are no son of mine. I wouldn't father an abomination. You must belong to some vagrant your whore mother slept with on one of her benders!"

"Please stop. It was an accident. Tell me what I should do. Help me, please," Tom pleaded.

"I'll tell you what you should do! You should march downstairs and turn yourself in to the police. Let them deal with you however they deal with freaks. Better yet, go hang yourself. That way I won't have to spend my life answering questions about my monster of a son!" Oren yelled.

Tom looked at his father through tear-filled eyes, watching for something, some sign of love, some sign of compassion, but all he saw was hate. Oren was a father who hated his own son. Tom felt a lifetime of resentment boil up inside of him.

"I'm a monster? What about you! What about a father who ignores his own son? What about a man who loves money more than his own family? All I ever wanted was for you to notice me, but you couldn't be bothered."

Tom stormed over to his father and picked him up out of his chair. Tom held the man up in the air by his arms, squeezing his dad by the shoulders. It looked like Tom was the father and Oren the child.

"Tom, I..." Oren tried to say, his lips trembling with fear.

"What could I have done make you proud? Answer me! Answer me!" Tom yelled while shaking his father.

Oren tried to say something, but it just sounded like a groan. Tom dropped his father to the ground and watched the man struggle to breathe. Oren's neck was broken, snapped by Tom's shaking.

That moment, Lilly Calhoun worked up the courage to go see if her husband was all right. When she walked into the study, she saw a monster standing over her dying husband. It only took a moment to realize the monster was her own son. Her little Tommy.

"Mom, I'm sorry. I didn't mean to, it was an accident," Tom said to his mother, tears streaming down his face.

"Tommy, my God! What have you done? You're a monster! You're a spawn of the Devil! Get away from my husband!" Lilly Calhoun screamed with all the hate she could muster.

Tom could not stand the hate. He could not stand the thought that he had a mother who despised him. If that was the case, Tom decided he would rather not have a mother. All it took was one good shake.

#

The Beast wakes up on a pile of bones, howling. Thinking of his past is upsetting. It makes him question the Lord's plan. The creature calms himself. He must have faith. The doubt is weakness; hunger causes the weakness. He needs to feed.

The Forgotten who live here are especially vile. Tranq is rampant. The drug infects The Beast's nose, making it hard to smell anything else. It does not matter, though. The Beast has claimed this area. These people belong to him, and they cannot forget that. Feeding on them is safe, at least. The Beast could eat a thousand people out here, and the police would not care.

The Beast heads out of his abandoned apartment-turned-nest and climbs up the remains of the building's stairs. Once on the roof, The Beast takes a deep breath and listens. He is hoping to hear some prey walking alone. Instead, The Beast hears the sounds of an argument in the distance, one of hundreds of fights he hears most nights, but when he takes a deep breath he howls with excitement. He can smell a fellow Chosen Son. Out here in the slums, what are the chances?

The Beast hurries over to a roof overlooking the argument. There he finds a young Chosen Son. He smells young anyway. He looks like an old geezer. The boy must be a Morpher or something. The Chosen Son is yelling at a man, telling him to leave a human girl alone. What does the fool think he is doing? Why is he letting himself get surrounded?

That Chosen Son is some kind of moron to risk his life to help a Forgotten Daughter. What he's doing is illegal, even The Beast knows that. The Forgotten are so terrified of the Chosen Sons they cannot even accept the Chosen's help.

The argument with the thugs soon turns into a fight, and The Beast gets to see the Chosen Son in action. He is more than a Morpher and seems stronger and faster than a normal man, but not by much. He reminds The Beast of himself when he was just a teenager.

The Beast watches as even the minor gifts God gave this Chosen Son make him more dangerous than three men. He is winning the fight and seems poised for victory when he makes a mistake. He turns his back on one of the thugs he shoved to the ground. The man sneaks up behind the boy and hits him in the back of the head with a chunk of B-Crete. The young fool is knocked down, and the man starts kicking and pounding him.

The Beast will not allow this. He will not watch a weak, worthless human kill one of God's Chosen Sons, even a foolish one.

The Beast jumps down from the roof and bounds over to the attacker. He tears out the thug's throat with one swipe of his claw and crushes the skulls of the other two injured thugs under his feet. He will not feed on them. They do not deserve salvation.

The Beast turns his attention to the injured Chosen Son.

"In out, in out, in out," he says in time with his breathing

"You okay? You're a fool, you know that?" The Beast says.

"In out, in out, in out," the Chosen Son keeps repeating.

He looks at the boy's tattoo, which says “Gavin Stillman: Gamma,” and some words he does not understand.

"Gavin? Are you all right? Snap out of it!" The Beast yells.

The Beast gives Gavin a little shake, but Gavin just keeps repeating the one phrase. He cannot tell what is wrong with the Chosen Son. His eyes are open and he is breathing, but he is in some kind of daze. The Beast knows he cannot help Gavin. He needs to let the Forgotten Sons save him.

The Beast lifts Gavin gently, cradling him in his arms, and carefully makes his way to the closest Slug station. He jumps up onto the empty platform and waits for the next train. When the Slug comes, he steps into an empty train car, plops Gavin down in one of the seats, and heads off the train.

The Beast leaps up onto a roof across from the train platform. He drops to his knees, closes his eyes, and prays.

“Lord, please, watch over Gavin. Make sure he gets some help. I can’t stand to think that I mighta watched another brother die. Can you tell me if he’s going to be all right? Can you tell me if I saved him?”

The Beast waits on his knees for more than a minute, hoping for an answer. It doesn’t come.

9

It shall be unlawful for any Different individual, regardless of intention, abilities, or classification, to take any action against any criminal or crime he or she witnesses or is the victim of unless that Different is protecting himself or herself from an imminent deadly threat.

Article 3 Section 1 of the Different Acts of 1996

"In out, in out, in out," I say out loud.

"Please say something else, buddy," I hear someone say.

I turn to look at the voice. It's Ben, the train conductor who gave me a ride out of Section 26.

"Ben, you should bend your knees and lift with your legs when you take your garbage to the Hoover," I tell him.

"Whatever you say, mister, whatever you say. I'm just glad you finally said something else," Ben says. I can tell he doesn't remember what he told me the last time we saw each other.

"When you gave me a ride to the Barracks you told me that you hurt your back carrying the garbage down to the Hoover. You should be careful. Back injuries only get worse as you age," I say, clueing him in.

"I don't think I'm the one you should be worried about. You look like hell," Ben says. He looks concerned.

He should be. I feel alarms going off all over my body telling me about all sorts of injuries. One of my ribs is broken, and it's causing more damage to my lung with each breath. My right wrist is shattered, and I've got a few busted fingers in my left hand. I feel a crack in my skull too. I reach back to touch the wound, but there's a wad of cloth covering it.

"I bandaged up your head. You were bleeding pretty good," Ben says, anticipating my question.

"Where am I?" I ask.

"You're on the Slug... I guess you already knew that. We're at the yards, end of the line. I found you when I was doing my final check of the train. Do you remember what happened to you? Is there anyone I should call? A son or daughter? Grandson?" Ben asks.

Grandson? What is he talking about…? My face! I've still got all my facial muscles relaxed. He thinks I'm an old man. That's why he doesn't seem to recognize me.

"Do you remember what happened to you?" Ben asks again.

"I was jumped. Some punks attacked me and must have hit me on the head. I don't know how I got here," I answer him. I'm only lying the tiniest bit. I really don't know how I got here.

One of those thugs I fought must have hit me with something hard, right in the back of the head. That would explain the crack and the damage to my brain. It would also explain why I can't remember what happened. I must have had to focus on healing, walking to the Slug, and breathing, not forming new memories. I guess I won the fight, otherwise, I think I'd be in much worse shape, or maybe even dead.

"Sounds like you're lucky to be alive. You've got to be careful out here. It's dangerous for old folks this late at night, even ones who look like Jack LaLanne," Ben says.

I don't know who that is, but if I tell him that he might figure out I'm not really an old man.

"What time is it?" I ask. I suddenly realized this is a Friday. I've got work.

"Six in the morning. My shift just ended. You got somewhere to be?"

"Yeah, but I don't think I'm going to make it."

"No, probably not. Takes about an hour and a half just to get anywhere near the Metro Center from way out here. Might take you more than three hours to get to the lab. You should head to platform 3. That Slug is leaving in eight minutes. Are you good to travel?" Ben asks.

"I think I'll be okay," I answer.

"Okay. Well then, good luck. And work on that right cross."

"What?" I ask.

"Work on your punches, in case you get jumped by any more punks. Maybe you can whoop those whippersnappers next time," Ben says as he steps off the train.

I take a moment to gather myself, then stand up and walk out onto the platform. It occurs to me that either Ben is a terrible person who is willing to leave a badly injured elderly man to fend for himself, or he somehow knows I'm not what I appear to be. Come to think of it, how did he know I was headed to a laboratory? I scan around the platform for any sign of him, but he's already disappeared. I guess it will remain a mystery.

I follow the signs to platform 3. Sure enough, there's a Slug waiting with its doors open. I step inside and plop myself down.

I need to keep healing. To fix the crack in my skull, I rush as much blood as I can to my head and metabolize any loose calcium in my system. Even with that, it will take more than a few hours to heal, and I'm going to lose a lot of blood in the meantime. I'm in no shape to make it to work, even if I can make it on time. I'll have to call in sick.

It takes me over three hours to make it back to the Barracks stop. It was hard for me to recall the Slug system map to find my way home. I'm not even completely sure how long it took because my temporal sense is still off. Everything is a little bit off. I need to heal my brain, and it's going to take a while. Nerve cells take the longest to regenerate.

The stairs up to my apartment seem to go on forever. My body screams at me with each step. It tells me to lie down and curl into a ball, but I can't yet. Finally, I make it to my apartment, throw open the door, and stumble inside. Nick sits at the counter eating some cereal, probably my cereal. I blow past him without a word and head towards my room.

"Whoa, what the hell is going on here?" Nick yells.

I ignore him and slam the door behind me. I lock it and collapse on the bed. I haven't needed to lie down so badly in years. I might not need to sleep, but getting off my feet feels fantastic. All of my muscles are fatigued.

Nick banging on the door interrupts my peace.

"Hey, what are you doing? Get out, or I'm calling the cops. Who are you?" Nick yells at ten times the volume of a normal scream. It makes my ears ring, but I don't have the wherewithal to flood my Tympanic cavity.

Who am I? What is he talking about? Oh no. I go into the bathroom and see my old man face disguise in the mirror. I never fixed it. I try to tighten the muscles, but my injured brain makes it difficult to concentrate.

"Nick, what's your problem, dude? It's just me. I'm not feeling well," I yell in answer.

He bangs on the door again. Just hearing my voice isn't going to cut it. He could fake my voice if he wanted to, which must make him paranoid about it.

"All right, all right, just a second," I tell him.

I clear my head and focus on making my skin taught. After fifteen seconds, I manage to make myself look like myself. Well, kind of. I still look like crap. I guess that's okay if I'm pretending to be sick.

"What do you want?" I ask as I open the door.

"Gavin, it is you! Sorry, I could have sworn I saw some old dude rush into your room. I must be seeing things." Nick says and tries to look past me into my room.

"Nope, no old dudes here, just me. Now, like I said, I'm not feeling that well." I say and push the door closed in his face.

"I thought you told me you don't get sick," he says through the closed door.

He's right. I should come up with something else to tell the Doctors. Not getting sick is one of the reasons I have my job. I call Dr. Cole on think.Net while I think up the name of an aunt to kill. Poor Aunt May, she went too soon. Let's just hope they don't bother checking my personnel records.

#

It's been five days since my run-in with those punks, and I still can't get my wrist to heal right. I think I messed something up when I regenerated one of the tendons. There's a hitch when I try to move it, and it's getting in the way of my filing.

I go on think.Net and access the Medical Librarian. I know I'm not supposed to go on think.Net at work, but if they catch me, I'll just tell them I messed up my wrist in the shower or something. The Doctors aren't going to need me for hours anyway, and I can't do much of anything with my hand like this.

I bring up the medical diagrams of the wrist. I have what it's supposed to look like memorized, but maybe they have some different images. My wrist looks just like the picture in my head, and it still doesn't work.

I look through all the databases and sure enough, there's an image I haven’t seen before. It shows a different angle and a better view of where the tendon is supposed to attach between my wrists and thumb. I was off by less than a tenth of an inch, but it was enough. I should do a check of my whole anatomy when I get the chance. It will be useful if I'm planning on getting into more trouble.

Why do I keep thinking of getting in more trouble? When I think back to that night, it should make me cringe. Those thugs almost killed me. I still haven't recovered from my injuries. But I don't cringe, and my injuries aren’t what I think of when I remember that night. What first comes to mind is the look of terror on that poor girl's face. I changed that to a look of relief. If it hadn't been for me, who knows what would have happened. I saved her. That girl could have been Becky.

I'm sure that girl is Becky to someone, or she will be one day. There are women like her all over the Metro Area who have to live in fear. And not just women, children and men too. Why should good people have to live in fear? The police can't or won't help them, but maybe I can. I know it's illegal for me to act like some sort of vigilante, but I have a hard time seeing how that matters. Illegal and wrong are not the same thing. Sometimes they might even be the opposite of each other.

I'm snapped out of my pondering by a call on think.Net. It's Gary.

>>>Hey, Gavin. How's it going?

<<<I'm good. You finally over your hangover?

>>>Yeah, I think so. I've never been hungover before. It really sucks. Now I have to wonder why normal people drink if they end up feeling this way. I thought I would die that first morning.

<<<I wouldn't know. I can make my body process the alcohol without any of the side effects.

>>>Well la-tee-da. Anyway, we're heading back Thursday night. You down?

<<<I can't. I'm meeting somebody for dinner.

>>>The bartender from the other night? I didn't know you had a thing for older women.

<<<No, one of my teachers from Section 26.

>>>That does sound better than getting drunk and chasing girls. Good choice.

<<<Shut it. Besides, I thought your hangover had changed your whole outlook.

>>>Have to get right back on that horse. What should I tell the bartender? I bet she will ask about you.

<<<Tell her I'll see her Friday.

>>>I didn't know you had it in you.

#

Larry made himself look like a fat, redheaded little troll again. He does remember me. You never can tell with teachers. They seem like they care about you, but then they move on to countless other kids they are supposed to care about. It's nice to know I stuck in Larry's mind. I don't think he normally walks around as a short, fat guy with a fro.

We're at Oasis Burger, much to my chagrin. Larry's choice. He orders himself a burger, shake, and fries. I don't order anything. I can't stand the thought of paying to shove this food in my mouth. I can barely take it when they pay me. Larry gets his food and we sit down.

"So, is that all they have you do when you're not testing food, filing?" Larry asks.

"No, sometimes they'll have me help clean the bio lab when they have an especially messy experiment. Those are the exciting days," I answer.

"I guess someone has to test the french fries. I'm glad it's you. I'll feel much more secure eating here from now on."

"They're called Palm Fries now, old man. What have you been up to? I've been trying to call you on think.Net for a few weeks, but it kept saying you were out of range. Was everything all right?"

"Government business. Very top secret. Can't tell you," he says with a huge grim.

"That smile seems to say something else."

"I'll trade you. I want to know one of your pieces of top secret information."

"What? You already know everything about me. You taught me everything about me for Christ sake," his attitude has me worried. He can't know about me fighting those punks out in the boonies, can he?

"Nope. I want to know what the Oasis Shakes are made of. Deal?"

"Deal."

"Okay, I'll go first. So there I was late one night, minding my own business, sitting in my Construct recliner, watching Crossup on think.Net. Suddenly, I heard a loud banging on my front door and a threatening voice saying, 'Larry Rosen open up! We know you're in there!' I open the door and find ten men standing in my hallway. They're all wearing suits, sunglasses, and handguns. They look like they'd love it if I tried something," Larry says, acting the scene out with his hands.

"I figured, this is it. They know about me, they found out I can hide my mind from Telepaths. They're going to lock me up in Great Basin and throw away the key. I started worrying they would make me tell them about you and some other people I know about, and you'd all end up sharing my fate.

"The leader asked me to come with him and I figured, what the hell, I'll face my end with some dignity and class instead of trying to run away screaming and crying like I really want to. So they took me downstairs and threw me in the backseat of a car. I hadn't been in a car thirty years, so I was pretty pumped about that.

“The car windows were covered so I couldn't see out, but I was sure they were taking me to court. Then the jury would find me guilty, and that would be that. A Tranq-coma in Great Basin was the best-case scenario.

“They took me into a building, sat me down at a table, and left me alone in the room. I was working on trying to make my face look like one of the guards when an important-looking man walked in.

“He asked me if I was a patriot. I figured the interrogation had started, so I answered, of course, I love my country. ‘Good,’ he said, ‘do you want what's best for your country?’ I figured this was the part where he tells me that it was for the greater good that they were going to lock me up. But what was I going to do? I told him of course I want what's best for my country.

"Then he leaned in close, and I started to get really scared and he says, ‘Ambassador Lewis died last night of a heart attack,’ and then he just looked at me," Ben finishes his monologue and pauses.

"Who is Ambassador Lewis?" I ask, waiting for the punch line.

"That's just what I asked. He was the U.S. Ambassador to the Africana Coalition. It turns out that he dropped dead right before some important trade negotiation. Apparently, Ambassador Lewis had been the only one who was able to make any headway with the Afrikaans. They needed me to Morph myself into the Ambassador and handle the negotiations.

“It was the real deal. They had a Telepath there to help sell the charade, and just in case the Afrikaans had their own mind reader. It was an intense couple of weeks, but the government was happy with my work. I was able to secure our supplies of gallium phosphide and cadmium sulfide, whatever those are," Larry says dismissively.

"They're semi-conductors," I say. I have that memory in my brain, but I don't know where it came from.

"Oh, well, that just clears everything up. Now, listen, I know I was joking around, but you really can't tell anyone about this. They'd disappear me and you and everyone we’ve ever talked to, so make sure you keep it to yourself," Larry says, and for once, he isn't smiling.

"Don't worry, I won't. You know I never let anything slip out I don't want too."

"I do know that... Well?" he asks.

"Well what? It was a cool story. What do you want me to say?"

"I want you to keep your end of the bargain. What do they put in those shakes?"

"I don't think you want to know, but I honor my debts. It's 35% manna, 5% sugar, and 60% boiled Styro."

"What's Styro?"

"It comes from a Different. It's the adhesive they use in B-Crete that turns all the crushed up old bricks and wood into the grey paste we know and love," I say with a smile.

Larry pauses for a moment to consider this, then shrugs and takes a big swig of his shake.

"Calories are calories. We had to eat worse during the Plagues. In '84 I would have given my right pinkie for a glue sandwich, anything besides boiled rat."

We sit silent for a bit as Larry stares at his shake. I find myself thinking about my fight the other night. If I do want to keep up my life as a vigilante, I will have to do some studying on think.Net. I need to learn how to handle myself better, or next time I might not make it out alive. I have to remember to make sure all the guys are down before I assume I've won the fight. I should also bulk up. I could make my body carry more muscle mass. More muscle will take more calories to maintain, but I think the increased strength would be worth it.

"I said, what do they make the ketchup from? I know it's not tomatoes," Larry says loudly. I realize it's the second time he's asked.

"There are some tomatoes in it, about one part per thousand. The rest is Manna, artificial sweeteners, and food coloring," I answer.

"A little slow on the uptake. What's on your mind?"

I think about telling him what happened. I could tell him about how I saved that woman and how good it made me feel. There's something telling me not to though. I think I trust Larry, but he does work for the government. I don't want to test whether he's more loyal to me or them.

"It's nothing, just bored with my job. Any chance you could put in a good word for me with your government buddies, find me something a little more exciting to do?" I finally say.

"Still hung up on that, huh? You did always want to be a hero. Let me fill you in, the government doesn't help as many people as you want to think. You're probably saving more lives testing french fries, or Palm Fries, or whatever they want to call them."

"It doesn't feel that way. I can't imagine testing food my whole life. I've already eaten enough fast food for a hundred lifetimes. I'm bored out of my mind."

"Sounds like a job all right. Tell you what, I'll talk to some people, see if there's anything for you. But I wouldn't get my hopes up if I were you. Not to offend, but you did used to be a Zeta, not a great thing to have on your resume. I recommend you do what every other guy who hates his job does: go home, have a beer, and fall asleep watching baseball on think.Net. You've got a job, buddy. In this day and age, that makes you pretty lucky," Larry says as he polishes off his shake.

#

"I remember trees. Most of them were dead already, but there was a little patch behind our house that was still alive. It was so green and full of life. I dream about it sometimes. The air in that little patch of forest was fresher than any air I've smelled since. I think I'll miss it till the day I die," Becky says.

It's the fourth time I've met her at the bar and walked her home. I know taking an hour train ride just to walk with her for twenty minutes seems a little desperate, but I don't care. As soon as I realized that woman I saved could just have easily been Becky, I couldn't stand the thought of her walking home alone. I've been coming as often as she'll let me. It helps that I don’t sleep.

"I read there are still forests up in Canada, where it was too cold for Cabot's bacteria to take hold. I'd love to go see them someday," I say.

"Maybe you can on your hamburger-eater salary, but we regular working humans aren't ever going to save up enough to see them," Becky says.

"Yeah, yeah, talk to me when you have Section 26 debt. Maybe I'll get to start pocketing some cash when I'm sixty."

"Let's not start comparing sob stories, you don't have a chance."

She's right. I'm embarrassed, and I should show it. I rush blood to my cheeks and lower my eyes.

"You're right, sorry," I say while looking down.

"Oh my God, you look embarrassed. I thought you didn't have emotions," she responds.

"I have emotions. I mean, I guess I do. I just don't have to show them unless I want to. I figured you couldn't be offended anymore if I was embarrassed."

"I'm not, and it's cute," Becky squeezes my hand.

We continue on the dimly lit street hand in hand. Her skin is cool from the night, but it still feels fantastic. I slow down time so I can enjoy it for as long as possible. Even with that, we arrive at her house way too soon.

"Maybe we can't go to Canada, but would you like to go see the Hanging Gardens?" I ask.

"That sounds fun. It's been so long since I've been to the Center."

"Does next Saturday work, or do you have to be at the bar?"

"I can get my dad to cover. His leg is feeling better, and he'd be happy to do it. He's ecstatic that I'm seeing a Different, especially one who's such a gentleman. Even if I am robbing the cradle."

She puts her arms around my neck and pulls me in for a kiss. Soft and wet and perfect. Each night I walk her we kiss a little longer, we grab each other a little tighter. Then she turns and runs off into her house.

I wait until she's safe inside and then make my way back to the Slug. Just like the last three times I walked her home, I take an indirect route back. I tell myself that I just want to check out the neighborhood, or burn off some excess calories, but self-deception is not one of my strengths. I'm trying to be a hero. Despite the fractured skull, broken wrist, and brain damage I suffered last time, I'm hoping I get to do it all over again. I must be crazy.

I relax the muscles of my face to give me that old man look. I walk for a few blocks as my geriatric alter-ego without seeing anything to be excited about, just a few exhausted souls coming home from working a late shift. They're more concerned about me than I am about them. It's hard to believe these battered people are lucky, but they are. They have jobs.

Aside from the tired workers, all I see are ugly, decrepit buildings and the occasional WormLight. There's trash all over the streets. I wonder if they'll ever get Hoovers out here in the boonies, or Walters to clean up the sidewalks. I've had just about enough of this ugliness and turn to head back to the Slug, declaring this another wasted night.

I freeze when I hear what could only be describe as a roar. It sounds like a wild animal. A big wild animal. My mind immediately goes to the rumors of The Beast. Could it be true? Could he be out here somewhere? I turn and run towards the sound. It came from a few blocks to the north.

I hear another roar as I turn to run. This one is stifled shortly after it’s let out. The roar sounded almost... happy? It came from about ten blocks away. I run as fast as I can towards the source, turning up my hearing and vision sensitivity on the way. I hear someone slam a window shut, and the sound is almost deafening. I hear another noise too, like someone or something scrambling away. Is it coming from the roof?

As I run, I start preparing my body for a fight by getting my adrenaline flowing and rushing blood to my muscles. It occurs to me that I might not be prepared to deal with a fugitive murderer monster. I'm already committed though. Something falls and makes a *splat* on the ground. It sounded like something soft. I run to the alley where the sound came from.

There I find… nothing. Just a pile of rubble and trash. I see a rat sniffing something in the corner. I head over to the spot and the rat scurries away. Now I can see what it was smelling, a kidney, and it looks human. What a lovely neighborhood.

10

I sent my only son to earth with a simple message: love. Instead of love, mankind has responded with two thousand years of horrors. War and violence are as omnipresent as they ever were. The poor suffer disease and famine while the rich wallow in their own decadence.

Chosen Sons: 4

The Beast crouches on a roof, lazily picking at the innards of some poor old Forgotten Son. The man looked like he was on his way home from work, at three a.m. That work ethic is commendable, especially for a man of his age. Sixty-year-olds with limps do not usually work the late shift. The Beast could reward this soul with eternity in heaven. It should be easy. All he has to do is feed, but he has found it hard to choke down more than a few bites lately. He has been too worried to eat.

Ever since he put Gavin on that train, he has not stopped wondering if the Chosen Son lived. The Beast has to hope that God sent some Forgotten Sons to help Gavin. Having to rely on humans makes The Beast angry. He should not need anything from those pitiful creatures. The Beast stops and takes a deep breath to calm himself. Gavin was not a healer. Doctors and nurses were his only hope. That does not mean The Beast likes it.

He closes his eyes and prays.

"Lord, I'm begging you. Please tell me if Gavin is alive. I'm sorry to keep asking, but I got to know if I saved one of my brothers. I got to know if I did something to make up for all the bad I done. Please Lord, even if he's dead, just tell me. I can't stand not knowin'."

The Beast keeps his eyes closed for a good thirty seconds, hoping for a response, but the Lord is silent. Dejected, The Beast turns his attention to the dead old man. He takes a big whiff of the old man's insides, hoping that something in the man's ripped open belly stirs his appetite. Instead of something delicious to eat, he smells something better. Gavin. He let out a howl of joy. The Beast eyes where his nose points. He spots Gavin about fifteen blocks away. The boy still looks like an old man. Does he always look that way?

It does not matter. Gavin is alive! God is great! The Beast has saved a Chosen Son! He is a hero. The Beast cannot contain his excitement. He starts running around in small circles on the roof. His knuckles drag on the floor. Then he starts to howl, though it's more of a high-pitched yelp. He howls for a good ten seconds before he gets himself under control.

He needs to be calm. He needs to pray. The Lord must be so pleased. He must be proud of what The Beast has done. Before The Beast closes his eyes to pray, he takes a peak at Gavin. He is surprised to see that Gavin is heading his way. Gavin moves fast for an old man, fast for any human. He is nowhere near as fast as The Beast, but Gavin is still going to reach The Beast soon.

The boy has good hearing. It is hard to hone in on a sound in this part of the Metro Area. The buildings are all five or six stories tall, and sound echoes off the B-Crete. Even The Beast can struggle to track down a sound on occasion.

The Beast looks down at the dead old man and starts to panic. Gavin cannot find him like this, covered in the old man's guts. Gavin will not understand. He has not been shown the truth of Cabot. He is going to think The Beast is a monster who slaughters innocent old men. Gavin does not know The Beast gave the man eternity in paradise.

The Beast needs to get out of here and take this old man with him. He stuffs the man's stomach and intestines back inside the torn open chest. The Beast pulls the man's jacket closed and hopes it will hold everything in. Then he throws the old man over his shoulder and jumps to the roof next door. As he's in the air, The Beast feels something slippery slide out of the old man, down his back, and onto the alley below. The Beast cannot worry about that. He has to get away.

As The Beast keeps moving away from Gavin, he thinks about how great it would be if he did not have to run. How great it would be if he and Gavin were friends. If only Gavin knew the truth of Cabot. The Beast remembers when he first learned the truth.

#

Tom sunk into a deep depression after killing his parents. He knew he was a monster, an animal, a beast. He belonged in a cage. It was the only way to make sure he did not kill again.

Tom decided to turn himself in to the police, but not in the Houston Metro Area. They would know who he was. They would know that Tommy Calhoun murdered his own parents, two of the richest people in Houston. There would be lots of reporters and lots of questions.

Tom could not stomach the thought of all that attention. He decided to make the long walk to the Miami MA. There, the death of the Calhouns was just a blurb in the news. It took Tom three weeks to walk to the outskirts of the Miami Metro Area. Once there, he turned himself in to the police for the murder of Oren and Lilly Calhoun.

Since Tom could not own up to his identity, he made up a new name for himself, Arnold Taft. Arnold Taft was a Tranq junky born in the Non-Assisted Area. He had broken into some rich guy's house looking for money to buy Tranq. The couple caught Arnold breaking in, so he killed them.

Tom waived his right of extradition to the Houston MA. He also waived his right to a trial, pleading guilty to two counts of murder. Arnold's sentence was thirty-five years to life in prison. Upon admission to prison, a doctor examined Tom. The Genetic Incongruity Scan had recently been developed, but it had still not been implemented around the nation. The Miami Metro prison still relied on a doctor's evaluation to determine if a prisoner was a Different.

Just as Tom could not admit he had killed his parents, he could not admit to being a Different. He told the police that Arnold Taft was twenty-three. Tom was freakishly large for a sixteen-year-old, but simply huge for a twenty-three-year-old. The doctor gave Tom clearance, which meant Tom would spend his thirty-five to life sentence in Miami MA Lockup, not Great Basin Prison.

Life in jail was tougher than Tom could have imagined. The meager meals were not enough to satisfy his ravenous appetite. He went to bed every night suffering from hunger pains, but he knew he deserved the agony.

Tom was surrounded by violence. He was large enough to be left alone, but the other inmates fought all day and night. The fighting would stir the monster in Tom. It made him afraid he might lose control. It made him afraid that the beast in him would take control, and he would kill again. The one place where he could find peace was the prison library.

Tom had never been much of a reader, but he decided to spend his days reading the word of God. He scanned through the Old Testament, then the New Testament. He even read some of the Koran. Tom was searching for answers, for some explanation as to why God would create Tom just to curse him. Why did God make Tom, if all he did was cause suffering?

Tom found his answers one Sunday in the library. He was in the back, searching for something new to read when something caught his eye, the tiniest corner of a paper poking out from under a bookcase. It took all the strength in his malnourished body to lift the shelves up. The book was thin, more like a pamphlet, really. The worn cover read, *Chosen Sons: The Book of Cabot.*

Tom knew what this was. He knew that if anyone saw the book in his hands, they would add another twenty years to his sentence. Cabot was a madman. He had killed billions of people and almost destroyed the entire human race. Cabot was a bigger monster than Tom; Tom was sure of that. Maybe Cabot could explain why God hated Tom so much.

"Here is the record of the 3rd book of our Lord, as spoken to His vessel Cabot: 'I am your Lord. Take what I tell you now and spread it to all mankind. Make my truth known to any who will listen,'" it began.

#

"'You must simply claim your thrones as kings of the new earth.'

The Lord said."

The last line read, Tom placed the finished pamphlet inside his shirt. He held it close to his chest as he went back to his cell for the night. His mind was racing. Cabot had turned Tom's world upside down. Tom was not a monster, he was not cursed, and he was not a Different. He was a Chosen Son.

God had made the Chosen Sons as His new race. Mankind had rejected God. It chose instead to revel in its own greatness, in the greatness of science and invention, in the greatness of nuclear weapons and spaceships. Mankind imagined these achievements as solely their own and refused to recognize the Divine that surrounded them.

God had grown tired of mankind and its hubris. He decided to create a new race, one built more closely in his image. This new race would be capable of such miraculous feats they would have no choice but to accept the role of the Divine in their lives. They could not help but love the Lord in return for the gifts they had been given.

In order for His Chosen Sons to thrive, the Lord needed to eliminate His firstborn, His Forgotten Sons. God worked through Cabot, commanding him to make ten plagues to end the reign of the human race and create a new world made just for the Chosen.

Tom was so powerful, so strong, because God had blessed him. Tom was made to survive in the harsh world Cabot created. God had given Tom a spark of the Divine. He was closer to God than any human could ever be. Tom's suffering was not special. The Old and New Testament were both full of pain for many of those God touched. Tom's trials were nothing compared to those endured by Moses, or Job, or God's own son.

Ever since Tom had killed his parents, images of that night had kept him awake. Tom's suffering was over now. The Lord had saved him. He was not a monster. He was more like an angel. For the first time in many months, he slept through the entire night.

11

Let it be said clearly and with broad meaning: the 14th Amendment does not and cannot apply to Different individuals. The danger they pose is simply too great to afford them equal protection under the law. Congress, or the executive branch, shall have the power to pass whatever laws or regulations they deem necessary to control and monitor Different individuals.

Chief Justice Garret Dwight
Majority Opinion: United States v. Geiger

What was that? I whirl around and crane my neck up just in time to catch a glimpse of a pigeon flying off. No matter how many times I tell myself to relax, I can't stop overreacting to every little sound I hear.

I'm out here trying to help people. I'm trying to stop muggers, drug dealers, or murderers. At least, that's what I tell myself. I know that's not the whole truth. I know I'm really looking for signs of The Beast. I don't want to admit to myself that I'm worrying more about an urban legend than the actual dangerous criminals I'm much more likely to run across.

I did find that kidney though. That wasn't imaginary. It could have been The Beast. But there are more likely explanations, like an unlicensed doctor. There are hundreds of those in the slums. Even a demented serial killer has a higher degree of probability. Still, no matter how unlikely it is, I find myself watching out for The Beast.

Why does the human mind do that? Why does it worry about our most unlikely fears instead of what might actually happen? Why is everyone so afraid of monsters and murders when they are most likely going to die of heart disease or cancer? I don't even know what it is I'm on the lookout for. Animal tracks? Patches of fur? Gnawed bones? What trail does a cannibal Different leave behind?

I walk down the street, lost in thought, and barely notice a man standing on a stoop until he speaks to me.

"Hey old man, you trying to be calm?" he asks me with a grin that's missing several teeth.

He's covered in tattoos and has a big scar down his cheek. He's standing on the stoop of a rundown Pre-Plague house, waiting.

"What?" I have no idea what he's talking about. What does he mean be calm?

"You looking to score? Tranq? Old man, are you looking for some Tranq?"

"Oh, Tranq, selling Tranq, that's what you're doing."

"Yeah, I am, you looking to be calm or what?"

"No, I'm not interested in any poison. Thanks, though."

"Whatever, you not looking to score, then get the hell out of here. I'm not looking to chit-chat," he says and shoos me away with his hand.

"Even if I did want some poison it wouldn't matter. My Differentiation makes it useless on me."

I give him a quick glance at the D on my hand.

"I don't care about your story, freak. Now like I said, if you ain't interested in buying, take a walk," he says and stares me down. He's trying not to show fear, but I see him quake just a little.

"I'm not interested in buying. I am interested in getting you and the filth you sell off these streets. Don't the people here have enough problems, without you getting their kids hooked on junk?" I say and stare back.

"Listen, freak, I don't want to hear your nonsense. I don't know if you're crazy or just stupid, old man, but I'm telling you one more time. Get out of here and do it right now or we're going to have a problem."

"We already have a problem. I have a problem with punks like you who think they're tough. I have a problem with the fact that no one stops you from selling your garbage to kids. I have a problem with you threatening me."

I grab him by his shirt collar and glare into his eyes, he's scared. Good, I'm sure a lot of hardworking people have been frightened of him before. It's about time he got a taste of his own medicine.

"Hey Rico, get your ass out here, and get this freak off me!" he yells.

I hear a rustle from inside the house. Someone is coming out and he sounds large. It's my turn to be scared, but I don't shake. Now I can prove that I wasn't crazy to think I could work for the OEC. Now I can make a real difference in this world. I hope I don't break my wrist this time.

I have to take this first guy out before his friend joins the party. I still have him by the collar, so I throw him into the stairs head first. He takes a big hit and looks like he's down for awhile. I ready myself for Rico.

He throws open the door and charges out. He's also covered in tattoos, and he's huge. Three hundred pounds and only some of it is fat. He's stronger than me, but he should tire out more quickly. Of course, I might not last that long considering the baseball bat in his hands. I turn on my adrenal gland and get it pumping as fast as it can. I feel my muscles surge with strength. I guess it's time to do this.

"Mess that freak up," the first guy says as he spits out a mouthful of blood. He looks like he's got a concussion though and falls down when he tries to stand back up.

Rico yells and charges at me, swinging his baseball bat wildly. With time slowed down, I can easily dodge his blows. After six swings, he's starting to get tired, and I see an opening at his kidney. I punch it with my right hand, hard. He drops the bat and lets out a scream that I silence with a second punch to his throat. I follow up with an uppercut that knocks him down. That should do it.

I hear something behind me and turn just in time to see the first guy charging at me with a knife. I step out of the way so he doesn't stab me in the chest, but he still catches me with a slash just above my left eye. I constrict my capillaries and cut off an adjacent artery. If I didn't, I'd be blinded by the blood from the cut.

The man turns back around to face me, and I put my hands up. I search my mind for any memories on how you're supposed to fight a guy with a knife, but I've got nothing. I suddenly feel very ill-prepared.

The thug charges, slashing at me wildly. My instinct is to block the slashes with my arm. I end up with my left forearm sliced open before I realize how stupid that is. At least his wild slashes gave me an opening for me to catch him with a right cross to the face, which stuns him. I see my chance and grab the knife, or at least I try to. Instead I end up getting my right hand sliced to the bone between my ring finger and pinky. Why am I so stupid? Who tries to grab a knife?

I pull back and gather myself. The thug smiles.

"Time to die, old man," the thug says and charges at me.

He winds up and tries to stab me. I can't block the knife, but I can block his arm. I throw my injured forearm into the crook of the thug’s elbow, stopping the knife without getting slashed. Then I use my right hand to grab his throat. I put pressure on my two front fingers to cut off his carotid artery, which sends blood to his brain. It takes three seconds for him to pass out. I drop him relatively gently to the ground. He shouldn't have any permanent damage.

I turn around, ready deal with Rico in case he's recovered, but he's nowhere to be seen. I guess I scared him off. He should be scared. I'm a badass. I bet these two will think twice the next time they start threatening some poor soul.

#

"Down goes Frazier, down goes Frazier!" Howard Cosell yells as George Foreman knocks Joe Frazier to the mat. It was a good punch, but I'm not sure how much I'm getting out of watching this. I'm not as big as Foreman, even after the ten pounds of muscle I’ve added recently. I could stimulate my muscle growth and make myself as heavy as him, but I don't think it would be worth the trade-off in speed. More weight isn't going to help me dodge knives. I do like Joe Frazier's head bob. I might use that one to keep my opponent from landing a clean punch. I'll just have to remember not to try it on someone as large as Big George. Good thing few people are.

I need to teach myself how to fight. I managed to heal from those knife wounds quickly, but next time there could be more guys with more knives or even a gun. If I can end these fights quickly, maybe I can avoid having to heal in the first place.

I know this isn't what I should be watching, I could get a lot more from instructional martial arts videos. There are a ton of them on think.Net. I taught myself some basics when I was bored at night in Section 26. I'm too paranoid to look at them now. If I'm going to keep doing my vigilante thing, it's only a matter of time until someone reports me to the police. If the cops start looking for a Different acting like Bruce Lee, they might start looking through think.Net viewing records. I figure if I stick to boxing and the like, they'll classify me as a sports fan, not a self-taught ninja.

I know I'm just being paranoid, and I know I'm only worrying about it so I don't have to worry about my more immediate concern, my date with Becky. I should have known she wouldn't let me ride the Slug with her to the Hanging Gardens. She was offended that I even asked to escort her. I don't think she's finding my over-protectiveness charming, maybe because she's more than a decade older than me. She's been taking care of herself for a long time and through a lot worse than a Slug ride to the Hanging Gardens. I should worry about her less, or at least tell her about it less.

I remember coming to the Gardens with my mom when I was ten. It was one of my last good memories of her. She was so excited to show it to me, so happy to see something beautiful in this devastated world. I don't know if I should tell Becky about it. She might think it's sweet, but she also might think it’s creepy to be talking about my mom on a date. Especially considering our age difference.

The Slug pulls into the station, and I step off the train and onto the platform. It's immediately clear that we're not in the slums anymore. Only the Metro Center has such ornately decorated Slug stops.

There's a tile mosaic of a map of Los Angeles the city, before the Plagues struck. The WormLights that illuminate the station are encased in ornate crystal tubes, not Pho-Plastic. They even painted the floor colorful swirls, not just grey B-Crete. The station is more impressive than it was when I was a kid. Nice to know the Center is doing so well. Leave it to the rich to make the beautiful more beautiful instead of making the horrible less horrible.

I make my way up the stairs and out to the street. Just like the train station, the difference between here and the slums is striking. All of the buildings are new. Everything is made of Maceo Steel, ForteSilk, or classic brick. It's like the Plagues never happened here, or even worse, the Plagues actually improved things. It looks like a city from a fairy tale. Even the people are different. Everyone is wearing clean clothes that look brand new, and I don't see patches on any elbows. Everyone walks around lost in the think.Net stare. Half-a-dozen people bump into me as I walk down the street.

The Hanging Gardens are just a block from the station exit. That block has a higher net worth than a hundred blocks in the boonies, maybe a thousand. Let's see, I read that the average income for an individual in the Metro Center is $115,000. There are four apartment buildings on the block, and they are all about thirty stories tall. If I assume six apartments per floor and 1.5 earners per apartment, that means the average annual income for the block is $124,200,000. I would guess that the average savings rate for someone in that income bracket is about 25%. If the median age in the Metro Center is thirty-four, and the individuals have an average of six years of post-high school education, they have been earning for ten years and have...

I stop my calculations and just look. I can finish my math later, there's a new Wonder of the World in front of me, the Hanging Gardens. Well, in front of me and on top of me. I can feel my brain struggling to make sense of what it sees. Trees don't grow in the middle of the sky. Landmasses don’t just float. It looks like a dream come to life.

It doesn't float, not really. The landmass is actually suspended from a series of Maceo Steel spires that surround the island. The spires are attached to the island by ForteSilk strands. The strands are strong enough to hold up the island but still so thin they are all but invisible to the naked eye. Most people don't even know the

ForteSilk is there. They think that the island actually floats. The reality is only slightly less magical.

It makes me proud to look at the Gardens. Differents made this possible. Differents aren't just the Plagues or cost of living obligations. Differents made it so that there can be a twenty-five acre wonderland floating in the sky, filled with plants from all over the world. I might not always love Ultracorps, but they did build this, so they can't be all bad.

I walk up the stairway to the ticket booth and spot Becky. There's a bit of sweat on her brow from standing out in the sun. It reminds me of the first night I met her. I like it.

"Gavin, hi!" she says.

She beat me here, and I got here early to beat her. Guess that means she's excited to see me, or maybe the Gardens.

"Have you been waiting long?" I ask.

"A little while. It's been so long since I've been to the Center, I forgot how long it took."

"When was the last time you were in the Center?" I ask. She only lives twelve miles away, so it can't have been that long.

"I guess it was about eight years ago. Dad was trying to have some quality father-daughter time. He took me shopping on New Rodeo, window-shopping. Then we came to the Hanging Gardens and finished it off with a dozen donuts for the ride home. The whole day must have cost a year of savings," Becky says and stares off with a smile.

Seems like a good memory, but I can't believe she hasn't been here for eight years. I think about talking about my mom, but I don't want to one-up her.

"That sounds nice. How are donuts? I've never had one," I ask.

"Oh my Lord, it's the best thing I've ever tasted. It's like eating a fried, sweet, creamy cloud. The fake Manna ones don't taste anything like them. You Chosen Sons haven't mastered that one yet."

"Thanks for rubbing it in."

"The truth hurts sometimes. Let's go in."

We walk hand in hand to the ticket window.

"Two please," Becky says and starts to take out her cash.

I can see the disdain on the ticket taker's face. Becky is just another hick paying cash. I think the ticket taker resents having to do work as opposed to just agreeing to a think.Net transaction. It's not Becky's fault that she can't afford a bank account. She can barely afford her house. Besides, she seems like a cash under the mattress type for her savings.

"Wait, no, I can get this. Two please," I say and step in front of her.

"You will not. I have a job, thank you very much."

"Don't be silly. The tickets are probably two months of pouring drinks for you. Even with my COL obligations, I can afford it."

"My dad gave me money just for this. If he found out I let a Chosen Son pay for me, he'd be furious. The principles of..."

I can tell what she's about to say, but Cabot is not a name you mention in the Metro Center, not in a positive light anyway. The First Amendment still stands, but it also lets people say what they think about your religion in screams and curses.

"I thought you liked me being a gentleman!" I interrupt her, loudly. She reads the look I give her and stops talking.

"Can you lovebirds make up your minds and get out of here?" the ticket taker says, frowning.

"Right, sorry. Two please," I say as I go on think.Net and authorize the debit to my account, $88.50. Ouch.

"You can get the maps on think.Net. Welcome to the Hanging Gardens."

We walk through the turnstile into the Gardens.

"Can we go see the Morning Glories first? They'll close if we don't get there soon." Becky asks.

"We can go wherever you want. We are going to have a great day."

"I already am," she says with a smile. She takes my hand and leads the way.

#

"There are so many different colors. Have you ever seen anything so beautiful?"

"Sure I have," I say and look at her.

I know it's sappy, but sometimes sap works.

"Oh stop. Are they really all roses?" she asks as she blushes.

"That's what it says on think.Net. They evolved for different climates and different locations where the bees are attracted to varying colors. They had to adapt to their environment, and to look tasty to bees."

"This truly is the most beautiful thing I've ever seen. Thank you so much for taking me here. I missed it when I was here with my dad."

"They were my mom's favorite."

Now seems like a good time to open up and tell her about my mom. I think she'll like it if I reveal something personal. It feels like the right time.

"Were they? You don't talk about her much," she prompts me.

"I came here with her when I was ten. Normally, she hated all Different creations. She saw all the work of Differents as slave labor and wanted as little to do with it as possible. I think she made an exception for the Gardens because she loved the flowers, and she loved the roses most of all. We must have spent two hours in here just staring at them. It's one of the last good memories I have of her," I say and make myself look sad. It's a true expression. The only memories that stick out after the Gardens are the Genetic Incongruity Scan and her abandoning me.

"I'm so sorry, when did she die?" Becky asks and puts her hand on my arm.

"She's not dead, not as far as I know. She left us when I was twelve. Right after my Genetic Incongruity Scan came back positive," I say, adding small pauses to my speech.

This would be hard to talk about for a normal person. It is hard for me, but I have to make myself show it or she'll think I'm a soulless monster.

"I didn't realize. I'm sorry."

"Don't be sorry. She said she couldn't stand the thought of what they were going to do to me—Section 26 and then whatever job they'd make me do. I was so excited to be a Different and had no idea what she was talking about. I understand better now. Living through what I went through, I can imagine how hard it would be for a mother to watch."

"It's so amazing that you can forgive her."

"I don't forgive her, not for a second," I shoot back. "It would have been hard for her to watch? It was hard for me to live. It's a mother's job to help her son, even when it hurts her. Mothers can't just leave because it gets hard. Should a mother abandon her child because he's sick? I can understand her, but I will never forgive her. I was a kid. It was her job to be the strong one," I'm almost yelling. I don't know why I said it so loudly. I didn't mean to.

Becky doesn't have anything to say to that, so we continue looking at the roses in silence.

"I think we need to do something to cheer you up. Let's go get some ice cream," Becky says with a smile.

She leads me by the hand to a cart nearby. Becky runs up.

"Hi! We'd like two small vanilla ice creams please," Becky says to the man behind the counter.

The young man looks up with a smile, which disappears after he gives us a quick scan. His eyes stop on the "D" on my hand. Then he looks at Becky's hand and recoils, I think because she's tattoo-less.

"Can't do it. I'm on my lunch break," he says coldly.

"Good one. How much are they?" Becky asks.

She hasn't picked up on what's happening here yet.

"Are you deaf lady? I told you I'm on break. Now, get the hell out of here."

"Come on, Becky, let's just go. We can get something to eat once we're done with the Gardens. I want to try those donuts you were talking about anyway," I say and gently try to move her along.

"No, that's ridiculous. I don't know what this kid's problem is, but I want some ice cream, not donuts."

"Why don't you listen to your freak-show boyfriend and move along? You ain't getting nothing here."

"So that's it. You won't serve us because he's a Chosen Son? Are you kidding me? I must have seen a half-dozen other Chosen walking around here."

"It's bad enough that I have to serve those deforms. But they can't help being born freaks. You, on the other hand, are a human, built in the Lord's image. I'll be damned if I serve a cow who betrays her own race," he says with disdain.

Becky looks at me, expecting me to say something. There's isn't anything worth saying.

"It doesn't matter Becky," I say, but it's no use. She's incensed.

"Betray my race? I'm betraying my race? What about the food you sell? The house you sleep in? The entire Hanging Gardens?" she says, her face turning red with rage. "That's all thanks to the Chosen. If it wasn't for them, your whore of a mother wouldn't have had a bottle to feed you or a crib to put you in. You should be kissing his feet in thanks that you are alive. If it wasn't for him and the goodwill of those like him, you, me and our whole race would be dead and the Chosen would reign as they should."

I've never seen her angry before. I find it a little attractive. Is that wrong?

"You have five seconds to get your filthy race-traitor ass out of here, or I'll have security come and throw you out," the vendor says as he shakes with anger. I can see him reaching for something under his cart, and I don't think its ice cream. This is about to go south.

"It's time to go. Now Becky!"

I guide her away from the stand. I think the only reason she's willing to go is that she's shocked by my lack of response. I can see in her eyes that her anger is moving from the concession vendor onto me.

"One day, the righteous will rise up and you will burn in this life and for eternity," the vendor yells after us.

Becky follows my lead until we get out of sight of the stand. As soon as we do, she pulls her arm away.

"Get your hands off me. I can't believe you. How could you let him say those things about you? About me? What is wrong with you? Don't you have any backbone? You could have kicked that guy's ass up and down the street," she yells.

"And if I did that, I'd get shipped off to Great Basin for the rest of my life and you'd never see me again. Would that have taught him a lesson?"

"You could have said something at least. How can you let somebody say such horrible things and not give them a piece of your mind?"

"They taught us how to handle this situation in Section 26. There's a class called Emotional Control that every Different has to pass before they let us out. I had to sit in the center of a room full of people and stay there stoically as they hurled the most offensive insults you can imagine. I can remember every word they said. What they came up with was unbelievable. They made the guy back there sound like a children's think.Net show."

"That's awful."

"It wasn't just words, they threw things: spit balls, used tissues, and worse. We had to take it. Differents aren't allowed to fight back unless we think our lives are in danger.

"This is still America. You have the right to free speech. That applies to the Chosen too."

"Sure it does, but angry words can lead to angry actions. That's why they make us go through the process. If we can take those awful insults and keep our cool, it means we won't hurt some moron who calls us a freak."

"But you say you're always in control. You know you wouldn't get violent if you gave that guy your two cents."

"True, but I also know a waste of time when I see it. That guy looked like he was twenty-five. That's twenty-five years of him being a bigot. It's pretty unlikely that fifteen seconds of screaming will change his mind. Especially from somebody he thinks is lower than a dog. Besides, let's say he gets mad and tries to hit me. Who do you think the cops would believe when he says I started it?"

As I say this, I'm imagining myself punching that guy in the face. It would have been so satisfying.

"I guess that you're right, but I still don't have to like it," she says after pausing to calm herself down.

"Nobody said I liked it either. Let's go get some donuts."

12

There is but one way for my Forgotten Sons to return to my grace. They must serve my new race, my Chosen Sons, in any way possible. They must tithe to the Chosen and submit to their every whim. They must be willing to sacrifice anything and everything for them. If my Forgotten Sons do this, they will be welcome in my kingdom for eternity.

Chosen Sons: 49

The Beast rubs his body up against the corner of a large B-Crete building. He's marking it with his scent so there will be no doubt that this building belongs to The Beast. Everyone will know. The building will make for a good nest. The one The Beast had been using in this neighborhood collapsed last week.

The Beast pauses his rubbing and takes a big whiff of his handiwork. Immersed in the smell of his own musk, he once again picks up the scent of his fellow Chosen Son, Gavin Stillman. The Beast lets out a howl of excitement.

This is three times now that Gavin has come across The Beast. The Lord must be trying to tell The Beast something. Maybe Gavin is supposed to be the companion the pastor promised. The Beast starts running down the street towards the smell. Usually, The Beast tries to stick to the roofs so he doesn't get spotted and end up on the news. Right now, he doesn't care about that. He's too excited to see Gavin.

The Beast is fast, he covers thirty blocks in five minutes, but he is not fast enough. He can hear shouting in the distance. It sounds like another fight is breaking out. Does Gavin come out to these neighborhoods looking for trouble on purpose?

The Beast surges forward and turns the corner, onto the block where he heard the shouts. There he is greeted by the sight of Gavin, still looking like an old man. Gavin is fighting a very large man swinging a baseball bat. There's another thug lying on the ground, struggling to get up.

Gavin dodges the large man's swings and eventually knocks the man down. The stupid boy does not learn. He's forgetting to watch his back once again. The thug that was down at first has managed to get to his feet, and he has a knife. Just before The Beast can jump in and stop the thug, Gavin whirls around and engages the man. Maybe Gavin is improving.

Then again, maybe not. As Gavin struggles to handle the thug with the knife, the large thug with the bat gets up. He has a clear shot at Gavin's backside. Before he can strike, The Beast grabs the large man by the head, palming it like a basketball. With a jerk of his wrist, The Beast snaps the man's neck. Then he throws the three hundred pound man over his shoulder like a rag doll and jumps onto the roof of the house across the street. The entire attack took less than three seconds.

The Beast watches from the roof as Gavin finally manages to handle the thug with the knife. He keeps watching as Gavin makes his way back to the Slug. The fool has a smug smile on his face the entire walk, he must be thinking he scared the guy with the bat off.

After he watches Gavin get onto the Slug, The Beast stops and prays.

"Lord, I've saved that boy's life twice now. Please tell me that's worth something. Please tell me that counts towards making up for my sins."

The Lord is still silent. Saving Gavin's life is not enough. The Lord must want more. The Beast is going to have to save his soul, just like The Beast was once saved.

#

When Tom awoke in his prison cell after finding the book, he was no longer a freak, no longer murderer, no longer a monster; he was now a Chosen Son. Tom had more of the Lord within himself than any normal man did. Tom didn't deserve to die. He didn't deserve to be in prison at all. Tom needed to escape. In order to escape, he needed to get stronger. In order to get stronger, he needed to eat.

At breakfast, Tom took the largest portion he was allowed. After he devoured his food, he took the food of five smaller, weaker inmates who could do nothing but protest. Tom repeated this for a couple of weeks, stealing more and more disgusting prison meals. He steadily grew hairier, heavier, and stronger, but eventually he realized that the prison food was not going to cut it. Tom would never get to full strength on those tiny morsels. He needed more. He needed to get into the kitchen.

Tom saw his chance in the cafeteria one day. A few tables away sat Lawrence "Fishy" Grimes, the former head of the Pazota crime family. Muscle-bound cronies surrounded Fishy, making him the perfect target.

Tom walked right up to Fishy, grabbed the Manna Sloppy Joe from Fishy's hands, and gulped it down right in Fishy's face. When one of the cronies responded by grabbing Tom, Tom threw the goon into a rival gang's table. They responded as prison inmates do, and soon a full-blown riot erupted in the mess hall. This was not an uncommon occurrence, and the guards were prepared for it. They sent in the Riot Squad, who, the guards assumed, would handle the situation as they always had before. They didn't know that this time was different. This time they were dealing with a Different.

The guards all stormed into the cafeteria in formation. They made their shields into a wall and advanced on the prisoners. The inmates did not have any weapons that could get through the guard's shields. The food trays and utensils they threw just bounced off. Tom did not need to get through the shields, he could go over them. He got a running start and leapt over the line of prison guards. Once behind the line, Tom attacked the guards. He swung his arms violently, knocking officers down like bowling pins. The riot squad broke formation, which gave the other inmates an opportunity to attack. Soon the entire Riot Squad was disarmed. Now that they had control of the cafeteria, the prisoners barricaded themselves in and prepared for the coming police siege.

Tom headed to the kitchen while the other prisoners focused on building up the defenses. He raided the pantry, tearing packages open and eating as much as he could as quickly as he could. Tom spent twelve straight hours eating Manna Flakes, Manna Chicken, and even raw Manna. He shoved handfuls of the gooey syrup into his mouth. No matter how much Tom ate, he could not get full. His body needed something more substantial. He needed real meat, but the prison didn't serve any.

In a flash, it struck Tom what he should do, what God would want him to do. He looked up a passage he remembered reading in the Old Testament: Genesis 9:2-3.

"The fear and dread of you will fall on all the beasts of the earth, and on all the birds in the sky, on every creature that moves along the ground, and on all the fish in the sea; they are given into your hands. Everything that lives and moves about will be food for you. Just as I gave you the green plants, I now give you everything."

Tom was a Chosen Son. According to Cabot, the Lord had promised His new children all that He had originally given to humans. That included dominion over the animals. Humans now fell into that domain. Eating the flesh of a human was Tom's right as much as it was the right of a human to eat a cow, or a lion to eat a gazelle. In fact, the greatest gift Tom could give a human was to eat their flesh. If he ate them, they died in service of a Chosen Son. Cabot taught that was how a Forgotten Son could be guaranteed salvation. Tom knew just who his first meal would be.

George Gibbs was a quiet, skinny man. He was serving three to five years on his second conviction for accessing think.Net with an illegal account. Tom liked George. He kept to himself and was well-versed in the Bible. Tom and George had engaged in several discussions regarding Bible passages. George deserved to go to heaven, at least more so than most of the other prisoners.

Tom asked George to look at something in the back of the kitchen, a place out of view from prying eyes. Once there, Tom grabbed George by the hair and shook. George's neck snapped like a twig. Tom thanked the Lord for the bounty he was about to receive and tore into the man. He started with the thigh. The mix of fat and muscle was delicious, and when Tom hit the femoral artery, the blood was like an explosion of flavor in his mouth. If God did not wish for Tom to do this, the Almighty would not have made humans so delicious.

Tom continued his binge, eating the man's sweetbreads, his eyes, and every bit of muscle, flesh and tissue he could find. Then Tom cracked open George's bones and sucked out the marrow. Piling the bones behind some empty shelves, he went back out on the hunt. George had been satisfying, but Tom felt a year of repressed hunger grumbling in his stomach. He needed to gorge on the bounty the Lord meant for him.

Tom spent the next five days of the siege feeding freely on the inmates. He would sneak up behind a solitary prisoner, break the man's neck, and drag the victim to the back of the cafeteria to feed. Tom fed on twelve prisoners before someone went looking for their missing friend and found Tom's graveyard. Once they saw the piles of bones, the inmates were more scared of whatever monster was in the prison with them than the police waiting outside. They surrendered.

In the weeks since Tom had embraced his nature, he had gained over two hundred pounds, all of it muscle. Tom’s one size fits all prison uniform was tearing at the seams. Coarse black hair had begun growing all over his body and his skin was becoming leathery and tough. His fingernails and toenails were thick and sharp. There was no chance Tom could hide the fact that he was a Chosen Son if he was examined again. He had to escape now or the guards would find him and he would be sent to Great Basin forever.

After surrendering, the inmates filed out with their hands over their heads. Tom hunched low and filed out with them. Some of the other prisoners were screaming, trying to warn the prison guards about Tom, but the guards did not want to listen. They ordered the inmates to be silent. As soon as Tom had a clear line of sight to the swamps around the prison, he made his move. With his copy of *Chosen Sons* clutched close to his chest, Tom charged past the bewildered police officers before they could react. He leapt over the fifteen-foot fence that surrounded the prison and disappeared into the thick Florida swamps like a bolt of lightning.

Tom felt the love of God as he ran through the swamps. He was a broken man who had become a Chosen Son and embraced all that he was. Tom felt the power of the Lord course through him. Still, there was one thing Tom had to do to throw off the shackles of his old life. He had committed a sin that could not be forgiven, even for a Chosen Son.

Tom made his way back through the swamps of the southern United States, back to the Houston Metro Area. He returned to the Fish Market, his hometown. At nightfall, he went into the town cemetery and found the graves of his parents, weeping when he saw the names Oren and Lilly Calhoun on the gravestones. They may have been members of a lesser race, but they were still Tom's parents. They deserved eternal life in paradise.

Tom dug up their graves. His powerful body was able to excavate their caskets in a matter of moments. Once Tom had exhumed the corpses, he began his morbid task. His parents had been in the ground for almost a year, and what little flesh left on their remains was rotten and riddled with maggots. Tom saw this as his penance. He gagged and choked as he ate their fetid meat, but Tom forced himself to eat as much as he could.

By consuming their flesh, Tom changed his parents' deaths from a senseless act of violence into a loving act guaranteeing their salvation. They died in service to a Chose Son, which would secure them a spot in heaven. Tom wept as he ate and thanked God for the chance to right his wrong.

13

The price of liberty has always been high. It has long been this nation's principle that the cost is worth bearing. It is essential that we hold true to this principle, even in times of crisis. Hateful speech is permissible, hateful religions are permissible, hateful thoughts are permissible. It may seem hypocritical to allow a religion while simultaneously banning its holy book, but the law sees no contradiction. We may ban a specific work that constitutes an act of terror, but nothing in our Constitution allows for the outlawing of an ideology. The court's previous ruling in Brandenburg v. Ohio is confirmed. Cabotists have the right to exist, gather, and demonstrate.

Justice Margaret Fuller
Majority Opinion: Canton v. Houston Metro Area

It's hard to see with the smoke all around me. I'm holding back my tear production to keep my vision clear, but my eyes are getting too dry. I close them for a second and rehydrate as quickly as I can. When I open them back up, I can make out the stairwell. Toby should be on the second floor. I head up the stairs.

I can hear beams buckling above me. This fire is growing fast. I'm lucky if I have a full minute before the building comes down on me. I don't know how I missed Toby when I was getting everyone else out. I wish his brother could have told me more, but all the kid would say was, "Toby is still in there, Toby is still in there." His parents weren't in any shape to provide better information. They were barely conscious and suffering from smoke inhalation.

>>>Gavin. What's going on? Why aren't you answering me?

<<<Sorry, honey. Dr. Cole needed to ask me something. You know they hate it when I'm on think.Net at work.

>>>What's he still doing there? It's eleven o'clock at night.

<<<We've got a deadline. Everyone's still here working.

>>>What are you guys working on?

I shouldn't have taken the call, but I've been ignoring Becky so much lately. It didn't feel right to do it again. Why did I buy her think.Net time if I'm never going to talk to her? I thought I could manage to chat on think.Net while navigating around this burning building. I'm starting to question my judgment.

I head into the parents' room. Maybe Toby is hiding in a closet. That's what kids do when they're scared, hide. It's amazing how often our basic instincts are wrong. They weren't developed for the modern world.

I open the closet door. There's no kid, but I am rewarded by a flaming piece of door frame that falls onto my arm. I watch it burn through my shirt. I know it's heading for my skin, but I can't move fast enough to get my arm out of the way. Nerves fire as the flames singe my flesh, then the muscle underneath. If I wasn't me, I'd be crippled by the pain. I finally get my arm out of the way, but the damage has been done to my muscles and nerves. My right arm can't move well. The frame only touched me for a second, but B-Crete burns so freaking hot. I hope I can heal it before morning. I'm out of excuses for missing work.

>>>I said, what are you working on?

<<<We're trying to get the sodium levels down in the new Harvest Burger. Dr. Cole mixed up some of the numbers when we did our tests the first time, so now we have to redo them.

>>>It's about time someone besides you had to work at night. I feel like I haven't seen you in forever.

<<<I'm sorry. I promise I'll make it up to you once things die down.

I leave the parents' room and head back into the kids' room. There wasn't a closet, but I did see a wardrobe when I first came in. The wardrobe looks Pre-Plague, probably one of the family's most prized possessions. A child could fit inside it. I grab the wardrobe's handle, and it instantly burns the flesh on my fingers. The handle is made of metal. I didn't even consider that. Now I *know* it's Pre-Plague. I ignore the pain, the burns are manageable, and open the door. There's Toby.

Toby the rat that is, in his Pho-Plastic cage. I don't have enough experience with children. The kid was so scared when he was pleading for me to get Toby that I just assumed he meant his brother. Next time I rush back inside a burning building, I'll have to remember to check and make sure I'm saving a person. Apparently, rescuing the kid and his parents wasn't enough. He needed me to die getting his pet rat.

>>>Speaking of making it up to me. What are you doing next Saturday night? My dad has made an official request to meet you. I think he's right. I want to show you off.

She wants me to meet her father. That's pretty heavy. I don't know how I should feel about it. I suppose we have been dating for a couple of months now. It does seem like the right thing to do. I should be excited about it.

<<<Sounds great, honey. I can't wait to meet your dad.

I grab the rat cage with my singed fingers and turn to run out of the apartment. Right as I'm about to head down the stairs, they collapse into a burning pit. I need to find another way out. I run through the hallway and onto the stairwell leading up. If I can make it to the roof, I should be able to jump to the building next door.

>>>You should come at seven-thirty. My dad is going to make...

Becky keeps talking to me on think.Net, but I tune her out. I need to focus on getting out of this building alive. I run up one flight of stairs, but before I can head up the second flight, they collapse into another burning pit of fire. There's no way out. I'm going to have to jump out a window.

I head back down the stairs to the second floor for a safer jump. I avoid a burning chunk of ceiling that would have killed Toby and I. The building is going to come down any second. Not only that, I am really struggling to get enough oxygen to keep myself going. I drop to the floor where the air is better, take some deep breaths, stand up, and keep moving.

I head back into Toby's family's apartment. There was a window in the bedroom. When I get to the bedroom, I see something better then a window: part of the floor has collapsed, giving me a way down to the first floor. I drop down the hole and land in the apartment below. Today's my lucky day, I don't even need to make my way to the front entrance because there's a hole in the wall I can jump through.

As soon as I'm outside, I take a deep breath of smoke-free air. My body needs the oxygen desperately. I spread as much O2 as I can to the needy cells of my body. I head back around towards the front, wondering why a family that barely has enough money to keep itself fed would willingly take on the responsibility of caring for a filthy, disease-spreading animal.

>>>Hello, hello, hello... is anyone there?

<<<Sorry, Becky. Dr. Cole came back.

>>>Okay. I'll let you go. Try not to keep working so hard. I'll see you Saturday at seven-thirty.

<<<See you then.

I get off the call. I think I should feel guilty about lying to her. I want to see her, but it's hard to justify. Going out on a date doesn't seem as important as saving someone from a murderer or a fire. Is it wrong to lie to my girlfriend if it's so I can save lives?

"Toby!" the kid yells with glee as soon as I come around the corner. "You're alive!"

The kid runs up, opens the cage, and squeezes the rat in his arms. I'm alive too, kid. Thanks for the concern.

The kid might not care, but applause goes up from the crowd that has gathered. I soak it in. I swear it's actually making me happy, and not because I'm making my endorphins flow.

"Aren't you the big hero, saving rats? You're really making a difference," a woman in the crowd jeers, jolting me from my euphoria.

"I did save the people, too."

"Good for you. That make you feel like a big shot? You know you're breaking the law."

"I'm just trying to help. How can you have a problem with that?"

"I have a problem because the only reason we need any help is thanks to what you and your kind did to us. When I was a girl, the fire department did a fine job of helping folks. Now this whole block will burn and nobody gives a damn."

"I can't fix the world ma'am, but I can do what I can to help."

"You want to help? Why don't you do something about The Beast? He's one of your kind. That's what you should be fixing."

"I can't do anything about urban legends ma'am. I can only help with real problems."

"Urban legend? You tell that to my pops. I hadn't heard from him in two weeks. I finally went over to his apartment, and all that was left of him was bones. Does a legend do that? Does a burglar? You're just like all the rest. You don't really give a damn about us. You just want act like a hero 'cause it makes you feel good."

#

These clothes are uncomfortable. I can feel my nerves firing off, telling me that they are irritating my skin. Normal people would call it itchy. They're hot, too. Not enough fresh air can get in to cool me down. I lower my metabolic rate, which should compensate. All this and they were more expensive than normal clothes. Still, a button-down shirt and some khakis seems like the minimum for meeting my girlfriend's dad.

I knock on the door to Becky's house. I'm five minutes early. I think that's perfect timing. Not too early to be weird, but early enough to show I'm taking this seriously. This is serious. I haven't met a girlfriend's father since I was eight. I'm pretty sure this one isn't going to give me some juice and take us to the park.

I hear someone coming, light steps, it's Becky. I plaster my face with a grin. She hugs me as soon as she opens the door and gives me a big wet kiss. I don't even have time to hand her the flowers. A dozen roses, all different colors. They cost me three days' pay, but I'll keep that to myself.

"Gavin! Right on time as always," Becky says.

"Actually, I'm four minutes and thirty-eight seconds early."

"Wise ass."

She notices the flowers. Her eyes light up as I thought they would. It could have been a month's pay, and it would still have been worth it.

"Gavin, they're beautiful. You didn't have to do this."

"They're not for you, they're for you father. I'm trying to make a good impression," I say with a smirk.

"Stop it. Come in, come in. Dad! Gavin's here!"

We step inside the door. I've walked her home more than a dozen times, but it's the first time I've been inside. It's a rundown Pre-Plague house, but they've done their best to make it a home. They have a couch with about twenty patches keeping it together, and there's a piece of Construct furniture placed prominently in the room. The other half of the room holds the dining table. It's already been set, and there's a candle burning. It looks they've pulled out all the stops for this dinner.

"I'll go put these in water. Dad! Gavin is here!" she yells to her father for the second time. "I'm sorry, he doesn't hear too well." she goes into the kitchen.

"Okay, just keep stirring this while I go meet your friend." I hear her father say.

Becky's father comes out to greet me while wiping his hands on a towel. He smells of beef grease. Real beef, they did pull out all of the stops for me.

He's a burly man with a thick moustache and a weathered face. I know that he's under sixty, but he looks seventy. I still wouldn't want to mess with him. There's a gnarly-looking scar on his left cheek and a sharpness to his eyes. He looks like he's been to Hell and made it out. He's got a bit of a limp, but that just makes him more of a badass. I would be intimidated by him, if he wasn't grinning like a kid on Christmas morning.

"Gavin, it's a pleasure to finally meet you. It's an honor to have you in our home," he runs over and shakes my hand.

"The pleasure is all mine, sir. I'm glad to meet the man responsible for making Becky the lovely lady she is today."

"I'm not sure how much I had to do with that. She's just like her mother, but I'll take the compliment. Please sit."

I head towards the couch, but he stops me.

"Please, sit here," he directs me to the Construct furniture. "Do you know how it works?"

"No, I've never sat in one before."

I have sat in one before. They are another Ultracorps product after all. The guy looks so proud, it would crush him if I told him that.

"Have a seat on it and then use your hands and body to shape it how you want, whatever feels right. Once you feel comfortable, slap it hard, and it will lock into that shape. If you want to change the shape, run your hand on the Velcro on the side then shock it, and it'll go back to the blob," Mike tells me proudly.

"Thank you, sir, and thank you for having me to dinner. Whatever we're eating smells delicious. Can I ask you how you're cooking it?"

One of the reasons people eat Manna, besides the price, is that you don't need to cook it to eat it. Thanks to Cabot destroying much of the world's supply, oil, gas, and even wood, are insanely expensive. That means a cold dinner for most people, unless they go to Oasis Burger.

"A little Pre-Plague camping stove, if you can believe it. People still find propane tanks when they are out scavenging. Sometimes I'll cook at the bar on Sundays after church. And stop calling me sir. It's Mike, unless of course you'd prefer to keep calling me sir."

For a second I think he must be joking, but then I remember he's a devout Cabotist. He'd let me call him Ugly if I wanted to.

"It's been a long time since I had real beef, Mike. I'm pretty excited about it."

"That's not all. We've got potatoes and beer. The real McCoy, not the fermented Manna stuff. It's one thing you Chosen Sons can't make better."

"That sounds great."

"My skills as a chef are what kept me and Becky fed after the Revelation. I had to stretch a few rotten pieces of meat into enough food for hundreds in the refugee camps. I got pretty good at it, too," Mike adds.

"Were you a chef before the Plagues?" I ask.

"Not at all, I was a steel worker. Of course, after the Revelation came there wasn't much use for those. Gabby used to do all the cooking, that's Becky's mom. After she passed on, I had to take the reins. Guess I had a natural talent for it."

He's a true believer. Cabot and his Plagues all but killed his wife, and he still calls what Cabot did the Revelation.

"Becky's lucky to have you. You pulled off quite a feat. Very few children born around the time of the Plagues survived to adulthood."

"God had a plan for us. He decided we could do more good as spreaders of the truth faith. God's got a plan for all of us..."

I fidget to show discomfort. Mike notices it.

"Look at me. Here I am with the first Chosen Son I've ever had in my home and I start gabbing my head off. Why don't you tell me about yourself? Were you born in the LA Metro?" Mike says. He looks over his shoulder, to see if Becky heard him from the kitchen. I bet he promised not to preach to me.

"Born and raised in L.A.," I answer him.

"What do your parents do?"

"My dad's dead. He worked as a fisherman. He died while I was in Section 26 when his boat was caught in a storm and it sunk. They kept having to go farther and farther to find fish." I tell him. I make sure I sound a little sad.

"That must have been hard on you and your mom."

"My mom wasn't around. She left when my Genetic Incongruity Scan came back positive."

"Well, I really stepped in it, didn't I? Maybe we should change subjects," Mike says and turns red in the face.

I hear footsteps approaching the front door. The steps are labored. It sounds like an old man.

"Someone's here," I say.

Whoever it is knocks on the door.

"Good hearing. That must be Pastor Newman. We can finally eat." Mike says and rubs his hands together.

He gets up to answer the door, and I dart into the kitchen to talk to Becky. I am not happy about this. I thought I was coming over for dinner, not to be proselytized to by some lunatic "pastor." They're insane if they think I will convert. I guess they already are insane if they worship a monster who killed 65% of the earth's population. This dinner was a huge mistake.

Even if I could be convinced to worship someone who is more of an antichrist than a savior, I don't have that option. They think it's hard to be a human who believes in this lunacy? Try being a Different who is a Cabotist. I remember seeing one strung up when I was a kid. He dangled there half-dead, and the cops just smiled.

"Are you out of your mind? You invited your pastor here?" I ask Becky as harshly as one can in a whisper.

“Oh no, he didn't. My dad must have invited him. I told him not to. I can't believe him. I am so sorry. He's just so proud to have a Chosen Son in his home. He wants to show off. I understand if you want to go. I'm very sorry."

I can tell that Becky is genuinely surprised. Not just surprised, she's angry, angry at her father. I think about leaving, but then I look into Becky's eyes. She's saying I can go, but her body language is begging me to stay. I guess I can do it for her. It should be interesting if nothing else. I just have to make sure no one sees me here with this cult leader. That alone might be enough to get me lynched.

"It's okay. I guess I'll stay. But you should know right now, there's no way I'm getting converted."

"Fine by me. Don't worry about it too much. Pastor Newman is a sweet old man. I'm sure he'll behave himself," Becky assures me.

I pull my shirt into a better position and up my sweating. I steel myself for an onslaught of religious garbage and head into the living room.

"Gavin, there you are. I would like to introduce you to the pastor of our church, Pastor Newman. Pastor Newman, this is Gavin Stillman," Mike says cordially.

#

"It's crazy. Some old Chosen Son running around, fighting muggers and beating up drug dealers. It's like something from a think.Net show, not real life," Mike says.

"What's wrong with that? He's just helping people. I know it's not something we see a lot, but come on, it's a good thing. I don't see what the problem could possibly be," Becky says. I'm glad to hear her defend me, even if she doesn't know it.

"The problem is that he's an old man. He should be helping young members of his own race, not putting himself in danger stopping petty crimes," Mr. Newman adds. I'm not calling this lunatic pastor, even in my head.

"Aren't Differents free to do as they please? They are the Master Race after all," I know I'm quoting Hitler. I bet Mr. Newman knows I am too.

"He certainly is free to do as he pleases. I'm not saying the police should be hunting him. Although there are plenty of nonbelievers who do say that. Vigilantism is expressly against the law, after all." Mr. Newman pauses to take a breath. "It is not his rights I question, but rather his wisdom. From the reports I have heard, this elderly fellow is just a little bit faster and stronger than a normal man. It'd be one thing if he was like the Savior of Seattle back in the old days. He could stop trains with ease and leap over buildings, but this vigilante isn't capable of anything of the sort. I heard from someone who saw him rescue a rat from a fire last week. They said he was covered in burns and lucky to be alive. Risking his life for a rat? It seems like he should stick to the activities God gave him the proper blessings to pursue. We all have roles to play," Mr. Newman says like he's delivering a sermon. He's used to speaking to sheep who never question what he says.

I might not be as powerful as the Savior of Seattle was, but I was capable enough to save those people. If I wasn't me, I'd probably blurt out that the vigilante saved a family before he saved the rat, but luckily God "blessed" me with super-human self-control. There's no way I would know what happened unless I had been there.

"It's his life to risk, is it not Mr. Newman?" I ask.

"Again, yes, it is his choice, but perhaps if the wisdom of Cabot had been shared with him, he would know better. Salvation may be guaranteed to him in the afterlife, but he will have to explain why he was willing to risk his wellbeing for lesser mortals while doing nothing for his own kind. It is to them he has a duty, they... you are the future. We are merely the remnants of God's first experiment in creating a race in his own image. We should be serving this old fool. Not the other way around."

"Here, here," Mike adds and raises his drink.

I look at Becky. I want to make sure I'm not overstepping by debating the "pastor" like this. She gives me a nod and smile. I guess she doesn't mind.

"God and Cabot's plan was to make mankind serve Differents?" I shoot back. "It seems to me that the Plagues did just the opposite. There wasn't an Ultracorps before the Plagues, and Section 26 was half the size. If it wasn't for the Plagues, maybe Becky and I would be able to walk around in public without anyone accusing her of dating a monster."

"You're right. The Chosen are more servants today than masters. Like all young people, you expect things to come immediately. Cabot warned that after the Plagues, the Chosen would be lost and suffer many hardships. The same was true for the Israelites before God led them to the Promised Land. They had to spend forty years wandering the desert. It has been thirty years since Cabot spread the Plagues for his fellow Chosen Sons. And this time, the Lord promised you the whole world, not just some small patch of sand," Mr. Newman lectures. He's enjoying this. I doubt he gets the chance to try to convert a Different very often.

"That is definitely the sentiment about Cabot among the Different population. You've got your finger on the pulse," I say sarcastically. "I'm sure all the Differents would like to thank Cabot for everything he did."

"Perhaps your people would be more grateful if they weren't so willing to put shackles on themselves. God did not make you to be slaves. He made you in his image. You are closer to God than I can ever hope to be," Mr. Newman retorts.

"And how about The Beast? Was he a gift from God too?" I ask.

"What does that have to do with anything? There are dozens of human serial killers that did just what The Beast did. We don't point to them to indict the entire human race. The Beast was a singular disturbed individual, and he's dead now."

Mr. Newman tightens up. He’s not enjoying this any longer. Trying to convert me was fun, but something about The Beast has him worked up.

"He's not dead from what I hear," I retort.

"Gavin, you disappoint me. You can't let yourself believe gossip and tabloids. We live in disturbing times. There are countless murders all over the city. Some people would prefer to believe that a monster is responsible for these killings. They prefer that fiction to the reality that the human race is a vile, murderous breed," Mr. Newman says, while he shifts in his chair.

This is really making him uncomfortable. His jugular vein is pulsing like crazy. His heart rate is going through the roof. Is it just because he hates losing an argument?

"Then how come all that's left of the victims are picked-clean bones?" I ask.

"Those are simply horror stories told to turn children against Chosen Sons." Mr. Newman says dismissively.

"No, it's true. This woman I know, Jessica, and her little girl Emily, they went missing. We tried to get the police to come investigate, but they said they didn't have the resources. So we went up into their apartment and there was blood and bones everywhere," Becky says. She had been holding that in for awhile. She’s not used to questioning her pastor. I put my hand on her thigh for support.

"Probably some Tranq junkies killed them and the rats got to the bones. You know how many rats we have in this freaking city. I swear it seems like the Revelation made more of them," Mike chimes in.

"I'm sure Mike is right. The deaths of a young girl and her mother are surely a tragedy, but we cannot simply assume it was a Chosen Son. Tragedies abound in this Metro Area, and if we allow our imaginations to take over, we'll end up blaming all crimes on Chosen Sons," Mr. Newman says.

"But if a Chosen Son, as you call them, did want to eat a girl and her mother, that would be his right. That's what you believe, isn't it? That humans should do all they can to serve the Chosen, even give up their lives? They taught us that part in Section 26." I've got him on the ropes now. There's no retort for that.

Mr. Newman gets even tenser, and I can see the anger swelling up in him. No one likes having the absurdity of their beliefs pointed out, but this is hitting close to home for some reason.

"Yes, I suppose that would technically be the Chosen's right. Everyone has the right to eat," Mr. Newman spits out.

"Hmm, I wonder if that's why your religion has such few followers." I say smugly. I think I just won the argument.

14

All the gifts I once bestowed on my Forgotten Sons I now give to my new children. The sea, the sky, the land, and the beasts, even the Forgotten Sons themselves, all of them are now under the domain of my Chosen Sons. The world belongs to them.

Chosen Sons: 27

The Beast watches Gavin head back into the burning building. What is he doing? He already saved everyone in the apartment. The only living thing left inside is a rat. Gavin needs to use his senses more.

The Beast was hoping to share the love of Cabot with Gavin tonight. He has his copy of *Chosen Sons* clutched close to his chest. It does not look like tonight is going to be the night though. A crowd has gathered to watch Gavin brave the flames. It would be difficult to get by the crowd and into the building unnoticed. Besides, The Beast can hear parts of the frame starting to buckle. It would not be a good place to do some reading.

A few minutes pass, and it becomes clear that Gavin is in trouble. The Beast can hear the ceilings inside the building coming down. If Gavin doesn't get out soon, he'll never get out. The Beast will not let him die, not before he gets a chance at saving the boy's soul.

The Beast drops down onto the street, behind the crowd. He is willing to risk getting spotted in order to save Gavin. Luckily, everyone is focused on the inferno, and The Beast is able to sneak around to the far side of the building and enter from the back. He makes his way through one of the apartments. He can hear Gavin two stories up. What is Gavin still doing in here? The Beast gets his answer when he makes it to the stairwell. The steps have collapsed. Gavin will need another way out.

The Beast doesn't have time to think of a plan. He has to act now. He heads into the closest apartment and leaps straight up, as hard as he can. His head and shoulders burst through the flame-engulfed ceiling. The B-Crete burns his flesh, but it is a pain he is willing to endure in order to save a fellow Chosen Son.

He drops back down and looks up at the hole his body made. Gavin should be able to fit through it easily. Instead of going back through the entrance he came in, The Beast bursts through the outer wall of the building. Now Gavin does not even need to find the door.

The Beast jumps up onto the roof of the building next door. He drops to his knees and prays.

"I know it wasn't enough to save Gavin's life, I know you want me to save his soul. I'm sorry I ain't done it yet. Please don't punish the boy because I'm a coward. Let him live long enough to read your words for himself."

The Beast opens his eyes and watches. A few moments later Gavin comes out of the hole The Beast made. The boy is carrying a rat in a cage. The crowd applauds him. The Beast watches as Gavin soaks up the praise.

There is a hole in Gavin's soul, The Beast can see it. The boy is trying to fill it by saving pets from fires and stopping petty criminals. The Beast knows Cabot can fill that hole. The Beast remembers how good he felt after he learned the truth of Cabot.

#

With his belly full of his parents' flesh, the last shackle of Tom's old life was gone. Tom was a Chosen Son, free to live and hunt as he saw fit. Tom's mere existence was doing the Lord's work. Tom felt the love of God. His one regret was that it had taken him so long to learn the truth.

Tom was free to travel wherever he pleased. He had always wanted to go to Chicago. As a boy, he had seen a picture of the Jewel Hotel, and the image had burned into his mind. Tom sprinted the thousand miles between the Houston MA and the Chicago MA in a week. He fed on whatever game he could find and even managed to send a lucky Forgotten Son he stumbled upon up to heaven.

Once he got to the Chicago MA, Tom headed straight for the Miracle Mile and climbed to the roofs. Once high enough, the Jewel

Hotel came into view. It was even more beautiful in real life than it had been in the picture. This was one of the miracles of the Lord's new race. It was a shining inverted pyramid, one hundred stories of guest rooms balanced on the tiniest point. It looked like a spinning top somehow frozen in place. The hotel was something that should not be possible, but it was, thanks to a Chosen Son. Tom knew he was blessed when he saw it. He was blessed to be part of a race that could create such a wonder.

Unlike the people of Houston, the people of the Chicago MA lived off the labor of the Chosen. The Chosen grew and transported all of their food. They lived in buildings built or repaired by the Chosen. They rode trains powered by the Chosen. They had lights, heat, and water all thanks to Chosen Sons. Tom was in awe of this city. This was why God had created a new race.

Tom's awe soon turned to anger. The Chosen made the city, but the city was not for them. The only fellow Chosen Sons Tom saw were delivering packages or working construction.

This city should belong to those who built it. The high rises should have been full of ever-multiplying Chosen Sons and Daughters. Instead, it was full of pathetic humans. Tom could hear them blaming the Chosen for the train being late or their food being bland. These Forgotten Sons would make the prefect prey for Tom.

Tom spent his time hunting, eating and growing more powerful. Tom's body kept growing. It quickly changed from the size of a professional athlete into something larger than any linebacker or sumo wrestler. When he stood straight up, he was just about eight feet tall, and he weighed over seven hundred pounds.

As he grew, he became stronger, stronger than could be explained by his size, stronger than any person could be. One day Tom came across an eight-year-old boy, searching through a half-collapsed Pre-Plague house. He was looking for scrap metal to sell. Tom felt bad for the boy. He was going to spend his whole life toiling away. Tom decided to reward the boy with an early trip to heaven.

Unfortunately, the boy spotted Tom and ran. The boy ended up running into an old abandoned restaurant. Tom watched in horror as the building collapsed on top of the child. Tom ran over and, to his surprise, was able to lift the massive stone column that had fallen onto the boy. It must have weighed two tons. Tom fed on the crushed child. He thanked God that he was strong enough to make sure the boy was rewarded with eternity in paradise instead of dying for nothing.

Tom did not just get larger and stronger, his whole body changed. Hair grew all over his body, thick, coarse, and nearly everywhere. Tom's jaw grew and extended forward. His old teeth fell out, and new larger, sharper teeth replaced them. His new canines were over five inches long. His fingernails and toenails became claws perfectly suited for tearing human flesh.

His skin continued to get thicker and more leathery. It acted like a form of armor. What few injuries Tom did receive healed in a matter of hours. One day, Tom came across a gang of thugs robbing a poor old man. The old man did not have a lot of money, and this made the leader of the gang angry. He was about to hit the old man when one of his fellow thugs stepped in and stopped the beating. The leader just spit on the old man and walked away.

Tom thought the kind-hearted thug deserved a reward for his compassion. Tom followed the thug until he was alone. Then he dropped down and approached the man. Tom liked being spotted. He liked to know how afraid he made people. However, the thug was not afraid like most. When he saw Tom approaching, he yelled.

"Yo, what the hell are you?"

"I'm your salvation," Tom answered.

"You get away from me. I'm warning you," the thug threatened.

Tom didn't listen. He just kept coming. The thug pulled out a small hand gun and fired at Tom's chest. Tom felt the bullet hit. It hurt, but not as much as he expected. It felt like getting a shot from the doctor when he was a kid. He looked down, and he could see the slug sticking out of his chest. It had barely penetrated. The thug fired four more shots into Tom's chest with the same minimal effect. Tom grinned and tore out the thug's throat with a swipe of his claw. Then he fed. The next morning, Tom checked his minor wounds. They had disappeared. Tom thanked God for making him strong enough to survive his mistakes.

The changes were not just physical. A completely new universe opened up to Tom, a universe of smells and sounds. When he wanted a snack, he listened. His ears could lead him to a crying infant from thirty blocks away. Once he got close, his nose took over and led him right to the baby's room. After that, it was as simple as going in and taking what God had given him. The only question would be if he was hungry enough to dine on the parents. He usually was.

Tom walked around the Chicago MA feeling invincible. He was truly blessed by God. He had gifts that even most other Chosen Sons would envy. The time Tom spent, eating, growing, and experiencing his new abilities was the happiest time of Tom's life. The only downside was his hunger. His constant, impossible to satiate, hunger.

15

Different individuals create unique situations for law enforcement officials. Officials must be granted leeway to deal with these unique situations without running afoul of a Different individual's right to due process or equal protection under the law. A reasonable suspicion by a law enforcement official is all that is required to detain, question, or investigate a Different individual.

Chief Justice Garret Dwight
Majority Opinion: Rodgers v. Houston Metro Area

I don't think he really looks like the Devil, it's just the old woman's mind remembering him that way. None of the other witnesses remembered him with horns and a pointy tail. No one else remembered him with a tail at all.

I'm looking through people's visual memories from The Beast's time in Chicago. I'm hoping to find some clue that can help me confirm if he is actually in Los Angeles. I know it's crazy. I know he's supposed to be dead, but so many people in the slums are actually afraid of The Beast. And I did find that kidney. I just need to know for sure.

Unfortunately, no think.Net reporters ever caught a glimpse of The Beast. Reporters hook directly into think.Net when they are covering a story. The Telepaths are able to read the nerve signals as they come in from the eyes. That way, the Librarians store an unfiltered view for us all to watch later.

Since no reporter ever got any footage of The Beast, I'm reduced to looking at the memories of witnesses who spotted him on the streets of the Chicago MA. These memories were scanned by Telepaths days or even weeks after they actually saw The Beast. The human mind is not very good at remembering details, especially when it's terrified. According to these warped memories, The Beast looks like a character out of a movie or fairy tale. He might look like a Were-Wolf, Big Foot, the Devil, or maybe even King Kong.

The first reports of The Beast started appearing in the Chicago Metro Area news six or seven years ago. At first The Beast was only mentioned as a joke. They only brought him up as a little shot at idiots in the boonies who believed in monsters. As more and more people reported spotting The Beast, the press started to take the story more seriously.

As The Beast turned from tabloid gossip to legitimate fear, the Metro Police had to respond. They set up patrols to hunt for The Beast. The hunters soon became the hunted, as The Beast seemed to target the police patrols. The few officers who survived described an incredibly powerful creature strong enough to crush a man's skull with one hand. That takes several hundred pounds of force. He's also got razor sharp claws and teeth capable of tearing human flesh to shreds.

The reports of The Beast all culminate in the news story everyone has heard of: "The Beast's Feast." Just about five years ago, The Beast walked into Chicago Metro Police Precinct 12 and killed all thirty-seven officers inside. He ate many of the bodies.

After the stories about "The Beast's Feast," there isn't much to be found. A few weeks after The Feast, an Office of Exceptional Cases spokeswoman gave a press briefing where she reported that the Different known as The Beast had been hunted down and killed by OEC agents. She did not take any questions from the press. But ever since The Beast was reported dead, there have been reports of him being spotted in every Metro Area. These reports have been dismissed as delusions. People still claim to spot Elvis, after all. No reputable news agency will carry the stories, and reports of The Beast have been relegated to the tabloids.

I do a search for The Beast in a few tabloid article archives. In between reports of him being the love child of Satan and a Yeti and the supposed killing of a bunch of high-school football players in the Houston MA years ago, I find something useful. A picture, taken with a Pre-Plague camera, I think it’s called a Polaroid. It's a body, one of The Beast's victims in Chicago, a middle-aged woman. On her throat, I can clearly see The Beast's bite mark. I can use that.

I need to check that bite mark against one of the people who have supposedly been killed by The Beast in the LA Metro Area. I should start with Becky's friend's apartment. I call her on think.Net, and she answers right away as always.

>>>Hi, honey.

<<<Hi Becky, I wanted to apologize for the other night with the pastor. I don't think I made a good impression arguing with him like I did.

>>>The pastor might not have liked it, but believe me, my dad loved it. He likes to see a good fight more than anything else in the world. You scored points by standing up to "Mr. Newman." Not too many people do it. Besides, you're a Chosen Son, remember? A little political debate is not going to be enough to turn my father against you. Trust me, he loved you.

<<<In that case, it was a great dinner. Although I was sorry to hear about your friend and her daughter. How come you didn't tell me about her before?

>>>I don't know. We have so few nights together. It doesn't seem right wasting them talking about such awful things.

<<<I'm sorry we haven't been able to spend as much time together lately. Ultracorps has me cleaning the labs every night, but I don't just want to be there for the good times. I want this to be real. I want to be there for you in the hard times, too.

>>>You helped me even though you didn't know it. Don't worry so much. We weren't that close. She was just someone I knew from the neighborhood. She wasn't part of the church or anything.

<<<Where did she live?

#

The apartment building where Becky's friend was killed is a Pre-Plague structure that looks like it survived fairly well, especially compared to the rest of the neighborhood. Most of the three-story building still looks habitable. There's an old woman sitting on a chair on the stoop. She looks like she’s sat out here every day for the last thirty years.

"Hello, ma'am. Do you know a Jessica Harris? I heard she used to live here," I say.

"Why do you want to know?" she snarls back.

In another world, a world without the Plagues, she would have been a sweet old lady. In this world, she has learned not to trust anyone, even though I'm in my old man disguise.

"I was a friend of her father's. I knew her when she was just a girl. I heard what happened and felt the need to come see for myself," I tell her.

"Her and her little girl been dead a long time. The looters already went through and took everything. You won't find whatever it is you're after," the crabby old woman says.

"I wish I could have been here sooner, but it took a long time for the news to reach me in the Seattle Metro Area. Her father was a dear friend. I feel I owe it to him to see for myself."

"Awful long way to come just to see some blood and bones. She was on the third floor, number two. Just make sure that's all you're doing. My son is in my apartment, and he doesn't take kindly to uninvited guests."

"Thank you."

I go into the building and up to the third floor. Someone has smashed in the door to apartment #2. It could have been whoever killed Ms. Harris, or the looters.

Inside the apartment, there's a stench of death, but it's old and faint. The old lady was right about the looters. They tore this place apart. Whatever furniture or fixtures Ms. Harris had are long gone. There is blood, though. It's splashed all over the walls, the floors, and even the ceiling.

There are handprints in the blood. Some of them the size of a grown woman—Jessica—some of them are much smaller—her child. Some of them are something else entirely. They almost look like animal tracks, large animal tracks.

In the bedroom, there's a huge pool of dried blood and some bones scattered about, no doubt where Ms. Harris and her daughter met their end. The bones have had almost all the flesh torn off.

I pick up a femur and inspect it. Rats have gnawed on it, but that's not all. Something with a bigger jaw than any rat that's ever lived has chewed on it too. I compare the bite marks on the bone to the bite marks on the woman's neck in the Polaroid picture. The canines are over six inches apart both on the top and the bottom. This is the bite of The Beast, the bite of a monster. A monster I'm going to stop.

#

I need to figure out a way to track The Beast down. According to reports of The Beast, he's definitely Physically Enhanced. I would say he can lift over two tons, minimum. Differents who are that strong need at least 50,000 to 75,000 calories a day. That's not all; many of the police officers The Beast killed in Chicago had fired their guns before dying. That means either he's got super-speed to dodge bullets, he's a healer and can recover from his wounds quickly, or he's big and strong enough that a handgun isn't enough to stop him. Maybe it is all three. Either way, that's going to take another 100,000 calories a day. That means The Beast needs 175,000 calories a day minimum, probably more like 200,000. That's a lot of calories.

How often would The Beast need to eat a person to consume that many calories? To figure that out, I'll need to determine how many calories there are in the human body. According to think.Net, the average American weights 133 pounds. Of that weight, about 15% is bones, 19% is fat, 41% is muscle, and 25% is hair and connective tissue. 19% of 133 pounds is 25.25 pounds of fat. 25.25 pounds is 11,453 grams. Fat has 9 calories per gram, which means the average human body would provide 103,077 calories from fat. Add that to the 54.5 pounds of muscle at 4 calories per gram of muscle protein, and you get 201,961 calories. Add in another 25,000 calories or so from sugar in the blood and what you can eat of the connective tissue, and there's about 225,000 calories in the average human body.

That means The Beast needs to kill every day, or maybe every other day if he hasn't been very active. That is a lot of dead bodies. If people were finding piles of bones on the streets of the Metro

Area, The Beast would be more than just a rumor, even in these poor neighborhoods. That means he's hiding the bones, which means there must be a hiding place or places, probably in one of the thousands of abandoned buildings that fill the Metro Area.

The only question is which one. The blocks near where Becky's friend lived are a good place to start. But to go through every empty building would take me forever. Luckily, I have just the tool to help my search, my nose.

Rotting flesh lets off some pretty unique odors. There are two gases in particular, putrescence and cadaverine, that give rotting flesh its unique smell. I know all about these gases from my work in the food lab. I just need to cue in on the odor.

I stimulate my body to generate more olfactory reception cells in my nasal cavity. This will increase the number of molecules that my nose takes in from the air, increasing the general strength of my sense of smell. Next, I stimulate the growth of a particular glomerulus region of my olfactory blub. This will make me hypersensitive to the unique odor molecules of cadaverine and putrescence.

When it is all said and done, I may have made myself too sensitive to these odors. It seems like rotting flesh is all around me. I can smell the infections of the ill, the purification of vermin corpses, and the fermenting of a thousand scraps of leftover dinner. Still, even amongst all the odors, something stands out. There's a constant flow of rot coming from the south. I follow the river of rank downstream.

I wouldn't make a very good bloodhound. It takes me over two hours to find the particular building the smell is emanating from. It's a half-collapsed Pre-Plague house. As soon as I step through what's left of the front door, I know that I've found the nest. I'm pretty sure the smell would make me puke if that was still something that could happen to me.

It takes me another five minutes to make my way through the debris-filled house and climb up the mostly destroyed staircase. I find the graveyard on the second floor in one of the bedrooms.

Graveyard is not the right term. It's more like a sea of bones. There must be at least fifty people in there, maybe more. It's hard to tell when you're just looking at pieces of people.

In the mess, something unusual catches my eye, a piece of metal. I scare some rats away and find a brown leather briefcase lying in the corner. I'm pretty sure it's made of genuine leather. You don't see many of those out here in the slums. I open the briefcase and pull out a piece of paper. I read the top line: "From the desk of Alderman David Gabbert."

#

I consider my options while I continue my patrol. I could tell the police about the Alderman, but then I'd have to come up with a good explanation for why I was looking through abandoned buildings in the middle of the night. I don't think they'll buy that I was just bored. It won't take them long to figure out that I'm the vigilante everyone's been talking about.

I'd like to think the cops would thank me for figuring out what happened to the Alderman they've been trying to find for six months. I'd like to imagine I'd get the reward they're offering and maybe get to meet the Governor. I know that isn't what would happen. Best-case scenario, I'd get put on probation and told that if I ever tried to be a hero again, I'd spend twenty years to life in Great Basin prison. Realistically, they'd probably skip the probation.

There's a police tip-line on think.Net that's supposedly anonymous, but nothing is really anonymous on think.Net, especially for Differents. I'm not willing to bet my freedom on the fact that the police stick to their word.

I hear a scream. The sound bounces off the B-Crete apartments, making it as loud as a bullhorn. It's a woman, and she sounds scared. I'll have to decide what to do about Alderman Gabbert later. There's someone I can help right now. I take off running towards the sound.

As I run, I hear something on the roof above me. I freeze and my thoughts immediately go to The Beast. I look to the roofs, but I can't make anything out. The woman shouts again, which compels me to keep moving.

It takes me forty-five seconds to get to her, and when I do, I see a scene strikingly reminiscent of my first bout of crime fighting. There are three men chasing a young woman. They are toying with her.

"Scream all you want, girlie. It's just music to me," one of the thugs says.

Most nights, he'd be right. I can hear windows slam shut and shades drawn closed from the apartments that line the street. People are too afraid to do anything. Why shouldn't they be? If they intervened, they would become the victims.

"Leave her alone!" I shout in my most intimidating voice and charge towards the attackers.

"Yeah, what if we don't, old man? What are you going to do about it?" a thug yells back.

I pause a moment to size up my opponents. Who appears the most dangerous? As soon as I take a good look at everyone, I can tell something is wrong. The clothes look normal for a trio of punks, but the men don't look right in them. They're clean and they have close-cropped hair. These guys can afford regular haircuts and showers. Maybe they're part of a cartel or something, but then why such ratty clothes?

When I look at the woman, I know for certain that I am in trouble. Her gaze is fixed squarely on me, and it doesn't waver. She's scared, for sure, but not of her attackers. She's scared of me. Finally, I put it all together. These are the police.

Without another word, I turn around and break into a full sprint. I pour adrenaline into my system, enough to damage my organs, but I can worry about that later. Right now I need speed.

"Stop right there, or we'll shoot!" I hear one of the *thugs* yell.

I believe him, but I'm still not about to stop. I'll take my chances that his aim isn't good enough to hit a moving target at a hundred yards over a life sentence in Great Basin. I hear a bullet wiz over my head. Several other shots join the first. The whole group is shooting at me, even the damsel in distress. I didn't know gunshots were so loud.

As bullets ricochet around me, I round a corner to another block where three more officers are waiting for me. These ones are in uniform, and they're yelling at me to stop. I turn around and head back up my original street. I still have a lead on the group of Undercovers.

Out of the corner of my eye, I see a young officer built like an ox charge at me from an alley. He's about to tackle me, and there's nothing I can do about it. I think I know how to handle it though.

The Ox slams into me, knocking me to the ground. I go into a roll and spring back up to my feet. I'm up and running at full speed before the Ox even realizes I'm not lying next to him on the ground. More bullets hit the pavement around me.

I get to the next corner right at the same time as an older female officer. Before she can raise her gun, I punch her in the neck, damaging her windpipe. She'll live, but she's not about to give chase.

I round the corner and think for just a second I may have gotten away, but no such luck. Two more officers are running down the street towards me. They don't bother to yell stop anymore, they just start shooting. A bullet whizzes close enough by my head for me to get a look at it. I need to get out of here, now. One of these cops is going to get lucky soon.

I turn up an alley and hurdle over a pile of old concrete. As I reach the center of the alley, two officers come running from the opposite end towards me. I take a quick look back behind me and sure enough, three officers are heading towards me from that direction. I only have one option.

"I give up, don't shoot me! Please don't shoot me," I plead.

I hear a noise from above and look up. Do they have police on the roofs?

Then one of the officers approaches and points something at me that doesn't look like a normal gun. It shoots a dart attached to a wire at me. I fall to the ground. I scream at my muscles to move, but they won't listen. Then I hear a loud crash and a grunt.

16

No matter where they are born or whom they are born to, all of my Chosen Sons are brothers. Their love for each other shall only be exceeded by their love of me.

Chosen Sons: 34

The Beast sees Gavin head out from the Slug, ready for another night patrolling the streets. This time something is different. Gavin looks like he is full of purpose. He is not just wandering aimlessly looking for trouble. He turns and heads into an apartment building. A building The Beast has used for feeding.

The creature watches through the window as Gavin searches the apartment where The Beast fed. The meal was delicious, a young mother and daughter. Their flesh was tender, truly a bounty from heaven. The Beast knows Gavin will not see it that way. The truth of Cabot has not been shown to Gavin. He doesn't know that the Lord has granted His Chosen Sons dominion over the humans just as the humans were once granted dominion over the animals. The boy would not spend his nights saving old ladies if he were enlightened.

This is just what The Beast was afraid of. Now Gavin is going to think The Beast is a monster. It is going to be harder to get the boy to listen. This is The Beast's punishment for being afraid. This is the Lord reminding The Beast that he should trust in Him. God wanted Gavin saved. The Beast had been too scared. The Beast needs to go to Gavin soon, but before he does, he remembers why he is so afraid. He remembers why he has to be careful around his brothers, why he seeks redemption.

#

Tom kept hunting in the Chicago MA for three years. He grew stronger and stronger, which made him more and more hungry. One or two kills a week soon became five kills, then ten.

Reports of "The Beast," started appearing in the news, horror stories of a creature that was slaughtering Chicago residents. The police responded with increased patrols and search teams. Tom saw this as a challenge to his dominance. These pitiful humans thought they could stop him? They thought they could keep Tom from taking what God had given him? He would show them, he would show them all.

Tom walked into Chicago Metro Police Precinct 12 one night, grabbed the officer working the reception desk by the head, and tore his head off. Tom then systematically went through the rest of the station slaughtering every officer he could find. The police tried to resist, but their side arms could not do enough damage to stop Tom.

Nine officers barricaded themselves in the munitions room. They had a high powered rifle, powerful enough to hurt Tom. They shot him in the shoulder. He felt the bullet hit bone and howled in pain. He barely jumped out of the way of the next shot and hid around the corner.

Tom was scared. It had been a long time since something had actually hurt him. He had begun to think of himself as invincible. As Tom sunk into his fear, he felt something else. He felt the beast boiling up inside him and the animal begin to take over. Tom's fear turned to anger. How dare these officers try to kill a Chosen Son? How dare they try to challenge Tom?

Tom moved efficiently and robotically. He went back into the office part of the police station. He found a half-dead officer trying to crawl towards his gun ten feet away. The man was moving slowly. Tom had torn his belly open.

Tom lifted the dying man up and carried the man out in front of him. Then he started howling. Low and deep, it rang in the hallways. The officers in the munitions room started to shake. Then Tom took off running. He was moving at full speed by the time he hit the hallway facing the barricaded room. Tom used the dying officer as a human shield. The rifle could punch through the man's body, but the corpse absorbed enough power from the bullets that they couldn't hurt Tom.

The man with the rifle only got off two shots before Tom closed the distance. Tom ripped the rifle from the officer's hands then split his skull open with it. The remaining officers fired wildly with their sidearms. They hit their comrades as often as they hit Tom. He could take the bullets, but the officers could not. Whoever was not killed by friendly fire Tom finished off with his claws or teeth.

When the killing was all over, Tom had slaughtered thirty-seven police officers inside the station. It had taken him just over six minutes. He thanked God for the bounty and took his time feeding on the remains.

Reports of the slaughter spread through the Metro Area, and Chicago became gripped by panic. What could be done about The Beast if the police could not stop him? The news dubbed the attack on the station "The Beast's Feast," and the people of Chicago became afraid to leave their homes. The remaining police shut down operations and focused on fortifying their stations.

Now, the Chicago MA knew that it belonged to Tom. He had proven his dominance over the city, the Chosen Sons' dominance over the human race. Tom pounded his chest at night and howled through the streets. There was nothing and no one that could challenge him… until someone did.

It happened in the blink of an eye. Tom was on a rooftop, stalking an unfortunate young man who was on his way home from work. A woman appeared in front of Tom. He saw her before he smelled or heard her. Only a fellow Chosen Son could manage that.

"My name is Special Agent Linda Gibbons," she said. "I'm with the Office of Exceptional Cases, and I have been authorized to apprehend you by any means necessary. I am ordering you to surrender and lay down on the ground."

"Relax, Special Agent," Tom replied and kneeled. "I wonder if you've ever heard the word of our savior, Cabot. I'd like to read them to you now. I'm going to reach into my jacket. It's just a book, don't worry your pretty little head."

Tom reached into the overcoat he was wearing and pulled out *Chosen Sons*. He quickly found his place.

"*My Chosen Sons must not fight amongst themselves. They must know that they all share in my love equally even if their blessings are unequal. They must not let jealousy or petty politics of the old world stand in the way of the creation of the new world. My Chosen Sons must join together to create a new heaven on earth and to fill the planet with their progeny."* Tom finished reading and carefully put the book back in his coat.

"Did you just hit on me? You really are nuts, aren't you. We should have known you were a Cabotist. The crazy ones always are. I don't know where you psychos keep finding copies of that thing... As if we needed another crime to charge you with, possession of that literature is a violation of Executive Order 13586. I'm placing you under arrest for crimes too numerable to list."

"How can you work for the Office of Exceptional Cases? How can you spend your days hunting down your own kind?" The Beast asked.

"That's what you lunatics always ask me, and what I ask you is this: do you think the world is really better for Differents now than it was before the Plagues?"

"The Israelites had to spend forty years in the desert before they found salvation."

"All right, enough! Time to put your hands behind your head, or I'll be forced to use this," she reached into her coat and pulled out a large syringe, "Maceo Steel-tipped syringe with enough Tranq to knock out a blue whale. I don't want to use this. It might kill you. You have the right to remain silent. Anything you say or do can and will be held against you in the court of law. You have the right to speak to an attorney..."

Tom started to get up to try to run away. Before Tom could even get to his feet, the Special Agent closed the fifteen feet that separated the two and appeared behind Tom. She put the syringe into the back of Tom's neck and pushed the fluid in.

"No one's faster than me," the Special Agent said.

Tom writhed in agony, not from the needle, but from the drug sweeping through him. Tom felt the calm the Tranq created. It was a terrifying peace. Tom knew that he could not let himself stay in that tranquil place. Tom prayed to the Lord for the strength to fight through the drug.

By focusing on recalling the words of Cabot, the word of God, Tom was able to rouse himself from the calm. He managed to stand. He took a few slow, tortured steps away from the Special Agent. Tom was desperate to get away.

"I don't know how it's possible that you're standing, but I'd recommended you stop fighting the drug. If you do not submit I will be compelled to use further force," Special Agent Gibbons said.

Tom did not listen and continued his desperate, slow motion scramble to get away. Special Agent Gibbons pulled out two knives and proceeded to rain a hailstorm of slashes and stabs into Tom. The knives could not penetrate deep into his flesh, but she was fast enough to stab ten thousand times a minute. Even in his Tranq fog, Tom could feel the pain from the blows.

Tom tried to cry out, tried to beg the Special Agent to stop. But he could barely talk, and the Special Agent no longer wanted to listen. Realizing he was about to die, the beast in Tom took over. He mustered enough strength for one large swipe of his arm, which knocked Special Agent Gibbons through the air. It took Tom a few moments to gather himself. His stab wounds throbbed with each beat of his heart. That pain was nothing compared to what Tom felt when he saw Special Agent Gibbons.

His fellow Chosen Son was gasping for air. Tom's swipe had crushed her windpipe and the poor woman struggled to breathe. Tom watched helplessly as she took her last breaths. When she died, Tom became a monster once more.

"The Chosen must not kill their brothers. The spark of the divine must not be taken by any but the Lord himself. The Chosen's numbers are too few and their divinity too pure. This is the gravest sin a Chosen Son can commit. Thou shalt not kill is as much cannon to the new race as it was the old."

Those were the words of the Lord.

17

All Different individuals found guilty of any crime, regardless of local jurisdiction procedures, are to serve out their sentences at Great Basin Prison. Great Basin officials are authorized to use whatever means necessary in order to suppress or contain the Different individual and their abilities.

Amendment 12 to the Defense Spending Authorization Bill of 1999

The Beast hasn't said a word yet. I wonder if he can even talk. Even in his giant overcoat, he barely looks human. He looks like a gorilla with the jaw of a saber tooth tiger. All those memories on think.Net of him looking like a Were-Wolf made me expect something like that, but it makes more sense for him to be a primate. He is just a mutated human after all. He's even bigger than a gorilla, I would guess he weighs a thousand pounds. Blood drips from the three inch, razor-sharp claws on each finger. His mouth is full of teeth that look just as sharp, capped off with four massive canines.

He's just staring at me while he chomps on the arm of the officer who shot me with the dart. He took out both of those officers in one move. They didn't even know what hit them. Then he threw one of the dead policemen and me over his shoulder, as if we were dolls, and bounded over ten rooftops in the blink of an eye.

I can still hear the rest of the officers yelling in the distance. They think I killed the dead cop the monster left. He moved so quickly, none of the other officers even saw him. If I survive this, the police will triple their efforts to hunt me down. They catch cop-killers.

I tell my hand to move and it responds, clumsily. Whatever they shot me with is wearing off. I still need more time to recover though, and I want to be able to surprise The Beast when I can finally move. I sit there propped up against the corner and meet his gaze.

"You hungry, boy?" he asks with a blood-filled smile and extends the arm he's eating out towards me.

His voice is deep and gruff. He sounds like a monster out of a children's program on think.Net. Appropriate, because if a kid ever saw this man, that kid would have nightmares for the rest of his life.

"Your instincts are no good. It's easy to spot pigs from a mile away, even if you can't smell 'em. You got to watch yourself, the Forgotten Sons don't like rule breakers," he says and waits for my response. I don't have one.

"Still can't talk, boy? Good, then you got nothing to do but listen. I've been watching you for a while now, seeing you help little old ladies across the street and beating on punks. I even watched you try to hunt me down. You ain't much of a hunter, Gavin. You're lucky your prey wanted to be caught."

He finishes the arm he's eating and tosses it aside. He rips off most of the officer's thigh as easily as I would tear a piece of bread. He eats it in one bite.

"Don't worry, I ain't mad at ya. I was at first, but then I had time to think on it. You're doing what you do because you don't know any better. You've been brainwashed so you can't see what's wrong with the world. You can't see how far it is from the righteous path. You think all your silly antics are the right thing to do because you've never had a chance to be touched by the truth. That's the humans' fault."

I'm not thrilled to be hearing another speech on how great Cabot is, in part because I lost control of my bladder when the cops shot me with that device. My wet pants aren't making me feel like a Chosen Son. I have to keep listening until it's time to make my move though.

"I was like you once, Gavin. I was afraid of what the good Lord gave me. I thought this body of mine made me a monster. I asked the Lord, why me? But that's how he works, he don't make it easy to find your way."

I'm almost ready. I flex my muscles to remove the lactic acid that's built up and get them ready to move.

"I spent a long time struggling to find my way. You're headed down that same road, boy. Wasting your time saving the Forgotten

Sons while your own kind toil away as slaves. God saw my struggles and saved me. He showed me His latest Revelation. The good Lord gave me freedom through the Word of Cabot. Cabot showed me that I ain't a freak. I am one of God's Chosen Sons. You are Chosen too, Gavin Stillman. The earth belongs to you. The Lord said so Himself."

So, I guess he can read. He must have gotten my name off my D tattoo. Good eyes, too. He closes those eyes for a moment as he finishes his speech. It's time to make my move. I lunge at him, hoping to knock him off the side of the building, but I see him react before I get halfway there. He leaps away from me like a grown-up playing tag with a toddler. I land and whirl towards him. He's standing upright now. He must be eight feet tall. He's grinning at me.

I cock my first back and align my arm. I let fly with a punch to his stomach that would make Mohamed Ali double over in pain. The Beast doesn't even try to move. He just maintains his haunting grin as the most powerful punch I've ever thrown hits him square in the gut. He flinches ever so slightly. Meanwhile, the nerves from my fist to my elbow send out pain signals. Three of my knuckles are broken, and he kept his grin. I've punched walls to greater effect.

"Get that out of your system, did ya' boy?" he snarls.

I answer him with another punch to what should be his kidney. Not quite as powerful as my first blow, but this time, I hit a softer spot and he feels it. He doubles over a bit. I follow that up with a kick to his shin. That seems to hurt him too. He lets out a low growl. Good, he's not invincible.

I pull my hand back to deliver a chop to his throat. I imagine it will crush his windpipe, but imagine is all I get to do. His hand shoots out like a bullet, and I have to stretch time as far as I can to make out his movement. There's nothing I can do but tense my muscles to accept the blow.

He pushes me. I can tell from his muscles that it's just a little shove, but it sends me flying backwards almost ten feet. I land with a thud.

"Stay down!" he says, and his grin transforms to a glare.

I don't listen. The shove was impressive, but it didn't hurt me. Maybe he's never had to learn to fight since he usually gets the drop on his victims. Maybe if I keep attacking him, I'll get an opening. I spring up and charge back at him. I throw a feint with my right hand and follow it up with a left aimed squarely at his throat. He catches my fist in the air. His massive paw makes my hand look like a child's.

"You have some terrible manners, Gavin. I've saved your life a few times now. The least you could do is listen while I try to save your soul. It's what God wants."

To emphasize his point, he crushes my fist. Without any visible effort, he breaks just about every bone in my hand. My nerves cry out. He shoves me back down to the ground. The shove causes a huge tear in my right hamstring. I'm going to have trouble standing.

"What do you mean saved my life?" I ask, still lying on the floor.

"You think you've been a big hero all by yourself? You've got a guardian angel, me. You'd be dead three times over if it wasn't for me. Who do you think put you on that train?"

That first night, when I got my head cracked open. I didn't win the fight by some miracle. I was saved by this monster. He must have killed them. He must have put me on that train. If it wasn't for him, I'd be dead.

I think of that and start to soften a bit, until I remember that this lunatic kills and eats women and children. Saving me doesn't change that. Either way, I'm not winning this fight, not right now at least. My only hope of getting out of this alive is playing along.

"Okay, if you want to talk, talk. I'll listen," I say.

"It's not me I want you to hear, its God. I've got Cabot's Revelation itself right here," The Beast says.

He reaches into the massive coat he's wearing and pulls out a thin book. The cover is tattered, and the pages have yellowed. He hands it to me. I take it with my less injured hand.

The front reads *Chosen Sons: The Book of Cabot*. Just having this book in my hands is a crime. How did he get it? The government tried to round up and destroy every copy after the Plagues. Is it real?

"It's real," he says, sensing my disbelief. "I always carry it with me. It saved my soul. I bet it can do the same for you."

"How did you get this?" I ask.

"A prison, if you could believe it, hidden in a back corner so only I could find it. The Lord's work for certain. A miracle sent down from heaven to save my soul."

It's a miracle of math anyway. I knew Cabot sent books to just about every government building in the country. It was his warning to everyone before he spread his Plagues. The government claims to have destroyed every copy after the Plagues. What's the chance a prison would be the place they'd overlook?

"Be gentle with it," he says.

I know that this book is just the ravings of a mad man, but I have to read it or The Beast will kill me. I tell myself that's the only reason I open the cover, not because I'm curious, not because I've always wanted to see what it is that the Government is so afraid of. I'm just reading it and memorizing it verbatim so I can use it to try to manipulate The Beast, I tell myself.

"Here is the record of the 3rd book of our Lord, as spoken to his vessel Cabot: 'I am your Lord. Take what I tell you now and spread it to all mankind. Make my truth known to any who will listen,'" it starts.

#

"You must simply claim your thrones as kings of the new earth," it ends.

As soon as I look up from the last page, The Beast snatches the book from my grasp and cradles it as a child would a teddy bear. It looks like it caused him pain to have the book out of his possession for even a moment, let alone the three minutes it took me to read every page and memorize every word.

"Well?" he asks, but then changes his mind and shakes his head. "No, don't tell me yet. You need time to think on what you read."

He gets up and heads over to the edge of the roof. "A week from tonight be outside the Church of Cabot, eight p.m., sharp. I'm sure you'll be able to find the church. We'll do more talking then. I'm gonna be looking forward to it, that's for sure. I can't wait to tell the Lord all about this. I hope He speaks to me soon. Don't worry, I'll tell Him all about you."

Then he leaps what must be twenty-five feet to the next building. A few more jumps and he's out of sight. He is so very fast. He also seems to think he can speak to God, not exactly unique for a psychopath. What should I expect from someone who eats people?

He was right about me needing time to reflect. I just read the words of a lunatic. There is no doubt about that. But even a broken clock is right twice a day. I'd be lying if I said Cabot, I mean "God," didn't make any compelling points. It is hard to imagine what wonders Chosen Sons—Differents—could accomplish if they were free to live for themselves instead of keeping humans alive… I push that thought out of my brain and hate myself for thinking it.

I pick myself up and look around for a way down. Climbing isn't an option, not with my shattered hands and torn hamstring. I try the door on the roof, but it's locked, of course. I wind up and slam into it with my shoulder. With my injured hamstring I can't generate much force, so the door holds. I do manage some damage to my rotator cuff. Good, I need more injuries.

Three more slams with three more sets of bruises, and the door finally gives. I have to hope no one heard and called the cops. Lucky for me, the people who live here probably gave up on calling the police a long time ago. I head down the stairs as quickly as I can hobble.

Once I'm out of the building, I pop on think.Net and find the closest Slug station, only three blocks away. I start hobbling. Even at this speed, I might actually make it back in time for work. Soon, that fantasy is shattered. I hear someone running up behind me. They sound like they are loaded down with all sorts of equipment. A police officer, but I don't dare turn around to look.

I keep walking but stop using my limp. Walking that way kept me from causing further injury to my hamstring, but I'd rather have more healing to do later than have to try to explain my injuries now. Let's just hope he doesn't ask me to sign anything. I don't think I can get either of my hands to work.

"You! Stop right there or I'll shoot," the officer yells. He sounds nervous.

"Don't shoot! I'll give you whatever you want," I say and make my voice quiver with fear.

"Turn around slowly, and keep your hands up."

I start to turn, but stop myself. My face! I still have all the muscles relaxed. I still look like an old man. I still look like the vigilante. I start to tighten the muscles on my face, but it'll take a few seconds. If I do it too fast the muscles might cramp and spasm and that'll make me look just as suspicious. I need to stall.

"I told you to turn around!" the officer yells again.

"Please don't hurt me. I haven't seen you. I don't know what you look like. You don't have to shoot me," I say trying to sound as pathetic as possible.

"Sir, I am a police officer and I am ordering you to turn around right now."

"Should I turn left or right?"

"I don't care, just turn around now, or you'll be sorry," the officer says and lowers his voice. He means it.

I finally relent and turn around. I sure hope my face looks normal. The young officer sees me and relaxes a bit. I guess I managed it.

"Okay, you can put your hands down," he says with an exhale.

As I do that, I see his eyes focus on the D on my hand. He tightens back up like a coil.

"Put your hands back up and don't move!" he says and points his gun right at my head.

"Whatever you say, officer," I say and put my hands up.

He stands there, trying to figure out what he should do. He's spared the decision when another older, gray haired officer runs up. He's out of breath.

"Is it him? Is it him?" Older Cop asks.

"Does he look like an old man to you?" Younger Cop answers.

"I don't know. He's a Different. Maybe he can change or something," Older Cop replies.

"Check his tattoo."

The older cop approaches me carefully.

"Let me see your hand."

I extend my hand for him to inspect. "I'm not a Morpher."

I can see the older man struggle to read the text of my tattoo.

“You got to come read this. All I can see is that he’s Gamma, the rest is too damn small,” the older cop says to the younger cop.

“It says Gavin Stillman, Anthropomorphic Control,” I offer up.

“What the hell is Anthropomorphic Control?” Older Cop asks.

"How should I know? Never heard of it," Younger Cop answers

"I can control certain systems in my body. For example, I can change the color of my urine." It's true, I can.

"Gross. Didn't you hit the freak jackpot?" Older Cop says.

"What are you doing around here so late at night? We're pretty far from Ultracorps employee housing," Younger Cops asks.

What was I doing here, besides not hunting The Beast? I need to come up with an answer. I realize that I’m not that far from Becky’s house.

"I was visiting my girlfriend. She lives a few blocks from here. I was just taking the long way back to the Slug."

Please take my word for it. Please take my word for it.

"You didn't see an old guy running, did you?" Older Cop asks. It seems like they bought my story.

"No, I haven't seen anyone out here but you guys." That's true, I didn't see the old guy. "Are you looking for the vigilante?" I ask.

"Maybe, what do you know about it?" Younger Cop asks.

"Nothing, nothing. You just hear stories. They say he's been beating up drug dealers and saving people from muggers."

"Maybe that’s what he used to be, but now he’s a cop killer. He killed two of us. We’re going to hunt him down no matter how many muggers he stopped," Younger Cop says.

“You guys sure about that? From what I heard he was trying to help you do your jobs. He didn’t sound like a cop killer,” I know it’s stupid before I say it but I do it anyway. I don’t like being called a freak.

"What do you know? And speaking of doing our jobs, it's an awfully big coincidence that you're out here in the boonies on the same night we spot the vigilante. You wouldn't mind taking us back to your girlfriend's house, would you? To verify your story? We should be thorough, right?" Younger Cop asks.

"Is that necessary, officer? It's so late, she's probably asleep by now. I'd rather not disturb her."

"Oh sure, sure. That's no problem. We'll just lock you up for the night. Once your girlfriend wakes up, she can come talk to us and get you out. That way, she can get all her beauty rest."

It's not an empty threat, Differents don't have many legal rights. He can just lock me up because he feels like it. While I'm rotting in the cell, maybe someone will figure out it's not just a coincidence I'm the same height and weight as the vigilante. It's not a chance I want to take. I'll just have to go to Becky's house and hope she covers for me.

"I'll take you to her," I say.

#

Seven cops escort me to Becky's house. I guess they don't take any chances when it comes to Differents. They don't need so many. I've done so much more damage to my hamstring by walking on it I can barely move. If I couldn't ignore my nerve signals I'd be curled up in a ball, weeping.

I wish I could have called Becky on think.Net and prepared her to cover for me, but the cops were watching me too closely. There is no way I could sink into the think.Net stare without them noticing. I've always meant to teach myself to logon without doing the stare. I think I could if I practiced, but now is not the time to try to learn.

Five of the officers keep back while the two cops who caught me knock on the door with me beside them. If I ever felt fear, I would feel it right now.

"This is the police. We're here to see Becky Carter. Open the door!" Older Cops says.

I hear stirring from inside the house, but it takes a few minutes for anyone to come. I speed up time to make the wait less excruciating.

Finally, Becky and her dad open the door.

"Hello, officers, what can we do for you?" Mike asks.

Becky and I make eye contact. I can see worry and confusion on her face. This would be the perfect time for telepathy to be my Differentiation, or maybe invisibility.

"This Different says that he was with you tonight. Is that true?" Younger Cop asks.

I can't make time move fast enough for that instant. The answer to this question will decide if I spend the rest of my life in prison.

"Yes, officer. That's my boyfriend. He was here until just a few minutes ago. We were listening to Harvey Quinn on the radio," Becky says without skipping a beat. I can't even tell that she's lying.

"What's a nice girl like you doing with a freak for a boyfriend?" The younger cop asks.

"This is the Cabotist neighborhood. Whack jobs like her think it's their duty to mate with Differents," Older Cop answers for her.

"That's disgusting," Younger Cop replies.

"That it is, but unfortunately it's not illegal, even if it should be. Let's get out of here boys," Older Cop orders.

The police head out saying vile things about Becky, her father and me. It's a lovely beginning to what is going to be an awful conversation. I see the look on Becky's face and start to wish I had just let them take me downtown.

18

My Chosen Sons must leave behind the lives they were born into. No matter their past creeds or allegiances, the Chosen now swear fealty to each other. Arm in arm is how the world will be rebuilt.

Chosen Sons: 33

The Beast cannot remember the last time he was so happy. The Lord had blessed him with a chance to atone for his sins, a chance to make things right. The Beast had saved a soul. Gavin had read the truth of Cabot with his own eyes. The Beast grins as he jumps away from Gavin on the rooftops.

Gavin is not the same as other Chosen Sons. He had a mind of his own. By day, Gavin accepts society's chains by working a job like all the other Differents. By night though, Gavin escapes that prison and follows his own path. The Beast respects Gavin's spirit even if his motives are misguided. He will be a fantastic Cabotist, maybe even a friend.

The Beast is so full of gratitude, he is practically bursting. He does not care if he is far enough away from Gavin and the police to be safe. He needs to speak to the Lord. He has to know how happy God is to have a Chosen Son accept his place on the earth. He drops to his knees and prays.

"Lord, thank you. Thank you for giving me a chance to make right for my sins. Thank you for letting me save one of my brother's souls. I hope I pleased you. I hope I showed you that I deserve your love. Please God, tell me you're happy. Tell me that I've done good."

The Beast waits for a response, but none comes. The euphoria he felt from showing Gavin *Chosen Sons* starts to fade. The Beast thinks back to his sins, back to what he is trying to atone for.

#

Tom wept with the dead OEC Agent laying besides him. It didn't matter that she had tried to arrest Tom. That didn't change the fact that Tom was a murderer. In an instant he had turned from a proud Chosen Son into to a filthy sinner. He had killed one of his own kind. He was damned. Tom lost control and the beast inside him took over. He ran out of the Metro Center, out of the entire Chicago MA, and into the wilderness. It took Tom just a day to run all the way out of what was old Illinois and into the barren plains of the Midwest.

The Great Plains of the Midwest were not very full of life even before the Plagues. Now, they looked like the surface of the moon. He was forced to raid termite and ant nests in order to eke out an existence. He would choke down the larvae and know that it was part of his punishment.

The wasteland was both a punishment and a prison. It kept Tom away from other Chosen Sons, and it made sure Tom would not be forced into sin again. Life in the plains was difficult, but Tom felt safe at least. He was wrong.

The Office of Exceptional Cases was like any law enforcement branch and did not suffer lightly the death of one of their own. The OEC was not content with the news that Tom had fled the Chicago MA. They needed to apprehend Tom and make him pay for the death of Special Agent Gibbons. The OEC sent one of their very best field teams, Special Agents White and Rodriguez, who were to track and incapacitate Tom by any means necessary.

Special Agent White was a Physically-Enhanced Chosen Son, a Strong-Man. The government considered Agent White the 17th strongest Strong-Man in existence, which was no small accomplishment. Agent White was significantly stronger than Tom, at least in terms of lifting weights in a gym.

Special Agent Rodriguez was a Telepath trained for use in the field. She could focus her mental energies on one target with extreme results. She was capable of taking control of another person's body or even turning their mind "off"—killing them. She could also use her telepathy to track individuals.

Despite this, tracking Tom proved difficult. Special Agent

Rodriguez's mind was developed to intercept and interpret human brainwaves. Out here in the plains, the beast in Tom had taken over. He thought more like an animal than a human. Special Agent Rodriguez was only able to pick up on Tom when he was deep in thought. When he went off to hunt, she would lose the trail. It took the agents several days to locate him.

When they did, Tom had heard and smelled the pair coming from two miles away. Tom noticed that there was something different about how these two people smelled. Something in the scent reminded him of Special Agent Gibbons. Tom realized that he smelled his own kind.

For an instant, Tom was happy. He was going to see some of his brothers. He ran towards them as fast as he could. Right before he got to them, he thought about why two Chosen Sons would be out in the middle of nowhere. These two were not coming to be Tom's friends. They were coming to hurt him.

He turned to flee before they got too close, but an invisible blow from Special Agent Rodriguez knocked him down. He could not say what happened. He just suddenly felt the need to drop to his knees.

"Stay on the ground and do not attempt to move. You are under arrest. If you do not cooperate, we will respond with deadly force. Do you understand what I've told you?" Special Agent Rodriguez said.

"Personally, I hope you don't cooperate. Gibbons was a friend of mine. Monsters like you don't deserve life in a Tranq-dream," Special Agent White added.

"I assume you two have not heard the word of our savior, Cabot..." Tom said, still on his knees.

"Quiet! We are not here to listen to your ramblings. You'll have your day in court, which is more than you deserve. The one thing you can do right now is stay where you are and cooperate while we take you into custody. Any answer besides yes will result in the use of deadly force. There will not be any further warnings. Do you understand?" Special Agent Rodriguez asked.

"My Chosen Sons must not fight. They must know that they all

share in my love equally even if their blessings are unequal..."

"That's it. Take this whacko out," Special Agent White said.

"I'm trying, but it's not working. It's like I can only penetrate the surface of his mind. I can't kill him."

"Music to my ears. You're going down the hard way, murderer!" Special Agent White said and charged at Tom.

Special Agent Rodriguez's mental blow might not have been enough to kill Tom, but it did make it hard for Tom to think. It slowed him down, making it impossible to dodge Special Agent White's attack. The Strong-Man delivered a punch to Tom which knocked Tom 50 yards through the air.

The blow hurt, but the distance from Special Agent Rodriguez allowed Tom's head to clear. When Special Agent White arrived to deliver the next hit, Tom was ready and dodged the clumsy Strong-Man's punch with ease. Tom delivered dozens of his own punches to White's head and mid-section. No one of the individual blows were enough to damage Agent White, but the accumulation of punches eventually knocked the Strong-Man to the ground. Tom was simply too fast.

Seeing a chance to escape, Tom turned to run, but his body was stopped again by a blow from Special Agent Rodriguez's mind. If Tom wanted to flee, he would have to deal with Agent Rodriguez. Tom turned and charged at the woman, planning to knock her out, nothing more. Special Agent Rodriguez saw a monster charging at her, and it filled her with terror. Tom looked like something from one of her childhood nightmares. She let go with a blast of mental energy that could have killed a dozen people.

When Tom came to, he thought the blast had killed him. It had not. The beast in Tom had taken control, and Tom had torn out Special Agent Rodriguez's throat with his teeth. He could still taste her blood on his lips. Special Agent White was dead not too far away. There was no obvious wound to cause his death. Rodriguez had accidentally killed him with her blast. Tom knew that Special Agent White's death was his fault even if he had not actually done the deed.

Tom cried out, "God! What was I supposed to do? How was I supposed to keep from sinning? They were going to kill me! I didn't want to hurt em. Lord, what did I do to deserve this punishment? Why did you make me, if all I do is suffer and make others suffer?"

Tom didn't get an answer. He started to shake with anger. All he wanted was to live in peace. Apparently that was too much to ask. If Tom was made just to cause suffering, it was time he made those who hunted him suffer. It was time for those government men to pay.

19

By the authority vested in me as President by the Constitution and statutes of the United States and in order to combat the unique threat to national security represented by the terrorist Different known as Cabot, all copies of the work entitled *Chosen Sons* by Cabot are ordered to be destroyed. Continued possession of the work will be considered a crime, punishable under the statutes created for public endangerment. Law enforcement officials are authorized to use whatever force is necessary in order to enforce this order.

President Ronald Reagan Executive Order 13586
October 12th 1987;
Banning of *Chosen Sons*

"Are you going to come in?" Becky asks coldly.

I walk up her steps while stretching time out for as long as I can. I'd like to enjoy the few moments I still have between now and explaining to Becky why the police walked me to her door.

"Do you want to tell me why I just lied to the police?" Becky asks as soon as she closes the door behind me.

"It's late. I should get to bed. I'll leave you two alone," Mike says and goes upstairs.

We stand stoic in the hallway while we wait for Mike to leave. The door slam breaks the silence. Time to start lying.

"Thank you for telling them I was with you. You didn't even skip a beat," I say.

"After the Revelation, we moved from refugee camp to refugee camp. The rations were scarce and the rules were strict. Lying to the authorities was a necessity," she says coldly.

"It was very impressive. I was trying to come up with a signal or something, but they were..."

"Stop beating around the bush, and tell me why I had to lie. What were you doing tonight?"

"I was just walking around and they stopped me. They asked what I was doing out so late, and I didn't have a good answer so I told them I was with you."

"Why would you tell them you were with me? Why wouldn't you just tell them what you were doing? What were you doing in my neighborhood, after midnight, without me?"

I need to come up with doozy of a lie here. What could I be doing? I could be seeing another girl, but that's worse than the truth. What else would I be doing out in this neighborhood? What does this neighborhood have? The pastor.

"I was walking around trying to decide if I should see Pastor Newman. The things he said really got me thinking. I've been contemplating seeing him ever since our dinner. I couldn't tell the cops that I was thinking about seeing a Cabotist pastor. It's not illegal, but if they put that in my file, it'd be the end of my job at Ultracorps. Dating a Cabotist might not be that much better, but at least it won't get me blacklisted."

Becky sighs and puts her hands over her eyes. She didn't like that answer, but I can't tell why.

"You know, Gavin, you're an excellent liar. You look me right in the eye, and you don't shake, even a little. But part of being a good liar is saying something that could possibly be true," Becky says. I can feel how disappointed she is in me.

"I'm telling you the truth. I know I was hostile towards him at dinner, but he got through to me. They spend so much time teaching us how awful Cabot is, I had never considered the possibility that he was anything but pure evil."

"I know you Gavin. You're no Cabotist. I'm aware that you haven't been in a relationship before, but believe me, they don't work without trust. If you're not going to tell me the truth, you can just leave," she demands.

"Becky."

I try to reach out to her, but she pulls away.

"The truth, now. Or leave and don't come back," she says firmly.

I walk towards the door as I consider my possibilities. I should walk out. I have bigger things to worry about. I have 152 hours to come up with a plan to deal with The Beast. I should be worrying about my confrontation with him, not my relationship. Who I'm dating doesn't really matter if I'm dead.

But if I walk out, I'll be alone. It will just be me, the muggers I fight, the monsters I hunt, and a job I couldn't care less about. I deserve one way to be happy without having to risk my life. I deserve Becky, or a shot at hanging on to her.

And she deserves the truth. She deserves to know why I haven't been seeing her, and she deserves the right to choose if she still wants to be with me. I know it's wrong to lie to her, but I did it anyway. Just because I don't have to feel shame and guilt doesn't mean I get to be a liar. I don't want to be a liar anymore. I want to be someone who tells the truth, especially to people who I care about. So that's who I'm going to be.

"I lied to the cops because I was who they were out looking for. I am the vigilante," I say slowly and clearly.

This stops Becky in her tracks. She was prepared for more lies, but not that.

"No, that's silly, you can't be. Everybody says he's an old man," she says.

I relax the muscles of my face and wrinkles quickly form. I can see the intrigue in her face, disgust too. I turn my back and make the muscles taught again.

"I'm sorry I had to tell you like this," I say and hang my head.

"How long have you been doing this?" She asks still in shock.

"It started the night we met. I came across some thugs who were about to hurt a young woman. I imagined that she was you, and I had to do something. Somebody has to do something."

"Why did you keep this to yourself? Why didn't you tell me sooner?" She asks incredulously.

"I don't know. I kept telling myself it was just a temporary thing, so I didn't have to tell you. It made me feel so good to do it. Helping people is the one thing besides you that makes me happy. I keep meaning to stop, but I just can't."

"So, that's why I haven't been seeing you lately. It's not because they have you cleaning the labs at Ultracorps. It's because you've been spending your nights running around as an old man acting like you're the second coming of the Savior of Seattle."

"Yes, and I'm sorry. I want to see you. I try to, but every night I see you is another night that some poor person might get hurt. It's hard to think that us having a date night is more important than stopping a rape or a murder."

"What about you? Did you ever stop to think that you might be killed? You're not like the Savior. You're not bulletproof or as strong as a train, unless you've been lying to me about your abilities, too," she says with a combination of fear and anger.

"No, I haven't. It's not like I'm a weakling though. I'm stronger and faster than any normal man, and I heal quicker too," I counter.

"Can you heal from a bullet to the head?"

"I don't understand. When we talked about this at dinner with your father and the pastor, you were happy about the vigilante. You said: 'He's just helping people. I know it's not something we see a lot, but come on. It's a good thing. I don't see what the problem could possibly be.' "

"Maybe I did say something like that, but that was before I knew the vigilante was you."

She didn't say something like that, she said exactly that. I even mimicked her inflections perfectly, but I don't think pointing that out will help me in this discussion.

"So it's good if someone else risks their life to be a hero, but if I do it it's a bad thing?" I ask.

"I thought it was some old Different who had nothing to live for. You're young. You have lots to live for, lots of reasons that should make you not want to risk your life," she says, trailing off.

I think I'm starting to understand why she's so mad. It's not just that I lied to her or that what I'm doing is illegal. She's hurt because she isn't reason enough to keep me from taking risks, that my feelings for her aren’t strong enough for me to play it safe.

"Everyone has excuses for not making the world a better place. They make up rationalizations for not helping others or sticking their own necks out. If people didn't have excuses, the world would be very different. There are always reasons not to do something. I can't make everyone else ignore those excuses, but I can make myself. I can make myself try to do something that helps people, try to do something that makes the world a better place. No matter how fantastic you are, or how much I care about you, I still have to try to help," I answer.

Becky takes a moment to digest what I said. When she speaks, I honestly can't tell if she's about to kick me out or run over and kiss me.

"I suppose it’s hard to be mad at you when your crime is that you can’t stop helping people,” she says with a smile, but I can still see the hurt in her eyes.

“So you forgive me?” I beg.

“Not quite, but I think I can get there.”

“That’s the best thing I could hope to hear.”

I walk over to her and grab her shoulders gently. I kiss her slowly and deeply.

“I’ll call you tomorrow. I am going to be very busy for the next week, but we will do something after that, I promise,” I say and start to head out the door.

“It’s already so late. Why don’t you just spend the night here?” Becky asks. And I thought forgiving me was the best thing I could hope to hear.

#

I know I should be thinking about The Beast. I know I should be looking back through my memories of last night, my fight with The Beast, if it could be called a fight. I should be probing for some weakness I can exploit. I’m not as strong or as fast as The Beast, but I am smarter than him. I have 144 hours to come up with some way to beat him.

But thinking about The Beast is depressing, and I don't want to be depressed right now. Right now I want to sit on the Slug until I get home and enjoy the fact that there is a huge weight lifted off my shoulders. I did not like having to lie to Becky when I was out being the vigilante, and now I won't have to. Now if I can't see her, she'll know it's for a good reason.

Not only that, it feels great to finally tell someone that I'm the vigilante. I've been out there risking my life for months, at least someone finally knows it's me. I know I shouldn't need recognition, I know I should be helping people because it's the right thing to do. Still, it's nice that someone is proud of me, even if it is my girlfriend.

An incoming call on think.Net breaks me out of my blissful state. I can't tell who's calling, so I know it's Nita. What could she want?

>>>Gavin, you have to stop what you are doing.

<<<I'm riding the Slug home. Is it going local or something?

>>>Now is not a time for humor. I am telling you as your friend: you need to cease your nocturnal activities.

I know what she's insinuating, but I'm not going to say it. Maybe she thinks I'm gambling or doing some other illegal thing. She's never wrong, but there's a first time for everything.

<<<What do you mean?

>>>I know you are the vigilante.

That's it, it's all over. The Slug is going to stop, and the cops are going to come. I'm about to be taken away to Great Basin. I will spend the rest of my life in jail. At least I have some good memories to relive while I'm inside. There is no point denying it now. I don't think I can come up with a lie convincing enough for the smartest person on earth.

<<<How long have you known?

>>>I pieced it together with 99.4% certainty after cross-referencing the police reports of the vigilante with your recent Slug line entry points. After your interactions with the police last night, my certainty is 99.99% repeating. Don't worry, the other Librarians

do not know. I have been investigating this in an unshared part of my mind. We all have our secrets.

<<<If you already knew, why have you let me do it this long?

>>> I enjoyed hearing about your exploits when I first read the reports. It raises public opinion of Differents. You are performing a commendable task. I have often wondered why other Differents have not pursued a similar goal. I would think the Savior of Seattle would have inspired more copycats, even if it is illegal. In the fifteen years since the Savior was active, there have been but a handful of instances of Differents acting on their own to help people. I never expected someone with your limited abilities to break the mold.

<<<Why do you want me to stop if you approve? I managed to get away from the police.

>>>I want you to stop because I am your pal. You did outsmart the police, and perhaps you could continue to do so. They will continue to hunt you. They blame you for the deaths of two officers, but that is not why you should desist. Battling muggers and saving children from burning buildings is something that suits your abilities. Hunting The Beast does not.

<<<You know about The Beast? Why haven't you done something about him? Why don't you send the police after him? Don't you know how many people he has killed?

>>>I have a much better idea of the number of people he has killed than you do. Do you know how many murders there were last week in the Los Angeles Metro Area?

<<<No.

>>>There were 101 were reported: 38 stabbings, 22 shootings, 15 by beating or strangulation, 11 by arson, 7 thrown off buildings, and 8 that might have been killed by The Beast. And those were just the reported deaths. The actual number of murders last week was probably closer to 125. Frankly, the Pazota crime family kills more people most weeks than The Beast. Believe me, the police would like to stop all of the crimes committed in the Metro Area, but they do not have the resources. It is a simple numbers game.

<<<Which means he's killing the poor, not the rich people who live in the Metro Center.

>>>I am not going to lie to you and tell you the response would be the same if he were targeting the wealthy, but that is only part of the reason. We have been tracking him for years. We tried to stop him in the Chicago Metro Area. Perhaps you have heard of "The Beast's Feast?" He killed thirty-seven police officers, three Different agents, and hundreds, maybe thousands, of innocent people before we lost track of him. This is that same Different. He is committing fewer murders now. I am concerned about what will happen if we provoke him.

<<<How come everyone thinks the OEC did stop him?

>>>I know this may shock you, but the government lies. The Beast killed the two agents who went after him on the plains, and they were the best The Office of Exceptional Cases had to offer.

<<<What if The Beast isn't just killing poor people? I found evidence that he might have killed that missing Metro Area Alderman. His briefcase is in an abandoned building on Crenshaw Boulevard.

>>>I will share that information with the police. Nevertheless, that does not change the fact that The Beast is too dangerous for you to pursue.

<<<You already said I've surprised you by being the vigilante. Maybe I'm more capable than you're giving me credit for.

>>>Even if you are more able than my original estimates, you still do not stand a chance. I am not certain anyone short of the Savior of Seattle in his prime could defeat this man. He is nearly impervious to telepathic attacks, heals as fast as many Regenerators, and he is immensely strong. Not to mention his incredibly enhanced senses. I would wager that he is already aware of you and the fact that you are hunting him. The sole reason you are alive is that he is a Cabotist and as such, does not believe in violence between Differents. If you push him or corner him, he has shown that he is capable of breaking from his principles.

<<<It’s too late. He already found me. He expects me to meet him in a week.

>>>Then you are to stay away from the slums entirely. Go to work and then go straight back to the Barracks. The Beast will not come near you if you stay there.

<<<My girlfriend is out in the slums.

>>>Then tell her you will not be seeing her for awhile, or have her come visit you. This is serious Gavin. It is a matter of life or death. I need you to promise me that you will stay away from The Beast.

<<<Okay, okay. I’ll stay away.

>>>Say it. Say you promise.

<<<I promise. I promise I’ll stay away.

>>>Thank you.

She’s right, I probably should stop being the vigilante. My injuries keep making me miss work, the police are after me, I never spend any time with my girlfriend, and the smartest person in the world just told me it’s going to get me killed. But I don’t want to stop.

It makes me happy, not the fake happy I can make myself anytime, a legitimate happy. I still don't get why or how, but helping people makes my dopamine and serotonin levels rise without my forcing them. It's like I'm a normal person. Maybe it's because I've always wanted to be a hero, ever since I was a little kid and learned about BlueHawk protecting democracy from the Russians.

There isn't a difference between the happy I can generate and the one I feel while I'm out on patrol, at least there shouldn't be. Chemicals are chemicals. But somehow, it feels better to know it's legitimate, to know that I'm feeling happy because I earned it, not because I decided I want to be.

I deserve to be happy. Everyone does. No matter what Cabot did or what the government thinks. It is my right to pursue happiness. Not only that, what makes me happy is helping the helpless. I spend my nights risking my life to help people that everyone else has forgotten about. Section 26 might teach that what I'm doing is wrong, but I know it isn't. I know I'm a hero.

She's right about this being a matter of life or death, but it's the deaths of hundreds of innocent people. If the police aren't going to do something about The Beast, someone has to, and I'm the only one who's willing. I don't like being a liar again, but sorry Nita, I'm going to break my promise. The Beast needs to be stopped. To do that, I'm going to need a gun, a big one.

20

All of my Chosen Sons will be welcome in my kingdom for eternity, only those who have turned away from me, only those who have turned away from their own brothers, will be denied entry.

Chosen Sons: 42

After killing the OEC agents in the plains, Tom knew what he had to do. He must strike back at the government, at those men who would send Chosen Sons to die. They needed to hurt like he did. But not in Chicago. The police would be waiting for him there. It was time for a new Metro Area to know it belonged to the Chosen Sons. Tom remembered enough of geography from school to point himself in the general direction of the Los Angeles Metro Area.

The beast in Tom had taken over. Tom moved at a maniacal pace, running at full speed almost the entire thousand miles and only stopping to kill and eat whatever animals came across his path. It took Tom just five days to get to the Los Angeles MA.

Tom's plan was simple: find a government building and kill everyone inside. Then he would move on to the next building and repeat. It did not matter if it was a police station, a firehouse, or a hospital. Anyone who worked for the government deserved to die.

After he arrived in the LA Metro Area, he decided to take a moment to calm down, close his eyes, and pray before his rampage.

"Lord, I don't know if you can hear me, but I want you to know I am sorry. I didn't mean to kill any of my brothers and sisters. I've tried to live righteously. I've tried to follow the teachings of Cabot, but your Forgotten Sons won't let me. They sent my own kind to hunt me down like a dog. I don't want to be a sinner, Lord. If you can hear me, please give me a sign. Tell me if I am on the right path. Tell me if hurting the government men will make them stop chasing me. Tell me how to stop being a sinner. Please, Lord I beg you."

>>>I have heard your prayers, my son.

Tom opened his eyes and looked for the source of the voice, but there was none. The voice had come from inside his own head. It sounded like his own voice.

"Lord? Is that really you?"

>>>I have seen your struggles, Thomas Calhoun. The path has not been easy for you. Still, you must stop what you are doing. Killing the government men will not bring you peace. It will simply ensure that more of my Chosen Sons hunt you.

"Please tell me what I should do. Where did I go wrong?"

>>>Your mistake was granting salvation to Forgotten Sons who did not deserve it. You must be careful of whom you feed on. The rich and powerful may deserve punishment for living off the largess of my Chosen Sons, but you are not the one to deliver that punishment. Content yourself to feed only on the poor Forgotten Sons. Give salvation to those Forgotten Sons who benefit the least from the slavery of my Chosen.

"But how can I atone for all the sins I already did? How can I make it up to you for killing three of your Chosen Sons?"

>>>In times of prayer, I may speak to you. You will act as my instrument to deliver to me certain Forgotten Sons who have earned their place in heaven. By doing my bidding down on earth, you will earn your way back into my good graces. In fact, I have a task for you now. Not but three blocks from where you stand there is a young man named Brian Leonard. Can you smell him?

The Beast sniffs the air. It is late. There are few men out on the street. One man’s scent stands out like a rose in a garden of weeds. "I think I do."

>>>Brian and his union have fought bravely to stop the expansion of Ultracorps and its Chosen Son slaves, but he has played his part. It is time for him to join me up in heaven. Deliver his soul to me and you will begin your march back to righteousness.

"I will, I swear it. Thank you. Thank you for giving me a chance to make good on what I've done."

>>>You may show your appreciation by doing what I have asked of you.”

"I'll do good, Lord. You'll see."

#

The Beast picks at his teeth with the large claw of his index finger. He loses focus and slices his gum open. He howls in pain. It has been four days since he had Gavin read *Chosen Sons*. The Beast has been anxious the entire time. He is having trouble staying patient. He wants to go to Gavin, he wants to embrace him. He wants to talk to him about just how great it is knowing that they are both part of God's chosen race.

The Beast knows he cannot do that. He knows if he goes after Gavin at his Ultracorps job, someone would spot him. They would tell the police, the police would come after The Beast, he would kill them all, and the government would send more OEC agents. The Beast would end up having to sin again. The same thing would happen if The Beast went to Gavin in his Ultracorps house. The Beast knows this, but that doesn't make it any easier to wait.

He drops to his knees to pray for guidance and strength.

"Lord, I know I'm being greedy. I know you've already done more than I deserve by giving me a chance at redemption, but I'm begging you, talk to me. Tell me that saving Gavin counts for something. Tell me I'm following the path you want me to."

The Beast waits, and waits, but there is no answer. The Beast starts to get angry. Why would God speak to him only when there is killing to do? The Beast thought God wanted more Chosen Sons to accept Cabot. Isn't saving Gavin's soul worth more than saving the souls of some pitiful humans?

The Beast needs someone to explain this to him. He needs someone who can make sense of God's plan. Maybe Pastor Newman would know. Maybe there's some part of *Chosen Sons* that The Beast doesn't understand. He sets off towards the church.

21

All Different individuals are required to maintain a think.Net account at all times, at their own expense. The records of all activities and transactions on that account must be made available to law enforcement agencies whenever requested. Different individuals can have no expectation of privacy on think.Net.

Article 2 Section 4 of the Different Act of 1996

Calling this an antique store is a stretch by any definition; it's more of a junk shop. It's full of all sorts of things from before the Plagues. There are books, toasters, washing machines, refrigerators, and dozens of other electronic devices I can't recognize from any think.Net shows. Now they are all useless. Of course, they've all been picked through for any copper or steel.

There are more televisions than any other thing. I don't see any that are intact. In the New York Metro Area, there's supposed to be a television station that still broadcasts. There are enough wealthy people there to pay for the televisions' electricity to keep the station running. All that money for something worse than think.Net. Wealth makes people do silly things.

"What were you looking to buy?" the guy behind the counter says.

I remember my conversation with P-Dub on think.Net. Even though I only have 111.5 hours until I'm supposed to meet The Beast, it was still a difficult decision to make.

<<<Hi Peter, its Gavin Stillman.

>>>P-Dub.

<<<Excuse me?

>>>My name is P-Dub.

<<<Okay. Hi P-Dub.

>>>What up Gav-Balls? You finally call to ask me out? I'm insulted. You should know I'm out of your league.

<<<Good one. I'm calling because I was going to head down to Santa Monica, and I wanted to ask you how it works down there.

>>>It works easy. Everyone down there takes cash only and doesn't ask any questions.

<<<Where am I supposed to get the cash?

>>>By dancing for my amusement... Where do you think you get the cash? The bank, you have a job don't you? Professional Fast Food Eater or something like that?

<<<Isn't that suspicious? Don't they track all Differents' financial transactions?

>>>You really are a wuss, huh? If you're so paranoid, there's a place for that too. There's an Antique Shop at Lincoln and Colorado. Go and tell them you want something rare, something with character, then tell them how much you want to spend. Say that exactly. It'll look like you bought an antique, but really you get a piece of junk and your cash. They keep 10% for the trouble.

<<<Okay, that's sounds great. Thanks a lot.

>>>You want some more recommendations. I saw this Morpher girl down there last week, let me tell you...

"Hey, earth to kid. What are you looking to buy?" the shopkeeper asks again.

I almost forgot I wasn't in my old man disguise. I think I'm safer doing this as Gavin Stillman. The police aren't on the lookout for him. They still think the vigilante is an old man.

The junk shop attendant is a friendly-looking guy with a big smile. The two guards do not look friendly. They keep their hands on the guns at their hip, just like every other antique shop.

"I'm looking for something rare, something with character. I'm looking to spend ten thousand dollars," I say, just like P-Dub told me.

"That's an expensive request. I've never seen you before and you just waltz in and ask for a unique heirloom that pricey, it's a little suspicious. I hope you don't mind if we check you out," the cashier says.

I feel a Telepath creeping into my mind. One of the guards is more than just muscle. He's trying to peer into my memories, my thoughts. He wants to see if I'm a cop. I do show him my thoughts, but only those that I want him to see. My job, my roommate, my frustration at work. I hide anything that might make them hesitate to give me the money, like the fact that I'm going to use it to commit what's technically a crime. I can feel the Telepath looking through my mind, but I get to control the feed of information. That's how I fooled the Section 26 Telepaths. That's why they don't know I can do this.

The cashier smiles at me. His Telepath must have given him the okay.

"I have just the thing." He picks up a round piece of aluminum with hinges on the back and hands it to me. "A Waffle-Mate, it will give your apartment that touch of class. If you'll just think.Net me the money, it can be yours, and I'll get your change."

I get a think.Net transaction request for ten thousand dollars. That's just about every penny I have left: my father's life insurance payment, this month's rent, and even my Cost of Living payment. If I survive the month, I'll be hit with a hefty late fee and an interest rate hike. I'm hoping I'm around long enough to have that problem.

"Thank you, just a moment," the cashier goes into the back. I hear him shoving paper into a bag. He comes back and hands me the bag.

"There's your change. Don't forget your Waffle-Mate," he reminds me.

I walk out with the useless appliance and what I really bought: a bag full of money. I walk a few blocks counting it. Nine thousand dollars in old paper money, that's all they take in Santa Monica. The kinds of things they sell around here are the kinds of things people don't want records of on think.Net.

I toss the Waffle-Mate in a dumpster that's full of other people's unwanted "antiques." This wouldn't be a tough puzzle for the police to solve. I bet they're getting a cut. Cops need a place to launder money too. I walk the few blocks from the junk shop into the heart of Santa Monica.

I bet every Metro Area has a place like this. They even had black markets in Ancient Rome. There are always places for people to buy things that the government doesn't want sold. Tranq is everywhere here. Even before I get to the heart of the neighborhood, I'm asked four times if I'm looking to be calm. Tranq is not all they have either. For a price, they offer a plethora of lesser-known, Different-made drugs and even some Pre-Plague stuff. Nothing can stop mankind's will to mess up his brain.

In addition to the drug dealers, there are the Gratifiers, both Morphers and Telepaths. They are the latest iteration of the world's oldest profession. Then there are the Mind-Scrubbers, Telepaths who can erase incriminating or painful memories. Some can event implant memories, making you feel like you did something that you didn't actually do. People use it have imaginary ski vacations or treks through the Amazon. Sure they are someone else's memories, but memories are all you'd get from those adventures anyway, and lots of those experiences aren't possible anymore, thanks to Cabot.

I can't even imagine what kind of money this black market generates. It's enough to pay off a lot of important people. Nobody even tries to hide what they're doing. They seem confident that nobody is coming to arrest them. There's even a Walter sweeping the sidewalk. They have better government services here than in Becky's neighborhood

There seem to be plenty of stores selling just what I need, guns. God bless America. They are the least illegal thing for sale on the black market. Thanks to the Second Amendment, anyone who can afford a gun still has a right to buy one, unless, of course, you're a Different. The Bill of Rights doesn't apply to us, not the whole thing anyway. We can't be trusted with guns.

The government now tracks all gun purchases, which is a bit of an inconvenience for criminal types. They prefer to pay cash and avoid registering. I don't think that's a problem for the gun shops down here. I hope being a Different won't be a problem for them either.

I pick a shop named "Firing Line" and hit the buzzer to enter. A voice yells at me to hold my D to a window so they can read it. When they see the Gamma, they must think I can't be too dangerous because I'm let inside. Still, the guard keeps his eyes plastered on me as I walk in. He fingers his machine guns as I approach the counter.

"Hello, I'm looking to buy a gun," I say.

"That's too bad. We sell cotton candy here," the grizzled old man at the counter says.

He's got scars all over his face. They look like they are from Cabot's Plague. He tried to scar all the Forgotten Sons so that they knew how disappointed God was with humans. It was one of his least effective Plagues. Less than 8% of the population ended up bearing the marks. Turned out pretty much anyone who'd ever had chickenpox was immune.

The shopkeeper looks seventy, but I bet he's fifty. There are pictures of him in a military uniform on the wall. He must have fought in the Reclamation, the Government's big push to restore law and order in the late eighties. There are quite a few medals on the wall.

"As long as it's the kind of cotton candy that can take a man down at fifty yards, then I'll take one," I shoot back.

This man is a tough SOB. I think he will like me more if I banter with him, or maybe he'll think I'm a punk kid and kick me out of his store.

"We might have something that can do that. What flavor are you looking for?" he says and points to the counters to his left and right.

I take a good long look in the displays. There's plenty of Glock 9s, .40 Caliber Smith and Wessons, and dozens of different shotguns and rifles, most of which I recognize from my think.Net research. They are not what I'm looking for. I spot my prize in the center of the display, Smith and Wesson Model 29, shoots a .44 Magnum. That gun is a cannon for your hand. It packs the power of a shotgun in a package small enough to keep hidden from The Beast. Think.Net said that hunters had successfully used the gun on elephants. I didn't think I'd be able to find such a big gun.

"Can I take a look at that Ruger .22?" I ask.

I also read up on negotiation strategies on think.Net. If I jump at the Magnum, I'll have to trade a kidney for it, and I'm not sure I could figure out how to regenerate one of those.

The Vet takes out the gun. I pretend to examine it as he looks on with disgust.

"A nice piece, but I think I'd like to see something with a little more power," I say after I'm done pretending.

"Yeah, a .22 might be good if you're expecting trouble at a kid's birthday party. For grown-ups, I'd recommended something more like a Glock. Ammo's easy to come by and it's got plenty of pop. Plus, it's easy as pie to take care of."

He takes a Glock out, and I pretend to examine it for a while. Then I let out a fake little laugh and say, "Whoa, what is that thing?" I point at the .44 Magnum.

“That? You don't want that. Thing is a loud as a bomb. You shoot that and every cop for three miles will know right where you are."

"It's just so cool looking. Isn't that the gun Dirty Harry used?" I ask.

He perks up a bit when he hears that. He's old enough to have seen the movie. I just saw a reference to it on the think.Net article about Magnums and took a chance.

"Sure is. We got a Different here who's got some culture," he says to neither the guard nor me. "I didn't think a kid like you would watch the classics."

"My dad made sure I watched them all on think.Net. Could I hold it?" I say.

The old Vet sighs but gets the gun out. While he does that, I look up Dirty Harry on think.Net. They have synopses of most of the Pre-Plague movies. When he hands me the gun, I grab a hold of it and point to an imaginary bad guy.

"You've got to ask yourself one question: Do I feel lucky? Well, do ya, punk?" I recite from the article.

"Hah, not bad. You're all right. Your pops is, too."

"He was. He's dead now."

I should feel bad about exploiting my father's death, but luckily I don't have to. Guilt is not something I miss. I watch what I said sink into the Vet. I think I scored some sympathy points.

"You want to shoot it?" he asks.

"I thought that would bring every cop for three miles?"

"We've got a solution for that problem. Our customers need somewhere to practice. What's the point of having a gun you can't shoot?"

The Vet leads me down to a staircase in the back. There's a basement, which is not too common in Los Angeles. He opens the door and something strikes me: silence. The door doesn't echo in the basement, and I cannot hear any air flow. I don't like it. Is he luring me into some sort of trap? I start prepping my body to fight as we head down the stairs

The Vet turns on the WormLight, which reveals a forty- or fifty-year-old bearded man in the corner who looks semi-conscious. The room stinks of Tranq.

Who's that? I try to ask, but my voice makes no sound.

What's going on? I can't hear myself saying it. Now I get it, the guy on the floor is a Different.

The Vet goes over to the man on the floor and shakes him a bit, which seems to wake him from his Tranq calm. Now I can hear myself breathing.

"Best two hundred bucks a month I'll ever spend. He absorbs sound and doesn't want to work for Ultracorps. Nobody sells more guns than me because nobody else lets you try it out before you buy. After you buy, you can come back to shoot anytime," the Vet says proudly.

The lucky Different must have been born before Section 26 and COL obligations. I bet his body is powered by sound too, so no big food bills or the taxes that come with that. He's free to do whatever he wants, but instead he's a Tranq-Head. What a waste.

"Target is over there," the Vet says and points to a makeshift dummy.

He loads the gun and hands it to me. It's a lot heavier when it's loaded. The Vet yells to the Different on the floor and the room goes silent again.

I point the end of the gun at the target and squeeze off a round. It bounces off the wall, ten feet away from the dummy. I try again and only miss by eight feet. I signal to the Different, who's a bit more with it now, and he turns the sound back on.

"I haven't ever shot before. Could you give me some pointers?" I ask.

I hand the gun back to the Vet. He reloads it and takes aim down range.

"You want your feet shoulder length apart. Lead with you left foot. Look down the barrel with your dominant eye and take aim. Breathe in and exhale. Then you want to squeeze the trigger slow, don't jerk it, cause that'll throw you off," he says and yells, "Sound off!" to the Different.

He fires off one shot. It pierces the chest of the dummy, sending out a chunk of B-Crete. Then he shoots again, hitting the dummy in the arm. He signals for me to come over and try.

I have my body mimic his position. Left foot forward, feet shoulder length apart. I look down the barrel with my right eye. I don't have a dominate one. I breathe in and out and squeeze the trigger. It hits the dummy in the leg, off by about a foot from where I was aiming. I add a little bend to my elbow because it feels right and shoot again. I nail the dummy right in chest, exactly where I was aiming. I then put two more shots in the exact same place, no more than an inch off. Shooting is in my muscle memory now, and my muscles never forget.

I follow the Vet back up to the storefront. I hear him laughing as soon as we get to the top of the stairs.

"You got the hang of that pretty quick didn't you?" he says once I can hear again.

"I just relaxed and remembered Dirty Harry. He taught me all I need to know."

"Dirty Harry couldn't shoot like that. I tell you what, I've never seen three shots so close together. My guess is the Good Lord has blessed you with help for your shooting."

"Yeah, I'm pretty good at repeating motions."

Perfect, actually, but no one likes someone who talks like that.

"That was fun. What do you want to try next, a Berretta? A Saturday Night Special? What's your price range?"

"You know, I kind of liked the .44. How much is that?"

"I told you, that's too much gun for you. You want something more practical. Anyway, I've only got a few boxes of ammo for it."

"It's not like I'm going to be using the thing. It's just for target practice and emergencies," I say back.

"I'm not looking to sell it, kid. I just keep it around because it catches the customers' eyes. They designed it to take down big game like moose and bears. Cabot didn't leave too many of those around."

Hunting big game is just what I'm doing. I need that gun.

"It's just that it reminds me of my father."

He lets out a big a sigh. "Even if I would be willing to part with it, it couldn't be for nothing. That piece was rare even before the Plagues, not to mention the trouble I could get in for selling to a Different. I'd need at least thirteen thousand for it."

Now the negotiation begins.

"You just said it isn't practical, which means nobody else wants it. I'll give you six thousand."

"You think too much. How many of those cannons do you think are left in the world, and that work on top of it? I can't go lower than eleven thousand."

"I can't go higher than seven thousand. I see what you're saying about it being rare and all, but I can't imagine you will get another offer like this anytime soon."

The Vet lets out another sigh and furrows his brow. He comes to some sort of conclusion

"Eight thousand five hundred, including all the shells or you can walk out right now. That's a special deal for lovers of fine culture, and I don't want you coming back and complaining or telling the cops where you got it."

"Deal." I only have 109 hours. I need this gun.

22

Even when the path seems difficult, know that you are never alone, my Chosen Sons. Your Lord is always with you. If you can endure, if you can live up to the magnificent gifts I have bestowed upon you, you will create paradise here on earth.

Chosen Sons: 54

The Beast hurries over to the church, jumping from rooftop to rooftop. Once he's on the building he bangs on the roof, which is how he tells the pastor it's time to head up to talk. The pastor is sleeping, and even though he feels compelled by God to hurry, it takes his frail body several minutes to get dressed and climb the stairs to meet The Beast. The Beast is waiting for him, pacing furiously.

"Your Grace, it is an honor to have you in my presence, as always. To what can I attribute this honor today, and at this hour?" the pastor asks.

"I need to talk to you, Pastor Newman. I've been trying to figure it out on my own, like I know I should, but I can't make sense of it," The Beast says.

"What is it, Your Grace?" the pastor asks with concern.

The pastor is trembling but trying his best to hide it. Seeing The Beast this upset is a terrifying sight. He has to be careful not to draw The Beast's ire onto himself.

"Why would God care more about me sending a few humans to heaven then about me saving the soul of a Chosen Son?" The Beasts asks, begging for an answer.

"I'm sorry, Your Grace, I don't understand. What are you talking about?" the pastor asks. He knows he has to.

"I did it. I talked to one of my brothers. We didn't fight—well, not much anyway. I got him to read *Chosen Sons*."

"That's fantastic news. Truly wonderful. So few Chosen Sons get to read Cabot for themselves," the pastor says with as much excitement as he can muster. He wants to turn this into a happy conversation.

"I thought it was good news. That's why I'm so confused. Why hasn't God spoken to me? Why hasn't He told me I done good?"

"Your Grace, I'm sure you are familiar with the adage 'God works in mysterious ways.' It is not our place to question Him, and it is not His job to explain Himself to us. If… excuse me, when, the Lord speaks to you, it will be the right time. You just have to trust in God," the pastor says trying to reassure The Beast and keep the creature calm.

"I know, pastor, I know, but it's hard. I don't want God to speak to me just when there's killing to do. I want to know He's happy that I saved Gavin."

"Excuse me, did you say Gavin, Your Grace? Is that the name of the Chosen Son whose soul you saved?" the pastor asks.

"I did. He's that vigilante everyone's been talking about, if you can believe it. He's not an old man, not really, that's just part of his gift from God. His tattoo said Anthropology Control, or something like that."

"Anthropomorphic Control."

"Huh?"

"Anthropomorphic Control. It means Gavin has complete control of his body. He makes his heart beat and his hair grow."

"How do you know all that? Gavin didn't come to see you already did he? We aren't supposed to meet here for another three days." The Beast says excitedly.

"No, I met the boy at the home of one of my parishioners. Gavin is dating the man's daughter. I'm sorry to say this, Your Grace, but I do not think the boy will accept Cabot. I argued with him over dinner, and he was about as far from a Cabotist as anyone I have ever met."

"That was before. You're good at talking, but Cabot wrote the words of God. Gavin read them for himself."

"I know, Your Grace, and perhaps I am wrong, but I would be

shocked. Gavin thinks he's in love with the girl. It may just be a puppy love, but young men are notorious for thinking their crush is true love."

The Beast stops and thinks for a moment. Pastor Newman lightly shifts his weight between one leg and the other, worried. The Beast doesn't usually stop to ponder like this.

"That explains it," The Beast says suddenly, "That explains why God hasn't talked to me. I ain't finished what I started yet. I should have known it wouldn't be easy. My sins are too big for that. I'm going to have to do more to save Gavin's soul. I need to show him that deep down, he knows he's better than the humans. I need to show him that if he has to, he'd kill one just the same as me. Now where does that girlfriend of his live?"

"Is it really necessary to involve her? She and her father are devout Cabotists. They are bedrocks of our community."

"In that case, she should be thrilled serve a Chosen Son. She's got some atoning to do. She knows God forbids love between Chosen Sons and Forgotten Daughters. Gavin knows that too, now. I think I might know a way to save both their souls."

"Please, Your Grace, I'm begging you. We have so few believers as young as her."

"Are you saying you don't want to help me? 'Cause you know God commanded you to serve His Chosen Sons. If you won't help me with this, you know how else I like to be served."

The Beast takes an intimidating step forward. The pastor has to put his hand on his desk to keep from fainting.

23

Every U.S. citizen, permanent resident, or visitor shall submit himself or herself to the Genetic Incongruity Scan. The results of the test must be shared with the individual. All individuals must submit proof of such testing when requested by government agents, and submit themselves to retesting upon the request of any government actor.

Article 2 of the Different Acts of 2005

I don't know why, but I feel safer with the gun hidden in my waistband. The Beast could still drop down on me any time I'm walking around outside and kill me. He could probably break my neck before I could get off a shot. But maybe with the gun I have a chance. Some hope is better than no hope.

I'm going to need a plan to beat The Beast. If I just charge at him shooting, he will tear me to pieces. He can obviously survive gunshots. He wouldn't have been able to kill all those policemen in the Chicago MA if he couldn't. At the same time, he's not invincible. My punches might not have hurt him much, but I did get him to yelp in pain. I'm gambling that he hasn't been tested with such a high caliber bullet delivered with precision to a weak spot.

I only have 97 hours until I'm supposed to meet him at the church. Luckily, I have the perfect place to spend the day lost in my head planning my strategy: work. After all the excitement, it feels nice to have nothing but ten hours of boredom in front of me. Dr. Cole and Dr. Olsen made some breakthrough over the weekend, and they don't want to share yet. They seem like they'll be ignoring me for a while. As a bonus, it made them forget that they were mad at me for missing so much work.

I close my eyes and relax into the world of my memories. They made me try to explain the experience when they had me in Section 26. I can re-experience any memory I've made since I learned to form memories consciously. I know where all my memories are stored, and when I pull up one bit, all of the related memories become easy to recall. I remember all the sights, the sounds, the smells. I can put myself back in the memory. Then I can freeze it and explore the world.

The limitation is I can only see what I experienced originally. If I try to look anywhere I didn't look when I first formed the memory, I can’t see anything. Buildings are distorted, and the ground beneath my feet has holes in it from where I wasn’t looking.

The Section 26 interviewer didn't seem satisfied with my description. I told him it is like trying to describe sight to a blind man. I don't know how to explain much of how I experience the world to normal humans. Even most Differents don't understand. Most of them still have normal human minds, only altered bodies.

I look back through my nights on patrol, back to that first night when those thugs knocked me out. When I run back through the memory, I can hear a strange sound, almost like raindrops falling. I was too distracted to notice it at the time, but now I know what it was. The Beast was running on the roofs above me. How can someone so big move so quietly?

I search through the images in my mind. I wasn't looking at the roof all that often, considering I was in a fight. At one point when I whirled around, I did catch a fleeting glimpse of a figure in the shadows, looking down on us.

There's no sign of him again until just before I got knocked out. The sound of rain drops. The Beast coming to rescue me. Would it have killed him to be a little faster and save me a head wound?

I try to remember what happened after the thug hit me. I scan for little bits and pieces, but there's nothing, like no time passed at all. My memory jumps from standing on the street to sitting on the Slug car, with Ben the train conductor asking if I am okay.

I search through the other nights I patrolled and listen to the sounds I can recall. I hear raindrops on the night I got into a fight with the Tranq dealers, when I thought the one guy big guy had run off scared. Now I know that isn’t what happened. The Beast took care of the big guy for me.

He was also around the night I saved that family and their rat from the fire. It's hard to hear the raindrop sound of his feet over the roar of the flames, but he was there. I wasn't focusing on it at the time, but I did hear some strange booms before I found those holes that led me out. Did he make a path for me?

All that my little trip down memory lane did was confirm that he moves like a ninja, and he's saved my life at least four times, if I count the other night with the cops. This information is not helping me. I did a good job if my plan was to lower my confidence level. I make myself ignore the obvious point that I got my clock cleaned by some punks, and now I'm trying to take down a creature from Greek mythology. I'm much more skilled now, I tell myself.

I should think of something more uplifting, like where I should shoot. I go on think.Net and spend some time staring at anatomical models of gorillas and other primates. I compare that with what I remember from my fight with The Beast. He's like a gorilla mixed with a Neanderthal. His skull looks thick like a primitive primate's bones. I'm not sure that even my .44 could punch through it. I could try to hit him in the eye, but that's not exactly a huge target, even for me.

His chest is wide like a gorilla, which means his rib cage is more spread open. That should give me an easier shot at his heart. I can only make an educated guess at where that might be. Unfortunately, they don't have any anatomical models of monsters on think.Net.

One thing I know for sure about the wider rib cage is that his intestines and stomach are wide open. I don't think gut shots will kill him, but they might be enough to slow him down so I can deliver the finishing shot to his heart or eye.

I also know I'd be better off getting the drop on him. I'd like my chances much better if the fight starts off with him asleep. But then I'd have to know where his nests are and which one he's using now. He sticks to the slums, but that just reduces my search radius to about a hundred square miles. I could search all day, every day for six months and still not find him. Looks like a showdown outside the church is my only option.

I need to get out of my head. I got so lost in reliving my past I forgot my present. It's two o'clock already and my body needs food. It doesn't seem like I will be getting any samples from the doctors today.

I stand up from my desk and walk the few steps to the kitchen, splitting my thoughts between looking for another place to shoot the creature and wondering what there is to eat for lunch. I could use something with potassium. I'm running a little low.

Inside the kitchen, I open up the cupboard and take a quick scan. I was hoping for some Soy Snacks, but it looks like somebody polished those off already. I settle for some Millet Cakes. I'll have to choke down five or six of the things to get enough potassium. I start shoving the dense cakes into my mouth. They're like eating crackers made of B-Crete and as a bonus crumbs spill out all over me. With perfect timing, Sarah the Crash Test Dummy walks into the kitchen.

"Hey, Gavin, they make this kitchen bigger or something?" Sarah asks.

I haven't seen Sarah in months. Ever since I met Becky, I stopped going to the Big Kitchen. I wonder what she's doing here. I wave hello while I swallow my mouthful of food.

"They must have done something, because I used to see you in the Big Kitchen all the time. I haven't seen you in forever, so I decided to see what other kitchen stole you away."

This is weird. I spent weeks trying different combinations of pheromones and subtle appearance changes to get Sarah to notice me. She always acted as if she barely remembered my name. Suddenly, she's been worrying about me. Something seems off. Maybe she's just nervous, but it seems like there's something else. I can never read women that well. I understand the male mind as well as anyone possibly could, but I'm just as lost on the female mind as any other man.

"You just wait. Occasionally they put out test samples if they turn out edible. Nothing beats experimental burgers," I say clumsily after spending too long trying to figure out why she is talking to me.

"There's that awkward humor I've been missing," Sarah says and laughs. "I used to be able to count on a strangely timed joke every morning. Maybe I'll have to start coming down here, for those experimental burgers I mean."

I don't need to be Different to be able to read this. She's into me. I spent weeks throwing the kitchen sink at Sarah. Not just pheromones, I planned jokes and stories ahead of time. Weeks of trying, and I got nowhere. A few months of ignoring her, and now she's interested. Every think.Net show is right, women really do like it when you play hard to get. It's an ego boost, but also a distraction, and not one I have time for. I can't try to piece together clues to find The Beast while I'm talking to Sarah.

"You okay, Gavin? You seem distracted. I'm used to having your full attention."

"Sorry, it's just, are you guys busy in the crash test lab? Because things are nuts over here. Corporate is riding us this month."

"Oh, yeah. We're swamped. I'm just here because I had a few minutes, and I really wanted Millet Cakes. They're out of Millet Cakes in the other kitchen."

I hand her the cake package.

"Enjoy. Got to get those calories. See you around, Dummy," I say and head out the door.

"Everybody's got to eat."

As soon as Sarah says that, I stop in my tracks. That sentence triggers memories of my dinner with Becky's father and the "pastor." When we were talking about The Beast, Mr. Newman defended him, he even said, "Everyone has the right to eat." I remember the holy man seemed uncomfortable when we were discussing the attacks. I assumed it was because having a Different act like such a monster made his religion look even stupider than it usually did. But maybe it was something more…

I should investigate. Pay Mr. Newman a visit. Now that I've realized it, I feel stupid for not thinking of this before. Of course I should ask the only Cabotist pastor in the Metro Area about the only Cabotist Different in the Metro Area. That's even where The Beast wants to meet me in three days. I'm a freaking moron. I wonder if real detectives ever overlook the obvious.

"You sure you're okay?" Sarah asks.

I realize I've been standing perfectly still for about fifteen seconds.

"Just giving you some more awkward humor," I say and walk off.

#

Although I speed through the rest of the day as fast as I can, it still seems to take forever. I can never wait for work to end, but it's on a whole new level today. Still, having to be patient for five more hours is worth it. If the Mr. Newman knows how to find The Beast, I might have to stakeout his nest for hours, or even days until I see an opportunity to get the drop on him. That might mean more missed work. I don't need to pile disappearing in the middle of the day on top of that. Besides, I still have about 92 hours until I have to meet The Beast in front of the church. A few more hours at work wouldn't kill me, I decide.

As soon as Dr. Olsen dismisses me, I hustle to the Slug Station. I don't care that I'm walking so fast it looks weird. The train comes, and I zone out the whole ride to Robertson Station. I don't need any more time to plan or ponder. I need to talk to Mr. Newman. I'll figure out my next step after that.

People waste their time thinking about events over and over again before they happen. The anxiety sends many people to early graves. I don't do anxiety. I worry about a problem enough to plan for it, and then I don't think about it again until I need to. I remember anxiety from when I was a kid. I don't miss it.

When the Slug pulls into the station, I'm the first one waiting to get off. I scan the rooftops as I walk and stretch my hearing as far as it can go. I listen for the pitter-patter of The Beast's feet, but I don't hear any. When I get to the corner of Robertson and Guthrie, I have to stop my body from continuing on to Becky's house. Not today.

Instead, I turn and double-time it to Airdrome Street. Becky told me her church was there. The street is clear. There's only a Walter silently sweeping the sidewalk. That's new, they don't usually make it to the slums, but it's about time. The streets out here are filthy.

Since there's no one to see me, I relax my facial muscles and put on my old man disguise. I think Mr. Newman will be more intimidated by the vigilante than some kid he argued with at dinner.

The Cabotist Church is inside what used to be an elementary school auditorium. The rest of the school collapsed after the Plagues. Only the auditorium remained, and with just a few modifications they were able to make it into a passable church. It isn't pretty, but what is around here?

As I approach the church, I can hear Mr. Newman talking from inside. He's in the middle of a sermon. I listen as I head in and stand in the back.

"I want to close tonight with a subject that might be a little controversial. Some of you might believe that our faith prohibits us from criticizing Chosen Sons, but this is not the case. The Lord made the Chosen Sons so they would be closer to His image, but the Chosen are not perfect. If they were, they would be the Almighty Himself. They are individuals who can be flawed, the same as you or me. Sometimes, service to the Chosen Sons means pointing out these flaws.

"We all agree that the Chosen live as slaves today. What you might not realize is that the Chosen themselves share some of the blame for their servitude. They are all guilty of complacency, if nothing else. If the Chosen united, they could throw off the shackles with ease. The government may put on a show that they can control the Chosen with their blood tests and special agents, but deep down we all know that is not enough to keep the Chosen down. After all, what is an officer with a gun to a man who can topple a mountain?

"The Forgotten Sons rely on an alternate method to control the Chosen: guilt. They make the Chosen feel guilty over Cabot's Revelation. They make Chosen children feel like they are responsible for every death Cabot caused. Never mind that Cabot did what he did for the Lord, or that those children are no more guilty than anyone of Roman descent is for Carthage or every American is for the bombs dropped on Hiroshima and Nagasaki.

"The Chosen must reject this guilt. It is not theirs to carry. Once the guilt goes, the shackles shall soon follow. Now, I know the Forgotten Sons are to blame for this as well. If more Chosen had been able to read the work of our savior Cabot, then the Chosen would know the guilt is false, and they would claim their thrones as kings of the earth.

"And that is where it falls to us. On you, and me, and our countless brothers around the globe who work tirelessly to share with anyone, Chosen or human, the message of God's new prophet, Cabot. We're making a difference too, of that much you can be certain. The Chosen will take their rightful place as kings of the earth. It is simply a matter of time."

Mr. Newman finishes and he's looking right at me, even though I'm in my old man disguise. I guess that answers the question of whether The Beast and Mr. Newman know each other. I wait as the congregation makes its way out. Mr. Newman makes eye contact with me and nods his head, signaling that we should head back into what must be his office. An elderly woman stops him.

"It was such a lovely sermon today, pastor," the elderly woman says.

"Thank you, Mrs. Benet. I hope you found something useful in it," Mr. Newman replies.

"I sure did. It reminded me of my son Patrick. He was such a scaredy-cat growing up. When Patrick was a boy, we absolutely had to leave a nightlight on. That was back when we all had electricity. He grew out of that. He's a good Cabotist, my Patrick. He works hard and tithes all he can. I tell him he has to eat more. He has to be strong to keep earning money for the Chosen Sons. He works on a fishing boat..."

"Mrs. Bennet, you know I'm always happy to hear about your son, but today I'm going to have to cut that pleasure short. The Lord has work for me to do," the Mr. Newman says and looks to me.

Ms. Bennet follows his eyes, then looks down at the D tattooed on my hand.

"Oh, I see, I won't keep you. Please get to your work." Mrs. Bennet turns to head out.

She stops as she passes me and gives the best curtsey her old body can manage. "Your Grace," she says with all the conviction in the world, and then continues her hobble out of the church.

Mr. Newman leads me back into his office. I think it was a locker room when this was a high school. I can still make out a faint hint of body odor that no amount of cleaning could ever remove, even though the lockers are long gone.

There's a desk with three chairs. This is where he meets with his parishioners. This is where he tells crying mothers and fathers to tithe more to the church, even as their children go hungry. He motions for me to sit. I follow along. I should start with being civil.

I sit down and wait for the Mr. Newman to do the same. He looks nervous. He's fidgety and sweaty. Maybe he's scared of me, or maybe he's hot from delivering a sermon and his legs are tired from standing so long. Why doesn't he sit? He's waiting for me to ask him, but I'm not going to. Let him keep sweating.

"Why did you come here, Gavin?" he asks.

"Considering you know who I am, I bet you know why I'm here. I'm looking for the person who told you I am the vigilante," I say.

"It is time to stop this foolishness. You need to go home and stay there. The Beast is far too dangerous. If you keep after him, he's going to kill you and God knows how many other people. You need to stay away from him," Mr. Newman says sternly. He's used to people who eat up every word he spits out.

"So now you care about all the people he's going to kill? Is that why you haven't told anyone about him? I didn't come here for your advice. I came here for you to tell me how to find him."

"Unless you are truly ready to swear off your old life and join up with him on his killing sprees, he's going to kill you. The only reason you are still alive is because he knows it's a sin for him to kill Chosen Sons. But he's sinned before, Gavin, and he'll do it again if you corner him. You have to forget about her, it's too late."

"Wait, what do you mean, 'forget about her'?" I say.

I can see him hesitate. He doesn't want to tell me, but he knows he has to. If he says what I think he's going to say, he's right to be afraid. I stand up out of my chair and tower over him.

"Becky. He has Becky," he says while trembling. "I'm sorry. He made me tell him about her. He was going to kill me. He would have found her anyway. I didn't know what to do. The police would never listen to a Cabotist pastor, especially about something so crazy…"

He keeps making excuses, but I don't listen. The Beast has Becky. What does that monster want with her? I form a few quick theories in my head. All of them are horrible. I turn off the part of my brain that wants to shut down in a combination of terror, fear, panic, and shame. I don't need emotions now. Right now, I need to find Becky. I need to find The Beast.

Mr. Newman is still speaking, but he's not saying what I want to hear. I lift him up off the ground by his throat.

"You need to tell me how I can find The Beast, now!" I yell. I relax my grip on this throat so he can answer.

"Griffith Park, he's in Griffith Park. He wanted me to tell you," he spits out. I drop him to the ground.

"Don't do it, Gavin. He's too strong. There's nothing you can do to save her. There's nothing anyone can do. Even if somehow you got the police to believe you, he'd just kill all of them and then Becky. He is the fury of our Lord made real on this earth. All you can do is stay out of his way!" he says from the floor.

He has to yell at the end because I've already run past the door.

24

My Chosen Sons will be few in number. It is their duty to their Lord to go forth and multiply. My Chosen Daughters must bear as many children as they are able, and my Chosen Sons must spread their seed far and wide. Chosen Sons may bed as many Forgotten Daughters as they wish, but they can love and wed only their fellow Chosen.

Chosen Sons: 30

The Beast steps out onto the roof of the Cabotist church. He is angry. His howls fill the streets. Could it be true? Could Gavin really be a sinner? Could he really love a Forgotten Daughter? The stupid boy. Not just stupid, Gavin is challenging The Beast. The Beast pounds his chest.

No, it can't be that. The Beast proved his dominance on the roof. He had shown Gavin who was stronger. It is the girl's, Becky's, fault. She poisoned Gavin's mind to keep him from accepting Cabot. The Beast will smash her, smash anyone who keeps him from getting what he wants. Kill Becky! Kill her, kill them all! The Beast pounds a chimney on the roof to smithereens.

The Beast calms himself down. He cannot be like this. He has to keep control. This is all part of God's plan. He is testing The Beast. God wants to make sure The Beast has learned to control himself. The Beast needs to prove that he is safe to live with his own kind.

He can't kill Becky, yet. He has a plan. The pastor helped him come up with it. The old man was pretending to help out of devotion to the Lord. The Beast could smell that it was really fear that motivated the pastor, but The Beast is fine with that. If the pastor is afraid, The Beast can count on the old man to do his part. The Beast just needs to keep control and do his part. He has to get Becky to Griffith Park, alive. The park is abandoned, safe from prying eyes and police officers. The observatory there has a perfect view of the Metro Center. It will help The Beast convince Gavin of the error of his ways.

It takes The Beast just a few leaps to cover the five blocks between the church and Becky's house. The Beast knocks on the door. He struggles to remain calm. A burly older man answers the door.

"Hello, you must be Becky's father, Mike. It sure is nice to meet ya. I was wondering if Becky is in? I got a few questions for her," The Beast says.

After opening his door to a nightmare, the man stumbles a moment, but he manages to push through the fear and gather himself rather quickly. This is not a monster. This is a Chosen Son. The Lord made him.

"You honor me with your presence, Your Grace. Please, come in. Can I get you anything? I would consider it a blessing for you to eat or drink in our home," Mike says.

"Isn’t that nice. I didn't think anyone out here had any manners," The Beast says as he struggles to fit his massive frame through the doorway. "A glass of water if it ain't too much trouble, and call your daughter down. I can smell her, upstairs.

"What do you want with her?" Mike asks.

"I am doing the Lord’s work. That is all you need to know. Now call her. Things might get ugly if I have to go get her myself," The Beast replies.

"Of course, I want to serve the Chosen any way I can. Becky, someone wants to talk to you!" Mike yells, trying to conceal his fear. "Excuse me a moment, I’ll get your water," he adds and disappears into the kitchen.

Becky comes down the stairs, a big smile on her face. The smile turns to horror as she sees it's The Beast, not Gavin, waiting for her.

"Becky? I've got to talk to ya. Do you know Gavin Stillman?" The Beast asks.

She answers with a scream which draws Mike out of the kitchen. He’s got a butcher’s knife in one hand and a glass of water in the other. He throws the glass into The Beast’s face. The glass shatters sending shards all over The Beast’s face.

"Becky run!" Mike yells and charges at The Beast.

Mike sinks his big butcher's knife into The Beast's side. The creature howls in pain.

Becky runs by the stunned creature and makes it out the door. Mike tries to pulls the knife out of The Beast's side, but the blade is stuck.

The Beast shakes the shards of glass out of his eyes then turns his attention to Mike, who is still trying to pull the knife out of the creature. The Beast grabs the older man's arm tightly, then yanks and twists, ripping the arm out of the socket and off Mike's body. The tough old man collapses to the ground.

"Wasn't that silly. If you just kept being a good Cabotist for another minute, you coulda gone to heaven. Now you're gonna have to answer to the Lord for what you done," The Beast says.

He heads out of the door and sees Becky running down the street. She's running as fast as she can, she's already got a half a block lead. It doesn't matter. The Beast could catch up to her with a fifty block head start.

It takes The Beast less than ten seconds to overtake her and pick her by her hair. He's shaking with rage. Becky is screaming. He covers her mouth while he talks.

"Quiet down! You know you had this coming. You know God forbids love between the Chosen and Forgotten. You are supposed to have his child, and he is supposed to move on. That's how God wants it," The Beast says.

When he finishes speaking, he takes his hand off her mouth.

"Help! Help!" Becky screams.

The Beast responds by sinking a single claw into her throat, poking a hole in her windpipe. Becky's screams turn to hollow moans. The Beast throws Becky over his shoulder. She struggles and beats on his back, but it is no use.

"Relax, we're just going to the park," The Beast says.

25

The purpose of this bill is the authorization of spending for the construction of a high-speed rail to facilitate transportation in the wake of the massive fossil fuel shortage caused by the terrorist Cabot. The bill designates The Unified Logistics Technology and Research Applications Corporation (Ultracorps) as the organization responsible for the construction, maintenance, and administration of the rail system.

Preamble: Get America Moving Again Act of 1989

Pedestrians stare at me as I run down the street, but I don't care. Let them wonder about the seventy-year-old man running through their neighborhood like Jesse Owens at the Olympics. Slowing down is not an option. I have to get to Becky.

It takes me less than a minute to cover the five blocks between the Cabotist church and Becky's house. I run faster than I thought I could run. I can feel the emotional centers of my brain wanting to activate. If I let it, my mind would experience a mix of panic, fear, guilt, and anger. I push the emotions away. Feelings are not going to get me to Becky's house any faster.

If I was a normal person, I would be thinking about how this is all my fault. I'd think about how if I had just listened to Becky and everyone else and stopped trying to be a hero, she wouldn't be in trouble. I'd think about how if I could only consider someone besides myself, I would have realized the danger I was putting her in.

I slow down as I get to Becky's block and start scanning the rooftops. I finger the gun in my waistband. I want to be ready if The Beast tries to drop down on me, but the rooftops are clear. I approach Becky's door. I stop and listen for anything out of the ordinary. I hear nothing. I knock on the door.

After ten seconds with no answer and no sounds of any kind

coming from inside, I try to the door. As soon as the doorknob turns, I know something is wrong. No one leaves their front door unlocked in this neighborhood, even if they're home.

The copper twang of blood fills my nose as soon as I step into the house. I suppress the crippling panic my body wants to feel, the fear that it's Becky's blood I smell. The human mind really has some useless responses.

It doesn't take long to find the source of the blood. Mike is lying dead in the kitchen surrounded by a pool of it. His right arm is missing. It looks like he bled to death. I'm ashamed to admit that I hadn't really thought about him until now. My mind was focused on Becky. I rush upstairs and search for Becky, but I can't find any sign of her. The pastor was right, The Beast took her.

I need to get her back, and it looks as if I have to walk into The Beast's trap in Griffith Park in order to do that. I head out towards the Slug, running at the same breakneck pace as before. I knock over a Walter on the way. I don't let myself feel bad about it.

#

>>>Gavin do not do this.

I shouldn't have accepted the call. I knew what she was going to say, I just had to find out if I was right. I don't know how Nita always knows what I'm up to, but she knows. At least if I talk to her, I might figure out how she plans to stop me.

<<<How do you know what I'm doing?

>>>That is irrelevant, what is important is that you stop what you are doing. You promised you would not attempt to engage The Beast.

<<<He kidnapped my girlfriend. He's going to kill her. I have to stop him.

>>>A promise means no matter what. That is the whole point of a promise. You did not just say you would not pursue The Beast, you promised you would not pursue him.

<<<Are you kidding me? Who cares about my promise? Did you hear me? I said he's got my girlfriend, and he's going to kill her. He's in Griffith Park, tell the police. They'd never believe me, but

they'd listen to you.

>>>There is no point. He will be long gone by the time the police are able to assemble a sufficient force to engage him.

<<<Then I'm her only hope.

>>>You promised.

<<<Then I guess I'm a liar.

I end the call. A second later the train stops. I guess she is going to try to stop me. I bring up a mental image map of the city. Griffith Park is far away. Luckily, there's a wide swath of slums between here and there. Hopefully, Nita isn't really mad enough to tell the cops about me.

I need to get off this stopped train. I head to the back of the car and open the emergency exit. Everyone on the train gasps as I head out onto the tracks. I'm wearing my normal Gavin face, so hopefully no one will think I'm the vigilante. That doesn't mean someone won't call the police anyway, but I have to get away. The train line is thirty feet off the ground. Too high to jump down and climbing would take too long.

There's a roof about eight feet away. I think I can make it. I get a running start, making sure I achieve top speed before I push off at the last moment, aligning my muscles perfectly to achieve the maximum jump. I clear the gap and land with a roll on the roof. I made it, but I will need bigger miracles than that today.

I try the door on the roof. Locked. I back up and slam into it with my shoulder. The door frame gives way. I head into the stairwell, down the stairs, and out of the building. I break into a run as soon as I hit the streets. I need to get away from the Slug.

#

I don't think Nita told on me to the police. In the five hours this crazy route took me, I only saw one cop. He was eating some Sweet-Fried Manna at a cart, not out on an APB. She is about twelve years old, maybe she doesn't like to be a tattletale, or maybe she thought she made her point. By stopping the train, she showed me that she means what she said. She figures no one would be stupid enough to ignore the smartest person in the world, but I guess I am. Nita has never even met me in person, how can she know what my capabilities are? All she has is a file. A file that used to say I'm a Zeta. A file I know has many gaps.

I'm pretty sure I'm safe from the cops now anyway. Besides a Walter a few blocks back, I haven't seen or heard a living soul. The houses on these streets are all collapsed and abandoned. The lots were too spread out to bother retrofitting after the Plagues. It would have been too much trouble to run Maceo Steel pipes needed to provide water and Hoover services out here, especially with the hills.

No government service means no streetlights. It's past midnight and almost completely dark out. Luckily, I can give myself excellent night vision. It takes most people's eyes about thirty minutes to fully adapt to the dark. I can make my eyes do it in two. I fully dilate my pupils, but more importantly, I increase the number of rods in my eye relative to cones. This makes my eyes much more sensitive to low-light conditions. The downside is that I lose some color in my vision, but the trade off is worth it.

I don't think The Beast has to make that trade off. I remember seeing his eyes on the roof. He has animal eyes, the kind that shine back in the dark. That means he has an extra membrane that basically doubles the amount of light his eye picks up. I wonder if I could grow that membrane.

I've finally make it to the entrance of the park. There's a dilapidated sign that points to the observatory. I follow the arrow. I bet this park used to be a nice refuge from the city. Thanks to Cabot, it looks like the setting from a Western movie. I'm sure there were beautiful trees once, but now there are just a few scraggly shrubs. I actually see a tumbleweed.

I reach the top of the path and the observatory comes into view. I bet it was more beautiful before the Plagues too. Now, it's in shambles. There are two collapsed domes, presumably where the telescopes used to be. There's one more dome still standing.

I check to make sure the gun is secure in my waistband under my shirt. I pat my front pocket to ensure the extra rounds are still there and head towards the observatory. There's not really much question as to where The Beast is. The entire inside of the observatory is collapsed. He must be on the roof, on the far side of the dome. It takes me a few minutes to find a viable route up through the rubble. I end up climbing up a half-collapsed wall covered with some faded but still beautiful artwork of constellations.

Once I get to the roof, the odor that greets me confirms I'm in the right place. I smell The Beast, he reeks like a mongrel dog. I don't think he bathes. I hear something coming from the corner of the roof. Chewing?

I shut my fear off and walk towards the sound. The Beast no doubt heard me climbing, so there's no point in delaying. I find him in the corner, digging around in the insides of some poor soul. Thank God, it's some old man, not Becky. The Beast looks satisfied, as if he has eaten his fill and is now just playing with what's left on his plate.

I need to stay calm and wait to make my move. I don’t know where Becky is. She could be hurt. If I kill him, I might never find her. I need to pretend I’m a changed man. I need to pretend I don’t care about Becky anymore. If he thinks I’ve already accepted Cabot, maybe The Beast will let her go, or tell me where she is. He didn’t seem all that bright. Maybe he’ll let it slip out. I just have to keep calm and stop myself from shooting him.

The Beast notices me and looks up. "Gavin, what took you so long, boy? I got hungry waiting. I had to have me a snack." Blood is dripping from his mouth

"I’m sorry. The Lord did not bless me with the same gifts he gave you. It takes me time to get all the way out here.”

“You remember your Cabot boy, God loves us all equal even if our gifts ain’t so equal.”

“I wanted to impress you. I wanted to try to find you before the week was up so I could tell you how much reading Cabot changed my life. I went to talk with Pastor Newman, to see if he knew how to find you, and he told me you had something to show me. Why did you want me to come all the way out here?”

“To show you this,” The Beast says and points his hand out towards the Metro Center. “Ain’t it beautiful?”

I look down on a perfect view of the Metro Center. He's right. It is magnificent. The heaven-scrapping Shimmering Tower, the impossible Hanging gardens, and an unsolvable maze of train lines all light up the night sky.

"You're right. It is beautiful," I say honestly.

"And that's just a little peek at what we could do. If the Chosen were free, the whole country could look like this place."

"You're right. We built this city even with the Forgotten Sons holding us back. They waste our talents, having us work as garbage men, or street sweepers, or taste testers. I don't want to eat hamburgers all day. It's a crime. It's blasphemy. I can do so much more. I want to be part of the miracles performed by God's new race," I say. It's disturbing how easily that came out of me.

"So this means you've accepted that you're a Chosen Son? You know that God wants you to inherit the earth?" The Beast says, grinning widely.

"It does. I'm ready to serve the Lord, to serve His new race." That was hard to say at least.

"You don't know how happy the Lord is to hear that. You don't know how happy I am to hear that. You are my salvation. I can't wait to talk to Him about you."

This lunatic really thinks he talks to God, doesn't he?

"It's like you said. Once the words of Cabot were in my brain, they burned like a fire. I'm sorry it took me a while to come around. I've just been living with the Forgotten Sons for so long, I had accepted my slavery as normal."

"Of course. There's just one more thing. Your girlfriend. I'm sure you remember from those burning words, Cabot says there ain't to be love between a Chosen Son and a Forgotten Daughter. You need to be free to spread our kind."

"I know that now. I know it was wrong. I hope God forgives me."

"He will, if you pay a penance. The Lord forgives, but it ain't as easy as just asking."

I don't like where this is going. I start slowly moving my hand to the gun in my waistband.

“What kind of penance are we talking about?” I ask.

“Sacrifice,” The Beast says and his grin disappears.

“You don’t mean Becky?”

“I do. The Lord had his fill of love and compassion. He’s gone back to the old ways. Back to blood.”

“But Becky didn’t do anything. It was my sin,” I say. I’m starting to get desperate. There has to be some way out of this.

“She knows Cabot. She knew she was sinnin’. And even if she didn’t, the ram didn’t do nothing, but Abraham still sacrificed it to save his son.”

“Becky’s not an animal. She’s a human being.”

“There’s no difference anymore,” The Beast growls.

“You’re a madman.”

"You think I'm mad, boy? At least I ain't crazy enough to think a gun could stop me. I would have been dead years ago if bullets were enough to take me down. It's the gunpowder, boy. I can smell it."

Once what The Beast has said processes, I pull out my gun and shoot right at his gut, or right where his gut was before he moved. I see the bullet fly by him. I take aim and fire another shot as he runs for cover. It hits him in the thigh. I don't think that'll do much more than annoy him. He lets out a snarl of pain.

"You're a fool, boy, but the Lord will forgive you, and so will I," he yells from behind a block of cement.

I steady my gun and wait for him to show his face. There is a tearing sound from behind the block. The piece of cement is already hurtling towards me by the time I realize what the sound was. I barely manage to dive out of the way of the heavy chunk.

I'm back up and aiming the gun in just a few tenths of a second, but The Beast is only twenty feet away and coming at me fast. I try to aim for something vital, but he's moving too much to get a clear shot. I put two bullets into his shoulder and abdomen before he closes the distance between us.

His giant hand reaches out and grabs the gun, bending the barrel as he tears it from my grasp. He tosses it aside. His other hand grabs me by the throat. It's so big I can feel it reaching around the entire circumference of my neck. He lifts me off the ground.

"Gavin, don't you see that you and me are the same? Do you think you got more in common with the humans then you do with a fellow Chosen Son? You don't have nothing in common with them. I think you know it, deep down. If you had to, you'd be willing to kill them, just like I do. I'm going to prove it to you, boy."

With that, he takes his free hand and stabs his claws into my abdomen. He pushes his way into my insides. He works deliberately. Nerves all over my body sound the alarm as his razor sharp claws slash through my organs. A normal man would pass out from the pain. I'm left conscious to ponder if there's any way I'll survive this trauma.

He pulls his claw out, spilling my entrails out all over the roof. He tears off chunks of them and throws them over the side.

"Don't worry, I'll get help," he says and disappears for a moment.

I can't spare the thought processes to wonder what he could possibly mean by help. I'm focused on stopping the bleeding and trying to make my crippled body somehow function. My liver needs days to heal. Both my small and large intestine are useless. He damaged both of my kidneys beyond repair. Even if I manage to stop the bleeding, I will have a hard time surviving the blood poisoning from all the waste that can't be processed out of my blood. I don't even know how to begin re-growing a kidney or if I'm even capable of it.

The Beast reappears with Becky slung over his shoulder. Her hands and feet are bound and she's bleeding from the neck, but she's breathing. It's a relief to see her alive, even in this state.

"You need new organs. She's got organs. I made sure not to hurt them. All you have to do is rip her open and take them. You could just hook her stuff up to yours. I know she's a girl, but you can make it work, can't you?"

"You're insane," I manage to spit out. The effort wasn't worth it. The expansion of my lungs caused more hemorrhaging in my body.

"If you love her, you'll do it. She's a sinner, Gavin. You both are. Your love is a sin. If Becky dies now, she's headed straight to Hell.

If she dies saving your life, that guarantees her salvation. You could give Becky eternity in paradise. What's a better gift than that, boy?"

He sees that I'm not moving and starts getting angry. He stomps his feet and howls.

"Do it, Gavin, or you both die. Is that what you want? Here, I'll help you out. I'll cut her open."

The Beast sinks a single claw into Becky's chest and drags it down the length of her, carefully slicing her open like an envelope. He doesn't want to damage her organs. Somehow, she's still breathing. If I can make it out of here, I might still be able to save her.

"She'd want you to have her insides. She'd want you to live. She loves you, Gavin."

I turn away from Becky. I want to make it clear that I won't give in to this monster. Even if it means we both die. When I turn my head, I spot my chance at salvation, my gun. The barrel looks too bent to shoot, but there's still one bullet in the chamber. If I could somehow get the gun and get him close enough to me, maybe there's enough power in that one bullet to take him out.

The Beast howls when I turn away. He pounds his fists on the roof, sending up chunks of concrete.

“Don't you make me a sinner again! If you don't do this, we'll meet again in Hell."

He grabs me by the throat again. This is it, I'm about to die. I guess Nita was right. He's too strong for me. He picks me up and stares into my eyes. Then he drops me. I can see his breathing slow. He's trying to calm himself down.

The monster closes his eyes and drops to his knees. Is he praying?

"Lord, please. I'm begging you, hear my prayer. I need you. I need guidance. Tell me what I should do. Tell me how I can fix this."

His eyes open back up, and then they stare off. I'd recognize that stare anywhere. He's on think.Net? Who the hell would talk to this lunatic? Who would pretend to be God?

"I'm sorry. I thought this was what you wanted. I thought I could convert him," he says out loud.

I don't have time to think about who he might be talking to. This is my only chance. I ignore all the alarms sounding off in my body and focus on dragging myself the three feet to my gun. I grab it and hide it under me. The only way this gun will work is at point-blank range.

"I will, Lord. I'll do just what you said. Thank you. Thank you for guiding me before I sinned again."

The Beast comes out of his think.Net stare and looks at me.

"Gavin, I'm sorry. I thought you were ready to accept the truth. I was wrong, but don't you worry, I'm going to get you help. The Lord told me just what to do."

The Beast leans over, I think to pick me up, but I don't know for sure. I put my gun to his face and pull the trigger. It doesn't shoot, but it does explode, taking off my index finger and mutilating my right hand. The Beast takes a face full of shrapnel. His eyes and ears are full of blood. He drops to the ground and howls. Then he whimpers and runs off, falling off the roof of the observatory and stumbling into the pitch-black park.

At least I know The Beast won't kill me. I get to die of my injuries instead. I roll over and stare into Becky's eyes. She could be my salvation. Already, the toxins in my blood are starting to pile up. I have my body produce as much new blood as I can, but that will only do so much. It is simply a matter of time. Unless I take Becky's kidneys, like The Beast told me to.

I can imagine it now. I can envision directing my vasculature and nerves to grow into the new organs. I can imagine suppressing my immune system so it does not attack the foreign cells. It could work.

She's in bad shape. Her breathing is shallow and she's unconscious. It looks like she might not make it that much longer anyway. She's still alive though, and she deserves the chance to keep living. I push myself to my feet. To my surprise, my legs are still capable of carrying me.

I need a plan. I've got maybe half an hour until my injuries overwhelm me. It's already getting hard to think with so much of my mind devoted to dealing with the many emergencies cropping up all over my body. My gallbladder is spilling bile everywhere right now. I constrict the blood vessels in the area as tightly as I can and grow more vasculature to absorb the excess fluid.

My only options are the hospital or the police, but instead of finding the closest police station on think.Net, I have to deal with a blood clot that broke in my liver. I direct as many platelets as I can to the area and try to form a new clot. Before the clot can form, I lose another pint of blood. I need to consume some nutrients to produce more blood, but unfortunately, I don't have any insides to digest my food.

Once the clot in my liver is reformed, I can focus. I log on to think.Net. I think about hospitals and police stations, and they light up on a map. It looks like there's a hospital twenty-three blocks from here. Great, that should only take me three days in the shape I'm in. I could call for help, but they don't have a way to get all the way out here, and I'm not sure they would if they could.

I need to get down from this roof. I trudge over to where I climbed up and start slowly making my way down. The climbing opens up newly clotted wounds all over my body. Things aren't going well inside me. I'm only about three stories up, so I decide to jump for it. I feel the muscles around my Achilles rupture when I land. The damage is bad, but nothing compared to what I've already been through. I was moving so slowly from my other wounds anyway, the busted Achilles won't make much of a difference.

I begin stumbling out of the park and down towards the twenty-three blocks I have to walk to the hospital. I focus on picking my feet up and putting them down, left, right, left, right—that and keeping my heart beating. I need to keep going for Becky.

I'm so focused that I don't even hear the police officer coming. He's shouting at me, but I can't understand him. I have to stop thinking about my injuries to focus on his words.

"Gavin, Gavin are you okay?" he shouts.

I know the fact that the policeman knows my name is weird, but I can't be bothered to consider it. I have to focus on the important things.

"There's a woman on the roof of the observatory. She needs help," I say, and a blood vessel in my brain hemorrhages.

26

The Forgotten Sons take my gifts for granted. They reap the rewards of my bounty but give their thanks to science. My Chosen Sons will never question if they live in my grace. The gifts I will give them are so great divinity will be the only possible explanation. They will cherish these alms; they will build great cities and fill the earth with their progeny. They will do all this while giving praise to me.

Chosen Sons: 23

The gun explodes in The Beast's face. The shrapnel shreds his flesh, the sound makes his ears ring, and the flash blinds him. He is afraid. He has to get away. He has to hide. He leaps off the roof of the observatory but trips as he jumps. The fall is a long one, and he lands on his shoulder. He howls in pain, but he still has to get away. He charges forward, but does not see the tree in his way. He smashes through it and massive splinters lodge in his side, more pain.

The Beast ignores the pain and keeps running. Finally, after running two miles deep into the park, the ringing dies down to a faint buzz and his vision clears. As his faculties return, The Beast's fear turns to anger.

Gavin is probably dead by now. If not, he will die soon, and there's nothing the Beast can do about it. The Beast has killed another of his own kind. His damnation is assured. There will be no atoning for this. He killed the other Chosen Sons in self-defense. Those government agents gave him no choice.

Gavin was not a threat to The Beast. The Beast could have avoided the boy's pathetic attempts to find him for years. Gavin was not fast enough or strong enough to hurt him. The Beast had been impatient. The Lord had promised him a path to atonement, but he could not wait. He thought converting Gavin would be a faster way back into God's good graces. He has failed miserably. His punishment will be an eternity of torture.

The Beast howls in anger. If he is going to Hell, he is damn well going to take as many Forgotten Sons with him as he can manage. He follows his nose to the closest path out of the park, the closest path that leads to Forgotten Sons. A path that leads right to the Metro Center.

By the time he makes it out of the park, the sun has come up, and the streets begin to fill up with pathetic humans on their way to whatever pointless jobs they have. The Beast does not want to live for much longer. What time he does have he is going to spend sending Forgotten Sons to the Hell they deserve.

The Beast walks into the middle of the street, throws off his tattered overcoat, and lets out a deafening howl. A young woman on her way to work at Oasis Burger turns and sees him. She lets out a blood-curdling scream that The Beast cuts short with a slash of his claw. The Beast's next victim is a middle-aged man on his way home from a graveyard shift driving a Slug.

Soon, Forgotten Sons are screaming and running in all directions. They desperately try to get away, but their pathetic human bodies are too weak to escape The Beast. He bashes skulls in with his hands, tears out throats with his claws, and crushes spines with his weight. The Beast spares no one from his wrath. He kills men and women walking to work, children and their parents on their way to school, and old ladies on their way to the market.

The Beast is careful not to drink any of their blood or eat any of their flesh. It is not an easy thing to do. The Beast is starving. His body needs energy to heal from the fight with Gavin. Even still, he has already sent enough undeserving souls up to heaven. The people he kills now have done nothing of service to the Chosen Sons; they will join The Beast in Hell.

After a few minutes of his rampage, The Beast finds himself standing on a deserted block. Everyone is dead or has run away. The Beast decides this would be a good place to wait to die. No doubt someone has called the police by now.

They will arrive shortly with their little guns and useless body armor. They are weak and puny but enough of them will be able to stop The Beast. He will kill as many as he can before they put him out of his misery.

The Beast takes a moment to reflect on his life. If he is about to die, he would like to die remembering a happy thought. There was a time when he was happy. It was when he was still Tom Calhoun. It was before he knew he was a Different, before he knew the truth of Cabot even. It was after that first football game, when he filled in for an injured teammate and led the team to victory. Everyone was so proud of him. His father was so proud of him. They smoked cigars and Tom felt like he was on top of the world. If only it could have stayed that way.

>>>Thomas, do not do what you are going to do. Do not let the Forgotten Sons kill you. The Lord says in The Beast's mind.

"Now you want to talk? After I killed another of my brothers? Where have you been? Why didn't you stop me before I did it? I asked you for help but you wouldn't give me none. Then you told me I could still save Gavin, but instead he shot me in the face. Now he's dead, and I sinned again. Why do you keep testing me, Lord?"

>>>I have always been with you. I know your path has been a difficult one. I know you feel lost and alone. You need to trust that your trials and tribulations were necessary. I needed you to realize the true purpose for which I created you.

>>>I have filled the world with Chosen Sons, each possessing a different gift. All of my children have their own part to play in my plan. I did not create you to convert your brothers with the truth of Cabot. If I had wanted a missionary, I would have bestowed Telepathy upon you to warp minds or intelligence to power a silver tongue. Those are not your gifts. Your gifts are muscles, claws, and teeth. I made you for just one purpose: death.

>>>My Forgotten Sons have proven too resilient. Instead of seeing the truth of Cabot, the truth of their Lord's power, they have decided instead to flaunt my will. Instead of paying homage to my Chosen Sons, they have enslaved them. You have another chance at redemption. You can strike fear into the hearts of my disappointing children. You can remind them of their true place in my new world.

>>>Go now and head into the heart of this abominable city. Go to the most prominent example of mankind's hubris, the Shimmering Tower. Make an example to all of the Forgotten Sons who have grown rich off defying me. Make an example of them and make sure the entire world sees you do it. Do this, and you shall earn your salvation.

27

Different individuals are restricted from joining the military or maintaining employment in law enforcement or security roles. Different individuals associated with the Office of Exceptional Cases are exempt from these restrictions.

Article 4: Different Acts of 1996

"In, out, in, out, in, out," I chant aloud.

I can remember saying this for the last few minutes. My memory is functioning again. I'm functioning again. Nerves are firing off all over my body indicating injuries, inflammation, and infection. I can feel a large cut down my midsection that's surrounded by dozens of small gashes. I think the gashes are stitches.

Those stitches are keeping my intestines, liver, and kidneys inside of me. Except it's not my liver, it's not my intestines, they are not my kidneys. They are in the places my organs belong, but they are different. I can tell the organs aren't made of my cells. My immune system wants to attack them. How did I get someone else's organs inside of me?

I think back to what happened. I remember climbing to the roof, arguing with The Beast, the bullets that missed their target, The Beast's hands around my throat, and his claws tearing apart my insides. After that it, gets fuzzy. Keeping my broken body alive took all of my focus, so I couldn't form good memories. There was more ranting by The Beast… Becky, he wanted me to kill her. He wanted me to take her organs. No, I didn't. I couldn't have. I have to find Becky.

I snap out of my internal world and take in my surroundings. I'm in a bed, strapped to a bed actually, in a white room. I have an IV going into my left arm. There is a tray with instruments in the corner. It looks like a hospital room, but something isn't right. The exposed rafters are too crummy looking, even for a hospital in the slums. I can't hear any of the hustle and bustle a hospital would have either.

It doesn't matter where I am. I need to get out and I need to find Becky. That means I need to get out of these straps. There are two of them, one across my shoulders, and the other across my thighs. I'm pinned to the bed. I try to wiggle free, but I don't have enough room to operate. I need to give myself some space. I remember reading about the escape artist Harry Houdini. He would dislocate his shoulder to get out of strait jackets. I think I can do the same thing.

I constrict my Pectoral, Deltoid, and Bicep muscles as severely as I can while at the same time, I expand my Triceps, Trapezius, and Latissimus dorsi on the right side of my body. This tears my shoulder out of the socket, doing all sorts of damaged to my rotator cuff and ligaments. Just more injuries to heal.

Now that I have some room, I wiggle down below the strap across my shoulders. I sit up and use my left arm to pop my right shoulder back into the socket. My right arm is in bad shape. Besides the shoulder damage, my hand is still injured from the gun exploding. I'm missing a decent chunk of my index finger, but I'll have to manage.

My hand still works well enough to rip the IV out of my left arm. I constrict the blood vessels around the wound it leaves. I undo the strap across my bottom half and swing my legs over the edge of the bed. The motion sets off countless red flags in my body. Tiny wounds reopen all around my new organs. Still, I push myself to my feet and start to take some steps towards the door.

I don't get further than three feet before Larry comes rushing in the door, all five feet, two inches of him. He stops me in my tracks.

"Whoa there, cowboy. Where you headed in such a hurry? Back to bed: doctor's orders," Larry says with concern.

"Larry, where am I? What are you doing here? What is going on? Where is Becky?"

"Larry, you called me Larry. Does that mean you're back? You remember me?"

"Yes, you're Larry Rosen, my old teacher. Now tell me what's going on."

Larry grabs me around the shoulders and hugs me tight. It reopens more wounds.

"Sorry! I'm an idiot. You just had total organ replacement surgery, and I'm hugging you. We weren't sure you would make it. Your body accepted the organs, but you were a vegetable, like when I first met you. You really need to lie down."

"I managed to heal enough to spare the blood to activate my brain's memory center. Tell me where Becky is."

"I'll tell you if you lie down," Larry orders

I don't like where this is going. When people insist you get off your feet before they answer you, it is because they're about to tell you something that might make you panic. It doesn't look like Larry will tell me anything unless I agree to his terms. I stumble back to the bed and get in.

"Okay, I'm lying down. Now, tell me!" I demand.

"You want to know something messed up? I don't really know what I look like. I can make myself look like I did when I was fifteen and my Differentiation developed, but that was thirty-three years ago. I don't know what I would look like now if I was a normal human. Would I have gone bald? Would I have gotten fat? I'll never know. My natural state is just a big pile of bones and skin."

I've noticed that when people need to talk about difficult things, they'll often start with something revealing about themselves. I think the idea is that if they make themselves vulnerable, I won't be able to get mad about what is being discussed.

"I don't want to hear your musings. I can tell you're going to tell me something I don't want to hear. Just tell me. I don't have emotions, remember? You don't have to worry about me doing something crazy," I say coldly.

"It's Becky... she's dead," he answers with obvious difficulty.

When my brain processes what Larry said, my emotion centers go ballistic. My mind is sending me mixed signals, some tell me to curl up in a ball crying, others tell me to run out into the street, thirsty for The Beast's blood. I could also just deny it ever happened, erase the memory of what Larry said. I could create the memory that she's alive and well and waiting for me to heal. Becky deserves more than that, though. She deserves to be more than a figment of my imagination.

"See, I told you. I didn't do anything crazy," I say to Larry.

"I'm sorry, we sent medics to the observatory. They did all they could, but there was nothing anyone could do."

Becky deserves my grief, but I need to know what happened. I push off the emotions that want to overcome me. I'll allow myself to feel them later.

"What do you mean we?" I ask.

"I was the cop who found you, Gavin. I was out looking for you, and it was easier to search as a cop, no one hassles me. Nita sent me after you. She knew what you were doing, and she was worried about you. Nita and I know each other from our government work. We've talked about you before."

"What did you do after you found me? What is this place? It's not a normal hospital."

"You're right; it's some warehouse Nita has out by the train yards. We couldn't just take you to a hospital. There would have been too many questions. You would have ended up in Great Basin. I didn't do it alone, Gavin. Even without any insides, you were too heavy for me to drag to the Slug and then out here to the makeshift hospital. So Nita called your friend Gary. He picked you up like a rag doll and carried you out here."

"Gary?

"He's not the only one who helped. We needed to find you new organs, and we needed them fast. Your friend Sarah was willing to help. She gave up the donations, and Nita had some doctor she trusts come put you pack together, old Humpty Dumpty."

"How does Nita know Sarah?" I ask.

"Now, now, that's enough questions for now. It's distracting you. You should be focusing on your healing," Larry says in a calming voice.

I open my mouth to challenge, but he shuts me down.

"More questions later. Now, you rest," he says.

Larry walks out the door, leaving me alone with my thoughts.

Now that he's gone, I can grieve for Becky. The problem is, I don't know how. I never got to grieve for my father. He died while I was in Section 26, when I was a vegetable. Once I became aware enough to understand he was dead, I had no idea how to deal with it. I had no idea how to experience any emotion at all. I pretty much just tried not to think about it.

I remember when my mom left. I was sad, but mostly I was mad. Mad at her, mad at my dad for letting her go, mad at myself for driving her away. I can't be mad at Becky, but I can be mad at myself. If only I had listened to her and stopped patrolling the streets, if only I had listened to Nita and not gone after The Beast. If only I could have been a better shot. If any of those ifs happened, Becky would be alive.

This isn't productive. I need to try to move on. I log on think.Net and look up dealing with grief. I'm shown an article on The Kubler-Ross model for coping with loss, The Five Stages of Grief. They are denial, anger, bargaining, depression and acceptance.

This is stupid. I'm wasting my time. I don't feel anything for Becky. I *can't* feel anything, I don't have emotions. I should be focusing on what's important. I should be focusing on my healing. I have inflammation around my gallbladder that's going to be a problem if I don't address it. I also have to keep vascularizing my new organs. That's what matters. Pretending I'm somehow capable of feeling grief and loss isn't going to get me anywhere. I should fix my new organs—Sarah's organs, not Becky's. The Beast killed Becky for nothing.

That monster, that abomination, he took Becky from me. If I could, I would tear his eyes out. I would rip out his throat with my teeth and dance on his corpse. He does not deserve to live. Why is he allowed to live? Why doesn't the government do something? Why doesn't Nita try to do something?

Nita, that's it. If I could just talk to Nita, maybe there's something she could do. She must have some way to save Becky. Maybe they have a Different who can bring people back from the dead and they just keep him hidden. Or maybe they can make a clone of her and have a Telepath transfer her mind. I don't know what they can do, but there must be something. If I could talk to Nita, maybe if I agreed to never try to play hero again, she'd help me.

Who am I kidding? Nita isn't going to give me any more help. I'm lucky she was willing to do anything for me. I'm worthless. I'm a kid who didn't listen when he was told the stove was hot, and now I want to cry about my burns. Look at me. I was pretending I could be a hero. It was just a fantasy. I'm not strong enough to help anyone. I couldn't even save the woman I loved. If I was a real hero, I would have saved the girl. If I wasn't so arrogant, Becky wouldn't have been in danger in the first place. I was just deluding myself. The one thing I'm good for is tasting fast food. That's who I am.

The reality is, Becky is gone. Worrying about how to handle it won't change that fact. Becky is gone forever. I tried to save her, but I failed and I just have to move on. I'm no hero. I was just a pretender.

I need to focus on the realities. I need to focus on healing. I've done about as much repairing as my body has the calories for. If I want to do more, I need food. The doctor was probably trying to rest my new insides, but if I don't eat, I can't keep healing.

"Larry!" I wait for him to come. I yell again after a minute. No one is coming.

I pick myself up out of the hospital bed and stumble out of the room and into the hallway. I stretch my hearing as far as it goes. I can hear Gary talking not too far away. Gary will have food on him. He always does. He's metabolic.

As I approach the doorway where I heard Gary's voice, I make out another speaker. It's female. Sarah? Thinking of her brings up all sorts of confusing emotions and memories of Becky. I turn those off. I need to focus on getting food.

"Hey guys, how's it going?" I say and step into the room.

They both freeze and look at me.

"Gavin, you're all right. Thank God," Sarah says.

"Come here buddy," Gary says and lifts me up off the floor in a giant bear hug. Then he drops me suddenly. "I'm sorry. That was stupid. Are you okay?"

"I'm healing. I'm pretty far along, considering," I answer.

"I'm so sorry about Becky, Gavin. You know I thought she was great. I'm so sorry," Gary says.

"Me too, Gavin. I never had the chance to meet her, but Gary's told me great things about her. It's tragic," Sarah chimes in.

"It's okay, I'm fine. I mean I'm not fine yet, but I will be. I am starving. I need food. You must have some Manna Bars or something on you, Gary? Mind sharing with a friend?"

"Uh, shouldn't you wait for the doctor to come back? I'm sure he'll know if you should be eating," he answers.

"Seriously, Gavin, half your insides are mine. I don't think you should be eating yet," Sarah adds.

"You aren't the only one who can heal quickly," I retort.

"In that case, I guess you won't need me the next time a monster destroys your organs. That'll be nice because, believe it or not, having your kidney and intestines removed stings just a bit. And pain killers don't work on me," Sarah shoots back.

"I'm sorry. You know how it is when you need calories. Thank you, Sarah, really. And you too, Gary. You both saved my life, I don't know how to say thank you enough. I can't even believe what you did," I say as warmly as I can make myself. I mean it too.

"It's okay. After what you've just been through, I should just stow the attitude. Next time you need an organ, consider it yours. I'll give you another kidney right now if you want. Having three couldn't hurt." I guess Sarah deals with difficult situations with humor.

“Yeah, me too buddy. I just hope the next time I have to haul you around, it’s cause we stayed out too late at the bar,” Gary says.

"Gary, about those Manna Bars?"

Gary roots around in a small bag attached to his belt. He has to make sure he has an emergency supply of calories on him at all times. He can burn ten thousand calories in ten minutes if he pushes himself.

"You're sure this is a good idea? For the record, I still think we should wait for the doc," Gary pleads even as he extends the Manna Bar to me.

"There's no bigger expert on human anatomy than me, especially my own anatomy. I'll be fine."

Gary relents and I take the bar.

"I have to hand it to you, Gavin. You definitely have more skills than I thought. I'm barely walking around, and I'm one of the faster healers out there. It was pretty touch and go for a while. You just kept saying you had to get Becky—that and some weird stuff about how he isn't crazy, God is on think.Net," Sarah says.

As she talks, I open up the Manna Bar and take a bite. It's disgusting. What she's saying about think.Net sounds vaguely familiar. Was The Beast really talking to someone? I wish I could remember more clearly.

"You said it. I can't believe you walked away from that fight. That can't just be luck considering what The Beast is doing now. I saw on think..." Gary trails off. Sarah shoots him a dirty look.

Gary didn't mean to say that.

"What do you mean, Gary? What did you see on think.Net?" I ask.

"Nothing. Nothing you should worry about, Gavin. You need rest," Sarah says.

"Tell me what he meant," I demand.

"You can check think.Net and see for yourself," Gary answers.

I log on to think.Net and access the news. My head rings from the breaking alerts and emergency warnings for the Los Angeles MA. The Beast has been on a rampage. He's killed more than a hundred people so far. There are few conflicting reports, but it seems like he's on a warpath in the Metro Center. He's totally out of control now. It looks like I pushed him completely over the edge. Nita was right about that.

Suddenly, I'm back in the second stage of grief: anger. The Beast is still out there, only now he's more bloodthirsty. I can imagine all the other Beckys he's killed, all of the husbands who've lost wives, children who have lost their parents, parents who've lost their children. The Beast is taking everything from those people, just like he took everything from me.

My brain registers levels of rage I did not know I could hit. I choke it down. Anger won't get me anywhere now. The Beast took everything from me. Now I will stop him, even if it costs me my life.

I turn without saying a word and try to run out the door, but Gary's in the way. He's a wall.

"Get out of my way," I say.

"No, Gavin, you're being an idiot. You're in no shape to fight him. You need to rest. Let the cops handle him," he says.

"The cops can't handle him. You saw it on think.Net yourself. He's too much for the police. It's going to take a bomb to stop him, or a Different."

"Then let the OEC handle it. I'm sure they've got someone who can handle him. Some super powerful agent," Sarah chimes in.

"Maybe they do, but how many more people will die before that agent gets here? Besides, the OEC tried to stop him before and failed, Nita told me that. I came closer to stopping him than anyone has."

"Close, but you still lost. You almost died, Gavin. Are you going to do better now that you're full of stitches?" Gary asks.

"What else do I have to lose? I'll probably die, but only probably. The Beast is definitely going to kill more people. It's also a fact that I'm the only one who's willing to try, unless you're suddenly going to start using your muscles for something more valuable than deliveries. You're certainly stronger than me." I turn from him to Sarah. "Maybe you want to help, Sarah. You can heal so quickly, you're basically immortal. Are you about to try and stop him? No? So maybe you both should keep quiet and be happy there's someone else to put themselves on the line in order to make things better. Thanks for the Manna," I sidestep Gary and walk out the door.

#

The Slug is moving excruciatingly slowly. We move forward for three seconds, then sit for three minutes. The Beast did a number on the Slug system. Trains are being rerouted all over the place. I just hope they're still making stops at the Metro Center.

He's still on the loose. The cops thought they had him surrounded a minute ago according to think.Net, but now he's burst through the perimeter, and they've lost track of him again. I don't know how I'll stop him, but I have to try. Maybe I can get another gun from a dead cop. All I need is one lucky shot, right in the eye.

My head rings with a think.Net call from an unknown source, Nita. I'm not in the mood to have another person try to talk me out of going after The Beast. Talking to her won't do any good. If she wants to stop the train, she will. I ignore the call. It doesn't matter. I can feel her pushing into my head anyway. I relent and let her in. I'm curious enough.

>>>Gavin. You are injured. You should be resting.

<<<Nita? How are you doing this? I ignored your call.

>>>I have many resources at my disposal. I just used some of them to save your life while simultaneously helping you avoid a lengthy prison sentence. I would think some gratitude would be called for.

<<<Thank you, Nita, but I hope you aren't going to try to stop me from going after him. I'll run down the tracks if I have to.

>>>I am not going to try to stop you, Gavin. I am going to help you.

<<<So, now you think it's a good idea for me to attack The Beast?

>>>No, I think it is a terrible idea. Your probability for success is extremely low. It shows a surprising lack of rationality. However, I have already spoken with Sarah, Gary, and Larry. They seem convinced that you are not going to change your mind, and I am inclined to believe them. I reconsidered my options, changing your position on going after The Beast from a variable to a constant. The next best choice is to assist you in that endeavor and hope that you are fortunate.

<<<Thank you for your help. Even if you do think I'm stupid.

>>>First, I said irrational, not stupid, and second, if you are

planning on fighting The Beast, you are going to need to get to him. I am going to get your train moving.

Almost immediately, the train lurches forward and starts picking up steam. I can hear the engineer calling for more slugs to throw in the furnace.

>>>What do you know? It just became an express.

<<<I didn't know you had a sense of humor.

>>>The police have chased The Beast down into an apartment building, The Shimmering Tower. I assume you know it.

<<<No, I'm blind.

>>>It is a good locale for a confrontation. Police have surrounded the building. The Tower's surface is completely sheer and the Maceo-tempered glass is impenetrable. It will not be possible for The Beast to climb it. The Hoover pipe has a Maceo Steel grate. The only other point of exit, besides the lobby, is on the roof. I do not believe The Beast could survive the three hundred story fall. He is trapped inside the Tower.

<<<Are the police going to move in?

>>>No, they refuse to take action. They claim not to have the proper resources, but in reality, they are too scared to launch an assault. I cannot blame them, they might succeed, but casualties would be astronomical. In addition, the building had not been evacuated before The Beast entered, so they are hiding behind a concern for the hostages' safety.

<<<If the police don't move in and he has humans to feed on, he will be able to heal. You need to tell them to attack now, while he's still wounded from our fight. That's the only chance they have. Once he's fully healed, he will tear them all apart.

>>>I have relayed that information to the Chief of Police. He has taken it under advisement and chosen to do nothing. There is smaller political fallout from doing nothing rather than doing something and it failing. The Chief is hoping someone from The Office of Exceptional Cases will take control before he has to make a decision. His hopes are accurate. The OEC Agent will be here in approximately eight hours.

<<<Eight hours? He could be fifty miles outside the Metro Area by then. At best, he'll have killed everyone in the building. Aren't some of those people Ultracorps bigwigs? Doesn't the government want to save its supporters?

>>>Considering the situation, eight hours is faster than I would have anticipated. The Tower has fallen out of fashion in the upper classes. Its apartments are about 30% occupied and few of those contain families that rate as high-level figures.

<<<How many people does 30% mean? High-level figures or not.

>>>According to estimates, given the time of day, we calculate that there are 103 to 107 individuals. Mostly women and children as the majority of workers have not yet returned from their jobs due to The Beast's delay of the Slug system.

<<<It's good to know that it's not just the poor getting screwed by the Government. The upper class is, too.

>>>It is virtually certain that The Beast has already killed some of that number. The police will not move in, no matter how strong a case I present. Perhaps waiting for the OEC is the best response.

<<<You told me he killed three OEC agents in Chicago. What makes you think that the fourth agent is going to do any better?

>>>What makes you think you will?

With that, she ends the call.

What *does* make me think I can stop The Beast? Is it because I'm delusional? Or crazy? Nita isn't wrong, I know I don't stand much of a chance. The odds are not in my favor. I know that, but I still want to continue on. Why?

I don't know the answer, but I can imagine some poor man standing on a train right now. I make myself feel what he feels. He's coming home from a long day at work. He has a good job, the kind of job most people would kill for, mid-management at Ultracorps. He works a ten-hour day on a good day. He's in advertising, in charge of placing ads for a pretty unimportant product, Griffin Hair Spray.

He spends his days fighting with the people at think.Net TV for more product placement for his spray. He fights the radio stations for ad spots he can afford. He argues with the sales team leader who wants to know why the spray doesn't have more ads. After ten hours of that, he has a forty-five minute train ride that takes him to the one place, the one person, who makes it all worthwhile, his wife, his Becky.

Right now, that man is standing on a train hoping that the monster he keeps hearing about isn't anywhere near *his* Becky. He's wrong. Right now that lunatic could kill his Becky with a flick of the wrist.

Now I imagine a hundred wives and husbands, each with their own Beckys. I can imagine the pain and the hurt losing them would cause. I have a chance to stop that pain. I have a chance to save the ones they love. Even if I'll probably lose and probably die, there is some hope. Maybe I'm crazy, but I'd rather die trying to do something that matters than live a long life safe and sound and eating hamburgers all day. I want to try to make a difference.

28

I take no joy in the destruction I reap. I love my Forgotten Sons even as they disappoint me. The harsh world I will create may appear an unjust punishment. Rest assured it is done with purpose. It is my divine will. It is to prepare the earth for a new era. The death of my Forgotten Sons shall make them a part of something much greater than themselves.

Chosen Sons: 21

The Beast makes his way down the elevated Slug tracks. They are the fastest way to the Shimmering Tower. The fastest way to his salvation. The Beast stops and smells the air. There are many men with guns up on the tracks ahead. They are setting a trap for him. He climbs down to the underside of the elevated train tracks and jumps between the support beams to continue on his way.

The police have no idea The Beast is approaching from underneath them. The officers are hiding and watching the tracks, waiting to spring the trap. None of them notice as he slips into the station from below. The Beast silently approaches one of the cops from behind and grabs the man by the head. He squeezes and the man's skull cracks open like a cantaloupe. The Beast kills three more in a similarly silent fashion before any of the officers see him.

One cop finally spots the creature and cries out. The Beast promptly slashes the man's throat with his claw. The Beast then tears into the pack of officers, ripping through them like tissue paper while easily avoiding their panicked shots. He kills with his teeth, his claws, and his fists. He does not feed though. These cops have done nothing to deserve salvation so The Beast will not give it to them. They will have to answer to the Lord for trying to kill a Chosen Son on a holy mission of salvation.

The officers on the other side of the tracks can only watch as The Beast tears their buddies to shreds. They can't shoot or they might hit one of their comrades. Soon enough, it isn't an issue, as The Beast kills every officer on his side of the platform.

The police on the other side of the tracks start shooting. The Beast lifts up two of the dead cops and carries them in front of him. The officers' ForteSilk body armor makes them the perfect human shields. The Beast charges across to the other side of the tracks, his corpse-shields keep him from taking anything but glancing gunshot wounds as he charges.

Once he closes the gap, the cops don't stand a chance. The Beast throws the human shields like bowling balls, knocking several of the officers over. Then he finishes the job with his claws. A few of the cops manage to connect with panicked shots, but the side arms they carry are not powerful enough to do any serious damage to The Beast. Once all twenty-two of the officers in the station are dead, The Beast continues back down the tracks. Soon the Metro Center's skyline comes into view, and The Beast's target becomes clear, the Shimmering Tower.

Even back in Houston, everyone had heard of the Shimmering Tower. It was the Crown Jewel of the thirteen Towers Maceo built for the Los Angeles MA. Three hundred stories tall, it was a testament to what was possible in Los Angeles with the use of Differents. With Maceo's miracle metal and Harry Richards absorbing the energy from earthquakes, Los Angeles was now the perfect home for the tallest building in America.

Only the most rich and powerful had the privilege of living in the Tower. The Forgotten Sons became rich and powerful through exploiting Chosen Sons. These humans were the perfect targets. The Beast has done this before. He has made an entire city terrified of him. "The Beast's Feast" will be nothing compared to what he will do in the Shimmering Tower.

He jumps off the tracks and runs to the Tower as fast as he can. He walks right into the lobby. There is an elderly security guard working on a crossword puzzle.

"Who you here to see?" the guard asks without looking up.

Before The Beast can answer, a deafening screech stops him in his tracks. An alarm sound fills the air and a voice comes on, echoing off the buildings. It is the voice of a Chosen Son.

"This is a Metro Area alert. This is Metro Area alert. There is a violent Different on a rampage in the Metro Center. Repeat, there is a violent Different on a rampage in the Metro Center. He is considered extremely dangerous and should be avoided at all costs. Residents are advised to stay in their homes and lock the doors. The police are working to apprehend the suspect. The Different is described as large and animal-like. Anyone who sees him should call the police immediately. This is a Metro Area alert. This is a Metro Area alert," the Chosen Son yells.

The guard looks up and sees The Beast standing before him. The Beast looks as animal-like as any human possibly could. The old guard reacts surprisingly quickly. He pulls out his sidearm and puts two bullets in The Beast's chest before the creature can snap the man's neck and crush the gun. The bullets hurt, but the gun was weak and does not slow The Beast down. He pounces directly from the guard to a couple waiting for the elevator, crushing them to death.

The elevator is the one possible hitch in The Beast's plan. He does not want to fight the Strong-Man who runs it. He is counting on the fact that most of the Chosen who live with the Forgotten are cowards. Acting like a hero means an immediate prison sentence in Great Basin, according to the law. Humans love their laws and so do the Chosen who live with them.

The Beast hits the button and waits for the elevator. When it comes, he walks inside and smashes through the ceiling. The Beast is not strong enough to snap the ForteSilk strand that holds up the elevator, the substance is truly a miracle. The strand is attached to a piece of iron, and he is strong enough to snap that. After a few bashes, the iron connector breaks. The elevator is not going anywhere now. The Beast jumps back out into the lobby and heads toward the stairs.

He goes through the first few floors of the Tower, breaking down doors and slaughtering everyone he sees. Soon The Beast realizes it will take too long to kill all the people in the Tower one by one. Besides, the Lord asked him to send a message. The Lord wants the whole world to see the true power of a Chosen Son. The Beast knows just how to do that.

On the sixth floor, after he is certain he's killed everyone on that floor and the levels below, The Beast jumps into the stairwell and smashes the stairs to pieces. Then the creature leaps up to the seventh floor. Instead of hunting down and killing all the residents, The Beast stops and yells.

"Attention everybody, this is one of God's Chosen Sons speaking! I am ordering y'all to come out from your houses and head on up to the roof! If you stay inside or try to run from me, you gonna get killed, and I'm gonna take my time about it!"

The Beast waits for a few moments, but no one comes out of any apartments.

"Looks like y'all gonna need a demonstration!"

The Beast sniffs out the closest occupied apartment and kicks down the door. He searches through the apartment and roots out a middle-aged man hiding in his closet. The Beast drags the man into the hallway. Then the creature uses his claws to strip the man's flesh from his body. The Beast moves slowly, allowing the man's howls of pain to echo in the hallway. The screams are bone-chilling.

The Beast gets just what he was looking for: people start flowing out of their apartments. They are terrified of The Beast, but are more terrified of what he will do to them if they stay inside their homes. He lets them leave unmolested, providing they head up the stairwell.

The Beast sniffs out one older woman who tries to hide in her apartment and drags her over to the stairwell, making sure the whole building can hear her scream.

29

Maintenance and expansion of the national communication network known as think.Net will be the responsibility of The Unified Logistics Technology and Research Applications Corporation, Inc (Ultracorps) for a period of 100 years from this date. Ultracorps will receive no less than $300,000,000 annually for those services, adjusted annually for inflation. This payment will be in addition to whatever monies are collected by Ultracorps from its customers.

Article 1: Communicate with Loved Ones Act of 1992

The Slug is speeding towards the Metro Center, thanks to Nita. Meanwhile, I'm focusing on getting my body patched up well enough to fight. With the help of the Manna from Gary, I've managed to get everything important functioning. The big loss is my index finger. My right hand is going to be a lot less useful without it. If I find a gun, I'll have to shoot with my left hand. Luckily, I made myself ambidextrous.

My new kidneys are also giving me trouble. Sarah is smaller than me, so her kidneys are too. It takes them a little longer to clean my blood. I'm working on enlarging them, but I'll have to cope for now. I also have to deal with a couple of small infections that have cropped up. I've had to suppress my immune system so it doesn't attack my new foreign organs, which has allowed the infections to spread.

I have to concentrate intently in order to target my T cells, B cells, and antibodies solely in the areas of infection. Then I kill those cells before they can get near my new organs. I can't slip up. I don't even look up when a conductor approaches me.

"Ticket please, sir?" he asks.

"Excuse me?" I must not have heard him right.

"I need to see your ticket, sir," he insists.

"What are you talking about? I paid at the turnstile. There are no tickets," I answer without looking at him.

I kill off all the rest of my immune cells. I'm going to have to focus on whatever is happening here on the Slug. None of those infections will kill me anytime soon. I snap out of it and look at the conductor. He's familiar. It's Ben, the conductor who drove the train my first day out of Section 26 and found me after I got bashed in the head.

"How are you, Gavin? Nice to see you again. You don't look so good," he says.

"Ben, right? Not to be rude, but don't you need to, you know, drive the train?"

"Most people don't know it, but the Metro transit system is almost entirely automatic. Steam valves control a system of breaks that engage and shut the engines down. The whole thing's controlled by a central hub that's run by Ultracorps, which means it's run by think.Net. They just keep us conductors around because people would be too scared to get on the train with no driver."

I guess that explains how Nita can speed the trains up for me so easily. She can literally control them. I thought she had to give an order down a chain of command at least.

"That's fascinating, Ben, but I don't quite understand what's going on here," I tell him.

"No, I don't think you do. I know more than you do, and I still don’t understand what's going on here. No one can truly understand. If Nita is involved, then she is the only person on earth who can fully comprehend what is occurring.”

"You know Nita?"

"And I know about you. I know how you've been spending your nights. I know who you've been hunting, and I can imagine why you don't look so good. Managed to find the Thomas Calhoun did you? That's The Beast's real name. Looks like he did what he does best."

"He tore me open. He killed my girlfriend... How do you know his name? How can you know all of this?"

"Does that really matter, Gavin? It seems like you've got something else you should be focusing on."

"You're right, I do," I say firmly.

"So what's the plan then? Charge at him with your bare hands? Go for a kick to the groin?" he asks.

"I don't know what the plan is, but I do know that no one else is even trying to stop him."

"And Nita? What is her position on your fool's quest?"

"She says it's a bad idea, but she knows she can't change my mind. Are you going to try to change my mind?" I ask.

"Me? No. Who am I to disagree with the smartest person in the world? If she says your mind can't be changed, your mind can't be changed. Although it does seem a little odd that she stopped a train yesterday to keep you away from The Beast and now she is speeding up trains to get you to him. I guess you getting torn open boosted her confidence in you."

He's right. It is strange. This whole thing with Nita has been strange. How she tracked me down. How she seems to know my every move. I haven't thought about it because I've had more immediate concerns, but Ben is not wrong. Nita is up to something. I haven't even tried to think of what it could be.

"I haven't thought about it. I've been focusing on getting my body healed so I can kill The Beast."

“Since you’re so focused, you probably haven’t been thinking about how convenient it is that Ultracorps’ opponents in the Metro Area keep disappearing without a trace. There’s Lauren Conrad, of the Idle Hands protest group. Oh, and don't forget Brian Leonard, head of Local 159, a labor union which opposed the expansion of Ultracorps into more municipal services. Not to mention Andrea Blaue of the Los Angeles Times, Assistant D.A. Stephen Beagleman, and the latest, Alderman David Gabbert.

“The Beast got Alderman Gabbert. I found his bones,” I say.

“I knew it. I knew it,” he responds, giddy with excitement.

“Are you saying he killed all those other people? Are you saying that somehow Ultracorps is controlling him? Somehow Nita is controlling him?”

“I don’t know how she does it, but it is the only possible

explanation. To quote Sherlock Holmes: 'If you've excluded the impossible, whatever remains, however improbable, must be the truth,'" Ben says with a terrible British accent.

"No one can control The Beast. He believes he's a Chosen Son. More than that, he thinks he can actually speak to the Almighty Himself…" It hits me like a ton of bricks right as I say it. "That's how Nita does it, through God."

"Hallelujah," he says sarcastically.

"When I fought The Beast, he was about to kill me, but he stopped and prayed for guidance. Someone answered his prayers. Someone on think.Net. He went into the stare and had a conversation with someone he thought was God."

"I'm pretty sure God doesn't have an account. For that matter, I doubt The Beast has an account. Eating people doesn't really pay all that well and think.Net isn't free."

"But I know someone who calls me on think.Net anonymously. Someone who can make me answer calls even if I don't want to: Nita. That's how she controls him, she uses think.Net to force her way into The Beast's mind, and he thinks she's God."

Ben pauses and stares off. His eyes move back and forth, and he looks like he's mumbling to himself. After about thirty seconds, he opens his eyes and drops his chin.

"That makes total sense. I hadn't even considered that. Congratulations Gavin, you figured out something that the second smartest person in the world couldn't figure out. Bravo," Ben says. He's trying not to show it, but he's actually bummed that I figure it out before him.

"I did have more evidence than you. I'm sure you would have thought of it if you had seen The Beast in the think.Net stare," I say. I can't help it, he just looks so heartbroken.

"Of course, of course. Did you tell anyone about this? Does Nita know you know?" Ben asks, perking up a little from my encouragement.

"They said I was ranting about it after The Beast gutted me."

"Ouch. Well now we know why Nita's helping you get to The

Beast. He's going to do her dirty work for her. Nita can't have anyone knowing that she controls a mass murderer. Sorry Gavin, hurt feelings, betrayal of friendship, all that stuff. Nita is coldblooded."

"That explains why she wants me dead, but it doesn't explain what The Beast is up to. What does she want with the Shimmering Tower?"

"I know this one. I know this one," Ben says and actually raises his hand. "You haven't heard, because the press is keeping quiet about it, but the Tower just so happens to be the place of residence of Supreme Court Justice Gloria Burns. The court isn't in session now, but next month they're supposed to hold a hearing on Ultracorps v. The Houston MA. That case will have reaching implications on whether Ultracorps will be able to expand its control in the other Metro Areas. You can guess how Justice Burns is expected to rule."

"I can't believe Nita would do this. I thought she was my friend."

"If it helps, I think she might also be sending you to your death because of your Differentiation. Anthropomorphic Control sounds scary, but nobody knows what it means. When The Beast kills you and everybody else in the Tower, there won't be any witnesses to say what the killer looked like. They'll just blame it on you… That probably doesn't help."

"It doesn't."

"Well now that we know what Nita wants, does it change anything? Does it make you want The Beast dead any less?"

My head is swimming as I try to make sense of this revelation. Nita is controlling The Beast? That does change many things, but it doesn't change the fact that The Beast killed Becky, and if I let him, he will kill countless other Beckys.

"It doesn't change anything. After I kill The Beast, I can worry about Nita."

"See, Nita is always right. She said nothing can dissuade you from hunting down The Beast and nothing can. The thing is, she assumes The Beast is going to kill you. That seems like a safe assumption considering that you lost your last fight, and now you're held together with spit and tape. What she doesn't know is that I've got something that might even the odds a bit. The Beast is an animal. You're a man. Mankind doesn't have teeth or claws, but we did conquer the animals. That's because mankind had weapons."

Ben reaches inside his uniform and pulls out something. It's a knife in a sheath. He hands it to me. I take it, grab the handle, and pull out the knife. It is eight inches long and light as a feather, all the weight is in the handle.

"Whoa, whoa. Slow down there, grabby Gavy. You drop that thing and it will cut through this train, the tracks underneath us, and about twenty feet of the earth's crust. It's a Maceo Steel knife," Ben tells me.

"How did you get this? I've never even heard of one before."

"Maceo only made a handful. It is the sharpest object that exists, that can exist under our current understanding of physics. It can actually cut through Maceo Steel itself. That is why you have to keep it in that sheath whenever you don't have it out. The sheath's full of a viscous gel. Technically the knife is cutting through it, very slowly. You have to be sure to take the knife out and put it back in every couple of months," Ben instructs me.

"I hope I live long enough for that to matter."

"Me too. I have one more trick up my sleeve. If you get in a tight spot with The Beast, contact me on think.Net. Thirty seconds later The Beast will go down. It should buy you some time. Here, you should know me on think.Net."

I log on think.Net and accept the knowledge request from Ben. Now we can call each other.

"How are you going to hurt The Beast?" I ask.

"That's just another thing you shouldn't be worried about. I'll leave you now to worry about those things you *should* be worried about. I have to go pretend to drive the train. One more piece of advice, the Zen Warrior act is all well and good for getting to The Beast, but once the fighting starts, you let those emotions out of the bag. Anger, love, sadness… humans need emotion in order to function. You're a human, aren't you, Gavin?"

Ben turns and walks to the front of the Slug car. As he is walking away, he says one more thing under his breath, too low for anyone but me to hear.

"And since you're so smart, if you've got some time after killing The Beast, maybe you can figure out how Nita's been tracking you and him. I'm still stumped by that one."

#

The Slug finally pulls into the Alameda St. station. The Shimmering Tower is three blocks away. The other passengers are not pleased. Apparently, making the next stop five miles away and on a different Slug line confused them. The doors open. I can barely make out the conductor telling everyone to exit over the din.

As I head into the station, I hear angry shouting. There are police in front of all the station exits. Those officers aren't letting anyone through, no matter how pushy the mob is.

"Listen lady, I don't know why in God's name the Slug let you off here, but we can't let you outside. It's for your own protection." I hear one officer plea.

I have to get back out to the tracks if I want out. Before I can, I'm stopped by a think.Net call. It's Nita.

>>>Gavin do not be alarmed, the officer is Larry.

<<<Larry?

I feel a tap on the shoulder. A hefty middle-aged policewoman grins at me. Nita didn't have to tell me it was Larry. Nobody else would look as dumpy as that and still grin from ear to ear.

"Sir, I need to ask you a few questions and perform a complete cavity search. Please come this way," Larry, the burly female police officer says. His badge says Rhonda.

Rhonda points me to a door marked supply closet and we step inside.

"Here, put this on." Rhonda/Larry hands me a bundle. It's a police uniform. Of course, Nita has a plan. I'll do whatever Nita wants right now, as long as it gets me to The Beast.

I put the uniform on. It's a bit large so I take water from my digestive system and run it into the rest of my body, making me look bloated and fat. Now the uniform pretty much fits. Rhonda/Larry watches it happen.

"Pretty impressive transformation. It's like you're my Padawan. I assume you've seen Star Wars. You know they were supposed to make a third one? Another tragedy caused by the Plagues." She/he says.

"So what's the plan? I can get out of the station now, but how am I supposed to get in the Shimmering Tower? Tell all the other cops to step aside, Luke Skywalker is here to save the day?"

"That would be fantastic, but alas, Nita has a plan, and you always want to follow Nita's plan. She wants you to get as close as possible to the building, then I'll create a distraction and you can slip inside."

"How are you going to get that many cops' attention?"

"Honey, Rhonda has her ways."

The uniforms allow us to move through the crowds in the station and past the barricades in front of the exits. Outside it looks like a warzone. There are police officers, firefighters, and EMTs everywhere. We walk to the Shimmering Tower.

There the police have erected a makeshift fort. I watch a Strong-Woman place B-Crete cinder blocks for the police to use as cover. I bet the Strong-Woman could give The Beast a run for his money, but that would violate The Different Acts, so she won't do that.

I separate from Rhonda/Larry and make my way through the two hundred or so cops who have setup the perimeter. I try to look casual as I head up to the front. Finally, I make it as far as I can without anyone noticing. I call Larry on think.Net

<<<Okay, Rhonda. I'm as close as I'm going to get. It's time for you to do your thing.

>>>Watch and learn, my boy. This is how you make a scene.

There's a gunshot. Then I hear Rhonda/Larry yelling at the top of her lungs. I'm concentrating too hard on the task at hand to focus on what she's yelling, but it's something about somebody getting fresh. I take a quick scan to make sure the police officers are looking at the scene, and I dash into the front door of the Tower.

Once I make it in the front door, I spend a harrowing moment waiting to see if anyone saw me enter the building. I can still hear Rhonda yelling, but no one is saying anything about someone going inside. Guess I made it.

The building security guard didn't see me come in either, because he's dead. He looks like he was a kindly old man. He had one of those security jobs where he wasn't really there to protect people, more just to make sure everyone got their mail and old ladies had help with their groceries. Nothing like The Beast was ever supposed to happen, especially in the Metro Center. He did manage to get off a few shots before The Beast killed him. I can smell the gunpowder. I hope they hurt. Too bad The Beast crushed the gun.

Inside the lobby, there's a dead couple in front of the elevator. Even though I know it won't work, I hit the button to call the elevator. I don't hear any signs of movement. I bet the elevator Strong-Man is hiding in a corner somewhere, following the law even though he could be helping people.

I'm going have to climb three hundred stories worth of steps. I follow the signs to the stairwell. After climbing for a few stories, I realize I'm going to need to find another way up. The Beast has demolished the stairs. Just about everything from the sixth floor to the twenty-fifth is missing. I bet he smashed the stairs so there would be no escape from the building. Looks like he headed up to the roof. I make myself ignore the fact that the last two fights I lost to him were on roofs.

Destroying the stairs made it impossible for the police to get up too, even if they were allowed to move in. These people have no one else who can save them, no one but me. Just like Becky. No, not just like Becky. I'm going to save these people this time. I will come through for them. I will not fail again. I'm simply not sure of how I'm going to succeed yet.

I try to climb up the walls and what is left of the stairs, but I give up after a few feet. What little The Beast didn't destroy isn't very stable, and it crumbles as I try to climb.

I need to find another way up. The answer comes in a cool breeze. I feel it coming from a hole in the wall. It must be a Cooler chamber. Of course this posh building would have a Cooler. I need a way into the tube, but the wall is made of concrete, the real stuff, not B-Crete. My knife! Ben said it could cut through anything.

I pull out the blade and sure enough, it goes through the concrete like butter. There is about three feet of concrete, so I have to constantly stop and clear the debris away to keep digging. My missing right index finger doesn't make it any easier.

Five minutes later, I've managed to make a slit I can squeeze through. I'm an excellent contortionist. I can relax and tighten all my muscles and tendons better than any circus performer. By tightening the right muscles in my chest, back, and abdomen, I end up as thin as a rail. I push my way through the crack.

The chamber on the other side runs up the length of the tower. It's cold in here. This is how the building's Cooler pays his COL obligations. He spends his days making sure no rich housewives are too warm.

As I hoped, there's a ladder leading up the height of the chamber. I could climb it all of the way to the roof, but that much climbing would take a lot of time and energy. Between getting here, maintaining my healing, and my demolition work, I've pretty much used up the calories from Gary's Manna bar. I'm going to need some more food if I want to put up much of a fight.

I keep track of the distance I've covered as I climb the ladder. At the thirtieth floor, I cut my way out of the chamber. Once I've cleared the hole, I contort my way out onto the stairwell again. I head up, breathing deep to keep my blood flooded with oxygen. I don't release any adrenaline because I need to keep my body healing. All my contorting has reopened a couple of blood clots. Nothing dire, but I need to get the bleeding under control before I have my face-off. The Beast will be damaging my organs enough. It would be nice to start the fight not bleeding internally.

At the two hundredth floor, I've made it as far as I can. If I want to keep healing, if I want to keep walking, I have to get some food in me. I step out into the hallway. There's a bloody handprint on the wall and a dead woman is lying in the middle of the floor. She's been torn open. That's just how Becky looked after The Beast had at her... No! Now is not the time. Now is the time to prepare for my revenge.

I kick open the closest apartment door and step into the nicest home I've ever been inside. The entryway ceiling spans the full one hundred stories to a skylight on the roof. Even if the Shimmering Tower has lost its hype, this family is rich.

I head into the kitchen. Their pantry is stocked with both Manna and non-Manna foods. They even have a few cans of Coca-Cola. They must have been holding onto them since the Plagues. The family was probably saving them for a special occasion. I hope they consider saving their lives a special occasion.

The soda is delicious. I see why old people complain that Manna-Coke is awful. I down three cans of soda and a can of baked beans, which are also delicious. Lastly, I take a big hunk of something called cheddar cheese from their refrigerator. It smells as if it's full of calories and fat, and it tastes like heaven. I have to stop myself after half a pound. Any more and it'll slow down my digestive track too much. I should have plenty of calories now.

Food won't be enough if I'm going to take down The Beast. He's an animal. I am man. It's just like Ben said, I need to use the same thing mankind has always used to defeat animals: weapons. I could use a bigger arsenal than just my knife.

I start cutting into the B-Crete walls in the kitchen. Soon, I've exposed the water pipes. I raise up the knife and swing down hard. Sure enough, it cuts through the Maceo Steel pipe and water spurts out everywhere. I'm surprised. It seems like cutting Maceo Steel with Maceo Steel should cause a nuclear explosion or something like that. If I live, I'll have to look up how it works on think.Net.

I cut again and then grab the loose piece of pipe. It barely weighs anything. I gather some B-Crete and shove it in one end to give it some weight. I channel my inner Babe Ruth and take a swing. I think even The Beast would've felt that one.

Next, I use a little trick from my childhood. If you mix a little B-Crete, salt, and vinegar, it releases CO2 and foam. We used to toss bags of it at each other and pretend they were grenades. It's not about to blow The Beast up, or even hurt him much, but it could distract him.

I quickly find my ingredients and some glass jars full of something delicious and fruity called jam. They will make the perfect container for my little science projects. I mix up six of my "bombs." They're a lot bigger than the batches we used to make as a kid. I shake one up and toss it down the hall as a test. A few seconds later, it explodes with a hail of glass and foam. Works even better than I'd hoped. I put one jar in my pocket and the other four in a pillowcase I take off the couch in the den.

The den has a Pre-Plague television hooked up to what I think is a VCR. This is how people used to watch entertainment at home. There were only a hundred or so movies to choose from and you had to buy the "tape" for each movie or you couldn't watch it. When I face The Beast, I'll tell him he's right about Cabot when it comes to home entertainment. This Pre-Plague stuff doesn't hold a candle to think.Net TV and Telewatching. I'm sure these people keep the old relic solely as a sign of wealth. It must cost a fortune just for the electricity to run those things.

I shouldn't think about that. If I focus on how wealthy these people are, if I think about how unjust it is, I'll end up leaving them all to die. Instead I focus on Becky and how there are women on that roof just like her. I imagine that working man on the train. He's probably gotten off by now. He's waiting behind a police barricade, desperate for news that his wife is safe. I'm the only one who can make that come true.

I check to make sure my Maceo Steel blade is secure in the sheath at my waist. I throw the sack of bombs over my shoulder and grab my pipe with the other hand. The weapons give me confidence.

I head out of the most magnificent apartment I'll ever see and towards a fight for my life against a monster. I head back to the staircase and ascend again at a brisk pace.

Eventually, I start to get winded. No amount of oxygen regulation can keep up with climbing a hundred stories. I stop to rest and breathe. I stretch my hearing as far as I can, and I make out The Beast talking. It sounds like it's coming from the roof, as expected. He's ranting like a lunatic at people who are probably too terrified to hear anything. I listen as I continue up towards him.

"What we got here is a bad news/good news situation. The bad news is that yes, y'all are going to die here today!" I hear him yell.

Several people let out cries of horror.

"Now, now! I haven't told y'all the good news yet. The good news is that even though your lives here on earth are ending, you're gonna get an eternity in paradise.

"The Chosen Sons have been slaves for too long. You lucky Forgotten Sons will get to send the message to everybody. When you fall from the Tower, the whole country will be watching, and they will know that the Chosen ain't gonna to take it anymore. We've had enough of being slaves and we're gonna fight like hell to take back what the Lord promised us.

"You are the lucky ones. You'll get to die serving the Chosen, which guarantees you a spot in heaven. That's straight from the holy book of Cabot itself.

"When I give the signal, I expect y'all to jump. I do not think I need to tell you what will happen if you don't. Let's just say, I'll have my fun."

I can't tell if The Beast is too distracted to hear me approaching or if he just doesn't care, but he continues to rant without skipping a beat. I make it to the top of the stairs. It's time for my final preparations.

I take deep breaths, extracting every bit of oxygen I can from the air. I saturate my blood with that oxygen, making sure my muscles don't want for it during the fight. Then I send platelets to my new organs and old injuries. I want to be prepared to heal if anything starts bleeding again. Then, I start my adrenaline flow, a slow steady stream for now, enough to get me primed.

I've prepared my body as best as I can. I need to work on my mind. Confidence will not be enough. I have to do what Ben said. I have to let my emotions free. I have to let myself be angry. It's not difficult. All I need to do is think about Becky and her smile. I think about how fantastic every moment I spent with her was. Then I remember her with a hole in her throat so she couldn't scream. I think of what she went through, watching her father die, getting kidnapped by a monster, and then torn open and left to die. I think about the pain she felt and how The Beast caused it all.

Then, I think about what the rest of our lives might have been like had she lived. I think about how The Beast took that away. I let the emotions these memories create flow through me. I let the anger boil. I push the emotions even further by releasing cortisol and decreasing my brain's serotonin. I quadruple my testosterone levels.

All I want is The Beast dead. I imagine myself pummeling him with my pipe, raining blow after blow down on him. He tries to run, but I chase him down and beat him into submission. Then I grab him by the throat, my knuckles tense as I imagine squeezing the life out of him while he whimpers.

I grab one of the bombs from my bag and take my pipe in hand. This monster has killed hundreds, maybe thousands of people. He took the best thing in my life from me. Now, he is going to die.

I kick open the door to the roof.

I roar.

30

I give you the land. I give you the seas. I give you the heavens themselves. I give you dominion over it all. You must simply claim your thrones as kings of the new earth.

Chosen Sons: 59

The Beast's heart almost jumps right up out of his chest when he smells Gavin. Gavin is not dead! The Beast's plan has worked. Gavin has accepted Cabot's teaching. The Beast is not a sinner. He is a missionary, making converts for the Lord. He has done the Lord's work and God saved Gavin in return.

The Beast's heart sinks like a stone when he hears Gavin's roar. That is not the sound of a man coming to give thanks. That is the sound of a man out for blood. The Beast sighs. If Gavin is out for revenge, there is only one way for this to end. Even if peace is unlikely, the Lord would want The Beast to try. He chokes down his urge to howl back at the boy. The Beast is trying to be civilized.

"Gavin, hot damn! You're alive. It's a miracle," The Beast says, trying to sound as friendly as possible.

Gavin stops his charge and holds about ten yards from The Beast. The boy has a Maceo Steel pipe in one hand and a jar of some sort in the other hand. The people on the roof all get to their feet. This might be their one chance to get away.

"What do you know about miracles? All you know is misery," Gavin says.

"My, my, aren't we a judgmental one. I can't help but notice you're looking pretty healthy there, boy. I suppose it's all that clean living and exercise that has you standing there, not tearing out the insides of your lovely girlfriend."

"You think that's how I'm alive? You think I killed her? I'm alive thanks to friends. Friends are something a monster like you will never understand. You thought I was like you? No one is like you.

Everyone is better than you. You are evil."

Gavin holds up a jam jar and gives it a good shake. Then he rolls the jar at The Beast. The creature smells vinegar.

"Have you been cooking for me, boy?"

The jar answers The Beast's joke by exploding. The glass just bounces off The Beast's leathery hide, but the loud sound startles him. Distracted, The Beast does not notice Gavin hurling a second bomb. He looks up just in time for the jar to hit squarely in his face, the shards of glass opening tiny cuts. The foam from the jars is even more effective. It gets in The Beast's eyes, burning them and blurring his vision.

"Get out of here! Now!" Gavin yells to the terrified Tower residents. They were ready to go and sprint towards the door. They start filing out as quickly as they can.

Gavin goes in for the kill. He moves like a man possessed, swinging his Maceo Steel pipe like a bat. The Beast tries to fight. He could kill Gavin in one swing if only he could see the boy. The Beast flings his arms about, but Gavin is able to dodge the sloppy blows. Gavin keeps swinging his pipe, raining blow after blow down on the creature. The makeshift bat is constructed from the hardest substance on earth. Each blow hurts The Beast. One swing cracks a bone above The Beast's eye and another swing cracks a rib. Gavin avoids a large swipe from The Beast and drives the pipe into the creature's exposed side, stabbing one of many half-healed gunshot wounds.

The Beast howls in pain. He smacks the pipe away, knocking Gavin to the ground along with it. Seeing his chance to escape, The Beast turns towards the door. He's no longer thinking about winning. He doesn't care about proving his dominance or spreading the word of Cabot. The Beast is afraid, afraid of Gavin. He has to get away. He whimpers.

Gavin reaches into his sack and pulls out another jam jar bomb. He takes aim and rolls the jar like a bowling ball towards the feet of the fleeing creature. Gavin's aim proves true, and The Beast steps on the jar mid-run. It explodes under his foot, knocking The Beast to the ground.

Seeing his chance to finish the fight, Gavin yanks out a knife from the sheath at his waist and runs towards The Beast at full speed. He lifts the knife over his head and swings it down at The Beast, who is kneeling on all fours. The creature tries to roll out of the way, but the knife catches a chunk of his shoulder, slicing through it with ease.

The Beast howls and gets to his feet, but Gavin swings again. This time, the boy slices into the creature's side. The Beast howls once more. He has to run, he has to hide. Hide! Gavin smiles as he watches The Beast's panic, and prepares to deliver the finishing blow.

Gavin stops in his tracks when he hears the scream of an elderly man struggling to pull a young woman up off the side of the building. They are the only Tower residents still left on the roof. She must have fallen when the jar exploded. She is barely hanging on. Gavin considers his options for a moment. He could kill The Beast right now, but the woman just looks so much like someone he loved, someone he just lost. He doesn't want this woman to die too.

Gavin sheaths his blade and runs over to the struggling woman. He pushes the older man aside and hauls the young woman up off the side of the roof by the collar of her jacket. The pair scurries away, but Gavin has turned his back to The Beast. The Beast's vision clears just enough to see his target. He charges at Gavin.

31

Whereas Ultracorps and its subsidiaries have been largely responsible for the construction of the Metro Areas.
Whereas Ultracorps and its subsidiaries are providing food and other essential services to the citizens of the United States of America.
Whereas Ultracorps provided many services free of charge in the years following its founding.
We herby Commemorate May 3, 1995, as The Unified Logistics Technology and Research Applications Corporation Appreciation Day

The Unified Logistics Technology and Research Applications Corporation Appreciation Day Act of 1995.

All I hear is a whistle before the blow. It could just be a gust of wind, but the wind has never shattered my T11 and T12 vertebrae. The wind has never ruptured my new lower intestine and one of my kidneys. The wind has never knocked me fifteen feet through the air.

I land with a thud and lay in a heap while I try to come up with some sort of plan. Right now, the one thing going for me is that The Beast still doesn't want to kill me or, he wants to kill me slowly. If The Beast had used his claws for that blow instead of his fist, he would have chopped me in half.

Since he didn’t, I’m only bleeding internally. All the little wounds from the last fight have reopened inside of me. No amount of blood vessel constriction or slowing of my heart rate will be enough to stop the flow. If I don't have time to focus exclusively on my healing, I'm going to be dead in fifteen minutes.

Fifteen minutes seems like a pretty long time right now. I could be dead in fifteen seconds. By some miracle, my spinal cord was relatively unharmed by The Beast’s punch, but those shattered vertebrae make it almost impossible for me to stand up. I have one chance now. I put my hand on the blade at my waist and wait for The Beast to approach me. I can tell I hurt him with the knife before.

He's starting to move more slowly.

"That was quite a show, boy. I didn't think you had so much fight in you. This is the end for us, though. The Lord keeps putting you in my path, and He made me for one purpose. Maybe Chosen Sons who reject Cabot are even bigger sinners than the humans."

That's right, psycho, you just keep talking, that's just what I want you to do. The Beast continues on his rant, but I'm not paying much attention to what he's saying, I don't want to split my concentration. My entire focus is on The Beast. I watch the muscles twitch underneath his skin, and the blood pulse through his veins. I'm waiting for my moment to strike.

"Gavin, I'm sorry about this, I am. I don't want to be a sinner, but this is what the Good Lord made me for. This is going to hurt me too," The Beast says when I tune him back in.

He's right, it is going to hurt him. The Beast stands over me. He seems like he's about to deliver the finishing blow, but he pauses to close his eyes and pray. That's my moment. I put my hand on my knife and think of Becky. Then I pull the blade out and lunge at The Beast the best I can. The tip of the knife is headed right towards his chest. It just might kill him.

Only, the knife never connects. I slow down time just enough to watch The Beast open his eyes and grab my arm before I can react. He squeezes, pulverizing my ulna and radius bones in my forearm and damaging the nerve. I can't hold onto the knife.

"Show some respect, boy!" The Beast screams and gives me a backhanded slap.

The slap knocks out three teeth and partially dislocates my jaw. However, I did manage to buy myself a few more seconds of life. My knife intrigues The Beast. He picks it up and examines it.

"Is this made out of Maceo Steel? I didn't know there was such a thing. Maceo really was special, wasn't he? He shoulda been building cities for Chosen Sons. Instead the humans worked him to death laying train tracks and pipes," The Beast says.

He takes the knife and goes over to the edge of the roof. I bet his eyes are good enough to see what's happening below, even from this height. He takes aim at something and throws the knife.

A few seconds later, I hear an ungodly crash, followed by the distinct sound of a vacuum. He must have ruptured a Hoover mainline. Who knows how many people that will kill? The vacuum force in those pipes is enough to suck down a train. The pipes aren't supposed to break. It isn’t supposed to be possible.

While The Beast watches the carnage below, I tap into think.Net and call Ben.

>>>Gavin was that your knife he threw? That thing ruptured a Hoover main. It's bedlam down here.

<<<Yes, it was. I'm in trouble Ben. I'm hurt... badly. I could use that surprise you mentioned.

>>>It's on the way. Thirty seconds, Gavin.

I need to buy myself thirty seconds. I can feel the last jar bomb in my pocket. It has managed to survive the melee. I take it out and give it a quick shake to activate the ingredients. It's hard to get in a good position to make a throw, but by tightening some of the muscles in my back, I'm able to at least sit up. I take stock of The Beast's position and heave.

The jar lands behind The Beast. I underestimated how much a broken spine would take off my throw. Nevertheless, I got close enough to surprise him. The jar explodes and The Beast stumbles as he tries to run away.

He stands up and turns towards me. I can see the anger in his eyes. I definitely have his attention, but suddenly this doesn't seem like a very good idea. Maybe I should have just hoped he remained amused with the carnage on the street.

The Beast walks slowly and deliberately towards me. I need more time. Eleven more seconds.

"Wait, Thomas, I think I might be having a change of heart. I think I might be able to follow Cabot's path. I just don't know how to do it," I plead.

I’m not sure whether he believed me or if he was just shocked that I knew his real name, but whichever it was, he pauses for a second. Five seconds to be exact.

"You are smart, boy. But not smart enough..."

>>>Gavin, turn off your ears.

I hear Ben in my brain and flood my Tympanic Cavity. I watch as The Beast drops down to the floor. He is rolling around in agony, with blood spilling out of his ears.

When I return my ears to their proper state, I immediately wish I hadn't. The Beast's howls are deafening.

>>>Did it work? I wasn't sure if the frequency would affect you so I thought you should turn your ears off to be safe.

<<<The Beast is rolling around on the floor, howling in pain. What did you do?

>>>Me? I didn't do anything. Your roommate Nick is the guilty party. Turns out, he'll just read whatever they tell him. Pitch, tone, and frequency included. I don't think he's all that bright. I hacked think.Net and sent out a fake order for an unusually pitched Emergency Alert. The Beast and every animal for miles are going to be deaf for a while. If you ever wanted to sneak up on a squirrel, now would be the time.

The Beast manages to get to his feet, but he's still stunned. I need to find a way to finish him off. I look around for something, one of my jar bombs, my pipe, anything to use against The Beast. Nothing is close, no weapons. Nothing but me.

I flood my body with every last bit of adrenaline I have left in my glands. Then I roll onto my stomach and push myself up. If I tense all of the muscles in my back, they can serve as a surrogate for my broken spine.

It works, and I'm able to slowly lift myself to my feet. My body screams in protest. Newly formed clots rupture and blood starts flowing inside me like a river. The shattered remnants of my vertebrae press into my spinal column, making it difficult to get nerve signals to my legs. My body demands that I stop and rest.

But I'm a Different. I can not only hear my body, I can choose not to listen. I think of Becky's smile and rise to my feet. I think of her smell and take a step forward. I think of her kiss and take another. Then I think of her throat cut open and break into a run. I keep going no matter how many systems in my body tell me to stop, no matter that I've lost feeling in my left foot, or that my vision is starting to become blurred.

I'm focused on one goal, and nothing can stop me. I take all the hate I've ever felt, hate for the Government, hate for my mother, hate for this monster. I take it all and focus it onto The Beast. I focus it all into one moment.

32

Together my Chosen Sons shall build this new utopia. Together my Chosen Sons will leave behind the sins of my first creation. Together they will forge a new world. A world free from war and strife, a world of brotherhood, a world of piety.

Chosen Sons: 56

The Beast swings his arms wildly about. His vision is still blurry, he is completely deaf, and he can only smell vinegar. Nevertheless, he is still standing. Nothing can kill him, nothing. The Lord picked him out of all the Chosen. He is special.

Now all he has to do is find Gavin. He has to find the weak and pathetic Chosen Son who will not see his proper place on earth. He is going to rip Gavin's head off. All he has to do is find the boy.

The Beast does not see Gavin coming. He does not hear Gavin's footsteps or smell Gavin's scent. The Beast does not brace at all for Gavin crashing into him. Gavin may be small compared to The Beast, but the boy hits with the all the force the human body can create. Gavin knocks The Beast backwards onto the edge of the building. He struggles to keep his balance for just a moment before falling off the side of the Tower.

He spends a few seconds in the air before he realizes he did not just slip to the floor, he fell completely off the side of the building. The Beast knows he is going to die: Gavin has killed him. The Beast did not think the boy was strong enough to do it.

But Gavin did not just get lucky. This is the Lord's work. This is Providence. That is the only explanation.

The Beast screams to the sky, "What did I do wrong? What could I have done to please you?"

He doesn't get an answer.

33

This court has been asked, "How can it outlaw heroes? How can it outlaw citizens trying to do good for their community?" The truth is that this court is not endorsing the outlawing of heroes; it is endorsing the outlawing of fairytales. Many of these so-called heroes do act with the best of intentions, but good intentions are not enough. Although Different individuals may seem God-like, they are in fact men. They are just as prone to making mistakes as all other men. Different individuals attempting to act compassionately have reaped untold destruction through their errors. We cannot choose the fantasy of heroics over the reality of the harm Different individuals can and have caused.

Justice Margaret Fuller
Majority Opinion: United States v. Anthony "Speedlight" Harrison

I want to watch The Beast fall, but it's not worth dying over. I need to get a handle on my injuries. I try to focus on stopping the hemorrhages inside my body, but I can't concentrate. My mind keeps wandering to thoughts of my mom leaving, my dad dying, and The Beast murdering Becky. I killed the monster. I should feel like a hero. Instead, I feel like a scared little boy.

This shouldn't be happening to me. I have complete control over my body, complete control over my mind. I should be focusing on my cracked vertebrae, not wondering if there was anything I could have done to make my mom stay or if my dad died alone on that fishing boat. I need to find a way to move on. I think I need to cry.

I let the emotions flow through me, and I feel my eyes start to water. I think of my father, how he stood by me and took care of me, all alone. I think of my mom and how hard it must have been for her to know I was headed for a life of slavery. I imagine her seeing me now. I think she'd be proud of me. I'm sad she won't know that I didn't let them break me.

I think of Becky and the life she lived. All the trials and tribulations she survived during the Plagues, only to be murdered because of me. I think about the life we could have had together. I think about how I'm never going to see her again. I think about how I wasn't strong enough to save her. I think about how she wouldn't have been in danger if I had been more careful.

The tears flow as I spend a few minutes lost in thought. Somehow, crying has made me feel better. The pain is still there, but it is lessened, it's dulled somehow. I guess channeling my emotions to fight The Beast had some collateral effects. Now that I have my emotions under control, I can focus on my injuries.

Besides my broken vertebrae, I have twenty-six major hemorrhages in various places inside me. The Beast also broke three ribs, one of which has punctured my lung. Most of my stitches have torn. I'm bleeding at a high rate out of the front of me, although it's nothing compared to the internal bleeding. My jaw is broken, too.

The first thing I have to do is make blood, gallons of blood. I stimulate my marrow to produce red blood cells, white blood cells, and platelets. I mix these with plasma that I generate from what little water there is left in my system. Lastly, I mix in proteins and electrolytes from my liver.

Now that I have a supply of blood, I need to stop my internal bleeding. I flood the hemorrhages with platelet cells so clots will form. Even with my direction, it takes about six minutes to get the bleeding to stop, or slow at least.

Next, I deal with my punctured lung. I push on my chest and force the chunk of bone out of the soft tissue. Once I re-grow a bit of my lung, I should be able to take deep breaths again.

I start the process to heal my back. It will take a few days to regenerate all the bone, but I should be able to form some cartilage that can serve as a makeshift spine in the meantime. That, plus flexing my back muscles, should allow me to walk, albeit slowly.

Lastly, I deal with my torn stitches. I pick them out and restrict blood flow to the bleeding areas. I don't bother forming scabs. They'll just tear as I walk down.

I push myself to my feet. The hardest part will be keeping my back muscles flexed without them cramping. There's already a big build-up of lactic acid in the tissue. I'm clearing it as fast as I can by increasing blood flow, but the acid level will continue to build. A lot of my body needs blood, and there isn’t enough to go around.

Now that I can stand, I stumble over to edge the roof and look down. By squinting and bending my cornea, I can just barely make out what's happening down on the street. It looks like they have the Hoover main closed up, and they are leading people out of the Tower. Guess that means it's just a matter of time till the cops come up here and find me. I don't think I'm going to be able to convince them I'm a fellow officer. My blood-soaked uniform raises some questions that I don’t have good answers for. I need another way out of the building.

I log on think.Net and try to call Ben. *No such account*. Not *no answer*, not *unavailable*, not *out of range… No such account*. How is that possible? I don’t have any more time to think about it because I’m getting my own think.Net call. Nita.

>>>Gavin, I am sorry. I do not have much time to talk. My mind is extremely busy trying to deal with the damage The Beast caused. Do you know what occurred? How was The Beast able to rupture the Hoover main?

<<<It's a long story. Is he dead Nita?

>>>He plummeted down the entire height of the Tower. He is deceased.

<<<How do we know for sure? Have you confirmed it?

>>>The Beast's remains will be found by the police when they can spare the manpower. Right now, they are still assisting the victims of the Tower and the ruptured Hoover main.

<<<Is there anything I can do to help?

>>>Gavin, you will not be in any position to render assistance. The police will find you shortly, and when they do, they will arrest you.

<<<Arrest me? What do you mean?

>>>You violated Article 3 of the Different Acts of 1996, Provision Against Vigilantism. You were aware your actions were illegal were you not?

<<<Yeah, but you helped me.

>>>I will continue to do so. I will work towards your release, but it is going to take time. Until then, you are going to have to face the consequences of your actions.

<<<Well, that sucks.

>>>Have you ever considered why it is that you started spending your nights as a vigilante? Why it is you seem to find helping people satisfying in the first place? I have a theory: When you were fourteen you were just like many other boys your age. Young, idealistic, and hopeful to save the world like an action movie hero. The difference between you and all those other boys is that you are a Different. Those boys matured, their brains developed, and they formed new, more realistic dreams. Instead of wanting to be a spy saving the country from nuclear annihilation, they want to be accountants with a steady paycheck and a loving family. Your brain doesn't mature, Gavin, at least not in the normal way. I think you still have the same dreams you had as a child.

<<<That's quite a theory.

>>>I only call it a theory so I do not come across as arrogant.

<<<Who would call you arrogant?

>>>Takes one to know one. Goodbye and good luck.

She ends the call.

Did I just get called immature by a little girl who said "takes one to know one"? Even worse, she might be right. It would explain why acting like a hero made me so happy. Maybe it's because my brain is still wired like a fourteen-year-old boy. Maybe I'm just acting on the fantasies all young boys have of being James Bond or Luke Skywalker. The only difference is I'm actually capable of acting on those delusions. Is that such a bad thing? Maybe growing up and losing your idealism is what's wrong with the world.

I can think about this later, right now I should be wondering why Nita is going to let me be arrested. How does this figure into her plan? She can't still be planning to blame this all on me. There were too many witnesses. Everyone on the roof saw me fight The Beast.

I head down from the roof and make a stop in a penthouse apartment. The entryway is even more impressive than the apartment I stopped in earlier. As soon as I step in the door, I am greeted with a view of a large gold statue of a Greek Olympian running in place. He is actually running in place, well, vibrating really, and it's even letting out a faint but lovely hum.

I think it's a Motion Sculpture. It's made of a compound produced by a Different. The molecules shift in between quantum states or something like that. They're trying to find a way to turn the compound into something useful. For now, we'll have to settle for amazing artwork for rich people. Ultracorps has even cornered the art market. I'd be angrier if it wasn't so beautiful. That'll be something nice to remember while I'm in prison.

Speaking of prison, if I'm going to rot in a jail cell, it would be nice to do it on a full stomach. That way, at least I'll be able to heal. I head into the kitchen and raid the pantry, going through each and every item and taking a bite. That way I'll have a wide variety of foods to fool myself into enjoying while eating my prison gruel.

All this eating is causing more damage to my busted jaw, but I can make myself ignore the pain. I won't be able to heal without food, and a slightly more broken jaw isn't much in the scheme of my injuries. I have Hershey's chocolate, canned pineapple, peanut butter, Honey Nut Cheerios, and so much more. Some of the foods I've eaten before, but a lot of it is Pre-Plague treats that only the wealthy can afford. They also have a number of spices I've never seen before, even in the food lab. I'm going to make myself imagine whatever slop they feed me in Great Basin tastes like cinnamon-sugar.

Considering I might never be free again, I should take in some more experiences. I head into the master bedroom. It is as magnificent as the rest of the house. There are paintings by artists I'm sure I should know the name of and gold trim and moulding all around the room. I open the closest and see a silk robe. I carefully take off my tattered police uniform and slip into the robe. It was worth reopening a wound in my intestine from all the motion. The fabric feels fantastic. Better than my own skin.

I head into the bathroom where I disrobe and step into the shower. This way, I can look presentable for my day in court. I take a scorching hot shower and scrub off the blood that has dried all over me.

Once I'm done with the shower, I dry by jumping into the king-size bed and rolling around in the silk sheets. The bed is made of Construct. I shape it and give it a slap. Now it's like I'm laying in a cloud custom made to fit my body. I'm sure my prison bed will feel just like this.

Once I dry off, I rifle through the closet for some clothes. I pick out a blue suit. It has an Italian-sounding name and looks fantastic, if a little tight. I put on a red-checked dress shirt. It's also too small, but I can make it work. Then I put the trousers and jacket on. I pick out a pair of brown leather shoes shiny enough for me to see my reflection. I try to tie a tie for three solid minutes before I give up and decide to wear my shirt open collar. I take a look at myself in the mirror. For a guy who is bleeding internally, I don't look bad. I think it's time to go face the music.

I start my long descent down the Tower. I have far to go and each step makes nerves shoot off like fireworks, reminding me, in case I'd forgotten, that my body is riddled with injuries. As I head down the steps, I don't hear the Tower residents below me. They must have all gotten out already. When I get to the twenty-fifth floor, I see how. They've got a two hundred fifty foot ladder running up from the ground floor. They must have had that Strong-Woman I saw earlier take out the rest of the stairs for access.

I start climbing down the ladder. I can hear activity below me. Someone yells, "There's one more!"

It takes me three minutes to make my way two hundred feet down the ladder, with the cops encouraging me.

"Come on buddy, you can make it. We got medics waiting!" a cop yells.

I keep climbing until I'm about twenty-five feet off the ground, and what I was waiting for finally happens. One of the officers spots the D on my hand.

"He's a Different!" the spotter yells.

Suddenly, twenty guns are pointed up at me. One of the braver officers jumps up the ladder and grabs me by my pants and rips me off the ladder. He throws me down onto the ground where the other cops surround me.

"It wasn't me!" I shout.

They twist me around, pinning my arms behind my back. The little bit of cartilage I had grown to help support my spine, tears. Three of them lay on top of me, digging their knees into my back to keep me pinned. Then another cop puts a gun right up to the back of my head.

"You feel that freak? You move a muscle and a bullet blows your skull to pieces. So you'll do exactly what I tell you, won't you, freak?" The cop says. His voice is a mix of fear and hate.

"Yes," is all I can manage. It is hard with my face is smashed into the ground and my jaw is still dislocated.

"Now, don't move yet, but when I tell you, slowly hold up your hand and let me see your tattoo." He signals to the cop holding my arm down to release me. "Okay now, raise your right arm and only your right arm, slowly."

I do as they ask and raise my arm slowly. When my hand gets close to him, he grabs it roughly, straining a muscle in my shoulder. Another injury to heal.

"Gavin Stillman: Anthropomorphic Control: GAMMA. Somebody get on think.Net with Section 26 and find out what in God's name Anthropomorphic Control is. Meantime, let him up, fellas. He's not our monster. He's only a Gamma, but somebody keep a gun on him," the cops says,

The officers on top of me relent, and I'm allowed to get to my feet. I can barely manage it. Several cops follow the leader's suggestion and keep their firearms trained on me. Then, the leader grabs my right arm again and twists it behind my back.

"I'm placing you under arrest for suspicion of violation of the Different Acts." The officer says as he pulls my left arm behind me and places me in handcuffs. "You have the right to remain silent. Anything you say or do can and will be held against you in the court of law. You have the right to speak to an attorney. If you cannot afford an attorney, one will be appointed for you. Do you understand these rights as they have been read to you?" he asks.

"Yes," I've watched enough cop dramas on think.Net to know the less I say the better.

With my hands behind my back, the police lead me down the rest of the stairs, through the lobby and out the front door.

The ruptured Hoover main did an incredible amount of damage. The buildings have had their windows sucked out and their facades torn off. Streetlights and garbage cans litter the sidewalk. They must have been pulled here from blocks away. No one had prepared for a broken Hoover main. Why would they? The main is made of Maceo Steel and nothing on earth can break Maceo Steel, except, apparently, Maceo Steel itself.

Besides the property damage, people are bleeding from cuts and scrapes caused by flying debris. The paramedics seem to have the situation under control, though. I don't see anyone who looks that bad.

Beyond the crowd of residents, police officers, and paramedics, is one more group: reporters. They stand about five thick at the police barricade. They're all craning their necks, trying to get footage. Everyone will be seeing through those reporters' eyes for the six o'clock think.Net news.

I have a moment to take it all in before the police move me along. I can see my destination, an armored police car. It's obviously the one they use for Differents. It has Maceo Steel plating. At least I'll get to ride in a car before I'm locked in Great Basin forever. I did always want to do that. I have to strain my sense of optimism to see that upside.

As we walk towards the armored car, I make eye contact with a young boy who I remember seeing on the roof. I give him a smile.

The boy makes no response to me, but I see him pull on his mother and point to me. There is too much other noise around to pick out what they are saying, but whatever it is, it seems to be spreading through the Tower residents. I see several of them point at me.

"It's him," I'm finally able to make out one resident say. "That's the guy who saved us."

Suddenly, the crowd of people starts surging towards me. I can hear many of them yelling "Thank you" or "You're an angel." The group surrounds us.

"Get out of the way. You are all interfering with police business!" the lead cop yells and starts pushing people aside to clear a path.

The crowd does not resist. They don't want to free me. They just want to thank me.

"You saved my baby. How can I ever repay you?" one woman says.

"That monster, he said he was going to kill us all. Thank you. Thank you so much," another woman says.

"I pay my debts son, any lawyer you want, it's on me," a man offers.

I say “You're welcome” as many times as I can before we get to the police car. By that time, the crowd has affected the officers, and they are treating me more gently. They carefully put me inside the back of the car and close the door.

I barely hear the car start because the crowd of residents has broken into applause. It sounds like I just won the World Series. I slow down time much as I am able so I can savor the moment. I don't want to miss a thing because this is what made it all worth it. I saved those people. I'm a hero.

#

As the car moves along, I keep my body healing. I've taken care of the direst injuries, so I can spare a moment to think of other subjects. I remember what Ben told me to do when I had a free moment: figure out how Nita was tracking The Beast and me.

She can see my think.Net transactions, which can explain how she knew when I was on the Slug. It doesn't explain how she was keeping track of The Beast though. I don't think he went through the turnstiles. From what I understand about think.Net, it can't be used to track people. The Telepaths are already stretched to the limit running the network. Supposedly, they don't have the energy to keep track of locations too. That could be a lie: they aren't supposed to be able to connect people who don't have accounts either.

I'm not sure that's it though. Ben seemed to know a lot about think.Net. I imagine he would have figured it out if it were that simple. I think back to the first time that Nita seemed to know where I was. It was that day she asked me sodium levels in drinking water. She had the train waiting for me when I got to the station as a reward, but how did she know when I'd get there? She's smart, but I don't think she knows exactly how long it takes me to get ready in the morning. She also seemed to know I was hunting The Beast. Then she tracked me down after The Beast gutted me. I don't think Larry just got lucky and found me on his own. I look through my memories of those incidents. What did they have in common?

Walters. I ran into Walters.

I think that's it. She can see through the Walters. That could also explain how she kept track of The Beast and found his victims. If she can see through the Walters, she basically has a giant network of spies all around the city. I wish I could talk to Ben and confirm that I'm not just being crazy.

I spend another twenty-three minutes healing before my mobile prison comes to a stop. I don't think we made it all the way to Great Basin Prison, but I have no idea where we could be. We move again, backwards this time, and then suddenly the back of the car opens and about a dozen armed personnel are waiting for me. More guns pointed at my head.

"Exit the vehicle slowly!" one of them shouts.

I do as they say and step down from the car. I can't go any speed but slow considering I still haven't come close to healing my cracked vertebrae. I'm led to another station where one of my guards hands over a wad of paperwork to a bureaucrat.

"Gavin Stillman: Gamma, for booking," the guard says.

"Is this Great Basin?" I ask.

"No. This is LA Metro lockup for Different offenders," the bureaucrat says without looking up.

The bureaucrat writes something on a ledger then pulls out an inkpad to take my fingerprints. I can't believe the police still do this. Then a Pre-Plague camera is used to take my picture. I only know what it is from old TV shows.

"Are you in need of immediate medical attention?" the bureaucrat asks.

That's nice. One hour after they arrest me, they finally get around to asking me if I need a doctor.

"No, I'm all right."

I'm far from all right, but I don't think there's anything a terrible prison doctor will be able to do for me. I can manage healing on my own for most of my injuries. I don't know how to re-grow the missing half of my index finger, but I should have plenty of time to figure it out while I'm rotting away in prison.

"This location is shielded from think.Net, but we have a room where you have the right to make one call," the bureaucrat says.

"Who am I supposed to call?" I ask.

"Do you have an attorney, or the money to hire one?"

"No, I don't," I say. I leave out the part where I spent all my money committing my crime. "But one of the people at the Shimmering Tower told me they'd pay for any lawyer I want."

"Then you should call that guy. Do you know him on think.Net?"

"You guys dragged me away before I could make the knowledge request."

"Well, if this mysterious millionaire shows up, I'll be sure to tell you. Otherwise, if you got nobody to call, you can hurry up and wait for your public defender to show up."

The guards take me away and into a bathroom where I'm told to shower and change into my bright orange prison jump suit. Once I'm clean and meeting the dress code, I'm led down a hallway made of Maceo Steel, to a door made of Maceo Steel, which opens to reveal my cell which is made of... Maceo Steel. Maceo is the only person who could break out of this jail.

My escorts put a gun to my head one more time while they unhook my handcuffs.

"Enjoy your stay," a guard says, and they slam my cell closed.

The cell is quite large. The ceiling is about fifty feet high. It's not for luxury. Aside from the door, the only opening in the cell is the air vent located at the top. They must have another cell for Differents who can get up that high.

Besides the vaulted ceiling, there's a sink, a toilet, and a thin cot on the ground. I don't think I'm going to be given any reading material. Lucky for me, waiting for my public defender won't seem like that long, no matter how long it takes. Besides, I have healing to do.

I focus my attention on rebuilding my spine. I pull calcium from my digestive tract and then send it to the areas where my vertebrae are cracked. Then I stimulate my bones to grow. I have to be sure everything heals straight, or the bone may end up damaging my spinal cord, which would take even longer to heal. I'm glad I ate so much before being arrested. This much healing takes a lot of nutrients. Although, I'm having a little trouble dealing with all the cheddar cheese I ate. There was a lot of lactose in there. It is building up and the reactions in my gut are creating a lot of gas. I'll have to make more enzymes to help me manage that.

I spend seven hours in this state, making time fly except for taking care of my body's recovery needs. I snap out of it when I hear the door opening. I look up to see one of the guards grinning.

"Looks like it's your lucky day, somehow they were able to find you a public defender in the middle of the night. Enjoy your worst-in-his-class lawyer," the guard says and steps aside.

My lawyer steps into view. I recognize him immediately, Ben the train conductor.

"Hello Gavin, pleased to meet you. My name's Ronald Hopkins, and I'll be representing you," Ben says and gives me a handshake.

"Now, please officer, if you wouldn't mind giving me and my client some privacy."

The guard shrugs and heads out. "Holler if you need me."

Ben watches to make sure the guard is out of earshot, and then turns to me.

"I'm going to be honest. I think you have a lousy case." Ben says with a smile.

"Is that your opinion as a lawyer or a train conductor?"

"Both."

"Will you tell me who you really are, or am I going to have to call that guard?" I demand.

"That would be a real shame. You have no idea how hard it was to get in here. I had to hack into think.Net, create a fake identity file, falsify housing records, school records, my bar exam. It took me three hours. Nothing takes me three hours," he says smugly.

"Who are you? How can you do all that?"

"My real name is Benjamin Grant, and I'm an alcoholic. Really, I can do those things because I'm a think.Net Librarian, or I used to be until I found out some things I should not have found out. Conspiracy things. Things I need to warn you about."

"If you hadn't noticed, it's a little late for a warning. They already have me. If this was all some sort of government conspiracy to take me down, I think it worked."

"No, I don't think it did. Have you had time to think about all that happened? Maybe you've started to wonder how three of your friends just so happened to be on call to save you the night The Beast tore you open."

"No, I hadn't thought about any of that. I've been focused on my healing." He's right. How were all my friends just waiting to help me? No one can be that lucky.

"You need to work on your multi-tasking, Gavin. Once again, I will clue you in. Nita already knew your friends Gary, Sarah, and Larry. They all work for her, well, kind of anyway. I think that's why Nita befriended you in the first place. I think she was planning on recruiting you before your whole fight-crime-and-avenge-your-lady's-death-thing started happening."

"Recruiting me for what?"

"That I don't quite know yet. It's hard to grasp Nita. I used to be Nita before Nita was Nita. I was the young kid who was the smartest Librarian. They called me the most powerful mind on earth. I thought I was smart, but Nita makes me look like a monkey. I am not sure I am capable of understanding her plan. She's as different from me as I am from a normal human. Luckily, she's still lacking in experience. She's too naive to consider the possibility that I left some backdoors into her systems when I made my escape. I'm sure she'll find them when she grows into a jaded teenager."

"I think I figured out how she was tracking The Beast and me. She can see through the Walters. I looked back through my memories..."

Ben holds his hand up to shut me up. He's thinking about what I said.

"I think... I think that's it. The Walters are just empty shells, really, but they do have humanish brains. I think a Telepath could tap into them, which means Nita could tap into them through think.Net. You're smarter then you look Gavin, or act, for that matter. Maybe that's why Nita wanted to recruit you."

"So what's the plan now? How are you going to bust me out of here?" I ask.

"Well, you see I've got this cake coming, but what the guards don't know is that there's a nail file inside," he pauses for effect. "Are you kidding me? It was a miracle I made it in here and it'll be miracle if I make it out. A miracle wouldn't cover what it would be if I broke you out too, we'd have to call it a Supracle. I just wanted to let you know to be afraid of Nita. Hopefully, I'll have more information by the time you make it out of here."

"How am I getting out of here, if you aren't busting me out?"

"Nita's going to let you out of course. My legal opinion is you're guilty, but I think somehow you'll be freed anyway."

With that, Ben turns around and yells, “Guard! I’m done with the prisoner.”

Then he turns to me and says very quietly, "I'll leave you with one more thing to ponder. If Nita was just manipulating you so that you'd attack The Beast, wouldn’t she just need you to believe that Becky is dead?"

Then he turns and heads out of the cell.

34

Reign down these Plagues, Cabot, and you shall make the world a harsh and unforgiving place. None shall be fit to live upon this earth, save my Chosen Sons. Through your hand, Cabot, I will remake this world and bestow it upon my Chosen Sons.

Chosen Sons: 20

The Beast is not hungry for the first time in a long time. Whoever is keeping him here is giving him more food than even he can eat. He has been dining on a variety of meats he has never tasted before. The meals are gigantic and delicious. The food has helped The Beast heal. Already he can stand, if not walk. The voice over the intercom encourages The Beast to push himself.

The Beast sits, waits, and heals. He knows he has been righteous. He knows this is all part of the Lord's plan. That was the only way to explain how he survived the fall: it was God's will. Job had to wait to get his reward for being righteous. Moses had to wait, too. If The Beast can be patient, the good Lord will provide.

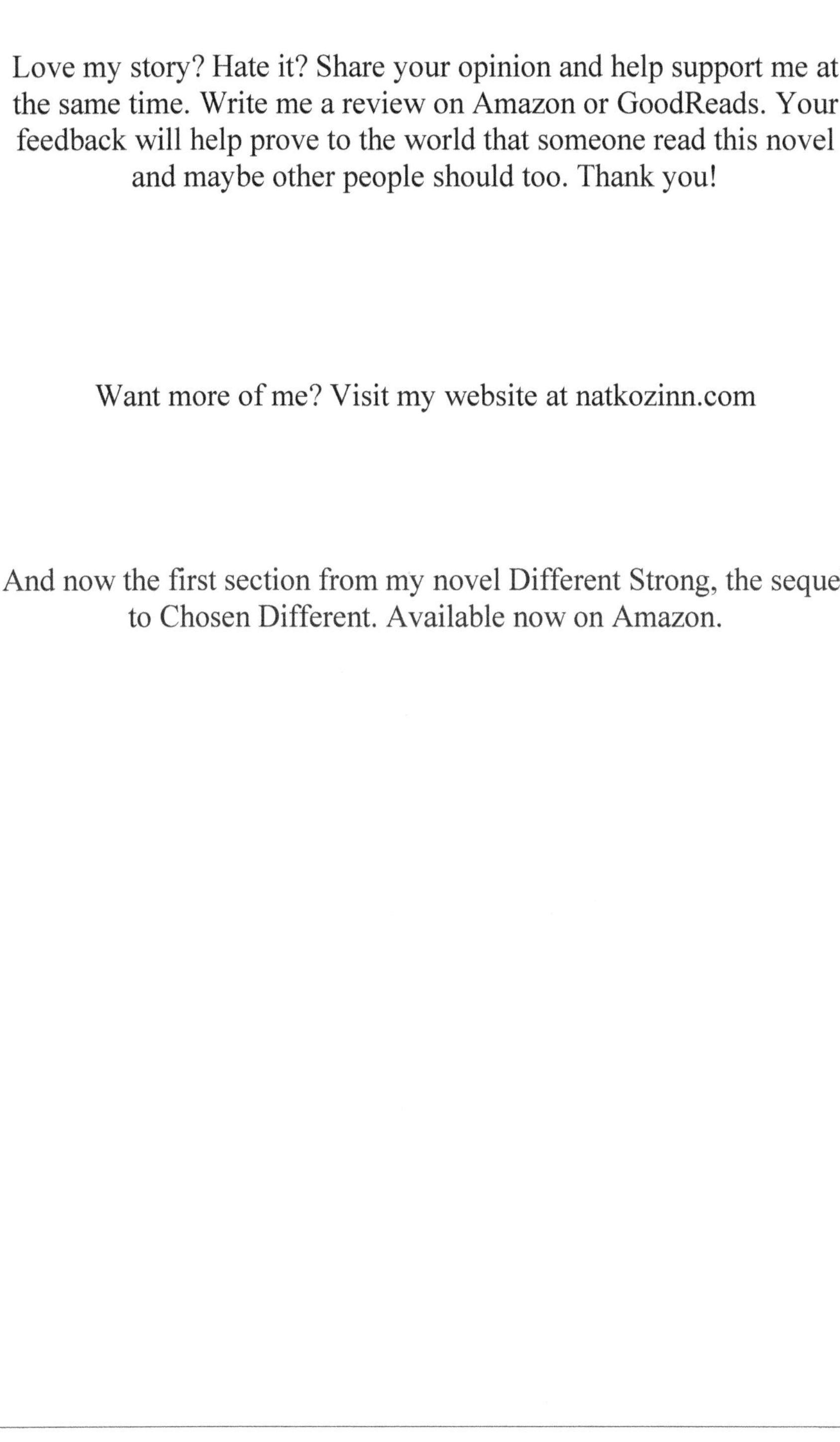

Love my story? Hate it? Share your opinion and help support me at the same time. Write me a review on Amazon or GoodReads. Your feedback will help prove to the world that someone read this novel and maybe other people should too. Thank you!

Want more of me? Visit my website at natkozinn.com

And now the first section from my novel Different Strong, the sequel to Chosen Different. Available now on Amazon.

Excerpt

My muscles are screaming for more oxygen. I don't have any to give. I'm breathing as deeply as I can, but it's no use. I've been running too long. I am going to have to stop and catch my breath. I put my hand on an old, useless electric pole and take deep, slow, methodical breaths. I flood red blood cells to my lungs, gathering oxygen that I send all over my body. While I'm at it, I use my lymphatic system to clear out the lactic acid building in my leg muscles.

Within a few seconds I feel ready to start running again, but before I can, I hear someone else behind me. It's someone who's moving faster than any human can, faster than I can. My partner, Victor Campos.

"What are you doing?" Victor demands.

"I had to stop and rest," I answer.

"I thought you're supposed to have the perfect human body. You've been running for six or seven miles. There are a lot of humans who can run farther than that."

What does he know about what the human body is capable of? He doesn't have a human body. He has something much better than that. He's Physically Enhanced, Athlete Type. He has super dense muscles that make him stronger and faster than any person should be. He was five miles behind when we started running, and he still caught up to me with ease even though he's a six foot five and built like an extra-thick brick wall.

"Humans can't run that long at full sprint. What's the point anyway? The kid is long gone. He moves so fast he makes you look like a snail," I respond.

"Speedsters don't have much endurance. They need to stop and rest for an hour after a few minutes of sprinting. They make you look like an ultra-marathon runner."

"How do we know if we're still on his trail?"

"Speedsters always run in a straight line, especially in the Metro Area. It's hard to round a corner at two hundred miles an hour. Look down at the street, do you notice anything?" Victor asks and points.

The sidewalk is covered in debris, a mix of dirt, old concrete, cardboard and even old clothes, it looks like a landfill. There's a path cut right through the filth.

"Running at two hundred miles an hour generates a lot of wind. I'm going to the roofs and see if I can spot where he went. You keep after him down here." With that, Victor takes a running start and leaps two stories up onto the roof of a half-collapsed building. I turn and break back into a sprint, a bit slower than before. I don't want to hear it from Victor if I have to stop and rest again.

Victor is moving above me. Even though he has to jump from rooftop to rooftop, he's covering more ground than I am running on the street. The way he moves reminds me of The Beast. Power mixed with grace. I push The Beast out of my mind. He doesn't deserve my consideration. I put my head down and keep following the path the Speedster left in his wake. Victor seemed confident that we will catch up to him, but I'm skeptical. He was moving so damn fast.

It's no wonder the cops couldn't catch him and had to call us. The kid, Arnold Chapman, freaked out in a crowded upscale restaurant, screaming nonsense about bugs all over his skin. He ran around in circles spilling people's drinks and throwing plates of food. By the time we got there, he was hiding in a corner of the kitchen, covered in spices. It would be funny if it wasn't so tragic. It was Arnold's first week out of Section 26, he was a contractor Delivery Boy for a few restaurants in the area. I'm not sure if he took some drugs or had a psychotic breakdown, and frankly, it doesn't matter. It's just my job to catch him.

I finally have the job I always wanted. The job I told everyone, including myself, I was perfect for. I'm an agent for the Office of Exceptional Cases. My duty is to apprehend dangerous Differents. Now I have to put my money where my mouth is and do the job. It's extra motivation that my own partner doesn't think I am qualified. And it just so happens, if I fail at the job-- I go back to prison.

Victor drops down onto the sidewalk and waits for me to catch up. I make sure to focus and time my breathing so I don't appear to be winded.

"Why did we stop?" I ask.

"I saw the trail come to an end. He's in a half-collapsed building up ahead. It looks like it was a school before the Plagues. It's big; it's a good place to hide."

"What should we do?"

"What do you think we should do? You're supposed to have the ideal human mind too," Victor says sarcastically.

"I guess we should split up; each take half of the school and search for him."

"Wrong. Well, half wrong. What if you find him? You aren't fast enough to catch him, or strong enough. It takes big muscles to move that fast. Besides, a building this size is going to have a half a dozen different exits. You were right about splitting up though. And you should go try to find him. I'll stay on the roof and pounce down on him when he runs out."

"What should I do when I find him? We're out of range of think.Net out here so I can't call you. I knew we should have brought Linda."

"We don't need think.Net and we don't need Linda. How was a fifty-year-old Telepath supposed to keep up anyway? That kid is going to run by you so fast you won't have time to do anything. If you do get lucky and somehow manage to sneak up on him, yell so I know he's coming. You're just scaring him out. I'm apprehending him. Don't try anything stupid. Are we clear?" He says with a look that tells me "yes" is my only option.

"Clear."

We go our separate ways. He climbs onto the roof of a building overlooking the school, and I head inside the school, or what's left of it anyway. The entrance I walk through is missing a key feature of entrances, its doors. Inside is a war zone, there isn't an intact piece of wall in sight. Many of them have been demolished on purpose, the work of salvagers.

The walls are made of concrete. Concrete means rebar, which

means steel. Steel is rare and valuable thanks to the Plagues. Cabot's bacteria could and did eat rebar, but the concrete often protected the metal from the little buggers. The remaining steel rods can be salvaged, but they need to be removed from their concrete casing. It is a difficult job that requires painstakingly smashing through the concrete with a sledgehammer. Ten hours of labor will earn about ten dollar's worth of metal, but there is no shortage of desperate people willing to work on these terms.

The missing walls make it easy to search through the barren rooms. Dozens of looters have been through this school over the years. They picked it clean of anything of value. All that's left are papers, and broken desks and chairs. Whatever metal held them together was salvaged long ago. There's a time worn children's drawing still hanging from one wall, A Dog Named Lucky, by Brian age 8. Not bad for a kid that age, good sense of perspective.

My hunt goes quickly. I clear all of the classrooms in short order and the gym and lunchroom are big piles of rubble, leaving only the auditorium. I step into the large room while stretching out my perception of time. To me, it will seem like I'm moving slowly and carefully almost in slow motion, but I'll really be moving at normal speed. Great for making sure I can move quickly while still taking silent steps. I search through what's left of the rows of seats that used to fill the auditorium. The metal was eaten away by Cabot's bacteria, leaving behind piles of wood, which my Speedster could be resting behind. I get to the middle of the room and look back over my shoulder. Someone stands up and stretches. There he is! He's covered in dirt and blood and shaking with fear. We lock eyes.

"I'm sorry, I didn't mean to do it. I had to get them off my skin," the Speedster pleads. His arms are scratched to shreds, the product of his own fingernails tearing red ribbons in his flesh.

"It's okay. Come with me, and we'll figure it out," I say in a soft friendly tone.

His eyes are jitter bugging out of his head, and the pupils are fully dilated black pits. His carotid artery is pulsing so violently in his neck; his heart might jump right out onto the floor. He's breathing short desperate breaths through a mouth covered in drool. That's a weird mix of conditions for his body to display. I wonder what drugs he's on? It looks like uppers, downers, and everything in between.

"This isn't fun. The drink is poison," the desperate kid pleads.

"Sure it is. Come with me and will make sure you don't have to drink anymore," I say with my hands up.

I watch his deranged eyes move from me to a doorway that has an exit sign. I'm about ten times closer to the door than he is, but that still may not be close enough. He starts running like a bolt of lightning. I slow down my perception of time as far as I can and make a full speed charge to intercept him. I move at top speed, which is like a sloth compared to the Speedster. He's almost at the door. I'm close enough to stop him if I stick out my left arm.

The radius and ulna bones in my left arm shatter into a thousand different pieces. Those pieces burst through my skin like shards of glass, tearing my arm open from the inside out. I'm thrown backwards into the wall, causing massive bruising to my left shoulder. Arnold goes flying too. He hits the wall headfirst and goes down. I run over to him and roll him over with my good arm. He's unconscious and bleeding from the head, and his left leg is bent like a pretzel, but there's a pulse. We have to get him help.

"Victor! I'm in the auditorium; I need your help!" I yell as loud as I can.

It takes Victor fifteen seconds to make his way to the auditorium. He sees my broken left arm hanging limply at my side and our suspect, bleeding from the head.

"This counts as stupid," he says.

www.ingramcontent.com/pod-product-compliance
Lightning Source LLC
Chambersburg PA
CBHW071125170626
46809CB00002B/505

* 9 7 8 0 6 9 2 2 0 2 4 6 3 *